Rave reviews for
Kimberly Cates's McDaniel trilogy

The Wedding Dress

"Once again, Cates creates characters so real they jump off the page as she takes readers on a journey into the depths of despair and the heights of happiness."
—*Booklist*

"A great story that is both heartfelt and sincere... you will not be disappointed."
—*The Romance Reader's Connection*

The Gazebo

"[A] delightful sequel....Readers will find this a great book for a winter's evening in front of the fire. Kimberly Cates has delivered up a winner with this one."
—*The Romance Reader's Connection*

Picket Fence

"Forgiveness and acceptance are key elements in this outstanding new family drama, which offers the deep insight into the human soul and the touching story that are hallmarks of a Cates novel."
—*Romantic Times BOOKreviews* (4½ stars)

"Cates weaves a tantalizing and emotional tale that strums the heartstrings and keeps the reader spellbound until the joyful, gratifying ending."
—*Booklist*

More praise for Kimberly Cates

"One of the brightest stars of the romance genre."
—*New York Times* bestselling author
Iris Johansen

Dear Reader,

I adore dogs. This is no news to anyone who comes to my house to be greeted by three Cavalier King Charles spaniels (Sir Tristan, Sailor and Huckleberry) and a black Lab (Jake). Nor is it a surprise to people who hear them barking when I'm on the phone. My theory is that the phone emits a high-pitched beep that only dogs and toddlers can hear—especially when your editor is on the line. I have used dogs in numerous books, delighting in their canine personalities, and have rescued more strays than my husband cares to count, determined to find them perfect homes. What most people *don't* know is how I started my love affair with all things furry—a juvenile delinquent dachshund my own "fairy godmother" filled my arms with when life suddenly got more complex than anyone could have guessed. I was eight years old and Humphrey was just the magic I needed.

This book is my tribute to families under fire, who face daunting odds with great courage. My loving thanks to parents who do daily battle to make their children walk, to "fairy godmothers" who make little girls' wishes come true, and of course to the pets who have brightened my world.

Here's to lint rollers, killer dust bunnies during shedding season and to the healing power of love. Real magic that makes little boys do karate and little girls dance, even when doctors don't believe they ever will.

Kimberly Cates

Kimberly Cates

the perfect match

HQN™

ISBN-13: 978-0-373-77265-0
ISBN-10:   0-373-77265-3

THE PERFECT MATCH

www.HQNBooks.com

Printed in U.S.A.

To "Dodo." Zora Miloradich Alpern, my very own "fairy godmother." Thank you for seeing me even when I felt invisible.

And in loving memory of the dog she gave me: Humphrey, the juvenile delinquent dachshund who changed my life.

CHAPTER ONE

THE TROUBLE WITH fairy godmothers was they never hung around long enough to see how their magic turned out, twenty-seven-year-old Rowena Brown thought, racing up the steps to the Whitewater Sheriff's office. Now, Cinderella—*she'd* gotten the lowdown about the coach turning back into a pumpkin come midnight. And in *Sleeping Beauty*—even the Disney version—Maleficent blabbed to the whole kingdom about the princess's pricking-her-finger-on-a-spindle clause.

But when great-auntie Maeve MacKinnon from County Meath had predicted Rowena would meet her soul mate in this quaint Illinois town, the ninety-year-old Irishwoman had failed to mention that three weeks after Rowena moved in, her personal bad boy would end up in the slammer for breaking and entering. God knew how much it was going to cost her to bail him out.

Rowena shook wisps of waist-long curls the color of daffodils out of her eyes and hugged her beloved red and gold tapestry bag tight against her in an effort to calm the butterflies rioting in her middle. Her sisters had claimed that Rowena could hide a kindergartener in the purse made out of a salvageable piece of antique Oriental rug she'd gotten at an art fair. Unfortunately at the moment, she was about as likely to find bail money inside the thing as she was a gap-toothed five-year-old.

Every cent Rowena had she'd invested in spiffing up her new

shop on Main Street: nailing on a roof that didn't leak, buying bright chrome cages to line the walls and putting in a "get acquainted" room designed to tempt even the most retiring wallflower to play. But if Clancy had already gotten himself in *this* much trouble, there was obviously one more accessory she needed to invest in. Stronger locks.

In a swirl of purple peasant skirt and jangling bracelets she shoved open the door to the drab brick building and rushed up to the desk labeled Information. Rowena couldn't help doing a double-take. The officer/receptionist who presided over the gateway to the room beyond looked disturbingly like one of those guys in the shako hats who guarded the Wicked Witch's castle in *The Wizard of Oz*.

He seemed as taken aback by Rowena's appearance as she was with his. She should be used to it by now. But then, ever since she'd set foot in Whitewater, the whole town had been gaping at her as she'd just dropped in from another planet. Maybe she had. Chicago, with its bustling streets and delicious diversity, seemed a galaxy away.

"I've come about Clancy Brown," Rowena told the receptionist as she tried to shake the image that kept popping into her mind—the pot-bellied deputy chatting it up with one of those creepy flying monkeys.

"Brown, Brown..." the man mumbled to himself as he scanned the register in front of him. "I'm sorry, ma'am. There's no one here by that name."

Panic buzzed in Rowena's veins. "Clancy *has* to be here! My neighbor said one of your deputies picked him up about an hour ago."

The deputy grabbed a mug that said Kiss My Bass. "Your neighbor must have been mistaken."

"That's impossible. The deputy gave her this card when he hauled Clancy off in his squad car."

Smith—that was the name on the officer's plastic name tag—slugged down a gulp of coffee as Rowena dug through her purse in search of the cardboard rectangle she'd plucked from Miss Marigold Pettigrew's frantically gesticulating hands twenty minutes ago. The sharp corner of the card jammed under Rowena's thumbnail. Breath hissed between her teeth at the sting, but she dragged the card out, triumphant.

"Here it is," Rowena said, resisting the temptation to pop her thumb in her mouth to cool the pain. Instead she squinted at the embossed lettering. "Deputy Cash Lawless, Whitewater Sheriff's Office."

"Cash? Holy sh—" Smith choked, coffee threatening to spray the papers on his desk. He thumped his chest in an obvious effort to clear his windpipe. He struggled to sober himself, but his eyes were actually watering with the effort it took. "Excuse me, ma'am," he said, clearing his throat. "I didn't realize that Deputy Lawless was the arresting officer in your case. The perpetrator you're looking for—Mr., um, Brown—is currently awaiting transport to—"

"Death row if Cash has anything to say about it," a rangy guy with a nose roughly the size of the Sears Tower called out, the room erupting in laughter.

"Death row?" Rowena's stomach whirled as the Brown family's hamster had the time her younger sister Ariel bounced Nibbles down the basement stairs in one of those clear plastic balls. "You can't mean that!"

"Potter, you're a real comedian." Smith shot a quelling glare into the cluster of desks and uniformed officers. "Can't you see the lady is upset? Hey, Cash?" he bellowed, angling his gaze in another direction. "The lady here needs to see you about that burglary you just busted up." Shuffling, scuffling sounds came from all over the office as everyone craned to see the scene unfolding.

Applause broke out as a man stood up from the desk in the far right corner of the room, his back to Rowena and the chorus of gibes ringing out from his coworkers.

"My hero…"

"…deserves a medal for courage under fire…"

But Rowena barely heard the teasing. The business card fluttered, unheeded, from her numb fingers as she focused on the rear view of the dark-haired man who was the focus of the whole room's attention. If Deputy Smith had reminded her of an evil castle guard, this Lawless seemed more like a general about to institute a Scorched Earth campaign and enjoy every minute of it.

Stiff shoulders stretched the back of a khaki shirt with sharp creases still ironed into the sleeves as he hung up the phone he was talking on. Dark hair cropped with almost military precision didn't come close to reaching his collar. His well-tailored pants skimmed an ass a jeans model would envy, muscular legs seeming almost too long to be real. And clean? Her mom could do surgery on that desk of his. Rowena figured there wasn't a speck of lint or dog hair in the world rash enough to cling to the man's clothing. Although women would probably stand in line to take them off.

She smoothed one hand down the crinkled fabric of her peasant skirt, reminding herself she'd rumpled it on purpose as Lawless turned around to face her. Every nerve in Rowena's body flashed an all-points bulletin: *Warning—subject armed and dangerous. Do not approach.*

The deputy even had warning flares of a sort emblazoned on his broad chest, Rowena gauged, his starched shirtfront splotched with vivid orange and yellow stains.

His features were harder to make out, half obscured as they were by the blue beanbag-shaped thing he clutched to the left side of his face. But she glimpsed a belligerent chin, a hawklike nose and a vein beating a very dangerous rhythm in his right temple.

"Head right on back there, Ms. Brown." Deputy Smith gestured with his coffee cup. "Deputy Lawless will see you now."

Rowena thanked him and started toward the far more intimidating man. Her heart raced. Deputy Lawless looked for all the world as if he was itching to shoot the place up. That is, if someone *could* shoot up a crowded sheriff's office with only one working eye.

And that was all Deputy Lawless had at the moment, from what Rowena could tell. The thing on his face was an icepack. His other eye, a penetrating whiskey brown, glowered at Rowena as if she'd just ripped off the collection box for the sheriff department's Widows and Orphans Christmas Fund.

Oh, God, Rowena thought as the man lowered the cold pack. His eye was almost swollen shut. This was not good. Clancy had really ticked this guy off. Was it possible that *her* Clancy had given him that shiner? No way, Rowena reassured herself quickly. Clancy might be completely out of control, but he would never hurt a flea.

Deputy Lawless crossed to a sink by a coffee station and dumped the icepack, then homed in on Rowena, his face unyielding as stone.

"Deputy Lawless." She started to offer him her hand, then thought better of it, winding her fingers in the strap of her bag instead. "I'm Rowena Brown. I own the new pet shop in town."

The deputy's disapproving gaze swept from the lingerie-inspired camisole clinging to her shoulders by thin spaghetti straps to the scuffed toes of the Frye boots one of her mother's friends had broken in at a protest march in the seventies. "I know who you are."

He didn't say "everybody in town does," but Rowena could hear what he was thinking. *You're the crazy lady who claims she can read animals' minds.*

Not that she could, exactly. It was more like being a sort of matchmaker. Sensing when a certain person and a certain pet were destined for each other. And once that instinct kicked in, she had no peace until she'd settled them together. Another supposed "gift" from Auntie Maeve, inspired by the old tin-whistle tucked in the desk drawer at the pet shop.

Wouldn't *that* be big fun to explain to the stone-faced man standing before her? A smear of red on the left side of his corded throat snagged her gaze. Blood? Her lungs squeezed shut. Better to get down to the crisis at hand.

"There's been a terrible misunderstanding." She couldn't stop staring at his neck, terrified she'd find broken skin.

Aware of the direction of Rowena's gaze, Lawless swiped one hand against the spot on his neck, then glanced down at his stained fingers. A muscle in his jaw knotted as he grabbed a tissue and scrubbed the color away. Thank God, Rowena thought. His skin was smooth, tanned—far too luscious looking for anybody as tightly wound as he was.

"Miss Marigold ran over to my shop the instant I got back and told me she'd called you," Rowena continued. "I'm so sorry for the inconvenience. She's flighty as a hummingbird trapped in a mason jar."

Lawless gave the best Medusa impression Rowena had ever seen—the guy should have been able to turn her into stone with a look like that. The last thing Rowena needed was to get this man's back up any more than it already was.

Rowena's hand fluttered as if to sweep her too-colorful description of Marigold Pettigrew away. "What I mean to say is that Miss Marigold is very excitable."

Lawless's scowl chilled even further. "Most people tend to get a little upset when they hear an intruder bashing around on the first floor of their house. Even in small towns bad things can happen to women who live alone."

Guilt elbowed Rowena as she imagined her neighbor terrified. "You're right, of course. I'm so sorry she was upset."

She was getting frostbite here. Lawless folded his arms over his chest. The stains on his shirt seemed as foreign to him as blacked-out teeth on Cary Grant. It looked to Rowena as if the deputy had tried to scrub out the spots peeking over those tautly muscled arms, but had given up. "By the time I got to Miss Marigold's place, her shop was in shambles," he said. "God knows how long it will take her to clean it up."

Chastened, Rowena swallowed hard. "I'm sure Clancy didn't mean to cause trouble."

"Clancy?" The deputy's gaze narrowed. He winced as the bruised skin around his eye tugged. "Who's Clancy?"

At Lawless' blank look, Rowena rushed to explain. "My dog. He's about this high." She held her hand mid-waist. "Black, with a white patch on his chest."

Lawless' lip curled, his voice rough around the edges as if he smoked a pack a day. Funny, he didn't smell of tobacco. "There's no Clancy here, Ms. Brown."

Rowena cocked her head to one side, confused. "But Miss Marigold said that my dog—"

"The dog that broke into the tea shop is named Destroyer."

Alarm bells jangled Rowena's nerves. Was it possible this Lawless man knew... She scrambled for a quick feint, settling on wide-eyed innocence. "No, Deputy. You're mistaken. My Clancy—"

Lawless cut her off. "*Destroyer* has a rap sheet of prior offenses three pages long. Most of which *I* had to file, since he has a rotten habit of popping up on my shift like Cujo out of a closet."

Rats. Rats. Double rats, Rowena thought, struggling to keep her voice calm. "First of all, Cujo was a Saint Bernard and Clancy is a Newfoundland. Second, Stephen King writes fiction, Deputy

Lawless. The dog in that novel was no more real than the crazed Chevy he wrote about in *Christine*."

"The King book this case reminds me of is *Pet Sematary*, where animals keep coming back from the dead. Three weeks ago, I delivered this very dog to Animal Control clear across the county and they swore I'd never see him again."

Outrage flared in Rowena's chest, drowning caution. "Animal Control?" She sputtered. "Don't you know how many animals they have to put down?"

"As a matter of fact, I do." Deputy Lawless planted his fists on his narrow hips. "They don't have any choice when an animal is out of control and a danger to others."

"Clancy's not a danger to anyone!" Rowena protested. "You're mixing him up with—with some other dog. It's a case of mistaken identity."

The chill in Lawless' tone snapped. "Lady, I could pick Destroyer out of any lineup you could name," he growled. "That dog has been a pain in my behind for almost a year. He's a public nuisance, running at large. And this time he added assaulting an officer to the mix."

"Assault?" Rowena's heart hit the floor. "Did he bite you?"

A barely stifled laugh came from somewhere in the room, the other officers enjoying the show. A muscle in the deputy's jaw jumped in irritation. "He slammed one of Ms. Marigold's swinging doors into my face." Color darkened Lawless' high-set cheekbones. "When I identified myself as law enforcement, the dog lunged through the swinging doors between the kitchen and the tea room and—"

"That was an accident," Rowena objected, imagining Clancy's joyful response to a human voice. "He was just trying to greet you."

"That dog couldn't have landed that blow any squarer if he'd aimed it!" Lawless challenged, his good eye blazing.

"You were probably in danger of being licked to death!" Rowena scoffed. "He loves people."

"Yeah. That dog adores me. About as much as I like him."

"If Clancy caused trouble, I'm the one to blame." Rowena thumped her chest with her flattened palm.

"*If* he caused trouble?" Lawless pointed to his injured eye.

Rowena swallowed hard. That *was* a really impressive shade of purple the deputy had going there. "What I'm trying to say is that Clancy's behavior is *my* responsibility."

"Then you should be damned glad it's my eye that's turning black and blue. If that little old lady had been walking into the dining room with those scones she'd just baked you'd have a hell of a lawsuit on your hands."

"Scones?" Rowena gasped. "Oh, God. *That* must've been what he was after." When she had researched the Newfie's history, she'd cried over the report about how badly his first owner had neglected him. Clancy still went a little postal when his dinner was late.

She'd love to get her hands on the monster that had left him to starve. "Deputy Lawless, if you only knew about what Clancy went through before I got him—"

"I'm more worried about what almost happened at that tea shop," Lawless cut in, judge, jury and executioner all rolled into one. "If that dog had bowled Miss Marigold over, he would have shattered her into a million pieces."

Rowena paled at the image the deputy painted in her mind. Her hand clenched around the strap of the tapestry bag. "But he didn't."

"*This time,*" Lawless asserted grimly. "Now I don't care how many aliases you and those bleeding heart animal lovers at the shelter give this monster. He's a menace. And it's my duty to make damned sure he doesn't get another chance to break someone's hip."

"But you don't have any legal recourse," Rowena said with an edge of desperation. "He didn't bite anybody. Besides, it's his first offense."

Lawless rolled his good eye. "And Charles Manson just crashed a few parties. Like I told you, Ms. Brown, Destroyer—"

"That's what I'm trying to tell you. This is just a case of mistaken identity. The dog in question isn't this Destroyer maniac you keep running on about. The dog you picked up is my dog, Clancy. He's had all his shots. All his registration stuff is filed. I'll pay for whatever damage he did to Miss Marigold's tea shop."

"You sure will. You're legally liable," Lawless said. "Once you take a look and add up the cost of what Destroyer's done you'll probably be begging me to take the dog back to the shelter. Any sane person would."

"And I'm not sane, is that what you're implying? Because I think an animal's life is worth more than—than a bunch of old china teapots?" Rowena craned up on tiptoe, peering around the room in an effort to find her dog. "I'll buy the woman new ones."

"She doesn't *want* new ones. Some of those had been in Ms. Marigold's family since the Revolutionary War. If you had seen that poor old woman picking up all those bits of broken china, crying her heart out…"

Rowena fretted her bottom lip at the picture Lawless painted, but a long, mournful howl from somewhere nearby drove back anything but fear for the animal in such danger. She edged around the deputy and tried to make a break toward the sound. But his hand closed around her arm, stopping her in her tracks. Rowena started at the feel of his callused palm against her bare skin, his fingers imbued with a more powerful authority than even the badge pinned on his shirt-pocket gave him.

"I know this is hard," Deputy Lawless said. "But there are

plenty of other dogs in the world who need homes. This one is hopeless."

Rowena pulled her arm out of his grasp. "Even a dog that really attacks someone gets a second chance! This was a mistake! Just a mistake!" *Like the ones you've been making lately?* her older sister Bryony's voice nagged in her head. "But then, I suppose you've never made one before, have you, Deputy Lawless?"

The man glanced away, something sparking in his eyes. Regret? Bitterness? It was gone before she could tell.

"Ms. Brown, I've had a very bad day." He enunciated so carefully she could almost feel black ice cracking under her feet. "Ten minutes before I got off duty I was called to Miss Marigold's Tea Shop to investigate a burglary in progress. I entered the premises with my gun drawn, and got a door slammed in my face. By a dog who proceeds to smear my uniform with the colored frosting for three birthday cakes. As if that wasn't bad enough, I have to haul Destroyer—"

"Clancy."

"Whatever. I had to haul that demon dog back to the station so that I could file a mountain of paperwork which made me late to a very important appointment."

"An appointment for what? The Cruella de Vil Fan Club?"

The man's jaw clenched so hard, Rowena bet he could have snapped a bullet in two between his teeth. *Keep your smart mouth under control, Rowena,* she thought. *Pulling the man's chain more than you already have isn't going to help.* Deputy Lawless looked as if he'd gone terminal when it came to a sense of humor.

Rowena strained up on tiptoe, finally seeing a familiar mountain of black fur in what must be some kind of holding cell. Clancy strained to squeeze his muzzle through the bars in an effort to lick the stout man next door who was obviously sleeping off last night's bender. Her heart twisted, eyes stung.

Even here the Newfie was trying to take care of whoever was within reach.

"Ms. Brown, I'm responsible for protecting the people of Whitewater County," Deputy Pompous said, as if she were a recalcitrant two-year-old. "I've called the shelter and told them Destroyer is coming."

Her chin bumped up. "Well, you'll have to call them back. This is *my* dog Clancy Brown, Deputy Lawless, and I'll fight you for him in any court you can name to prove it. And what's more, I'll *win*. Microchips don't lie."

"Micro what?"

"Take him to any shelter in the country and they'll wave their magic wand over him and—bingo!—my name will bleep up on their nifty little scanner screen. Any competent veterinarian can verify Clancy's identity under oath. If you persist in persecuting my dog—"

"Persecuting?" Lawless scoffed.

"—you're going to be spending an awful lot of time doing that paperwork you hate, preparing for a case you're going to lose. Is this unfortunate little grudge of yours really worth spending the taxpayers' money on?"

Rowena could see the deputy's control slip another notch. Steely eyes held hers for a long moment in a wrestling match of wills. She didn't like confrontation, but damned if she was going to back down. Lawless blinked first.

"Fine," he said at last through gritted teeth. "Take the damned dog. That is, if you've got enough nerve to take legal—and financial—responsibility for any damage he causes in the future."

"Absolutely." Rowena tried not to think about what her mother would have to say about her promise. But Dr. Nadine Brown's features swam into Rowena's consciousness, her mother's brow creased with all too familiar exasperation. *What are you thinking? That's a legally binding document he's*

*talking about. You don't even know how you're going to pay
for the tea shop debacle, let alone the next disaster!*

But Rowena would have signed a deal with the devil himself
to keep animal control from sticking a needle in Clancy's vein.
The moment she had glimpsed his big dark eyes from behind the
bars of the cage in "doggie death row" half an hour before he was
scheduled to be euthanized, she'd felt a shock down to her toes.
A wild, desperate need to swoop him into her arms, save him.

*And that would be different from the way you react to any
animal in trouble exactly* how? Rowena imagined her sister
Bryony taunting.

But Clancy *was* different. There was something special about
this dog. Rowena felt it in her bones. A life he needed to live,
work he was destined to do, a future he had to have or else…

"Ms. Brown?" Lawless' voice snapped Rowena back into
the sheriff's office to face yet another disapproving frown.
"I'm beginning a new file on the dog. If he ever gets loose
again, I'm going to have him legally declared a public nuisance.
And from that point on, I'll take every step the law allows to
see that he's off the streets permanently. Understand?"

"Yes, sir." She wondered if he was smart enough to know
she meant it as an insult.

Apparently so. His cheeks darkened. "You'll have to fill out
some paperwork before I can release him." He checked his
watch again, an even deeper frustration darkening his face.
"Which means I can pretty much kiss my appointment goodbye. They'll be closed before I—"

"It's an *appointment*," Rowena fired back, her temper
flaring. "People reschedule them all the time, Deputy."

"Is that so?"

"As a matter of fact, it is. This isn't the end of the world.
You aren't going to jail because of it. Small children aren't
going to die because of it."

Whoa! Rowena took a step backward at the rage in Lawless' eyes. What was she doing, poking him with a sharp stick? Clancy didn't have his get-out-of-jail-free card yet. Did she want Deputy Whiplash to change his mind?

She swallowed the rest of her anger and reached for the firm tone she used to calm hostile animals. "Listen. Obviously we're not going to agree on this. Just show me where to sign and Clancy and I will get out of your way."

The deputy sat down at his desk.

"Couldn't we let Clancy out first before you whip out his release papers? I hate the idea of him behind bars."

"And I hate the idea of him back on the street. Looks like we're both going to have to get used to disappointment. When I open that cell, all I want to see is the door hitting him in his backside. Give me any more time and I might just change my mind."

Rowena opened her mouth, closed it. Could the deputy do that? Keep Clancy here if Lawless decided to turn stubborn about it? She didn't know the legalities, but she didn't dare risk it. She sank down on the chair across from him and turned her attention to something she figured couldn't get her in trouble, digging the leash she'd brought with her out of her bag.

Satisfied with her concession, Lawless retrieved a set of forms from his desk and began to fill them in. After twenty-some minutes, he shoved them across the desk to her. Taking out her favorite pen, she scrawled her name in bright green ink.

"There," she said, adding a flourish. "As to the damages and such, you know where to find me if you've got any questions about—well, anything. My shop is—"

"I know where it is. If there isn't a law against building a pet shop across the street from an elementary school playground, there should be."

Rowena compressed her lips. "If you want to change the law you'll have to take that up with your alderman or councilman or whatever you have here. But it's only fair to tell you that they were pretty much thrilled when they heard a new business was coming to town."

"That was before they knew—"

"Knew what?" Rowena dared him to finish the sentence, even though she could have filled in the gist of it herself. *Before they knew some big-city nutcase was moving in.* But Lawless didn't rise to the bait, probably heeding some office policy about insulting the locals only when necessary.

"Never mind. Let's just get this over and done with." The deputy pushed himself to his feet and started toward the back of the building, nabbing a set of keys on the way. She followed him, straining to get a better view of the holding cell beyond his rigid silhouette.

Her heart leapt as she glimpsed the Newfoundland busily scratching at the wall to the cell next door, a worried look in those big brown eyes, as if Clancy knew something was wrong with the drunk on the other side. There was no way to tell the dog the human's problems were self-inflicted. Or that, at the moment, she and Clancy had enough trouble of their own. Still, she couldn't help but be grateful to the deputy—asshole though he was—for releasing her dog in the end.

"You won't regret this, Deputy Lawless," she said, itching to throw her arms around the Newfie.

"I already do."

Rowena swallowed hard. What could she say? "You'll never see either one of us again."

"Ms. Brown, I'm just not that lucky. In fact—wait." He pressed his fingertips to his temples, closed his eyes in a mock trance. "I'm peering into the future... I see..."

"I don't see into the future," Rowena cut in. "I just feel—" She stopped, cursing herself for a fool. Why did she even bother to attempt to explain her gift? She'd tried it before. But that was what had started the whispering behind her back, triggered the abrupt silences when she walked into a store or passed someone on Whitewater's streets.

"You don't know anything about me," Rowena said, trying hard not to hurt.

"Let's try and keep it that way."

"Deputy Lawless, I promise that Clancy—"

Lawless whipped around to face her, his features grim, the keys jangling in his hand. "Listen, lady, I don't care *how* many aliases you give that dog. He's *still* the same fence-breaking, tire-chewing, steak-stealing juvenile delinquent he always was."

"He is not!"

"Destroyer!" the deputy called sharply.

In the holding cell, the Newfoundland wheeled away from the wall and leaped up to plant his plate-sized paws on the bars. Eager canine eyes fastened on Lawless, the dog's bearlike body quivering in excitement as if to say *Here I am! Yeah, that's me, boss!* The Newfie's tongue lolled out of his cavernous mouth in a goofy grin, his giant tail wagging so hard it could have knocked someone out.

Lawless crossed his arms over his broad chest and pinned Rowena with his pointed glare. "I rest my case."

CHAPTER TWO

ELVIS WAS PRACTICING his pick-up lines again. Not a good idea, when the after-school crowd was due to burst into the pet shop at any moment. The irascible African Gray parrot's vocabulary wasn't exactly G-rated, and the last thing Rowena needed was for a mob of angry parents to storm into Open Arms, ready to burn the local witch at the stake.

If they made up their minds to do it there wouldn't be any problem finding a public official in Whitewater to light the fire. Deputy Lawless would be happy to donate a whole book of matches to the cause of ridding his town of an unsavory element.

Rowena grimaced. Fortunately for her, even the deputy would have a hard time getting a blaze going today. A miserable cold drizzle had been falling all day, leaving the world beyond her front window soggy and gray. That meant there would be an hour of mopping muddy footprints before she closed up for the night. One could hardly expect kids charging in to see puppies and kittens to stop to wipe their feet.

But while they were leaving all of those damp patches on her floor, she'd just as soon they didn't pick up any colorful language, courtesy of the store's most incorrigible rogue. She left off cleaning the gecko aquarium and went to fetch the black drape she used to throw over Elvis's cage to shut him up temporarily. Not that she had much hope her technique would work any better than her efforts to drive Cash Lawless out of her head.

Time and time again in the three days since she'd left the ill-tempered deputy's office his chiseled features flashed into focus just when she'd least expected it. Those heavy brows, the arrogant jut of his nose, his mouth drawn into a sneer that almost—*almost*—negated the sexy shape of his lips. Too bad the man had such rotten things to say to her. Her cheeks heated as she remembered him taunting: *Wait...just a minute...I'm peering into the future...*

Jerk face.

The name a freckle-faced sixth grader had called his class-mate in the shop the day before rose in her mind, the label not particularly eloquent, but describing Lawless to perfection, nonetheless.

He'd made it plain what he thought of her. He'd taken all of ten minutes to form his opinion. Less than that, really. He'd had his mind made up even before he met her. But then her "crimes" against Whitewater's social order reached even deeper than opening a pet shop across from the school, as far as Lawless was concerned. Like far too many of the people in this small town, he would've been happy to deem just being different a crime. And if Rowena was anything, she was different.

Rowena swallowed hard, her fingers tightening in the folds of the cage drape. A familiar awkwardness settled over her, in-escapable as the plaster dust when Open Arms was a construc-tion site. Self-doubt crowded her.

What if her move here had been exactly the reckless mistake her mother and sisters had predicted? She'd invested every cent of the legacy her godmother had left her, the money that was supposed to be her nest egg. Knowing that safety net existed had been the only thing that had comforted her mother when Rowena had dropped out of vet school last spring.

She closed her eyes, remembering how the painful scene had ended in the wee hours of the morning, once Nadine Brown had realized there was no budging Rowena from the course she'd chosen.

Gray-faced with exhaustion, bordering on tears the cool and capable Dr. Brown never shed, Rowena's mother had surrendered.

At least you'll always have your inheritance to rely on, Nadine had said a week after Maeve's funeral.

About my inheritance, Mom. While Auntie Maeve was in the hospital, we talked about how I should use it. She said it would help me find my destiny.

Your what?

My destiny. She didn't dare say "soul mate" as the irrepressible Maeve had. *Just listen, Mom. I've thought this whole plan out. You and Bryony and Ariel are right. I can't save every stray I run across. But just think how many I could place if I used that money to work in tandem with a shelter, helping rehabilitate rescue dogs and cats, finding them homes.*

And you're going to support yourself how?

I could design all kinds of stuff—collars and bowls—and, well, sell fun pet supplies for ready cash, and I'd keep the pets I'm working with at the shop all day, so I can match them with owners. I know it's a little unorthodox, but—

A little? her mother had exclaimed. *Rowena, I'm trying to understand this. I really am. But it bewilders me that a young woman as bright and talented as you are would fling away six years of education to open a pet shop anywhere, let alone in a town where you don't know a soul, hours away from your family. And with pets someone has already rejected? For heaven's sake, why?*

A question impossible to answer in a way her mother could understand.

Because I feel right *inside when I'm placing rescue pets, and in vet school I felt* wrong…

Rowena should have saved her breath. Article number one in the Brown Family Constitution was "logic above all," mere instinct far too messy. "Rowena's Voodoo," her younger sister Ariel called it. Even now, pushing twenty-five, she still made "woo woo" sound effects to tease.

Rowena tossed the drape over the parrot's cage in an effort to throw Elvis into a make-believe night, hoping that the wily bird would settle down, fall asleep and be blessedly silent.

Not that she had much hope that her ruse would work. Could you arrest a bird for profanity? Public indecency? Corrupting the innocence of a minor? Maybe she'd ask the good deputy, if she were ever unfortunate enough to run into him again.

Her mind filled with eyes that flashed, dark and angry, when she'd told him missing the appointment was no big deal. Talk about overreacting! And yet, didn't it stand to reason that anyone who worked in law enforcement was bound to be a control freak? At least on some level. And it seemed that the needle on Lawless' irritation meter jumped right off the charts where Rowena was concerned.

Guilt itched as she remembered the way he had chewed her out, describing Miss Marigold's despair over her broken treasures. Rowena's next-door neighbor *had* been heartbroken. Rowena had been hosing off some cage trays at the back of the shop the night of Clancy's Great Scone Raid when she had seen the sixty-year-old woman carrying out a big box of something that clinked as she moved. Before Clancy's escapade, Rowena might have plopped down the hose and hurried over to help, even if the lady *did* tend to look bug-eyed with alarm every time Rowena said hello.

But this time, Rowena had just stood rooted to the spot as Miss Marigold hauled her burden to where the garbage would be picked up the next morning. The older woman had been weeping, her nose chafed Rudolph-red, her eyes all swollen behind cat's-eye glasses she'd probably bought sometime during the 1960s.

Rowena had tried to apologize, her stomach as knotted as her garden hose. But before she could get out more than a few words, Miss Marigold had dropped her box with a horrific crash and fled back into the rear entrance of the tea shop, as if Rowena had set an attack dog snapping at her heels.

Rowena had crossed to where the box lay off-kilter on one side. A china tea spout decorated with a motif of peacock feathers lay in the gravel, a teapot lid with a finial shaped like a cat a few feet beyond. Rowena stooped to pick each up, amazed at the delicate work.

She stared down into the box. Lawless had been right about one thing. Even if she did pay for the damages, it wouldn't matter. She'd never be able to piece her neighbor's treasures together again.

She'd lifted Miss Marigold's box into her arms, holding it for a long time, not knowing exactly what to do with it. But somehow in spite of the wreckage she couldn't leave the broken china for the garbage man to take. Instead she'd stuck it in her back room.

And what are you going to do, oh brilliant one? Wave your hands and say abracadabra? Cast some magical spell that would make the teapots whole again? Now, *that* would be a gift she'd be grateful to have at the moment.

The school bell rang in the distance, bringing Rowena back to the moment at hand. A parade of delighted faces, kids jabbering and laughing and cajoling their parents to come into the shop just to take a look. She'd done her best to make Open Arms irresistible, and it seemed where Whitewater's children were concerned she'd succeeded.

At least with all of them except one.

Rowena turned away from the parrot's cage and glimpsed an all too familiar small figure scowling into the store's front window. Yes. Her crabby ghost was back again, hovering under the rainbow-striped awning, a few feet away from the door the kid had never once entered. Mousy brown hair was swept into a ponytail, exposing sharp drawn features. Her brow crinkled in aggravation, the folds of a duckling-yellow slicker gleaming from the rain.

The first time Rowena had seen the nine-or-so-year-old girl she'd assumed that the kid's disgruntled expression was due to the glare reflecting off the window into the child's eyes. But today there wasn't a sunbeam for miles and those eyes behind round silver wire glasses still glared into the shop's interior as if something about the place frustrated her beyond bearing.

Rowena had tried to imagine what could possibly have displeased the child, but she'd been so busy working the kinks out of the shop's layout that she'd pushed her questions to the back of her mind. But today, the ghost finally shoved Rowena's curiosity right over the edge.

In spite of the awning's shelter, the child was trying to keep an adult-sized purple umbrella over her head while she wrestled with a book the size of a dictionary. That was one serious piece of literature, Rowena thought. Wasn't that monstrosity of a volume a little much for a fourth grader to handle? Surely her ghost couldn't be reading something that advanced, even if the kid was one of those pint-sized geniuses that made the newspapers now and then.

All business under the wavering shelter of the umbrella, the girl balanced the volume between the pet shop's window ledge and her tummy and opened the book to one of about a dozen pages marked with scraps of orange construction paper.

Rowena watched the child study what must be pictures of

some kind, then raise those too-solemn eyes to peer intently back into the pet shop interior. Frowning in obvious frustration, the disgruntled little girl plunged on to the next marked page, studying the book again. The poor little thing was going to put herself in traction wrestling with a volume that heavy.

Rowena glanced around her store and, finding it empty for the moment, ducked outside. A gust of wind sprinkled her left side with rain, her orange linen tunic sticking in chill, damp patches to her arm. But the little scowler was so intent on whatever she was reading she didn't even notice anyone approach. Rowena couldn't help but be amused by the way the kid screwed her face up in fearsome concentration.

"Hi, there," Rowena said.

The child jumped as if Rowena had just yelled "boo," the book starting to tumble from her small hands. Rowena made a quick grab for the volume, nearly throwing her back out in her effort to keep the thing from landing in the rain puddle below.

"Whew, that was close," Rowena said, eyeing the murky pool that covered the bottom inch or so of the girl's green sneakers. The poor kid's feet must be soaked.

Stubbornly silent, the child looked up at Rowena with eyes a woodsy color, somewhere between green and brown. Rowena might have been tempted to laugh out loud if she weren't sure she'd wound the soggy little soul's dignity. Instead, she tried to lighten the mood.

"You know, you keep scrunching your face like that, it's going to freeze that way."

"Grownups always say that. But I never saw a single person's face freeze. Even the principal's and he looks grumpy all the time."

Smiling to herself at the girl's cranky response, Rowena glanced down at the volume in her hands. "This is some book you've got here. It's almost as big as you are."

"That's an exaggeration." The five-syllable word came so naturally from the child's mouth Rowena stared. "If the book was big as me I couldn't carry it at all."

"Right," Rowena said, nonplussed. She tapped the book's spine. "Still, it looks pretty heavy. Wouldn't it fit in your backpack?" Rowena nudged the olive drab bag slung over the child's narrow shoulders. "Most of the kids I see around here have pictures of superheroes or Disney princesses on theirs. Yours looks as if you could climb Mount Everest and not have to worry about it splitting."

She'd hoped to coax a smile out of the little girl. Instead, the child leveled her with a serious stare.

"I'm too young to climb Mount Everest. People freeze to death up there, you know."

"It was a joke…well, at least it was supposed to be."

The child peered at her, silent.

"You want to come in out of the rain?"

The child shook her head. A schoolbus passed by, splashing water in an arc that spattered the backs of Rowena's jeans. She sighed but tried again.

"My name is Rowena, what's yours?"

"Charlie." The little girl waited, as if expecting some comment about that being a boy's name.

Rowena had been teased on the playground because of her unusual name often enough to catch on. "I like it. Your name, I mean."

"I wasn't hurting anything," Charlie said.

"You're going to hurt *yourself,* lugging a book this size around," Rowena observed. She flipped to the cover and read the title aloud. *"MacGonagle's International Expert's Encyclopedia of Dog Breeds."* She flipped it open to a page, her own eyes crossing at the complex descriptions. "Whoa! You can read this stuff?"

The girl's lips pursed. "I'm only in fourth grade you know."

Okay, so the kid did have that fourth grade look—permanent teeth still too big for her face, marker-stained hands from some art project during the day. But her eyes looked far older than they should. Not to mention the child had been studying the book as if she were a zoologist trying to unlock the mystery of some exotic species.

"Do you like dogs?" Rowena asked.

Charlie nodded. "All three of them."

"You've got three dogs?" Rowena asked in surprise. She wouldn't have guessed it. The kid didn't have the look of someone who had a pet waiting at home to lavish her with unconditional love. "What are their names?"

"Tiffany and Sweet Pea and Sugar Cookie. But I don't have them now," Charlie said softly. "Mommy didn't like it when they weren't puppies anymore. She gave them away when they got big and then she'd get another puppy again. After last time, my daddy said absolutely no more dogs. Not ever." For the first time, Rowena saw vulnerability in the little girl's face. Charlie caught her bottom lip between her teeth and blinked hard. "Sugar Cookie liked me best."

Rowena's blood boiled. Anyone could make one mistake—get a dog that didn't work out for some unforeseen reason. But to bring home three different dogs and then dump them each in turn when Mom got tired of them...? It seemed Charlie's parents were exactly the kind of pet owners who abandoned the pets she was trying to save. Charlie had paid the price, too. The heartbreak was still in her eyes.

"So now that your puppies are gone you just look at pictures?"

"Not usually. It makes me sad. But since you moved in here, well, I just *have* to. It's driving me *crazy.*"

Deputy Lawless' disgust at the shop's location flashed into

Rowena's mind. She hadn't considered it from the perspective of a woebegone little waif like Charlie. Rowena laid the dog book gently into the girl's arms. "I'm sorry."

"Why are you sorry?"

"That my shop drives you crazy."

"It's the kids at school that make me crazy. They say you've got a bear in here. Even my best friend Hope Stone says so. It's all my little sister talks about. She says she wants to pet the grizzly bear." Charlie face crumpled in exasperation. "You can't pet a grizzly bear! They chew people's arms off. I saw it on *Animal Planet*."

Rowena bit back a smile. "I think I caught that show, too."

"So that big black thing you've got in here just *has* to be a dog. But I never saw one that big. Maybe you could just *tell* me what kind he is, because this book is getting real heavy."

"How about if I show you, instead? Would you like to give Clancy a treat?"

"I don't know…" Longing filled Charlie's eyes. She leaned her umbrella against the wall so she could check a watch a scuba diver would envy. She glanced nervously over her shoulder at the street. "Can you show me real fast?"

"You bet. I'll even mark his picture in your book. That way you can prove to the other kids you were right when you go to school tomorrow."

That offer clinched the deal. Charlie handed her the book, then took a deep breath. She slipped her hand into Rowena's as she walked through the door.

Rowena smiled as she led the little girl to the playroom where Clancy was tossing a regulation-size football into the air and trying to catch it. His white teeth flashed, and Rowena felt Charlie's hand tighten its hold on hers.

"That's the biggest dog I've ever seen." Charlie swallowed hard, her eyes wide as sunflowers.

"He's not even full grown yet. You should have seen the first Newfie I rescued. Huey was 200 pounds in his heyday."

Charlie slid the straps of her backpack down her arms and set the bag on the floor. She stared at the dog, fascinated. "Did Huey ever bite anybody? By mistake? I mean, my head kind of looks like a football."

"Your head isn't nearly pointy enough on top," Rowena said, ruffling the child's hair. "Besides, you're far too pretty to be mistaken for that chewed-up mess of a football."

Green eyes regarded her solemnly. "I'm not pretty. My best friend Hope says she wants the prettiest kitty in the whole wide world for her birthday. People only want the cute ones."

"People may *think* they want the cutest one at first. But sometimes I can change the way someone *sees* the kitty," Rowena tried to explain. "Make them see the 'pretty' in an animal that no one else can see. That's what I do. I take in animals that other people think are too broken—in their hearts, you know?—for anybody to take home. Then I find somebody to love them."

Charlie cocked her head to one side. "Doesn't anybody love him?" She pointed to Clancy.

As a matter of fact, Rowena thought, there were quite a few people who downright hated the poor dog. But Charlie didn't need to know about how quickly Clancy's official Whitewater lynch mob was growing.

"Someday, someone besides me will love him," Rowena said.

"Only if he's a real good, right? And he never, ever does anything bad again?"

Rowena chuckled. "I certainly hope that's not how it works or nobody would ever love me at all! I make mistakes all the time. I bet you do, too."

"Not anymore," Charlie said soberly. "Except for coming in here when I'm not supposed to."

"Ah." A lightbulb went off in Rowena's head. "So that's why you never came into the shop before." For a moment she considered ushering the child out the door. She didn't need some parent furious because she'd encouraged Charlie's disobedience. But Charlie seemed so sad, and Clancy's specialty was making people smile.

Decision made, Rowena gave Charlie a conspiratorial wink. "If this is supposed to be a secret mission we'd better hurry."

Rowena opened the gate to the playroom. Clancy bounded toward them. "Sit!" Rowena commanded. Clancy dropped like a rock, looking so virtuous she almost laughed aloud. But in spite of the halo Clancy appeared to have fixed over his head, the dog was scooting toward them, ever so surreptitiously, on his butt.

Rowena dug in her jeans pocket for the heartworm medicine she'd tucked in there earlier. Pulling out the packet, she pushed the cube through the foil on the back side of the plastic blister. She put the cube in the little girl's hand. "Here you go, Charlie."

Charlie looked from the little block on her hand to a glass jar filled with bone-shaped cookies. She regarded the cube warily. "How come this treat was all wrapped up like that?"

Rowena grinned at the child's quick intelligence. "I'll tell you a secret. That's really Clancy's heartworm medicine, so he won't get sick. But it tastes just like a treat."

"Sure it does." Charlie grimaced. She bit her bottom lip, her gaze skittering nervously to Rowena's. "What if he gets mad that I tricked him?"

"He won't hurt you. I promise," Rowena urged. "And just think about the story you'll have to tell Hope tomorrow. I'll even snap your picture with my camera." Rowena picked up her old instamatic from the ledge. "It spits the picture out right away. You can take it with you. Would you like that?"

Charlie nodded. "I could hide it in my secret place. That way Daddy would never know I was bad."

Rowena had had her own share of misadventures as a child, and while she'd dreaded being caught and the punishment that was sure to follow, she'd always been sure she'd be forgiven. There was something darker, deeper in Charlie's eyes, as if the child was walking on thin ice and waiting to fall through. Thank heavens Charlie's fascination with the dog ran greater than her fear.

Charlie looked deep into the dog's eyes then took a step toward him, the cube clutched in her hand. "I know she told you this is a treat, but it's not," Charlie said earnestly. "It's probably going to taste real yucky, but it'll be good for you." She uncurled her fingers. "Just close your eyes and swallow it real quick."

As if he understood every word, Clancy swept the chew into his mouth with one lick of his pink tongue and gulped it down, surprising a laugh out of the solemn child. Rowena snapped the picture, delighted.

"That tickles, huh?" Rowena asked as the dog wagged his giant-sized tail. "He likes you."

For the first time, the creases in Charlie's brow vanished, the tightness in her face softened. "I like him, too."

"Would you like to brush him while I mark that page in your book?"

Charlie nodded. Rowena took the picture the camera spit out and put it aside to develop. She set down her camera and fished a brush out of a basket filled with various grooming supplies on a ledge beside her.

"What kind of dog is he?" Charlie asked, sinking cross-legged onto the floor and starting to brush the dog with long, gentle strokes.

"He's a Newfoundland," Rowena said, retrieving the book and leafing through it. "They're so strong and brave and such great swimmers that they save people drowning in the water."

"Like taking lifesaving class at the Y?"

"Yeah. But sometimes they can save people even if nobody ever teaches them to. It's a natural gift."

"A New Found Land would be a good thing to have if there was a tidal wave." Charlie stroked the brush through Clancy's thick black coat. "My watch works underwater. Just in case."

"In case there's a tidal wave?" Rowena asked, astonished. "In Illinois?"

"I'm not stupid. I know you can't have a tidal wave here. But my daddy said he'd take me and my sister to Disney World sometime. There's an ocean there. It never hurts to be ready, just in case."

Rowena's chest squeezed. This poor little mite wasn't thinking of meeting Cinderella and seeing the castle or going on the rides when she went to Disney World. She was worried about a tidal wave. What had made Charlie so insecure that she was forever thinking of disaster? Did her parents have any idea how scared she was? And what on earth could calm the little girl's fears?

Charlie put the brush down and rose up on her knees to see the pictures in the book. A Newfie leapt out of a rescue helicopter into a rough sea. A second shot showed the same dog grabbing a rope with its teeth to haul a life raft full of people to shore. Another image captured a swimmer holding on to a dog's thick tail while the Newfoundland paddled to safety.

"Could your dog do that?" Charlie asked.

"I've been working with Clancy on water rescues. I hope next summer his new owner will take him for even more training."

"You mean he's not your dog?"

"Not for keeps. See, I always get this feeling about who a pet should belong to. I don't feel that when Clancy is with me, so I'm just taking care of him until I find him the right home."

Charlie's eyes widened, something sparkling in them for an instant before the little girl put the emotion out.

"Somebody's going to be so, so lucky," Charlie whispered, slipping her arms around the dog. "You'd never have to be scared if you had him around."

The child sounded so sure of it, her voice filled with yearning. Rowena felt Charlie's small hand close around her heart.

Charlie pressed her cheek against Clancy's side. She gasped. Shyness evaporated. The dread Rowena had sensed in Charlie's glances toward the door disappeared. "I can feel his heart beat!" Charlie marveled.

Rowena dropped to her knees beside the pair, her intuition singing. "I'll tell you a secret, Charlie." Charlie raised her head to peer into Clancy's face. Clancy tipped his head to one side, examining the little girl bare inches from his licorice black nose, as entranced with Charlie as Charlie was with him.

Rowena's heart nearly pounded its way out of her chest, the roaring of instinct inside her so loud she barely heard the bell above the shop door jangle behind her.

"Clancy's been wishing for someone to love him for a very long time."

"I'd love him," Charlie's so-sad eyes brightened, her pale face almost beautiful.

"I know you would." Caution struggled to surface in Rowena. *Don't get the child's hopes up...don't set her up for disappointment...*

But look at her, Rowena reasoned. *How sad she looks, how small...what kind of a parent would deny such a woebegone little girl a pet who could make her feel safe? Bring her back to joy? If she were my little girl...*

But she's not, her sister Bryony's voice chided gently.

Rowena tried to stop the words, but they spilled out in spite of her efforts. "It's obvious you're a very responsible girl. Maybe you're old enough to take care of a dog now."

Charlie shook her head gravely. "My daddy said no more."

"Maybe when he said that he didn't realize what a remarkable young lady you'd grow into. Maybe he didn't know…" Rowena hesitated.

"Know what?" Charlie asked with such hope in her eyes Rowena couldn't stop herself.

Rowena shoved back the last vestiges of caution as she cupped the girl's soft cheek, peered into Charlie's solemn eyes. So deep she could see the child's soul.

"Do you know what I think, Charlie?" she asked, more sure of what she was about to say than she'd ever been of anything before. "I think Clancy has been waiting for you his whole life."

"Really? But how—how do you know?"

"He told me." *Whoa, Rowena,* she thought. *A little too much honesty there.* The kind that tended to get her in trouble.

Doubt warred with a desperate need to believe in the little girl's eyes. "Dogs don't talk," Charlie said at last.

"Not like you and I do. But Clancy told you he likes you, didn't he? His tail wagged. He licked you. And just look at his eyes. He hasn't taken them off you for a second."

"Charlie!" A sharp masculine voice from the shop behind them cut through the magical web of understanding between Rowena, Charlie and the dog. They all three jumped, Charlie with a dismayed squeak, Rowena with an oath as Clancy's massive head slammed into her nose.

The big dog surged to all fours in front of them, instinctively putting his bearlike body between Charlie and the angry man stalking toward them.

"Daddy!" Charlie exclaimed, leaping to her feet as the thundering footsteps on the tile floor drew nearer.

Half blinded by the dog hair in her eyes, Rowena looped her arm around Charlie's shoulders, hating how stiff they'd become.

Rowena blinked hard to clear her blurry vision. When she managed to do it, she wished she hadn't.

Deputy Cash Lawless stormed toward her, another little girl in his arms, fury blazing in his eyes.

CHAPTER THREE

ROWENA TRIED TO REMEMBER how to breathe as her nemesis stalked toward them, six foot two inches of angry male. The child in his arms was swathed from hood to shoes in a purple unicorn raincoat, but Cash Lawless looked as if he'd stepped out of his morning shower fully dressed. His dark hair plastered to his head, the angles of his face even more forbidding gleaming wet.

His jacket, caught back by one of the little girl's legs, had left the front of his body exposed to the elements. His wet shirt stuck to the rippling muscles of a chest so broad he could probably bench press Rowena's weight without breaking a sweat.

And at the moment, he looked as if he'd like to toss her out of his way, Hulk style, to get to the little girl trembling in the curve of Rowena's arm.

Cash Lawless was Charlie's *daddy?*

Rowena's mind reeled as she tried to grasp the undeniable truth. This lost, lonely child who had already won Rowena's heart belonged to the hard-nosed deputy. The man who had a personal vendetta against the dog Charlie loved.

Rowena's ill-advised words of moments before played mercilessly in her head. She'd built the child's hopes up, so sure she could make Charlie's dream come true.

She'd have a better chance of turning Clancy into a cat.

"Charlotte Rose Lawless," the deputy snapped, "what do you think you're doing sneaking off like—"

Rowena could tell the instant he recognized Clancy.

"Charlie, get away from that dog!" Lawless ordered. "It's dangerous!"

"He is not!" Rowena exclaimed, as the deputy's long stride ate up the space between himself and his daughter.

"He gave me this black eye!"

Charlie nibbled on her lip, a little doubtful. Obviously the black eye had made an impression.

"It was an accident!" Rowena rushed to explain to the little girl. "Clancy just got overly excited and banged a door into your dad."

"Charlie, get over here right now," the deputy roared, flinging open the playroom gate.

"Yeah," the child in the deputy's arms piped up. "You are in *big* trouble, little girl." The mite thrust her hood back from a face straight out of the fairy book Auntie Maeve had sent Rowena from Ireland.

"Do you have any idea what could have happened to you, running off like that, Charlie?" Lawless demanded.

To give the man credit, he looked plenty shaken up. And Rowena tried to remember that, as a cop, he would have seen plenty of examples of bad things happening to children running wild. He had that if-you're-not-dead-in-a-ditch-I'm-going-to-kill-you-myself-for-scaring-me-spitless parental expression Rowena had seen on her mother's face a time or two.

Rowena searched for something to say, anything to defuse the situation. "We have to quit meeting like this, Deputy," she said, fighting a ridiculous urge to fold her arms over her breasts. "I'm happy to say, your eye is looking a whole lot less swollen than last time I saw you."

"Last time we met, you swore I'd never have to see you

again." He slashed Rowena a filthy look above the yellowish bruise shadowing his eye.

Rowena forced a smile for Charlie's sake. "Funny how life goes. God's sense of humor, you know. Tell him your plans and—" She sounded like an idiot, but deflecting Lawless' anger from Charlie to herself seemed like the only option.

Cash reached for Charlie's arm, but the child shrank back behind the mountain of Newfoundland, evading his grasp. Clancy shifted to block the deputy's path even more solidly and made a sound low in his throat.

Rowena gaped, as stunned as if the dog had just launched into a chorus of "Who Let The Dogs Out." That vein in the deputy's temple throbbed.

"Is that dog *growling at me?*" Lawless shot Clancy the Stare Of Death.

Oh, lord! Rowena thought, her nerves knotting. That's just what she needed. Lawless tallying up even more "incidents" to condemn Clancy as a vicious dog.

"You're upsetting the poor animal, stomping in here the way you did!" Rowena defended. "He thinks you might hurt Charlie!"

"Hurt my own daughter?" Dark eyes narrowed. "The last thing I need is parenting lessons from that juvenile delinquent of a dog!"

"If you'd just quit yelling—"

"*I'm not…*" Lawless seemed to start suddenly. His voice dropped to something a shade quieter, but no less emphatic. "Yelling," he finished, his cheekbones darkening.

"Yes, you were, Daddy," the child with Christmas tree angel curls corrected. "You got to use your indoor voice unless you're out for recess. Teacher says."

"Mac, I…"

Rowena raised a brow. What was it with this guy and names?

The five-or-so-year-old who looked as if she should be sleeping under a buttercup was named *Mac?*

Lawless hesitated for a moment, obviously grappling with his temper. "I'll try to keep that in mind," he told Mac. Rowena could see just how much effort it cost him to keep his voice below a roar.

He turned back to Charlie, who was clinging to Clancy's neck as if she really were afraid. Of her father? Rowena wondered. Or of being dragged away from the dog she already loved? The man didn't look particularly warm and fuzzy at the moment. No wonder Charlie figured Clancy was a better bet.

Rowena could see Lawless suck in a steadying breath. "Charlie, I thought we agreed this place was off-limits."

"Deputy Lawless," Rowena said, trying to catch hold of Clancy's collar before the dog assaulted the officer a second time. "Charlie just wanted to—"

"Sneak away from the car while I was talking to her sister's teacher? Cross the busiest street in town without the benefit of a crossing guard? Run off to a place I specifically told her not to go? If Mac hadn't noticed Charlie's umbrella by the store window I'd still be looking!"

Okay, Rowena admitted to herself. So it *did* sound like a pretty daunting rap sheet when he put it that way. "Let me explain," she said. "See, the problem is that the kids at school were saying I had a bear in here. Charlie's a smart girl and knew that wasn't possible. So she got this gigantic book of dog breeds to prove she was right, and…well, I'm the one who asked her into the shop. What harm is there in letting her get a closer look?"

That might have been fine, a voice in her head condemned, *but you took the child way past "getting a look" and deep into the realm of impossible dreams.*

"You know damned well what harm that could do to a lonely

little—" Lawless accused, then cut himself off. But not before she saw a flash of self-recrimination in his eyes.

So Lawless knew Charlie was lonely. But why? The child obviously had a father, a little sister and the dog-dumping mother waiting at home. Or was there a mother in the picture after all? Rowena glanced down at the deputy's ring finger. No glint of gold or telltale white line marked his skin where the ring would have been. Of course, there were plenty of married men who chose not to wear their wedding rings at all. And as for being lonely even in a crowd, Rowena knew from her own childhood how isolated a child could feel, even in a house full of people.

"Isn't this exactly the reason you opened your shop across from the playground?" Lawless challenged, gesturing to his daughter. "To prey on children and their parents? Con them into—"

"I'm hardly a criminal for wanting to help children find pets! A pet can be the most important relationship in a child's life!"

"Funny." Lawless looked her up and down with a glance so scathing it burned her. "I thought that was the parents' job."

"Dogs can teach children things they can never learn any other way! How to take care of a creature smaller than they are—"

"Smaller?" Lawless snorted, pointing at the Newfoundland.

"Well, a living being who depends on them, then. Someone they can take care of, tell their secrets to."

"Someone who tears up the yard, rips up the house and ends up making a hell of a lot of work for the parents? Kids get tired of pets just as soon as the Christmas shine rubs off. So don't give me the party line, Ms. Brown. I'm not about to fall for it."

"But, Daddy, if you'd let me have this puppy I'd do everything," Charlie pleaded. "He's been waiting for me his whole life!"

"Charlie—" Cash began.

"It's true!" Charlie burst out. "Rowena talks to animals, and they tell her who they want to love them and, oh, Daddy—" Awe filled the little girl's voice. "This dog loves me!"

"What the—?"

The deputy's eyes widened, his mouth twisting in outrage.

Charlie tightened her arms around Clancy's neck. The dog licked her face.

Lawless looked from Charlie to Rowena, his fury boiling over. "Oh, no, you don't, Ms. Brown. You tell her the truth, and I mean now! You aren't some wacko Doctor Doolittle who talks to animals. And that dog should have been—"

Rowena had to give the deputy some credit. Even angry as he was, he managed to stop himself cold before he told Charlie the dog would have been put down months ago if he'd had his way.

"Daddy, Clancy—"

"The dog's name isn't even Clancy."

"Oh, Lord, not that again." Rowena groaned.

"Its real name is Destroyer, Charlie. And there's a good reason for that. He chewed the tires off Jeff Jones's racing bike. He dug up every flower the Volunteer Garden Brigade planted in the park. He just wrecked up that tea shop where your sister had her last birthday party and broke all of that nice old lady's china."

"Not my kitty pot that spit tea out his tail!" Mac gasped.

Even Charlie's eyes widened at the list of Clancy's transgressions.

Rowena dove in to explain. "Clancy only did those naughty things because he was lonely and bored and wanted attention," she assured the girls. "He needed a job to do."

She turned to Lawless, praying she could somehow make him understand. "Working is in a Newfoundland's blood, and now he's finally found his life's work. His…destiny, if you will." Heat stole into her cheeks at the danger of exposing so many of her vulnerabilities to a man she knew scorned her. "Look in his eyes, Officer," she pleaded. "When he looks at Charlie, he…"

How could Rowena even begin to describe what she saw in the dog's expression? Something new, something wonderful, the budding of the nobility of spirit she'd sensed would grow in Clancy once he began taking care of the human he was meant to love.

Once he found Charlie Lawless.

Rowena tried to put it into words the child's father would understand, feared it was a hopeless endeavor. "Deputy, do you believe in love at first sight?"

"No," he snapped back so quickly it startled Rowena. Something hard, bleak, tightened the deputy's face. Then it turned to blistering scorn so quickly anyone but Rowena would have doubted it had been there at all. "Why is it, Ms. Brown, that I'm dead certain *you* do? Exactly how many times have you done it?"

"Fallen in love at first sight?" Rowena's cheeks burned even hotter. "Actually, never."

In fact, she was beginning to think she never would fall in love at all—at least not with anything that walked on two legs instead of four. How many times had her mother warned her that she was so wrapped up in saving everyone else, she'd end up with no life of her own?

Rowena fought back her own doubts and looked straight in Lawless' eyes. "Just because I've never done it myself, doesn't mean I don't know it when I see it."

"Know what?"

"Love, Deputy," she said, running her hand down Charlie's ponytail. "Look at your daughter. Before you came barging in here, her eyes were shining. She was absolutely glowing. So happy—"

The officer's jaw clenched.

"I may not ever have fallen in love at first sight myself," Rowena asserted, "but give me a little credit. I know soul mates when I see them. Charlie and Clancy were meant for each other. Take him home and I promise you won't be sorry."

"Please, Daddy," Charlie begged softly.

Lawless ran his hand over his close cropped dark hair. "Charlie, you know what I'm up against! I barely have time to take care of you and your sister, let alone a dog."

Rowena hoped for some defiance, some fight to flare in the little girl. Instead, any spark in Charlie was snuffed out. Charlie was surrendering. Rowena could see it in the child's eyes. Anger surged through her. "If you've got too many things inked into your precious schedule to give Charlie what she needs, then maybe you'd better reconsider your priorities, Deputy!"

"No!" Charlie exclaimed, looking from Rowena to her father in dismay. "No, it's okay, Rowena. Daddy's right."

"No, he's not!" Rowena exclaimed, feeling the little girl's desperate need. Knowing in her bones that Clancy could heal her.

Cash Lawless' lip curled. "Let's get this straight once and for all, Dr. Doolittle. The day I take *that* dog into *my* home is the day they haul me off to the insane asylum and lock me up. What the hell?" He gave a bitter laugh. "Maybe I should let them. Sometimes a quiet cell might be a relief."

"No!" Mac cried, suddenly tearful, her clinging arms all but cutting off the deputy's windpipe. "Daddy, no! Don't go to the 'sane asylum! You promised you'd never go 'way!"

Lawless flinched as if the girl had slapped him. Even Charlie looked ice-white, stricken, though she didn't say a word.

"I'm sorry, button," Lawless soothed, obviously appalled at his children's distress. He tamped down his anger at Rowena to comfort his little ones instead. He stroked a curl back from his daughter's cheek with a tenderness that surprised Rowena, confused her. "I'm not going anywhere, Mac. It was just a—a figure of speech. A grownup way of saying no."

"Well, it's a really bad way!" Mac plumped out a quivering bottom lip.

"It sure is, if it makes you cry. I won't do it again."

"Pinkie swear?" Mac demanded, holding out her tiny finger.

Lawless hooked his long, strong masculine finger with his daughter's. "Pinkie swear," he repeated, a sheepish flush spreading up his throat as he slanted a glance at Rowena. She didn't want to feel touched by his gesture. Didn't want to like him even a little.

Tears welled up in Charlie's eyes, rolled down the silent little girl's cheeks to plop on Clancy's fur. There was something horrible in the resignation on the child's face. Rowena fought back tears of her own. The child's heart was breaking. Rowena could see it.

Lawless held out his other hand to Charlie. "Come on, cupcake. Better get a move on or we'll be late."

"Late? Again?" Rowena grumbled. "If being late is more important than taking a little time with your daughter, to—to—"

"To what?"

"To soften this for her. To explain…"

Charlie was losing Clancy once and for all and the little girl knew it.

Fury bubbled up in Rowena. "Is your precious appointment schedule more important than taking time to pay attention to your daughter's needs?"

The deputy's jaw hardened, his eyes black ice. "Don't you *dare* tell me how to run my family! Look at you. Telling impressionable kids you can talk to animals when anyone with a brain knows that's a bald-faced lie. If that's how you get your kicks, lady, there's nothing I can do about it. But tell your bullshit fairy tales to *someone else's kids*. Not mine. Got it, Ms. Brown?"

Rowena stared at him, stunned at the rage in his face, the bitterness, an almost…hopeless edge.

Clancy's worried gaze flickered between the two grownups. He whined piteously.

"Don't yell!" Charlie cried. "You're scaring him!"

Cash fell silent. Rowena's throat closed, aching for the little girl as Charlie turned back to the Newfoundland, stroked him lovingly.

"Don't be sad," Charlie pleaded, giving the Newfie one last hug. Clancy looked up at the little girl, his eyes mournful as if he understood her every word. "Maybe Rowena was wrong," she tried to reassure him. "Maybe you've been waiting your whole life for some other girl to love. Maybe you'll be so happy you won't even remember me. Maybe…" Her voice choked. Lawless stepped forward, took her hand.

"We've got to go, Charlie." He drew her gently away. Then he leveled Rowena a glare filled with loathing and blame. "Looks like you and that dog have exactly the same M.O., Ms. Brown, bashing around in places you don't belong. Maybe next time you'll think about the damage you could do before you go interfering in a child's life. Unless you like breaking kids' hearts as much as Destroyer likes breaking china."

"I didn't…I mean I don't…" Rowena stammered, unable to shake the sick feeling the deputy was right. Why hadn't she listened to the warning in her head? Why hadn't she been more careful? Waited until she could be sure Charlie's father would welcome the dog into his home?

Because she'd been so certain this time. She would have wagered her shop, her last dime, her own life that Charlie

Lawless and the Newfoundland were a match made in heaven. But now the little girl looked as if she'd been through hell. What use was this "gift" Auntie Maeve had given Rowena if it could make such a painful mistake?

"How could I have been so wrong?" she murmured to herself as she watched Cash Lawless and his daughters disappear beyond the pet shop door.

The Newfie tugged at his collar, looking up at Rowena as if he were sure she would chase after them. As if she could fix things. Make things right.

But she couldn't mend the damage she'd done to Charlie Lawless anymore than she could make Miss Marigold's teapots whole. *This must be some kind of record, even for you,* Rowena chastened herself grimly. *Two mistakes impossible to mend. Two broken hearts in a matter of days.*

Maybe more, a voice inside her whispered. She couldn't help but wonder if Charlie had been the only Lawless she'd hurt moments ago. Had she bruised Cash Lawless's heart, as well?

Absurd. The man didn't *have* a heart if he could turn his back on the love in his daughter's eyes when she looked at Clancy, her desperate need for everything the dog could bring into her life. The dog would always be there when the little girl needed him, would love her even if she made the mistakes Charlie was so afraid of.

Clancy nudged the door with his big head, bulldozed past Rowena to run after Charlie. But it was too late. Through the shop's big front window Rowena could see Cash Lawless's forest-green SUV pull away.

Clancy scratched at the door, whining. Did even the New-foundland sense that he'd just lost his chance to be the magical dog she'd known from the first he could be?

She thought of Charlie Lawless with her tidal-wave-proof watch and little Mac in her sparkly raincoat with the unicorn on its front. And the deputy, their father, with his blasted appointments and his stubborn loathing of the dog that could bring his daughters such joy.

She wanted to hate him, and yet...he'd seemed so strong, so gentle, when he'd tried to soothe his daughters' fears. Solid in a way that surprised Rowena.

She hadn't expected that kind of tenderness. Not from Cash Lawless. Not when he was so angry, so harried, obviously so upset.

You promised you'd never go 'way... Mac's cry echoed through Rowena, wringing her heart.

So somebody had left the little girls. Their mother? Rowena couldn't help but wonder. But why? Death? Divorce? No, not divorce.

No woman would leave those beautiful girls by choice. If Miss Marigold was still speaking to Rowena, Rowena could just slip through the gate and ask her. Those bug eyes beneath the lenses of her cat's eye glasses had a knack for ferreting out top secret information the CIA would envy. The old woman was a more reliable source than the library archives when it came to unearthing town gossip. But Miss Marigold would welcome Attila the Hun and his barbarian hordes into her beloved tea shop before she would Rowena.

Clancy scrabbled at the door and whined again.

So, now what are you going to do? Rowena asked herself. *Sit down and cry? What good will that do Charlie and Clancy? You didn't go into this business to give up. Just think of all the matches you've made over time. How many people refused to believe you knew what was best for them where a pet was concerned. What makes this time any different?*

Cash Lawless.

There was something about the deputy that unnerved her. Irritated her. Confused her. Made her feel restless inside, the way she did when her intuition hit the 'on' switch, hard. But just because the man rattled her nerves was no reason to give up.

"Damned if Cash Lawless is going to make a quitter out of me!" she resolved aloud. "I have to make this happen. For Charlie. For Clancy." She grimaced wryly. "So I can get some sleep."

Because she wouldn't be sleeping anytime soon, now that she'd made that perfect match—it would churn inside her, keep her awake. Until she settled Clancy in that house it would make her half crazy—

Only half *crazy?* Deputy Lawless mocked in her mind. *Lady, you'd rate certifiable in any psych test I can name.*

Terrific, Rowena thought. Now I've got *him* talking in my head, as well. As if Bryony and Ariel and Mom and Auntie Maeve weren't enough.

Don't be fobbing me off, you cheeky lass, the old Irishwoman's voice whispered in Rowena's memory. *It's important work I've given you to do.* Rowena's palm tingled with cold, as if she could still feel the imprint of the tin whistle her godmother had pressed into her hand. *No one else in the wide world but you can do the task you've been given. This pipe, Cuchullain's own, holds the power to charm all broken creatures' hearts.*

"But what about my heart?" Rowena sank to her knees and hugged Clancy tight, sudden loneliness wrapping around her. She found so many ways for other people to give love. Had put so many pets in other people's arms. She'd never once found one her gift told her was destined to fill her own.

Temptation nudged her. Maybe Clancy could stay. Be her dog to love and come home to and laugh over.

No. Much as she loved the Newfoundland, he'd never be as happy with her as he would with Charlie. He wouldn't have a child to tend, to watch over, to guard. Never have the chance to wash away a little girl's tears with swipes of his big pink tongue.

Clancy was Charlie's miracle. Charlie's chance. And somehow Rowena was going to make certain the child and the dog got to realize every bit of the magic she sensed would blossom between them.

No matter what Cash Lawless had to say about it.

CHAPTER FOUR

THERE WAS A PINK concrete poodle in Cash Lawless's front yard.

Rowena shifted into Park in front of the tombstone gray house at 401 Briarwood Lane and stared out her van window. She blinked hard in disbelief, but the statue was still there.

For an instant Rowena wondered if Charlie was wrong about her mother giving the puppies away. Maybe the deputy had put a hex on the poor things and turned them into lawn ornaments. In fact, maybe the statuary-cluttered yard was the reason Charlie was so scared of making mistakes. One *pouf* and the poor kid could be condemned to spend eternity like the Asian-inspired turtles balancing shell-crackingly heavy pots on their backs.

Truth was that if someone had constructed one of those games where you matched the house to the person who lived there, this would be the *last* place Rowena would have connected to Cash Lawless' picture.

No iron bars across the windows, no dungeons to lock helpless stray dogs in. Okay, so maybe the dungeon thing *was* an exaggeration, as Charlie would chasten her, but the idea of Cash Lawless in this modernistic nightmare was almost as ridiculous.

No question about it. With all the gorgeous vintage houses and charming cottages in Whitewater, the deputy had chosen the ugliest place of all.

And as for the yard he was so worried about Clancy ruining—Rowena figured the dog would be doing the neighborhood a favor if he dug a hole big enough to dump those creepy sculptures in.

Rowena switched off her engine and sucked in a deep breath. *Okay,* she told herself in her most reasonable tone, *let's get real here. The deputy's lack of taste shouldn't be distracting you this much. It's not like anyone is forcing* you *to live in this place. The bottom line is you're stalling.*

She heard Clancy snuffle from the backseat in agreement. Rowena glanced back at the dog, who tossed his beloved football over the back of the seat. It landed in her lap as if to say, "it's your play, quarterback." Unfortunately, the whole sports analogy wasn't a helpful one. It rekindled the memory of when Rowena was a kid and her far more competitive sisters sank to bribery to keep her off their teams.

"That doesn't mean I'll screw this up, too," Rowena reassured Clancy.

After all, she'd argued the dog's way into the Lawless household a jillion times the past week and a half. Composed and discarded speech after speech in her head, as she worked in the shop or designed artsy new dog bowls or sifted through broken pieces of pottery. She'd hoped she wouldn't find the kitty teapot Mac Lawless had loved amongst the rubble. But there was no mistaking the deliciously snooty feline face captured on one of the fragments of china.

Unfortunately digging out all the shards of the cat, then trying to superglue them together, proved to be an exercise in frustration. She ended up with the cat's butt fused to her fingers and could have sworn the blasted critter smirked at her.

She'd mourned Miss Marigold's teapots more than ever after that. She adored whimsical designs, things to surprise smiles out of people when they least expected it. Like the birdhouse Rowena had hung outside her kitchen window: a cat with a red-checkered napkin tied around his neck, a fork and knife clutched in his paws and his mouth wide open, forming the hole for the bird to go in.

That was the problem with the Lawless house. It had absolutely no sense of humor or wonder, an astonishing fact in light of the concrete poodle. The only thing vaguely human about the place was a straggly marigold at the bottom of the stairs.

Rowena rolled down the van's back window just enough to give Clancy a bit of fresh air then climbed out of the car. "Wait here, pal," she said, straightening her clothes. She'd dressed sedately—at least for her. Black slacks, a sunshine yellow jacket she'd bought at an art fair and earrings she'd made herself out of art deco-era buttons. Best to look like a respectable member of society when she told Cash Lawless how to run his life, she thought with a wry smile.

She climbed up the steep flight of stairs and made her way toward a front porch that caught the light in spite of the dismal house paint. The windows and doors were wide open, as if the house was gasping to drink in some of the beautiful September day beyond.

But Rowena hadn't even reached the door when she heard something that raked her nerves. Sounds coming through the screen. A child sobbing.

"Hurts, Daddy!" Mac Lawless wailed. "You always hurt me!"

"I know." Cash Lawless' rough-edged voice answered. "I know it's tight, honey, but it'll loosen up if you just—"

The hairs on the back of Rowena's neck stood on end. What in the world was he doing to the child?

"I hate you when you hurt me!"

"I hate myself." Lawless said with fierce feeling. "But damn it, Mac, I won't stop. Got that? I'll never give up. Never. Now come on, sweetheart! Open your leg and—"

Rowena's stomach clenched with outrage at the child's tears, terrified at what might be happening behind the gray walls. Dread overpowered caution. Without stopping to think, she wrenched the screen door open and plunged in. Stripped down to a sleeveless white T-shirt and running shorts, the deputy had the child pinned on the floor, his big hands curved around her ankles...

"Leave her alone," Rowena cried, lunging to grab him around the neck and pull him off the child. But Lawless' reflexes were too good. Before she could get a solid grip he dodged to one side, catching her arm, using her own momentum against her. In a heartbeat she was hurtling over him, Mac's shrieks piercing the air.

Rowena flailed, kicked, terrified she'd crush Mac, but Lawless controlled her flight. One leg snagged something on a side table, the sound of glass shattering in its wake. Rowena caught a glimpse of something glittery, pink just a second before she collided with it.

Cash swore, trying to help her avoid the blow, but it was too late. The object she'd hit careened over from the impact, taking her with it, a horrendous racket making her ears ring. Pain burned under Rowena's right eye as she struggled to untangle herself from whatever she'd fallen on. But the instant her mind registered the lines and shape of it, her heart slammed to the floor.

It was a wheelchair.

A child-sized, glittery pink wheelchair.

She pressed her hand over her mouth, feeling sick, feeling foolish, feeling like...well...like she was about to be slapped in handcuffs and hauled down to the hoosegow. For breaking and entering. Assaulting an officer. Not to mention vandalizing his property. She stared down at the hideous lamp she'd shattered—well, his really ugly property.

Slowly she shifted her gaze to the little girl she'd been trying to defend. Mac-sized metal braces encircled the child's tiny legs. Elastic exercise bands and miniature weights scattered the mat rolled out on the taupe carpet. Stuff for physical therapy.

Cash Lawless faced her down like one of her sister Ariel's bad-cop fantasies, his broad chest heaving, his tanned shoulders sweat-damp, some kind of tattoo smudging his left biceps. He looked disoriented, hunted, his nerves stripped raw as if he'd just gotten up from a torture session on the rack. Maybe he had.

He seemed to shake himself, trying to clear his head. "You." He pinned her with eyes that were granite-hard beneath spiky black lashes. "What the hell are you doing in my living room?"

For a moment Rowena couldn't remember the answer to his question herself, let alone form it into a coherent explanation. At least, not with the deputy's gaze peeling back the layers of her soul that way. She sucked in a deep breath, trying to get a little oxygen to her brain.

"It was Mac…" Rowena stammered. "She was screaming, saying you were hurting her. I could see you bending over her from the door and I…" She faltered, remembering all too well the power in him, the size of him, leaning over the tiny child who seemed completely at his mercy.

Somehow Rowena doubted the deputy would appreciate what her snap judgment of the situation had been. "I, uh…" She shrugged, undoubtedly looking as guilty as she felt. "I thought you…"

His gaze narrowed. "It's obvious what you thought."

Obvious *and* embarrassing. Rowena's cheeks burned. The man would hate her worse than ever after this. She'd taken Clancy's chances of being placed in the Lawless household from slim to none in less than twenty seconds.

"What can I say?" Rowena swallowed a lump of defeat. "It's official. I'm an idiot."

She glimpsed Mac moving on the exercise mat, pushing herself up to a sitting position and scooting her way over to lean against the wall. At least Mac was able to move her legs, Rowena thought in relief. Still, they looked far too thin, way too frail sticking out from under the ruffle of the glittery purple tutu about the little girl's middle.

"It's a very bad thing to hit a policeman!" she accused with a formidable frown. "My daddy's going to have to 'rest you now. And you'll get handcuffs on and— Hey, Daddy. That lady's bleeding."

"Yes, she is." Was his voice a little softer, or had Rowena imagined it? The deputy probably came with that whole "if I get quiet be afraid—very afraid" warning Rowena's mother had.

Rowena's hand fluttered up to the crest of her cheekbone. It stung, felt a little sticky. Great. She hadn't just humiliated herself. She'd managed to get cut in the process. She could just imagine trying to explain the mark it would leave behind.

Cash righted the wheelchair. He gathered Mac, tutu and all, in his arms and put her into the seat. There was something heart-wrenching in the big man's gentleness as he buckled her in, set her feet in their tiny rainbow striped stockings on the footrests.

"Guess I get to stop therapy while you take that lady to jail, huh, Daddy?" Mac chirped.

Cash grabbed the white hand towel he'd looped around his neck, looking as uncomfortable as Rowena felt. "We'll finish later," he said. "Head on into your room and watch *Dora the Explorer.*"

"Watch TV?" If the kid could have danced a jig, she would have. "*Before* my therapy's finished?"

"You heard me. Get out of here before I change my mind."

Completely unfazed by his growl, Mac flashed him a gleeful smirk then wheeled her chair down the hallway. Lawless watched until she vanished into one of the rooms. Silence fell, his utter isolation crushing all the anger out of Rowena.

"I'm...so sorry," she said.

"Yeah. So am I."

He turned back to Rowena, but instead of slapping her in cuffs or bellowing at her or any one of a jillion characteristically hostile actions she expected from the deputy she loved to hate, he paced toward her, a bemused expression on his face.

"You're crazy." Why didn't the insult sound nearly as scathing as it should have?

"You should talk to my mother." She grimaced, then touched her cheek gingerly as her cut stung anew.

Lawless's eyes narrowed as if he'd just remembered the injury, as well, and he closed the space between them. Frowning in concentration, he grasped Rowena's chin, tipped her face into the light streaming through the window. With the corner of his towel, he dabbed at the cut.

"Doesn't look like you need a stitch," he muttered, more to himself than to her. "A butterfly bandage will work just as well."

"In your expert medical opinion?"

"As a matter of fact, yes. We're the first responders to accidents. We handle triage until the EMTs get there. Come on back to my bedroom."

Rowena's surprise must have shown in her face. She could see the instant he realized what had given her pause.

"I keep the first aid kit on the top shelf in my closet to keep it out of Charlie's reach," he explained. "That kid makes boxes of bandages disappear so fast I should've taken stock in the company."

Rowena hated the niggling suspicion he rekindled. Neglected dogs and neglected kids often had the same markers to indicate they were in danger. More injuries than usual were at the top of the clues to look for. "Does Charlie get hurt that often?" she asked, trying to sound casual.

Lawless gave her a long look, as if he knew exactly what she'd been thinking. "No. She just has this thing about Band-Aids. She's always afraid we're going to run out."

Rowena remembered Charlie's big eyes filled with dread as she'd talked about tidal waves. Was there a good reason the girl was busy making disaster plans for their future trip to Florida?

"She seems...very worried for a child her age. I know it's none of my business, but—"

"You're right. It's not."

She'd hoped for some sort of insight, but she couldn't exactly blame him for closing up tight. She was a stranger, after all.

"Listen, I should just go," she suggested. "You're being a really good sport about this, but you don't want me here, and after this is little debacle I sure don't want to be here."

"You're not going anywhere until I dress that cut. Move." He sounded like a drill sergeant, and she doubted he'd hesitate to grab her arm and march her down the hall if she resisted. Instead, she let him herd her down the corridor.

As they passed what must be Mac's room, the child howled for Cash to adjust the television. Rowena waited for him outside the door, her eyes finding a collage of pictures on the long sweep of wall, family pictures of the girls from babyhood until just a few years ago.

Rowena's heart ached at the images she saw. Mac dancing in some kind of recital, her fluffy little costume making her look like a plump yellow chick. Charlie and Mac in doll-sized karate outfits. So Mac had been able to walk at one time. What had happened to change that? Rowena wondered. An illness? An accident?

She examined the center shot of the collage—an eight by ten. One of those family holiday pictures Rowena had always dreaded when she and her sisters had gathered at the family brownstone. It pictured the Lawless girls in matching Easter finery on the front steps of the gray house, ribbon-festooned wicker baskets clutched in their white gloved hands. Mac appeared angelic in rose-petal pink while Charlie looked as if the ruffles that made up her collar had developed sharp little teeth that were gnawing into her neck.

Behind the girls, Cash Lawless stood, sexy as hell in a black suit and Kelly-green tie, his crisp white shirt making his tan seem darker, his angular face all the more arrestingly handsome. But in spite of the formal clothes that fit his athletic body to perfection, something primitive glinted in his eyes—as if he were constantly aware danger could be right around the corner, and he'd damned well be ready to meet it.

The exquisitely beautiful woman standing beside him was ice to his fire. Hair blond as Mac's framed the woman's face, but she possessed none of the fairy-like charm that surrounded the little girl. Cool, poised and elegant, the woman's face was reminiscent of a young Sharon Stone, stylish cream pencil skirt and a tailored jacket without a single crease skimming a figure Miss America would envy.

So this movie queen goddess clone was Cash Lawless's wife.

Rowena didn't know why the fact should bother her. No doubt it was a holdover from that whole "matching" curse Auntie Maeve had stirred up in her mind so long ago. Making people and animals fit where they belonged.

Obviously Cash Lawless had a strong opinion where Ice

Goddess belonged. In his bed, underneath him, fulfilling all those fantasies the woman must have inspired in every other red-blooded man she met.

The kind of hot fantasies Rowena would never inspire. Sighing, she smoothed a hand down her own jacket, realizing the man would be hard-pressed to discern whether she had breasts or not beneath the flowing yellow cloth. Not that she wanted Cash Lawless to notice her breasts, she amended hastily. Or anything else about her except what a perfect pet Clancy would be for his lonely daughter.

Rowena peered again at the woman's face in the picture, trying to probe beyond the one-dimensional image to the human qualities that ran far deeper. That made the woman a wife, a mother. One who seemed to have disappeared.

Was she the reason Charlie and Mac had seemed so terrified their father would leave them? What had happened to her? To *them*—the perfect little Stepford family in the Easter picture?

Rowena pulled her gaze away from the image and caught sight of a much smaller photo. It wasn't one of those perfectly posed varieties. Instead, it looked a bit off-center, a little blurry. Charlie perched high in the forked branches of a tree, bracing a board while her father nailed it to what must be the floor of a tree house.

Rowena scarce recognized the child in the picture as the ghost who'd scowled into her shop window for weeks. Charlie's eyes sparkled with excitement, her grin so wide and carefree.

Even more amazing was the difference in Cash's face. Dressed in a faded Police Academy sweatshirt with the sleeves torn out of it, he looked ages younger.

He wasn't even looking at the camera. His gaze fixed on Charlie's face as if there was nothing in the world more beautiful to him than his child, or more important to him than this moment he shared with her.

Rowena felt a jab of envy. Making memories, Auntie Maeve had called times like the tree house moment captured on film. Rowena could still remember the spry old woman warning the ever-busy Nadine Brown that such opportunities were fleeting. Once gone, they never came again. Lost in her own wistful memories, Rowena was startled by Cash's voice when he called out.

"This is taking a little longer than I thought. Head on back. Mine's the room at the end of the hall."

Rowena figured she could make a break for it, but if patching her up would make him feel better, she might as well let him. Besides, the man piqued her curiosity more than ever now.

The first two times she'd met him, he'd seemed so hard-edged, almost military in his need to be in control. But today with his disabled daughter, she'd glimpsed cracks in that facade. Saw in the desperation, the determination limning his face along with the sheen of sweat, a sense of isolation that yanked at her heart.

Hurts, Daddy... Mac's tear-choked voice raked Rowena's memory. *I hate you when you hurt me...*

I hate myself.

What must it be like for him? Suffering through Mac's tears day after day? Realizing that no matter how hard he fought, there were some things beyond his power to control? And that one of them was his daughter's pain?

Entering the room he'd indicated, she looked around, trying to connect the man to his surroundings. But again, the setting didn't fit him, his room yawning spaces of emptiness broken up by even more clusters of family pictures that marked places where furniture must have been.

A double-sized box springs and mattress sat on the floor, the bed made up so precisely Rowena could have bounced a quarter off of the simple navy spread. A folding TV tray to one side held a windup alarm clock, yet another ugly lamp and a James Patterson novel splayed pages down somewhere toward the beginning, the one and only thing in the house that actually had a thick layer of dust filming its cover.

After a moment, Cash strode in. "First aid kit's in the other room."

She jumped, feeling as if she'd intruded in something painful, something private. "Right. I, uh, was just looking at your pictures. The one of the tree house in the hall is terrific," she scrambled to explain, trying to break the sudden tension. "I always wanted a tree house when I was a kid. But my mom and dad weren't big on that kind of stuff. You know, doctors' schedules, volunteer work, making sure their kids had a jillion after-school activities that would look good on applications to Harvard Medical School."

What was she doing, telling him stuff like that? Next thing she knew he could ask the six million dollar question—with those family expectations, how did she end up here, in Whitewater, running a pet shop? Fortunately, he was too distracted by the picture tacked to his wall.

His gaze narrowed and he ran one fingertip over the tree house. "I never finished building it," he said. "Mac got hurt."

So Mac's disability had come from an accident of some kind. Had she fallen out of the tree? Rowena wondered. No wonder he'd quit working on the thing. But it seemed somehow cruel to ask him outright.

"How long has she been in a wheelchair?"

"Two and a half years."

"Mac's injuries…what did the doctors say? Are they permanent?"

His eyes blazed. "My little girl will walk again. Got that? She won't just walk, she'll dance the way she did when she was three. I won't let that wheelchair be all she ever knows."

"No. Of—of course not." Her chest ached as she remembered Mac in the little ruffled chick outfit, Mac with the purple tutu around her tummy when she'd been doing therapy.

Mac, the little fairy child…everyone knew that fairies had to dance.

"It must have been hard for you…and your wife." She couldn't help thinking about the perfect woman in the picture. The deputy's face went cold.

"Yeah," he said, scorn dripping from his voice. "It's been pure hell for Lisa."

Present tense. So the woman was alive. "Is their mother the reason the girls got so upset in the shop, worried about you leaving them?"

"We're divorced and they haven't seen her for months. Is that what you want to know?" he challenged, making her feel like a nosy jerk.

"I'm sorry."

"I'm sure as hell not. Let's get that cut taken care of and get you out of here. I've got Mac's therapy to finish."

Rowena fled into the master bath, its walls stark white, almost painfully clean, nothing on the counter to show a man actually lived here.

She stiffened, startled as Lawless's big hands closed around her waist, set her up on the bathroom counter as if she weighed no more than a cotton ball. She sensed he must've done the same with his daughters countless times. But there was nothing innocent in what Rowena felt in the wake of his touch.

His intensity seared into her, the imprint of his hands still burning as he opened the bathroom closet and stretched up to snag a Gortex bag from the highest shelf.

"Just hand me a bandage," Rowena said, not sure she wanted him to touch her again. "I'll get out of here before—" *Before you realize you flustered me so badly…*

Turned you on, you mean, she forced herself to acknowledge. *It's just a reflex, Rowena. With all that fire, all that passion in him you're off to save the world again. Cash Lawless might be hard on the outside, but inside, where no one can see, he's bleeding. And you could never stand for any living creature hurting that way to be alone...*

He dampened a corner of his white towel. "This will just take a second." He cupped her face with his long fingers, dabbed at the cut. Tingles shot down to Rowena's breasts. The man might not be able to see them with her jacket on, but apparently they sensed *him* just fine.

He took out some antibiotic lotion, the kid-friendly kind that didn't sting, and squeezed some onto an Elmo bandage. As he carefully stretched Elmo to hold the cut's edges together butterfly fashion, his forearm brushed the tip of one nipple. Her breath hissed between her teeth.

"Hurt?" He gave her a concerned glance. She shook her head, not trusting her voice.

Oh, Lord, don't let him feel how pointy I got...

"Looks like we'll be even after today," he said, unexpectedly trailing his fingertip down the side of her face. He had to feel the way her blood suddenly pounded in that tender spot where her jaw met her throat.

"Even?" Rowena squeaked.

"You'll probably have a shiner come morning."

A black eye? Rowena thought. That was all he was talking about? At least he didn't know what that casual touch of his had done to her long-dozing libido. An instant later relief gave way to alarm. Drat. Drat. Double drat. Cash wouldn't be the only one talking about her eye. Her bruise should be in all its purple glory by the time Wednesday hit.

"Great," Rowena muttered aloud, pointing to her bandage. "I can't wait to explain this to my mom when she stops by the shop on Wednesday."

"Aren't you a little old to be explaining things to your mom?"

"Heck, no. There's no statute of limitations when it comes to mom-worry. She'll be fussing over my scrapes and bruises until I'm eighty."

"You're lucky, then."

She saw Lawless's mouth tighten and thought of the blond goddess in the picture and his little girls, so afraid of being left by him.

Blast. She'd meant to make a joke. Instead she'd managed to stick her foot in her mouth again.

"Your family lives nearby?" he asked, ironing the emotion out of his face.

"No. Mom's just swinging by on her way home from a medical conference in Iowa City to check up on me. Perfect timing, as usual."

He stared at her, and she got that sensation she'd had before, that he was seeing things she'd rather keep hidden. "I'd love to be a fly on the wall when you tell the good doctor about your little performance today," he said.

"My sister Ariel says that fibbing is legal when it comes to soothing mom-worry. Why tell her things that will only get her upset?"

"In this case, she'd have every right to be. Anything could have happened. You charge in here, alone, and try to wrestle me to the floor. I outweigh you by at least fifty pounds. I'm a cop with a temper you know can be dangerous and I've made it clear I don't like you."

"First impressions are deceiving."

"Not in my experience." His gaze skimmed slowly from her wayward curls to her non-existent breasts, then back up to her face as he seemed to consider. "My gut's almost always right when it comes to getting a bead on someone's character. A cop's life depends on it. And on being smart about the risks he takes."

His eyes darkened for a moment. Rowena wondered if he was thinking of the chances he took every day when he put on that uniform, and about the possibility that his little girls' worst fears could be realized. Someday he might not come home.

"Is there a single soul on earth who knows where you are right now, Ms. Brown?" he asked.

"Well, um…" Clancy. But she supposed the deputy would say he didn't count. The dog was smart, but even a Newfoundland couldn't file a missing persons report.

"I thought not," the deputy said soberly. "If I *had* been in the middle of abusing my daughter when you interrupted me what did you think would happen? Did you think I'd just let you sashay out of here and report me?"

"No." She wasn't an idiot, after all.

"Didn't you have some sort of plan?"

"My plan was to stop you."

"And mine would have been to shut you up, once I knew you'd discovered my secret. The wrong kind of man could have hurt you." He touched her injured cheek so gently it rocked her to her core. "Could have killed you."

He was right.

The thought chilled her as his fingers fell away, but she raised her chin, defiant. "What was I supposed to do?" she demanded. "Stand out on the front porch with my cell phone and wait for help to come? I know you think I'm silly or naive or reckless, Deputy, but I'll be *damned* if I'd ever stand by and let anybody hurt an innocent little girl like Mac when I'm around!"

His eyes warmed, melting some of the hardness in his face. Revealing bare hints of a far different man buried beneath. "You know what, Ms. Brown? I actually believe you."

"Don't sound so surprised."

"But I am." A perplexed crease carved deep between straight dark brows. "Do you have any idea how many people I see every day who won't get involved? Something unthinkable happens right in front of their noses, but they turn away, pretend ignorance. Turn up the volume on the TV set so they can't hear the screams. They're too busy, too scared or too apathetic to take a risk or even just inconvenience themselves."

His tone softened, his gaze bound to hers by some fragile thread. Respect? Rowena wondered.

"I'll tell you this much for certain, Ms. Brown," he continued. "If either of my girls ever *did* wander off and run into trouble, I'd hope like hell that you were the one who saw them."

Rowena swallowed, astonished at just how much his admission meant to her. "Deputy, are you actually saying something nice to me?"

The left corner of his mouth ticked up. "Under the circumstances, maybe you should call me Cash."

"Okay. Cash." She fidgeted with a button on her jacket. Bad move. It just reminded her of that whole tingling breast episode. "And what—what are you going to call me?"

"Trouble." He smiled then. A real barn burner of a smile. For a minute Rowena forgot to breathe. "You know, you still haven't answered my question," he said. "Why did you show up on my doorstep in the first place?"

"Oh, it was nothing much," Rowena started to hedge, her cheeks burning. Then something in his face made her decide to go for broke. "I just stopped by to convince you to give up your egocentric ways and think about your girls for a change. After all, what's the big deal about adding a dog to the family?" She grimaced in self-disgust. "I figured maybe I could guilt you into letting Charlie have Clancy."

"And now?" Something in his eyes reminded her of Charlie, something tender, vulnerable, hurts she ached to heal.

"Now you've ruined my whole plan. You're not a self-absorbed ass. You obviously love your daughters. And maybe— just maybe, mind you—you don't need me to sweep in here on my broomstick and straighten your priorities out."

"Thank you for that."

"Deputy...I mean, Cash..." The name sounded so strange, intimate on her tongue. "I still wish there was some way to... I just can't help but feel that Charlie *needs* this dog."

The words hurt him. She could see his guilt twisting, a sense of inadequacy in this man that stunned her.

"If this was before the accident and Mac wasn't in a wheelchair..." He raked his hand through his hair. "Hell, I'd let Charlie get a dog. Not one the size of a Shetland pony, mind you. And sure as hell not Destroyer."

For the first time, Rowena didn't bother to correct him.

"But you have to see that under the circumstances it's impossible." It clearly mattered to him that *she* see what *he* saw, understood his reasons. The knowledge humbled Rowena, made her ache to close the distance between them. A distance far greater than this small room. A distance filled with pain she couldn't heal. Wounds she couldn't cure. Vulnerabilities he'd never allow anyone to understand.

She reached out and squeezed his hand. It felt so big, so strong beneath her fingers as he looked at her in surprise. Still, he didn't pull away.

"I don't believe in impossible," Rowena confessed, feeling somehow unutterably young.

"Then I envy you."

She could see from his haunted expression that he really did. "But Mac walking again...you believe in that."

"That's different." He tugged his hand free, his voice roughening. "She has to walk. If she doesn't I'll never forgive my-self." Self-blame twisted Cash's features, as if there were secrets inside him jagged as broken glass.

"Were you…with her when she got hurt?"

"No. Lisa was driving."

Driving. So it had been a car accident that injured the little girl. Rowena laid her hand on his arm. "There was nothing you could have done, then. It's not your fault."

He wheeled around, banged one fist on the wall. "Don't tell me what's my fault and what's not! You don't know what happened. Nobody does—" He broke off with an oath as a tense voice sounded from the far end of the hall, running foot-steps coming toward them.

"Daddy!"

Charlie. Rowena's heart sank. The child raced into the room, slammed to a halt, her glasses sliding askew. Charlie gripped her hands together tight as she saw Rowena.

"Oh, Daddy, is it true?"

Rowena felt Cash try to melt the tension in his shoulders, uncurl his fists by force of will. "Is what true, cupcake?"

"Hope says it's a surprise for me. I didn't believe her, but she says I must get to keep him. 'Cause why else…" Charlie hesitated, almost as if she didn't dare put it into words. "But, Daddy, why else would my dog come here?"

Such a wistfulness filled Charlie's old-soul eyes Rowena wanted to cry.

Rowena saw Cash's jaw harden in dismay, as if someone had twisted a knife in his chest. She was the one who had put it there.

"Hi, Charlie," Rowena said softly, sliding down from her perch on the counter.

"My dog. He's in the car. He—he threw the football right out the window to me." Charlie nibbled her bottom lip, looking from Cash to Rowena.

"I'm sorry I got you all excited," Rowena began, knowing the apology could never be enough for the pain she'd caused the little girl or her father. "I just stopped by to…um, apologize to your daddy. It was very wrong of me to get your hopes up the way I did, telling you that Clancy belonged with you. I didn't understand that…well, that your sister…"

"Oh." The tentative sparkle of hope vanished. It was as if the sun went behind a cloud. "It's okay, Rowena. I know. He might knock Mac down, or eat stuff off the kitchen counters or—or run away like my mom did."

The child was thinking in disasters again. Rowena wondered how long it had been since little Charlie had imagined unicorns and princesses and happy endings all her own.

Rowena hunkered down. She squeezed Charlie's hand. "I'm sorry, sweetheart. For making you sad."

"Oh, I'm never sad," Charlie protested, looking at her father in alarm.

"Everybody gets sad, honey," Rowena said. "I'm sad because what I did hurt you. And your daddy. I never meant to." She looked up into Cash's pain-filled eyes. "I'm so sorry."

"Maybe you'd better go," Cash said. He didn't say "so I can mop up the damage." He didn't have to.

She was ready to flee, but as she brushed past him, he caught her wrist for a moment, his hand warm around the fragile skin. She looked up to see his forced smile, his gaze pulling her in. "See you, Trouble."

Rowena's eyes stung at the unexpected tenderness in the words. Maybe the most merciful thing she could do from now on was to stay out of Cash Lawless's way. Because one thing she'd learned for certain by coming to his house.

When it came to trouble, the man had more than enough of his own.

CHAPTER FIVE

IT WAS GOING TO TAKE a hell of a lot of coffee to pry his eyes open this morning, Cash thought as he paced to the counter and grabbed the heart-spattered mug Charlie had painted for him last Father's Day. But once again, his former partner and current nanny, Vinny Scoglomiglio, didn't disappoint. The sixty-eight-year-old ex-cop brewed coffee so thick and black and strong Cash was convinced someday some archeologist was going to stumble on a cylinder-shaped object that would be a cup of Vinny-style joe standing on its own, even the mug crumbled away. Yep, after Armageddon, all that would be left were cockroaches, piles of Styrofoam and Vinny's coffee.

"You look like hell this morning."

The gravelly voice should have startled him, but he'd grown so used to the old man letting himself into the house at all hours, he didn't even flinch.

"Right back at you, Mr. Google," he said, casting a bleary glance over his shoulder. The girls had christened Vinny with that nickname soon after the man had started babysitting them. Cash still wasn't exactly sure if they'd just massacred the guy's last name or if the soubriquet came from the fact that Vinny spent every spare moment on the Internet.

Vinny shoved half-glasses up his nose, abandoning his morning crossword puzzle. "I should look like hell. I'm practically dead. Considering all the Jim Beam I drank and the cigars I smoked I expected to be six feet under thirty years ago. What's your excuse, junior?"

Cash Lawless took a long swallow of coffee, waiting for the bitter brew to do its stuff. "Haven't been getting much sleep lately." Lately? More like the past week and a half. Ever since Rowena Brown had walked out the door.

Vinny eyed him like a mother hen with one chick. "Been having those nightmares again?"

Cash's jaw tightened. He hated the damn things—flashbacks, the counselor the force had sent him to had told him. Perfectly understandable under the circumstances, the woman had soothed. Nothing to be ashamed of.

Except they made him feel like he was caught in a crossfire with his pistol jammed.

"Been a while since one of those sons of bitches laid into you," Vinny observed, squinting up at him. "Usually happens when your stress ratchets up. Something going on around here that you haven't told me about? That ex-wife of yours isn't causing you trouble?"

The very mention of Lisa usually sent a jolt of bitterness and anger through Cash. And yet, it wasn't his ex-wife's coolly elegant image that rippled across the surface of his mind today. It was a gypsy of a woman with sunshine hair and blind faith in her eyes, a woman who'd barreled into Cash's thoughts the way she'd charged into his house, with no thought at all to her personal safety.

Yes, Rowena Brown was trouble, all right. And she'd changed Cash's understanding of the word forever. Where had she gotten that fire of conviction, the courage that drove her? That fierce belief that she could make things better if she tried?

I don't believe in impossible...

Cash had to agree it was true. Anyone with half a brain would have known her trip to Cash's house could only end badly. If she'd actually knocked on the door instead of charging in, he would have verbally lambasted her so harshly for coming near his children again that her ears would still be ringing.

She had to have known the kind of reception she'd get. And yet the reckless woman had come to Briarwood Lane anyway, that menace of a dog of hers packed in the back of her van as if she actually thought she might have a chance to convince Cash to take Destroyer in.

If *that* wasn't evidence Rowena Brown believed in the impossible, then nothing was.

"Hey, there, buddy. I asked you what's wrong," Vinny grumbled. "And don't tell me nothing. I may be old, but I'm not dead yet. I can see something's eating at you."

Not a bad description, Cash admitted, though he'd never tell Vinny that. Rowena had been nibbling away at his concentration for days now. He'd remember the heat of her skin beneath his fingertips, the silk of her hair against the backs of his knuckles. The way her pulse had pounded when he'd touched her throat and how she'd gasped when he'd accidentally brushed her breast with his arm. Her gold-tipped lashes had flown wide and in spite of everything—in spite of himself— he'd felt himself hardening beneath the worn cotton of his running shorts.

She'd hardened, too. The tip of her nipple had teased his arm, and she'd looked at him as if he'd burned her. And for a moment, just a moment it was a fire they both wanted to dive into.

He'd almost forgotten how tempting a woman's skin could be, how tantalizingly different from his own. And for the first time in two years he had ached to sink himself deep into a woman's wet heat…

Vinny jabbed him with the SpongeBob pencil he was using for his morning crossword, and Cash jumped as if his friend had caught him in the act. Thank God Vinny couldn't read his mind. "Well? What's bothering you?"

"It's a woman." The confession slipped out before Cash could stop it. Weirdly, just saying it aloud was a relief.

"Thank you, Jesus!" Vinny flung SpongeBob to the table, the big Italian's face gleaming. "What'd she do? Club you over the head with a baseball bat to get your attention?"

"Actually, she tried to get me in a choke hold. I gave her a black eye."

Vinny scowled in confusion. "You what?"

"It was an accident," Cash said, suddenly enjoying his friend's discomfiture. "But I suppose my reaction was under-standable under the circumstances. She *was* breaking and entering."

Vinny glanced into his own cup, looking more worried than ever. "My coffee too weak to clear your head this morning, boy? You're not making any sense."

"She heard Mac crying through the screen door." Cash's amusement vanished in the wake of the memory. "We were working on that new set of exercises her therapist gave us last time."

"Oh."

There was no need to say more. Vinny was the only other person besides Cash and Mac's therapist, Janice Wilson, who knew what torture the sessions could be. It was grim work, strengthening little legs that had been broken, torn and patched back together. Scar tissue clenched the muscle fibers so tight that it was agony to stretch them.

"So what happened then?" Vinny prodded.

"Rowena blindsided me, charging through the door, grab-bing me around the neck. A sneak attack on a cop is never a good idea."

"Not to mention a combat vet. And you're both."

There were times Cash would have sold his soul to be in a firefight back in Kuwait instead of on that exercise mat in his own living room. War was hell, but at least he hadn't been waging it on his own child.

"What the hell was this woman thinking? Breaking into your house that way?"

"Rowena thought I was abusing Mac."

"Hell, whoever this Rowena is, she was lucky to get off with that black eye! If I'd been here, I'd have wrung her neck for suggesting such a thing. No wonder you're still seething."

"That's the funny thing, Vinny. Once I got the picture, I wasn't mad. I...liked her."

"Liked her? This...hey, Rowena—now I remember that name! Isn't that the same dame you were wanting to ride out of town on a rail a few weeks ago?"

"That's the one."

"Vern Hendersen down at the gas station went in her shop—his old lady made him, just to get the scoop after that smash and bash at the tea shop everybody was talking about."

Just as Cash had figured, the tale of the tea shop had leaked to the public and then some. A story like that was just too damned funny to most cops to keep to themselves.

"Vern says this Rowena person won't last long around here. In Whitewater, a dog's a dog. You can get everything you need for one at the Fleet and Farm. Folks around here are too smart to waste their money on those fancy big city gewgaws she's got in her windows."

"You're probably right," Cash agreed. And yet, now some part of him would be sorry to see her go.

Vinny swore under his breath in frustration. "Hell, when you said you weren't sleeping because of a woman, I thought maybe some female had stirred you up. Ain't been using your dick for much besides holding up your underpants for the past two years."

"For Cripe's sake, Vinny. I hope you don't talk like that around my kids!"

"Like what?" Vinny said, looking injured. "Working around here, my mouth's cleaner than the insides of most people's washing machines! So this woman—she didn't flip up your light switch?" The ex-cop looked nosy as an old maid, eager to get some tasty tidbit of gossip.

Cash pretended ignorance. "My what?"

"Never mind." Vinny heaved a sigh. "If I have to explain, it didn't happen. No chance you might actually get laid."

The image that sprang into his mind made a body part far lower than his head throb—Rowena Brown spread out across his bed while he set out to discover exactly what feminine curves lay underneath that loose yellow jacket she'd been wearing. Somehow the fantasy only made stark reality worse.

"Exactly when am I supposed to get laid?" Cash demanded. "In between *Dora the Explorer* and putting dinner on the table? Or maybe I could squeeze it in between Mac's therapy and her time in the swimming pool? I could just lock the kids in the bathroom and go at it right here on the kitchen table. Hell, Vinny, even if I *did* feel like having sex, no woman in her right mind would have me. One look around here and any sane person would run the other way."

"You can't be sure about that." Vinny crossed his arms over his barrel chest and shot Cash an appraising look. "There's no denying you're pit bull mean and you've got an ugly mug on you, but you never can tell what'll get a woman's motor running."

Cash chuckled, trying not to wince as a pain jabbed behind his left eyeball. He resolutely ignored it. He didn't have time for a migraine. "Thanks for the vote of confidence, Mom."

"So this woman. She tried to beat you up and then...what?"

"She tried to convince me to let Charlie have a dog."

"A dog, eh?" Vinny didn't look nearly as aghast as he should have. He picked up SpongeBob, rolling the pencil between his fingers until it settled between two like the cigars he'd had to give up after his heart attack. "A dog might not be a bad thing, kid. Little Miss Charlotte spends an awful lot of time squirreling herself away in hidey holes. Last Thursday it took me forty-five minutes to find her. She was asleep up in that tree in the backyard."

"Asleep up there?" Cash exclaimed, visions of trips to the emergency room dancing in his head. "She could have fallen— broken her neck!"

"Not that girl. She lashed herself to a branch with a chunk of rope. Said she read sailors did that sometimes when a killer storm blew up at sea—well, they lashed themselves to a mast instead of a branch, but you get the drift."

He did. Far too well. And the image of his little girl up in her unfinished tree house alone hurt him.

"She's too damned quiet for such a little thing, Cash," Vinny said.

"Her mother abandoned her. Her sister's in a wheelchair. What do you think she should be doing, Vinny?" Cash fired back. "Turning cartwheels?"

The ice pick jabbed behind his eye again. He went to the kitchen cupboard and reached for the bottle of pills on the top shelf. He shook one into his palm and slammed it back with a gulp of coffee. He knew Vinny had seen the prescription bottle. The older man's voice softened.

"I'm just saying it might not be such a crazy idea—getting a dog for around here," Vinny said. "If it would make Charlie happy."

"The dog Charlie wants is the size of the girls' playhouse and has the manners of a boatload of Vikings bent on pillage. Exactly where would you suggest we put the dog once I get

Mac up on crutches? One fall could tear out the screws that are holding her femur together. And then—"

"Alright! Alright! I get the picture." Vinny held his hands palms up in surrender. "But wouldn't there be plenty of time to worry about that if…" He stopped dead midsentence and looked away.

"If what?" Cash challenged.

Vinny met Cash's gaze with reluctance and very real love. "MacKenzie isn't up on crutches yet."

"And maybe she never will be? Is that what you're trying to say?" Fury blazed in Cash, turning the ice pick to fire.

"Cash, I—"

"If that's how you feel, maybe you shouldn't be watching the girls. I can't afford any negativity around here that Mac might pick up on."

Hell, Cash thought, he sounded like a first-class jerk. Vinny Scoglomiglio had saved his life in the chaotic weeks after Lisa had bailed on him and the girls. His friend had stepped into the role of nanny like a Mary Poppins in combat boots, taking on the mysterious woman-jobs of hair braiding and Barbie playing and birthday cake baking with Cash's daughters.

Okay, so the cakes were heavy as rocks, but they were home-made. Cash had almost humiliated himself by breaking down when the kids had surprised him on his birthday with his favorite German chocolate cake. Vinny and the girls had made it from scratch, using the recipe Lisa had left behind.

"I'm sorry. I'm an ungrateful bastard, and I wouldn't blame you if you never set foot back in this kitchen," Cash said, voice low. "But I hope you will."

"And miss the sour look on your face when you take that first drink of my coffee in the morning? No way. Can't shake me off that easily, boy. There's a new tuna casserole recipe I clipped out of the Sunday paper I'm dying to try."

Cash felt the throbbing in his head start to ease. "Glutton for punishment, huh?"

"Stayed married for twenty-six years. Be married still if Dolores hadn't divorced me. If that's not proof, what is?"

Cash laughed. "I always wanted to meet Dolores so I could thank her for that. If she hadn't served you with the papers, you'd never have quit the Chicago force, never have left the city and come here."

"Fate." Vinny said succinctly. "You know, I never was much use to my own kids. Working long hours, drinking away whatever was left, trying to drown out the pictures that inner-city hell painted in my head. I'm damned grateful to have a second chance, you know? To be something better to your kids than I was to my own."

"I was lucky as hell when I drew you as partner."

"Got stuck with the burned-out alcoholic, you mean."

"You were off the bottle by then." Cash remembered Lisa's reaction to the news when she heard it from one of the other deputies wives—that Cash had drawn the short straw, gotten the screw-up from the big city. They'd fought about it for hours. Truth was, Cash had volunteered to take Vinny on. Something in Vinny's face had made Cash trust the older man, first with his own life and later with the lives of his daughters.

"Bookmakers wouldn't have given me very good odds when it came to staying clean. Smart money would've been on the chance I'd get you killed."

"I placed the winning bet. Maybe I used all my luck up on that. What if there's none left for Mac?" The doubt slipped out. He met Vinny's eyes.

"Luck will have nothing to do with whether that little girl of yours walks or not. MacKenzie is your daughter, Cash. Stubborn as hell. She'll come through fine either way, no matter what happens. You'll see."

"Mac has to want to walk. But Janice says I can't—can't make her…"

Vinny's smile braced him. "Then Janice doesn't know you as well as I do, does she?"

Cash wished to hell he could be sure Vinny was right. There had been a time when Cash believed he could conquer anything. No battle was too tough, no challenge too great. He'd been a marine. His body tough and trained. His will invincible.

He'd taken on the Iraqi invaders with an almost suicidal belief in himself, defeat not a possibility in his world.

How odd to think Rowena Brown felt the same thing, especially now, when he'd learned the hard truth about limitations he'd once denied. He envied her that fierce ability to believe. In healing. In hope. In the future.

There were times Cash didn't believe in anything anymore. Not even himself.

NIGHT SHIFT STANK.

Cash slugged down the last of his tepid coffee from the Quick Mart and tried to keep his eyelids from caving on him. Not much going on in town—a few fender benders, a disturbing the peace call and a report that half a dozen kids were partying at Mose Dillon's abandoned boathouse down by the Mississippi.

No booze this time—at least, not where Cash could find it. But they had stockpiled enough illegal fireworks to start a brushfire if a stray spark had fallen on the dry leaves starting to blanket the ground.

Another deputy might have hauled them all in, but Cash and his five brothers had gotten into more than their share of mischief when they'd been that age. So he'd done his best to scare the shit out of them and followed their car to the place they were supposed to be staying overnight. He'd been relieved to see Jimmy Parker's mom in the window, probably demanding to know where the boys had been. Last party ol' Jimmy would be hosting for awhile, Cash had figured.

But as the rest of his shift crawled by, Cash's week's worth of insomnia started catching up with him until he was bone tired and bored as hell. And one thing he knew from years on the force: anybody—even a deputy—asleep at the wheel was a very bad thing.

Cash turned down Main Street on his patrol, looking over the row of buildings across from the school. The pet shop was still closed. Not that he'd expected Rowena Brown to open the shop for a blue light special on catnip at five in the morning, but from what he'd seen when he'd started his shift, she'd closed up the shop early the night before.

Not that it mattered. It was just that a cop needed to know the natural rhythm of the neighborhoods he patrolled. Yeah. The whole street lay quiet, Rowena's shop dark and shut up, Miss Marigold's kitchen window glowing in the corner of the tea shop. From what Cash could tell, the older woman slept as rarely as he did.

His cell buzzed—the ring tone set to the theme from *Dragnet* by Mr. Google himself, the techno whiz, when Cash hadn't been watching. Damned if Cash could figure out how to change the ring back.

Frowning, he scooped up the phone and hit the talk button.

"Lawless here."

"Miss me, candy ass?"

Vinny. The Italian's jovial voice told Cash it wasn't an emergency.

"I miss you all right. Like a toothache."

"You never write, you never call. Yada, yada, yada."

"What the hell are you calling me for in the middle of the night? I'm working, you know."

"More like you're about to fall asleep, and I'm saving your

butt again, junior. It's a tough job, but somebody's got to keep you on your toes." Vinny chuckled. "Quiet night, huh? Been listening to the scanner."

"Not much happening."

"Good, because you're going to have to be ready to party down when you drag your sorry ass in come morning."

"Party?" Cash echoed. "I didn't miss a holiday...or a birthday—no. Charlie's isn't for months. What's up?"

"Can't say for sure. Big secret. The girls are up to something for sure."

"What girls?" Cash asked tiredly.

"Mac and Charlie. You know. Your pride and joys. The fruits of your loins. Your—"

"Yeah, yeah. I get it. My girls. But both of them? Doing something together?"

"You got it, dude." Cash could almost hear Vinny grimace. "Damn. I've got to quit watching those Mary Kate and Ashley reruns with Mac."

"You made them, right? I mean, Mac and Charlie. Play together."

"I know I'm brilliant, but I can't take the credit. Charlie came up with this one all on her own—whatever this one is. I'm not quite clear about specifics. She had Mac in the corner whispering away the minute they came in from the bus, then out they go to Mac's playhouse. Tight as two ticks on a dog all evening. Even begged me to let Mac sleep in her room with her. Figured it couldn't hurt. Charlie's got that extra twin bed in there. Hope it's all right with you."

"No. I mean, yes. That's fine."

"It's a hell of a lot better than fine. It's a goddamned miracle if you ask me. Checked on 'em an hour ago and they were sleeping like angels. Charlie even insisted on leaving the window wide open so Mac could see the stars."

"Did she?" Cash felt a stirring of hope. One of the things Cash had hated most in the past two years was how his girls had grown apart. Charlie played with her sister out of duty now instead of love. Nothing could hide the wall that had grown between the girls or the fact that Charlie would far rather be alone.

"So they're playing together," Cash said. "That's good, right? So what's worrying you?"

"Nothing. Just wanted to give you the heads up. Had to swear in blood not to set foot in the playhouse or it would ruin the surprise."

"So why didn't you sneak out back before you hit the couch and see what they're up to?"

"You're kidding, right?" Vinny's dead seriousness made Cash crack a smile. "That cross your heart, hope to die bit is serious stuff. You want to stick a needle in *your* eye? No sir, Deputy Lawless. I don't think so."

"I see what you mean. But I didn't swear, so maybe as soon as I get home, I'll phone in to the Sheriff's office, have them stake out the playhouse."

"Might be a good idea."

He could hear Vinny yawn. The nights Mr. Google stayed over to watch the girls had to be hard on the older man. Stubborn cuss insisted on sacking out on the couch instead of using Cash's bed. Vinny said the couch kept him from getting too soft.

"Go to sleep, old man." Cash said with gruff affection. "I'm awake now."

"Good. I'm heading in to check on them one last time right now. Their father is a real pain, you know."

Cash heard the hall floorboards creak.

"Hey, Cash?"

"What?"

"It was fun watching the girls today. All that bustling back and forth, bowls and plates of food and such. Don't be eating any donuts on your way home. Probably have a heck of a tea party out there before they'll let you go to sleep. The works, you know? Stale bread and grape jelly and a bottle of pickles."

"I can't wait."

"It'll do your heart good to see them…happy, you know?"

Happy…

That was one emotion that had been in short supply at the Lawless house for quite awhile.

Hell, Cash didn't care if they'd used up a week's worth of peanut butter sandwiches and he had to take a handful of Tums to tamp down the heartburn he'd get from eating all those pickles. If he could just see his little girls smile…

The way they had before their whole world had shattered.

The way they had before they'd learned the truth. That their daddy couldn't protect them from the ugly things out there in the world. That their mommy wouldn't always be there to tuck them in at night.

Sometimes there really were monsters under the bed.

And even daddies could be afraid.

"Listen, buddy," Cash said. "I'm going to sign off now."

Cash heard Charlie's bedroom door squeak, and put oiling the hinges at the top of his to do list.

"See you when you get home," Vinny whispered. "Charlie kicked the covers off again. They're lying in a heap by her—sonofabitch!"

In a heartbeat, the world on the other end of the phone erupted. Vinny roared, a bloodcurdling cry of pain, the girls' startled screaming buried in the sounds of a horrific crash.

Cash's belly turned to ice.

"Vinny?" Cash yelled into the phone. "Vinny! Talk to me! What the hell's going on?"

Vinny didn't answer.

The cell went dead.

CHAPTER SIX

CASH'S TIRES SQUEALED as he turned down Briarwood Lane, his radio spitting static. He'd tried three times to connect to the house by the land line as he'd sped across town, but the relentless busy signal had ratcheted up his alarm.

"Got a 9-1-1 from your house, Cash," his radio warned through bursts of static. "Can't get much out of Charlie—she's hysterical—some kind of intruder. Cash, Vinny's down."

"Shots fired?"

"Not that we can tell. Help's on the way. Wait for backup."

"Like hell I will! My kids are in there."

He swerved into the driveway and slammed on his brakes. He was out of the squad a heartbeat later, sprinting up the stairs to the front door.

He tried the door. Locked tight. Not the point of entry. But hadn't Vinny said Charlie's bedroom window was open? Cut the screen, then—bingo—an intruder was in. He keyed the lock, opened the door, making no sound, but the living room was empty. Whatever was going on, the action had moved deeper into the house, where he couldn't see it.

He clenched his teeth against the sound of Mac's panicked wails, along with the scream of the sirens in the distance. Sounds he'd heard on instant replay in his worst nightmares. He crushed the instinct to rush to his daughter, knowing surprise was his best weapon.

Cold sweat broke out on Cash's body as he edged his way toward the hall, his pistol drawn, held at the ready.

The noise was coming from Charlie's room. He crept toward it, back against the wall. Just outside his goal, he paused, readying himself to wheel into the doorway, draw a bead on whatever lowlife scum was in there.

His trigger finger itched, fury and fear warring in his belly as he counted in his head. *One, two…*three.

Ten years of instinct and combat training kicked in as he swung around, filling the door.

"Freeze! Police!" He shouted. His pistol barrel swept the room. Glimpses of Charlie, Mac, Vinny flashed past.

Vinny's leg bent at a gut-churning angle where it should have been straight. Broken, Cash assessed with a combat vet's skill. Charlie huddled in a ball, her back against the bed. God, no. Had she been hit? Sonofabitch, Cash would kill the rotten bastard.

"Cash!" Vinny's voice, woozy as hell. "Put that damn pistol away. You're scaring the kids."

"The perp—" Cash snarled, everything feral in him wanting blood. "Where is he?"

Was Vinny actually smiling? A sick smile, a weak one. "Under the bed."

Hell, Vinny was right. The surface of Charlie's twin bed tilted wildly askew, even the headboard off the floor. It was moving…

Did the jerk have a gun pointed out at the room? Was that why the kid was shrunk up so tight in the corner?

Cash approached the suspect, every sense on alert. "You— scum bag—slide out from under there," he ordered. He kicked the teetering bed savagely with his boot. "You mess with my kids, I'd as soon shoot you as look at you."

"No!" Charlie shrilled, diving between Cash and the suspect.

Cash blanched, his daughter suddenly lined up in his pistol

sights. He swung his pistol upward, so it was pointing at the ceiling. "Charlotte! Get out of the way!"

"Don't shoot, Daddy! It's my fault!" she screeched wildly.

His gaze locked on his daughter, Charlie's face splotched red and white, soaked with tears, her whole body shaking under her Monkey Shines pajamas.

Mac wailed, scrabbling toward him across the floor, flinging her arms around his leg. "Pick me up, Daddy! Pick me up! Charlie sneaked—"

Sirens blared to a halt in front of the house. Backup, arriving at last.

"Damn it," Cash ordered the perp again. "Get out from under that bed before I forget I'm a cop!"

The bed shuddered, the intruder still blocked from view by fallen comforters, scattered stuffed animals and Charlie's quivering form. "Hands where I can see 'em."

"He can't put his hands up," Mac said. "He doesn't got any."

The front door slammed open, the rush of footsteps thundering toward them.

"What?" Cash asked.

"The bad guy gots paws."

"Paws?" Cash echoed, bewildered as his fellow officers stormed in.

"Lawless," Evander's voice broke in. "Where's your perp?"

The mass of covers twisted, a face nosing its way out into the open through the loop of Charlie's arms.

"Holy shit!" Evander swore as the perp dropped his weapon of choice. A chewed-up football plopped out of his mouth. "Is that who I think it is?"

"Destroyer," Cash growled. He holstered his gun as the Newfoundland peered up at him with shame-filled eyes.

THERE WAS NO DENYING IT any longer. Clancy was gone.

Rowena sank into her desk chair and buried her face in her

hands. She'd searched everywhere, scouring the streets from the moment she'd realized the Newfoundland had somehow escaped her fenced-in yard. She'd been so sure she'd find him—or that his stomach would win out over the adventure of wandering at will and he'd show up at her door, his pink tongue hanging out, his tail wagging and that sorrowful expression he got when he'd done something he knew was wrong. Head drooping, peering up from under his eyelashes as if begging forgiveness.

But two days had passed and hope was running thin.

"Maybe I should call Animal Control," she thought, then canned the idea of asking them outright. Surely Mindy, the girl Rowena channeled her rescues through, would recognize Clancy even without scanning for his microchip. Mindy would call her, and then...

Then what? Wouldn't the humane society have to enter in their logs somewhere that Clancy had, once again, darkened their doorstep? And what if they weren't the people who picked Clancy up? What if a patrol car saw him "running at large" and nabbed him? Cash Lawless had warned Rowena at the Sheriff's office that first day that if Clancy got one more strike against him, he'd be out.

Rowena swallowed a lump in her throat.

God, why had she taken Clancy with her to the Lawless house? Let the dog see Charlie again? Ever since that day, the Newfoundland hadn't been himself. He'd carried his mangled football with him everywhere, barely putting it down to eat. An anxiety behavior if Rowena had ever seen one. She'd worked so hard to obliterate those from Clancy's repertoire. But for some reason, Clancy's encounter with Charlie had brought the dog's insecurities flooding back.

Restless, whining, never settling down, Clancy behaved as if he knew as well as Rowena did how wrong things were with the solemn-eyed little girl and felt as if he should fix them.

Surely it wasn't possible that the dog…what? Rowena brought herself up sharply. Logged on to Map Quest when she wasn't looking and found Charlie Lawless's address? Then had Shakespeare the cat boost him up over the fence so he could navigate the streets of Whitewater and knock on Charlie's door?

Right, Rowena. Get real. There was no way Clancy could find the place, even if he wanted to.

And yet, it was as if the 175-pound dog had just vanished in a puff of smoke.

But she couldn't spend another day trolling the streets, looking for him. She had a shop full of other animals that needed to be cared for. A business that had to be open if it was going to bring in any money. And, as Rowena often told the pets who clamored for her attention when she needed to be re-stocking shelves and such—dog biscuits weren't free.

Rowena crossed to the nearby sink and splashed cold water onto her face. She caught a glimpse of her reflection in the mirror and tried to paste on a smile to fool any customer that happened by.

Not that she had been able to fool her mother into thinking everything in Whitewater was going as smoothly as Auntie Maeve had predicted the last time Rowena and Nadine Brown had stopped by the hospital room before the Irishwoman had died.

Rowena winced, remembering her mother's reaction, one that had only grown fiercer than ever since Rowena had moved to the town where her godmother had predicted her soul mate was waiting for her. *Whitewater, Illinois…* Maeve had said, pointing to a River Road tourist pamphlet someone had left in a magazine. *Rowena, that is where you will find him….*

Nadine Brown had blustered her protest the whole way home, and in the months that followed. *My God, Rowena, Maeve believes in fairies and the banshee and—and Santa*

Claus, for all I know! Building your whole future on the ramblings of a senile old woman is insane, no matter how much you love her!

But how could anyone as logical as Nadine Brown understand the connection between Rowena and Maeve? Or how completely Rowena trusted her godmother?

When Nadine Brown had made the visit Rowena dreaded, the reserved doctor had gotten so quiet it shook Rowena to the core.

Your eye. I suppose some stray did that to you? Or did you fall off a ladder fixing this place up?

This place has a name, Mom. It's called Open Arms. Couldn't you just look around a little? Rowena had been hoping for some sort of approval. Just a sliver of reaction to show her mother would eventually be reconciled to Rowena's decision as long as her daughter was happy.

Nadine had given a cursory glance to the bright colors, the shiny cages. *It's very cheerful, dear. But you won't be able to see it if you damaged your vision when you got that black eye. I know you didn't have a doctor look at it.*

I didn't need to. My eye is fine, Mom. And so is my life here.

Her mother had examined the bruise, shone a light into her eye. At last Nadine Brown had put the flashlight away. *I know you're a grown woman and you think I'm trying to interfere in your life. But you're still my daughter, Rowena. I'm worried about you.*

Rowena hadn't been able to resist the wistfulness in her mother's eyes. *I love you, too, Mom,* she had said, giving her mother a hug. Dr. Brown patted her back, then disengaged. Rowena let her, knowing her mother always felt uncomfortable with public displays of affection.

By the time Rowena had waved goodbye, she'd been relieved to see her mother leave and yet a little sad. She had wanted the visit to be different. But then, she was sure her mother had felt the same way.

Luckily Rowena had had the perfect antidote to her mood right at her fingertips. She'd given Clancy a bath. And no one could help but laugh at the Newfie's delight as he tried to bite the stream of water from the garden hose.

The memory of the irrepressible Clancy drew her back to the present with a sharp wrench of pain. She'd work in the shop today, she reasoned. Then as soon as she closed up, she'd start looking again and hope like hell she wouldn't find Clancy hit by a car on some highway or shut up in the backseat of Deputy Lawless's patrol car.

True, she didn't think of Cash as a dog-hating Attila the Hun any longer, but the man had made a pretty daunting list of Clancy's past transgressions and still considered the Newfie a danger to the people Cash was sworn to protect.

She knew now, as she hadn't before, just how seriously the deputy took his responsibilities.

A knock sounded at the shop's front door. Rowena glanced at the clock. Still ten minutes before she was scheduled to open. Swiping a brush through her hair, she grabbed a hand towel and scrubbed her face dry as she made her way to the front of the store.

She'd almost reached the glass door when her vision cleared enough to see who stood on the other side. Her breath clutched as she glimpsed broad shoulders, short, dark hair and the grimmest expression she'd ever seen on a man.

Cash.

Her heart slammed against her ribs, panic choking her. Oh, God. Had he found Clancy dead by the side of the road? Was he coming to tell her...

But the instant she turned the deadbolt in the door to let him in, she saw something cowering behind him. Something big. Black. Furry.

"Clancy!"

She cried out the dog's name as she flung open the door, then hurled herself at the Newfie, clutching the dog in her arms.

"Oh, thank God! Thank God!"

Cash hadn't taken the dog to the pound the way he'd threatened, Rowena thought, more grateful than he'd ever imagine. He'd brought Clancy back to her.

And yet, the dog shrank back, looking so dejected after his little escapade, Rowena couldn't help but laugh with relief.

"Yes, you are a bad, bad dog! Running away like that!" she scolded, unable to keep her voice from quavering. "I've been worried sick about you!"

Clancy swiped her cheek once with his tongue, then collapsed to the ground and hid his nose under one massive paw.

Rowena climbed to her feet, and shook the hair out of her eyes, beaming. "Oh, Cash! Thank you so much for bringing him back to me. I've been terrified with him lost. Anything could have happened to him."

"Something did."

He wasn't smiling. He wasn't irritated or put out or any one of a dozen other reactions she might have expected. Rowena stilled. Something was badly wrong.

"What—what happened?"

"While I was off working a double shift, Charlie found him wandering loose in our neighborhood. She and Mac hid him in the playhouse until after dark."

"Oh." Why on earth would Clancy end up clear across town? Maybe he really had been looking for his little girl. She imagined Charlie's excitement, her desperation to keep the dog. The lonely little girl trying to hide a mountain of a dog in plain sight. "Oh, Cash, I'm sorry."

"That's not all of it."

Rowena swallowed hard, peering up into the deputy's brown

eyes. Deep lines carved around his mouth, dark circles under his eyes, his face haggard, as if he hadn't slept any more than she had. "Then what…?"

"After their babysitter was asleep, Charlie climbed out her bedroom window and got the dog so it could sleep in her room. When their babysitter went in to check on them, there was some kind of commotion—the dog jumping up, the girls screaming. The damned dog tripped him."

"Oh, no." Rowena felt herself shrink inside, horrified.

"He broke his goddamned leg."

"Clancy? Oh Lord! I'll call the vet!"

"Not the dog. The girls' babysitter. Doctor says he'll be on crutches for eight weeks, maybe longer. Hell, he's sixty-eight years old."

Rowena felt the blood drain from her face. Guilt washed through her. "Oh, Cash. I…"

"I told you this dog is dangerous! But no. You wouldn't believe me."

"Did Clancy mean to—to hurt him?"

"Vinny says no. The dog was lying next to Charlie's bed and Vinny tripped over him. But what does it matter whether the dog ambushed him on purpose or not? Doesn't change the fact that Vinny's in a cast, or that there's no way he can handle Mac and her wheelchair."

Cash ran his splayed hand over his head in frustration. "What the hell am I supposed to do now?" he demanded. "My childcare is down the toilet. My girls are a mess. And I'm in the worst bind I've been in since my ex-wife took off."

"I'm so sorry," Rowena said, feeling helpless, completely to blame. Why hadn't she called the authorities two days ago, when she'd done her first sweep of the neighborhood and realized Clancy wasn't just nosing around the corner somewhere?

Because she'd taken Cash Lawless at his word when he said he'd only give the dog one last chance. And yet, if she had reported Clancy missing, any officer patrolling the town would have been on the lookout for the dog. Maybe none of this would have happened.

"This is my fault," Rowena whispered, heartsick.

"You think it's your fault. Charlie thinks it's her fault. Hell, look at your blasted dog's face! He thinks it's his fault." Cash thrust the rope Clancy was tied to into Rowena's hands. "Truth is, it doesn't matter who's to blame. Doesn't change a damned thing."

Rowena winced at the truth in his words. "Can you give me your—your sitter's name and address? I'd like to...to..."

To what? A voice demanded in her head. Pay for the guy's medical bills? And just where would you get the money?

"Vinny Scoglomiglio—631 Cameo Drive. Apartment 3."

Rowena didn't bother to write it down. She knew she'd remember every word. Guilt did that to her. She caught her lip between her teeth, searching for something to say.

"Tell me just one thing, will you?" Cash asked her, obviously at the end of his rope.

"What's that?" Rowena's hands trembled as she looked into his eyes.

"I'm supposed to be back on patrol in six hours. Who's going to watch my kids while I work?" Cash glared at her. She took a step back. Couldn't help herself.

"Don't know the answer to that one, do you?" His shoulders slumped. "Neither do I."

He sounded defeated, hopeless, alone. Rowena clutched the makeshift leash so tight bits of twine cut into her hands. He swung around, then stalked to where his dark-green SUV hugged the curb.

Rowena watched him open the door and climb in. His kids must both be in the back, strapped into their car seats. Charlie's face peered out the window, a pale smear of misery and huge, worried eyes.

Who would take care of the girls while the babysitter recovered? Rowena wondered as the vehicle pulled away down the street. Such sweet little things, so battered by forces beyond their control. Mac not able to walk. Charlie hurting deep inside where the scars didn't show. Their mother gone. Now, their caretaker was nursing a broken leg.

Rowena remembered the steep flight of steps that led up to the Lawless house. Even without a broken limb, it would have been difficult for whoever watched Mac to get the little girl and her wheelchair up to the landing or down to the street.

It was a daunting job. How was Cash Lawless going to find someone to help him in such short order?

Collaring Clancy, she went back into the shop and locked the door behind her. Suddenly she needed to hear a familiar voice.

Rowena went to the phone, punched in Bryony's number. It rang until the answering machine picked up. "Hey, Bry, it's me. I've um, got a situation here I'm not sure how to handle. Just wanted to talk—"

"Don't hang up!"

Her older sister's voice startled her. Rowena almost dropped the phone. "Bry?"

"Yeah, yeah, yeah. It's me. I was screening my calls. Hard to get any work done around here."

"Sorry for interrupting."

"Yeah, well. I almost managed to ignore you, but then I realized you've got your 'oh, shit' voice on so I couldn't do it. What's this situation?"

Rowena leaned against the wall. "You wouldn't believe what happened now."

"With you involved?" Bryony laughed wryly. "Try me."

Rowena spilled her guts to her sister, Bryony gasping and commiserating at all the right places until the tale was done.

"Listen, Rowena, I know you feel bad," Bryony said at last. "But this Lawless guy probably has plenty of other people to help him out of this jam once he stops to think about it. Friends, coworkers, women who'd love to get a shot at making themselves indispensable to a man who looks that hot."

"I didn't say what he looks like!"

"You didn't have to. I can tell from your voice. You've got a thing for him, don't you?"

"What do you mean, a thing?" Rowena demanded, feigning indignance.

"He's divorced. He's got two kids. One in a wheelchair and one who wants a dog. It's a typical Rowena to the Rescue scenario. Am I right?"

"Well...I..."

"Did he kiss you?"

"No! He barely touched me! Like only to put a bandage on...my eye...when I crashed into Mac's wheelchair."

"So that's the real scoop on that shiner mom was telling me about. Ariel thought your story of stepping on a rake and getting hit with the wooden handle was suspicious. I was going to give you the benefit of the doubt, even though it was a lame excuse."

"I saw it in a skit on *Saturday Night Live*. It was the only thing I could think of that would make a mark like the tube part of a wheelchair. Next time I'll call you and Arry for a consult."

"Not a bad idea. I'm way better at making up stories than you are."

"So how about writing me an ending for this one?" Rowena pleaded. "What do I do now?"

"Absolutely nothing." Bryony said. "I know you feel bad about those little girls. But consider the problem from all angles. Yes, your dog got loose, but you weren't the one who brought it into the Lawless house, were you?"

"No. But—"

"This babysitter—you said he's a man, right?"

"Right."

"Typical. He was responsible for keeping an eye on those kids. I mean, a Newfoundland isn't exactly something a kid could sneak in the house in a pocket, like that frog you sneaked in 'cause Bobby Keifer wanted to eat its legs. I think I still have hearing loss, the way Mom screamed when she found that thing in her bath tub."

"Listen, Bry. Listing off my previous disasters is not helpful. The frog deal is over and done with. It's this current mess I'm trying to sort out."

"That's what I'm trying to tell you. It's not your mess. I'm sure Bobby just went out and caught another frog to turn into sushi, and this guy—what was his name?"

"Cash Lawless."

"Oh, for God's sake. That doesn't even sound real. It could be an alias for all you know. Maybe he knocked off his wife, and the kid in the wheelchair is a con game, you know— and—"

"You should write that down—you'd have a thriller on your hands. The man is a deputy, Bry. You know. Badge. Gun. Protect and serve. You're not going to find him on *America's Most Wanted*."

"That's not the point."

"Then what is?"

"This is his problem, honey. Not yours. You've got a shop to run. Animals to take care of. Sisters to phone and a mother to bamboozle with stories about rogue rake-smacking incidents. This guy sounds like he has enough baggage to trek from that dinky little town you're in all the way up Mount Everest."

The reference carried Rowena back to the first time she'd talked to Charlie Lawless, teased her about her indestructible bookbag and the journey she could take with it. Charlie's words fell from Rowena's mouth. "People freeze up there, you know."

"Has this guy threatened to sue you? Or…"

"No!" Rowena stopped, her voice quieter. "No."

"Then stay away from him. I don't want you to get hurt, honey."

"I promise I'll be careful."

Bryony muttered under her breath. "Careful? Right. That's what you told me when you picked up that fox in the woods. The one in the trap?"

Rowena winced, hating the memory. Of all the mishaps of her childhood, that one had caused her the most heartache. She'd convinced Bryony to let her bundle the creature up in her jacket and hide it in the garden shed. While Bryony waited with the fox, Rowena had run inside, asked her father if she could rescue the animal. He'd told her to leave the thing alone! She could get rabies. But it hadn't stopped her. Trouble was, when those sharp white teeth had chewed up her hand, Bryony had tried to save her. Her sister had gotten bitten herself, and endured the painful shots that followed, as well.

"Hey, Bry. Thanks for…well, listening."

"Which is a nice way of telling me it doesn't matter what advice I've given you. You're going to do exactly what you want. Well? Isn't it?"

Rowena didn't answer.

Bryony sighed. "Row, you've got the biggest heart of anyone I know. I just wish it weren't so damned stubborn. What are you going to do?"

"I'll tell you when I figure it out."

"Terrific."

Rowena sobered, a wave of homesickness sweeping over her. She knew Bryony had inherited their mother's aversion to PDAs, but she wished she could give her sister a hug.

"You're the best," Rowena said.

She heard Bryony's disgruntled snort. "Then how come you never do what I tell you to?"

"Slow learner."

"I'll say. Honey, just make sure…"

"What?"

"That this time, you're not the one who gets bitten."

SO MUCH FOR SISTERLY advice, Rowena mused as she mounted the stairs to Cash's door three hours later. Her pulse was jumping, her nerves strained, Bryony's voice in her head telling her she was about to make a Clancy-sized mistake.

But Rowena just couldn't help herself. In spite of her sister's oh-so-logical insistence that the accident at the Lawless house wasn't Rowena's fault, she *had* to do something. And hopefully in the hour she'd spent in Vinny Scoglomiglio's comfortable apartment, she and Cash's ill-fated babysitter had come up with a solution that just might work.

Vinny had certainly been eager to give it a try. And Rowena had spent the best part of her drive to the Lawless place reassuring herself that the grizzled ex-cop hadn't just agreed with her because he'd been whacked out on the painkillers the doctor had given him before he set Vinny's leg.

With the Lawless girls in school, Vinny had insisted this was the perfect time for Rowena to pitch her idea to the deputy and get his reaction. Cash was sure to be home.

But when she knocked on the door, the house beyond stayed silent, still.

Of course, if Cash had seen her van with the vivid Open Arms logo, he might decide not to open the door, she thought wryly.

She waited a moment, then pressed the doorbell and knocked louder, her fist stinging from the impact. She chewed at her bottom lip, her nerves growing more ragged by the minute.

He had to be in there. Vinny had seemed so organized and insistent when he'd charted out Cash's schedule with her, sketching out every school project, every doctor's appointment and every spelling test day on the Lawless family calendar.

Cash must just be trying to avoid her. She winced at the thought. Well, she wasn't going anywhere until they talked about this like civilized human beings *and he did exactly what she wanted.*

When no one answered, she walked around the house to peek in the backyard. Empty. Then back to the window that looked into the house's living room. Her shoulders tensed as she remembered the one time she'd actually set foot in the room, the sting of the cut under her eye and the far more painful burn of embarrassment once she realized what a terrible mistake she'd made.

When she'd first realized Cash Lawless was a far different man that she'd imagined he was.

Is that what this offer of yours is really about? That jolt of sensation you felt when he put his hand on you? When you looked down at his mouth and wondered if he'd taste as good as he felt? As if he'd ever want someone like you. Especially after the wife he'd had...

Okay, so maybe—just maybe—she might have mixed motives. Wanting to reach out to Charlie, wanting to make up for Clancy's caper, wanting to test the hot waters Cash Lawless had stirred in her with his soul-weary eyes and his strong, healing hands. But if the guy thought she was just going to give up and go away if he ignored her long enough, he was wrong.

She pounded on the door one more time, then went to the picture window to see if there were any signs of life. Cupping her hands around her eyes to kill the glare off the glass, she squinted to see inside.

Bad idea!

Rowena's heart almost stopped as she saw a tall, wet, very naked Cash Lawless stalk out of the hallway, wrestling with the tangled up bath towel he was trying to cinch around his hips.

Too late.

Rowena had already gotten an eyeful—long, muscular legs, a toned curve of buttocks and…well, the most impressive equipment she'd ever seen. Not that she'd seen that many to compare it to.

Appalled at herself for staring, she straightened, fully intending to flee back to the front door and feign innocence. But she jerked up so fast her elbow hit the window. The glass rattled like thunder.

Cash spun toward the window, stepping on the tail of towel in the process, ripping the length of terrycloth completely out of his grasp.

His gaze locked with Rowena's through the glass, his incredible body frozen for an instant like one of those nude models Ariel had painted in art class.

No wonder her sister had flunked it on purpose so she could take it twice, Rowena thought, unable to tear her gaze away from him.

Oh, Lord, she thought wildly, what would Ariel do in a situation like this?

Jump his bones, her sister's voice whispered wickedly in her ear.

Rowena settled for the next best thing. She forced a wan smile to her face. Then she held up her hand and waved.

CHAPTER SEVEN

SHE WAS WAVING AT HIM. For a split second Cash froze in disbelief at the sight of Rowena in the window. Then a cool draft from the kitchen window he'd left open a few inches chilled the drops of water still clinging to his freshly showered skin, and startled him enough to shake him out of his trance.

Naked.

Hell, he was buck naked.

He dove for the towel, managing to wrench it out from under his foot, then scrambled to wrap the bath sheet around himself to cover the most vital parts.

But damned if Vinny hadn't shrunk the towel in the wash. The blasted thing seemed about the size of a postage stamp. Cash's cheeks burned, and yet, damn. He couldn't quite shake the memory of the expression he'd glimpsed on her face.

Her soft mouth parted as if she'd gone breathless. Her eyes sunflower-wide and hot as a July sky. And one thing he knew for sure. She hadn't been looking at his face.

Cash tamped down the unexpected surge of heat that pulsed through him and latched onto the question at hand. What the blazes was the woman doing on his doorstep? Again?

That demon dog of hers had better not have made another break for it or… Cash would save the dog the trouble of aggravating him to death and just shoot himself.

Cash opened the door just enough to talk while still trying to keep his neighbors from getting an eyeful.

"Hi," he said, clutching the towel together.

"Hi." Her face shone the hectic pink of the peonies his mother used to grow.

"I was in the shower."

"I see."

Yeah, she'd seen, all right. The shock of it still registered in her eyes. Along with something more. A little breathless, a little wicked, a lot tempting.

"I didn't mean to…well…bother you. But Vinny said this was a good time to catch you at home. Without the girls around. You know. Alone."

She *wanted* to catch him alone? Her gaze flicked to his mouth. Cash remembered some kind of body language thing one of the guys at the office had read in a men's magazine somewhere—that if a woman looked at a man's mouth she wanted to be kissed.

But who believed that bullshit anyway? Nobody with a brain. Unfortunately, it wasn't the part of his anatomy that was listening at the moment. It had been a long time since he'd seen that brand of appreciation in a woman's eyes.

Damn, what the hell was wrong with him? He had a full-fledged mess on his hands and Rowena Brown was at least partially to blame. It didn't matter that she was turned on by him, even a little. Having sex was the last thing on his current list of priorities. He needed to be in combat mode—that's what he and Vinny called times like these, when you needed to strip your life down to the bare essentials just to survive.

"This really isn't a good time," Cash said.

"Then I'll make this quick." Rowena fidgeted with the hem of her green T-shirt, looking at his chest, over his shoulder, anywhere but straight in his eyes. "Have you figured out what you're going to do with the girls while Mr. Scoglomiglio is out of commission?"

"I've got half a dozen calls in to different centers to try and arrange temporary day care, but it's complicated." Frustration gnawed inside him. "The girls don't do so well in crowds of strangers since their mother abandoned them. And wheelchair accessible is just one more thing to add on to my giant sized list of requirements. All the centers I've contacted want a full breakdown of Mac's medical records from her doctors before they'll admit her. That way the school understands what it would be dealing with in light of MacKenzie's *disability*."

God, how he hated that word.

He should have left it at that, but he found himself going on, drawn by Rowena's empathetic eyes. "Even once the medical data is cleared, there's still the issue of getting the girls wherever they need to go after school. Changing bus routes and working out how to get Mac to therapy, doctor's appointments and God knows what else." He kneaded his temple wearily. "Truth is, the situation looks damn near impossible with the way my work schedule bounces around."

"Maybe that won't be as big a problem as you think," Rowena said.

Cash's lip curled. "And maybe Santa Claus will come down the chimney Christmas morning. Listen, Rowena. I'm not sure why you're here. But I really don't have time for—"

"Anything, from what I can see," she cut in, a crease between her dark golden brows. "According to Vinny, you're exhausted. You're overwhelmed. You're overextended and now you're without a babysitter."

"Not exactly a newsflash—Vinny?" Cash frowned, readjusting his towel. "What do you mean according to Vinny?"

"Mr. Scoglomiglio and I have been discussing your problem, and we think we've come up with a solution."

"Whoa, there. Hold on a minute now," Cash growled. "I handle my own problems, got it? I don't need you—or even Vinny—to figure this out for me."

Her chin bumped up and she looked him straight in the eye. "That may be true, but it would sure make things a little easier if you let us help. You're going to have to trust somebody someday, Cash. And Vinny thinks you should trust me."

"Trust you to what?" Cash demanded.

"To take the edge off."

Her answer didn't help. He shifted uncomfortably, remembering his fantasies of a few minutes before. There were things he might like to have her take the edge off all right, like the hard-on that had threatened to spring up and embarrass the hell out of him when he'd realized she was staring at him through the window. Thank God he'd gotten to the towel before his growing arousal became too obvious.

"To take some of the pressure off you," Rowena continued. "You know, to help you out. The way I figure it, Vinny can't lift Mac with his broken leg, or carry her off and on the bus, or get her up and down the stairs. He really can't even drive until the doctors shorten his cast. So I was thinking, what if Vinny filled in some hours at the store for me, while I taxied your girls wherever they needed to go?"

"That's absurd."

"Is it? I could babysit Mac and Charlie while you're at work. And on the evenings when they didn't have appointments or whatever, the girls could come to the shop and help out. That way I could get my work done, too."

Christ, Cash thought, amazed. The woman really meant it. Irritation licked through him. "First of all, I barely even know you."

"Do a background check. I'm sure you've got access to that kind of stuff at work. I can even give you references if you want to check me out that way, too. Besides, Vinny will be around a lot of the time. He'll see me in action, and he doesn't seem to be the type to mince words if he thought I was screwing up."

Cash remembered plenty of times Vinny had given him a shakedown for something he didn't approve of. "I'll say this much. You've got him pegged right. But as for that whole hanging around the shop idea of yours—forget it. Things aren't tough enough around here? You want my kids to spend hours wandering around in a pet shop?"

"It's perfectly clean!" Rowena hastened to reassure him. "The health department—"

"It's not dog germs I'm worried about! It's the fact that the place is stuffed to the gills with animals my kids are going to want to bring home!"

Cash shuddered, just imagining it. A relentless hell of plaintive little voices begging him *please, Daddy, please. Please let me get a turtle!* A hamster. A guinea pig. A freaking boa constrictor.

And if they actually wore him down enough and he caved, with his luck the hamster would be pregnant, deliver the biggest litter of babies on record, and then promptly start to cannibalize its young right in front of his daughters' eyes.

"After what happened with Clancy, they'll understand your no dog rule," Rowena insisted. "But by spending time in the shop, they'll get some of the benefits of being around animals, as well. And—"

"This is insane," Cash said, as much to himself as to her. "I can't do this."

"What you can't do is work long hours, night shifts and the occasional weekend, watch your kids and get them to their activities after school all at the same time."

Good point, Cash thought, but he wasn't about to admit it to her. "That doesn't mean I should let you do it. No offense

intended, but it's not like you've been a stellar example of responsibility since you came to town. You lost that dog of yours,
for God's sake. What's to keep you from losing my kids?"

She flushed again. "That's the beauty of the plan. What red-
blooded American kid would wander away from a pet shop?"

"I suppose that's true, but—"

"You told me that a cop has to trust his instincts. Vinny
believes I can do this. Do you?"

She pierced him with those eyes of hers, so big, so full of
emotion his breath hitched in his throat. A wisp of golden hair
caught in the breeze and clung to the corner of her mouth.

"I don't know," he admitted. Against his better judgment he
reached up to brush the strand away. Her mouth was dewy soft,
warm to the touch. He felt her breath catch before he pulled
his hand back.

"That's fair enough," Rowena said, her voice just a tad unsteady. "Let's just try it this week, then. A trial run of sorts. You
can make up your mind after that."

Cash frowned and she must have sensed his indecision.

"If nothing more, it'll give you the time you need to research
the different day care centers thoroughly," she said. "What do
you have to lose?"

"My mind?" he suggested all too seriously.

"If you do, I promise I'll help you find it." She held out her
hand as if to shake on it, something endearing in the simple
gesture.

Cash hesitated a long moment, feeling like his wheels were
spinning out of control. A sensation he hated. Knew far too
well.

"Fine," he agreed at last, and shook the hand she offered.

KISSING THE BABYSITTER was a very bad idea. Cash had learned
this life lesson at a young age—fourteen to be exact, when his

parents had caught him laying one on Tilly Maloney while the busty high school sophomore was supposed to be watching his little brothers.

It wasn't as if he'd planned it—but who was he to argue when God dropped a cheerleader in his lap? Two years his senior, Tilly had been quite a catch, although she'd been less than pleased to find out that he was just a lowly eighth grader. Tilly had refused to babysit for Cash's mother ever again, and with six rambunctious boys running around like savages, reliable babysitters had been worth more than gold.

Question was, why had that old family story suddenly flared up in Cash's memory, flashing like a neon warning sign?

Yeah, it's a freaking mystery all right, you idiot, he mocked himself, glancing over at Rowena in the passenger seat of his SUV. First, she sees you naked and stares at you like that dog of hers would eye a T-bone steak. Then she saves your ass by volunteering to solve your babysitting crisis—hell, that would merit a kiss just out of pure gratitude. And now?

Cash gritted his teeth against the frisson of desire she stirred beneath the fly of his uniform pants. She was sitting so close to him in the car he could smell her lemon-scented shampoo and glimpse a sliver of breast where the shoulder harness pulled her V-necked tee askew. The aqua lace edging her bra cup peeped at him, made him want to pull the shirt aside to get a better look. Maybe he could appeal to her sense of fair play. After all, she'd looked him over, but good, when he'd dropped his towel.

The car behind them beeped its horn, startling Cash into seeing the stoplight had turned green. He hit the gas a little too forcefully through the intersection, then had to jerk to a stop to park in front of the school. He saw Rowena stomp her foot down on an imaginary brake and grimaced.

If Vinny had been in the seat beside him, Cash knew the crack the old man would make about the erratic ride. *Been driving long, junior?*

But then, if Vinny had been riding shotgun, Cash wouldn't have been distracted by his breasts. Had she noticed him giving her the once over? Cash wondered. Her cheeks looked a little pinker, her expression a little shy.

He climbed out of the vehicle, rounded the hood and opened her door for her.

"Come on in to the school office with me and I'll register you with the secretary so you can pick up the girls." He didn't know why he said it. That had been the plan, after all. She'd waited while he got dressed for that very reason.

He'd caught her at the kitchen window, looking out at the big oak tree, a quiet sadness in her eyes.

Sometimes he thought he should cut the damned thing down so he didn't have to look at it anymore. Be reminded of broken promises and unfinished business, of childhood interrupted and failures that still ate at him late at night.

The blasted tree was the thing he'd liked best about the house when Lisa had wanted to buy it. The oak seeming so solid, its branches spreading wide like open arms welcoming him home. He'd perched Charlie atop his shoulders and imagined the fun they'd have building a tree house, as soon as Mac was old enough not to get hurt climbing after her sister.

But Mac had just gotten hurt a different way. Now, with fall and winter coming, the wind would strip the oak's leaves away, until the wooden platform Cash had built a lifetime ago stood out, a stark reproach, amidst bare black branches.

Rowena pulled him back to the present, her long legs swinging toward him as she climbed out of the car. He pushed the bleak memories away, grateful for the distraction as she smoothed her shirt, hiding the aqua sliver of bra from view. A good idea since she was on her way to the principal's office. Still, Cash couldn't help but regret she'd done it.

By the time they reached the office, she looked so nervous even the secretary could see it.

"Something wrong, Deputy Lawless?"

"This is Rowena Brown. She'll be picking up the girls from now on."

"Well, isn't that nice." The secretary eyed Rowena with blatant curiosity. She handed Cash the forms and sent him to the table right outside the school office to fill them out.

When he heard the secretary whispering something to Rowena, all but dripping with sympathy, Cash screwed up his own address and had to start over. By the time he finished, his jaw clenched in irritation.

As they headed down the empty hallway to Mac's classroom, Cash pounced. "What was Mrs. Kettering saying while I was gone?"

Rowena actually gulped. "Nothing much."

"People don't whisper when they say 'nothing,'" Cash challenged.

Rowena sighed. "She said all the teachers have been worried about the girls. That it will be good for them to have a woman around."

"Did you tell her you won't be around? At least, not very long?"

"I tried to, but…well, she seemed to think you and I are an item."

"An item?" Cash echoed in disgust. "Can't a man just bring in his new babysitter without starting school gossip?"

"Only if that babysitter is a stout woman with warts on her nose and the man has a beer gut and a bad haircut." Rowena's eyes twinkled up at him. "Apparently our imaginary affair will not be good news to Mac's teacher, Ms. Daily.

She thinks you're hot. And she hasn't even seen you drop your towel."

What was Rowena doing? Cash thought, off balance. Teasing him? Yeah. And enjoying the hell out of it. So much for the woman being scared of him.

"Mac's teacher is barely more than a kid herself. She hardly says boo to me!" he groused. "There's no way she thinks I'm hot—oof."

The breath wooshed out of him as Rowena elbowed him in the ribs. He started to protest, but she was already turning to greet the pretty brunette who had somehow materialized before them. Plenty close enough to catch the gist of their conversation, if her fire-engine-red face was any indicator.

Perfect.

Ms. Daily looked at him with hurt puppy-dog eyes. The school secretary was right. The teacher did have that lovelorn look. Why hadn't he ever noticed it before?

Probably because he hadn't even noticed she was female. He'd barely noticed that Angelina Jolie was female since Lisa left him. That is, until he'd seen Rowena Brown staring at him through the picture window.

"I'm Rowena Brown, MacKenzie's new babysitter," Rowena jumped in, obviously trying to fill the awkward silence.

"I see."

Yeah. She saw, all right, Cash thought as Ms. Daily ushered him and Rowena into Mac's classroom. And by the time the day was over, the whole rest of the school would be in on Ms. Daily's little fantasy, too. They'd never believe his relationship with Rowena wasn't X-rated.

But then, maybe his life had been G far too long.

He smacked himself mentally to shut himself down. He'd decided two years ago that he'd never risk what he saw so many other single fathers do: install a revolving door on his daughters' home to admit a parade of women, meaningless fucks to take care of biological needs.

Charlie and Mac had been hurt enough by the one woman on earth who was supposed to love them. And since Cash had screwed up choosing a mother for his children so badly the first time, he wasn't about to chance it again.

Not that he'd really chosen Lisa for anything but a hot lay. Look at where that had gotten him.

Suddenly Mac's piping voice penetrated his thoughts.

"You're not my babysitter!" Mac exclaimed with a scowl, backing her wheelchair away from Rowena. "You're that very bad lady that hit my daddy. You should be in jail right now."

The other pre-kindergarten kids gasped, staring at Rowena as if she were a hardened criminal.

Rowena threw Cash a glare. "Jump in here any time, Deputy."

Cash grinned, liking the way the tables had turned. "Actually, Rowena *is* going to be taking care of you and Charlie for a little while, kitten. Until Mr. Google's leg gets better."

"Charlie was bad so he breaked it," Mac informed her teacher. "But that's what you get when you sneak a bear into the house."

"A bear?" Ms. Daily repeated, looking from MacKenzie to Cash in surprise.

"It's really a dog," he explained. "A very big dog."

"A Newfoundland," Rowena added.

"I adore Newfies!" Ms. Daily exclaimed, clasping her hands together. "You're that pet shop woman everybody's talking about, aren't you, Ms. Brown?"

"Arrested but never convicted," Rowena said, slanting Cash a saucy grin.

"I've been thinking about getting a dog," Ms. Daily told Rowena. "You know how it is. I'm a woman, living alone." She turned her attention to Cash, all but batting her eyes. "I asked Deputy Lawless at the beginning of the school year to come over to my house and check the windows and locks and such to make sure they're secure. He promised he'd try to stop by some night, but he never did."

"Oh," Rowena said politely. "That's too bad."

Yeah, Cash thought. *It's a crying shame.* He must have had some survival instinct still operating in his subconscious, staying away as he did. Ms. Daily obviously had a lot more in mind than home safety, and with her being Mac's teacher, it could have made things plenty awkward. Maybe it wasn't such a bad thing, letting the woman think he and Rowena had something besides babysitting on their agenda.

He walked over and slipped his arm lightly around Rowena's waist. Rowena went stone stiff, then looked at him as if his hair was on fire. In spite of that, she felt good to him, her waist trim beneath those baggy shirts she wore, her body warm underneath soft cotton.

"Rowena is just the person to set you up with a dog," Cash said, giving her an affectionate squeeze as he watched Ms. Daily's face fall. "And that Destroyer—he's one dog in a million."

"Really?" Ms. Daily said, perking up a little. "I'd love to meet him! I'm not doing anything right after school tonight."

Rowena pulled out of Cash's grasp, purposely stepping on his toe in the process. Luckily, it was hard to make an impression through steel-toed boots. "Clancy's not up for adoption," she said flatly.

Cash's jaw almost hit the floor. "What do you mean he's not up for adoption? You've been trying to unload him on me for— I mean, talk me into adding him to the family for three weeks," he amended, remembering his audience.

"You were going to adopt the Newfie, Deputy?" Ms. Daily

asked in surprise. "That would be wonderful for the girls! I wouldn't dream of snatching him from under your noses."

Please, Cash thought. *Snatch him. In fact, I'll pay you to take him...*

"A dog is more than we can handle at my house right now, isn't it, Mac?" He tried to enlist his daughter's help. After the disaster last night, he at least expected her to be on his side.

But even Mac looked wistful. "I love that doggy real much. But he breaks things, Ms. Daily. Like beds and legs and screens and stuff. He jumped right through the window so he could sleep with me an' my sister an' the policemen came with guns."

Terrific. Even Mac was in league against him.

"What happened last night was an accident, Mac. Just a misunderstanding." He tried to repair the damage. If the demon dog was sold to Ms. Daily, Cash's problems would be over. Charlie would have to accept the dog was out of her reach forever. She'd get over her infatuation with the animal, and life could go back to normal.

Or could it? Cash remembered Charlie's anguished tears as he'd driven the dog back to Rowena's shop. Charlie had clung to the Newfoundland as if it were a buoy in a flooded river, the only thing keeping swift currents from sucking her under.

Christ, it ripped his heart out seeing her that way, and yet what choice did he have? Look at the mayhem the dog had caused being in the house one lousy night.

Ms. Daily seemed to consider. "Well, accidents do happen, don't they, MacKenzie? And I really do want a Newfoundland."

"They're a wonderful breed as long as you don't mind shedding and drooling and your house isn't full of knickknacks," Rowena warned. "They can take out a table top full of knickknacks with one sweep of their tail."

"Oh, well..." Ms. Daily seemed to hesitate a moment.

"You never mentioned any of that to me," Cash complained.

"Once you research the breed, Ms. Daily, you know, do your homework, I'd be happy to put you in touch with the nearest Newf rescue organization," Rowena assured the teacher. "They do fantastic work with their dogs."

"A rescue what?"

"Volunteers that take in certain breeds when they end up in shelters or puppy mills or whose owners can't keep them anymore. They take the dogs into their homes and work out any kinks in their behavior. Then they match them with new owners. A quiet, single-dog home for more nervous types. Children if a dog is rambunctious and loves to play. I'd be happy to put you in touch with the rescue organization."

"But if Deputy Lawless doesn't want a dog, why can't I have the Newfie he was talking about? Destroyer?"

"His name is Clancy," Rowena said, looking Cash stubbornly in the eye. "And he already belongs to somebody else."

THE END-OF-DAY SCHOOL BELL rang outside the building as well as in. Ever since Rowena had opened her shop, the sound had measured out her day. The morning bell—cleaning cages, stocking shelves, preparing to greet customers. Moms who'd dropped off their older kids would wander over with toddlers in tow looking for goldfish food or hamster pellets or asking Rowena the kinds of questions she loved best.

Jaime's birthday is coming up. We're thinking of getting her a puppy.

Rowena still felt a thrill every time a parent trusted her, cared enough to ask her. She adored talking about the different breeds, the different personalities. Finding yet another perfect match. And the retired people—she might be the only person they talked to all day besides the cat or dog that had become their family now that the child who'd become a doctor had moved to California. Or the husband or wife they once bickered with disappeared through divorce or death.

The animals Rowena's clients took into their hearts, into their lives didn't replace the loved one lost to age or to distance. But at least another living creature helped to soothe the sting.

When the final bell rang, the bell that let school out, it ushered in a far more boisterous crowd. Freed from the grind of multiplication tables and fractions and adding two plus two, the five- to twelve-years-olds who were her customers were given free rein to explore the mysteries of how geckos' toes got sticky enough to walk up a glass aquarium side or how a parrot learned to talk.

But today's bell might as well have been the kind that signaled the start of a boxing match. From the minute Cash had rolled Mac's wheelchair out of the classroom, Rowena had sensed he was spoiling for a fight.

To his credit, he didn't succumb to the temptation of chewing her out—at least until he'd strapped Mac safely in her car seat.

He shut the door, and Rowena followed him and the wheelchair around to the back.

"Why don't you just tell me whatever is bugging you before the top of your head blows off?" Rowena challenged, knowing they had only so much time to get this scene over with before Charlie came out. "I know what you're going to say."

"Then why should I bother to say it?" Cash snarled.

"Because if you don't, the top of your head's going to blow off. That vein in your temple is beating so hard it looks like it's going to burst. And I'd just as soon not have a brain hemorrhage on my conscience."

"Fine, then. You want to know what I'm thinking? I'm wondering what the hell's the matter with you." Cash folded Mac's wheelchair up, putting it into the back of the SUV with a force that made the whole car bounce. "You own a pet store. You sell pets. Why the hell won't you sell one to Ms. Daily?"

"I'll be happy to sell her a dog. Just not *that* dog."

"Because he belongs to somebody else?" Cash slammed down the hatch. "What kind of bullshit excuse is that?"

Rowena looked across the playground, saw Charlie. Laughing clusters of children buzzed all around the open field, but Charlie walked alone, so solemn, so solitary, it broke Rowena's heart.

"You want to tell that little girl the connection she feels to that dog is bullshit?" Rowena argued. "She defied you, Cash. Tried to hide the dog from you."

"Hide that monster? Fat chance that was going to work!"

"You know that, and I know that, but she didn't. She was willing to risk it. Do you have any idea how desperate she had to be to do that?"

"Plenty of kids try to pull one over on their parents," Cash argued. "It's natural."

"Sure it is. All a part of growing up. Charlie should be testing the limits, trying your patience, making mistakes because she knows damned well you'll love her no matter what."

"Of course I'll love her! She knows that!"

"She *doesn't* know that. Charlie doesn't believe…"

"Don't tell me about my daughter," Cash warned, gritting his teeth. "You've barely met her, and I've been there for that child her whole life."

"You have. But her mother hasn't. In Charlie's world, that changed everything. Maybe Charlie can't own Clancy, but that doesn't mean somebody else can. If Clancy stays with me, she'll be able to see him, and—"

"Oh, so that's what this is all about, is it?" Cash folded his arms over his chest and stalked to the side of the car. "Your little altruistic *helping the single father out of a jam* bit. What you were *really* trying to do was weasel that dog into my house however you can."

Rowena's temper flared. "That's not true! I—"

"Maybe we should forget this whole thing," Cash said. "I don't know why I agreed to it in the first place."

"Because you need help, just as much as Charlie needs that dog!"

"We're not another pack of strays for you to take in." Pride, stubbornness etched his face, and yet Rowena saw something buried deeper. A vulnerability cloaked in anger.

"*I* take care of my family." He jabbed his thumb into his chest. "*I* do. No one else."

"I know you do." She said it so quietly she startled him. He glared down at her, muscles in his face tight, his eyes blazing. And suddenly she knew—the reason he'd gotten so angry, the reason for all his harsh words, the reason he was trying to shove her away as hard as he could...

She hadn't said anything to him that he hadn't said to himself.

What kind of poison was that for a proud man like Cash Lawless to swallow day after day? Rowena could guess the kind of creed the deputy would live by. *A man takes care of his own. Protects his children. Keeps them safe.* But Cash couldn't magically raise Mac from her wheelchair or make his little girl's legs whole. And he couldn't give Charlie back the bedrock every child deserved to build their lives on—that her mother would always be there for her, no matter what.

And every time he looked at Rowena, he had to face the decision he'd made not to give Charlie the dog Rowena believed could heal the child's broken heart.

Every time Cash looked at Rowena, he had to ask himself the question: *what if she was right?*

She sucked in a steadying breath, aching for him as Charlie skirted three boys with construction paper jack-o'-lanterns in their hands and approached the SUV. The emotional ravages of the night before chalked the child's face white and drew dark circles beneath her lashes. Charlie's hair looked as if it hadn't seen a brush in two days. But when would Cash have had time to do it in the confusion of dealing with the emergency room and trying to get Vinny's leg set and still getting the kids to school on time?

The mouse-brown strands hung limp against Charlie's cheeks, her hair as lifeless as her eyes. Eyes filled with confusion when they saw Rowena standing there. Mac must've rolled down her window, because the five-year-old leaned out of it, yelling to her sister.

"Hey, Charlie! The bad dog lady is going to be our Mr. Google until our real one gets better!"

"Really?" Charlie stubbed the toe of her tennis shoe on a bump in the asphalt. She righted herself, then looked from one adult to the other. "Is that true, Daddy?"

Rowena could see Cash wince as the little girl's face brightened just a whisper, like a parched flower at the first drop of rain. He rounded the car to where she now stood, barely a foot from Mac's window.

His jaw worked, and Rowena sensed what he was about to do. Call off the deal. "Charlie, I don't think…"

"—you girls can do without me," Rowena interrupted, jarring Cash with her elbow in the hopes she could knock some sense into him. "How else is your daddy going to pick you up from school every day or get Mac to therapy on time? And you girls can't stay alone in the house when your daddy's at work, can you?"

It was Cash she was talking to, reminding him of all the reasons this arrangement of theirs was a bitter necessity that he'd damned well better swallow. And she knew the stubborn deputy understood exactly what she was saying.

She heard him make a low sound of frustration in his throat. Charlie must have taken it for an assent. The child looked from her father to Rowena.

"That's what's going to happen?" Charlie asked in a small voice. "You—you'll take care of Mac and me?"

"That's the plan," Rowena told her.

"But what about the puppies and kitties and stuff in your shop?"

"I'll take care of them while you and Mac are in school or your daddy's home from work. And sometimes, you and Mac and I will go to the shop and you two can help me. If you don't mind too much."

Disbelief flooded Charlie's pinched features. "Maybe that isn't such a good idea." She peered up at Cash, all those little worry lines back in her face. "If I hadn't been naughty and gone in your shop when I wasn't supposed to I never would have loved Clancy and the bad stuff last night wouldn't have happened."

Rowena warmed as Cash stroked Charlie's tangled hair. "We'll bend the rules just this once," he told his daughter. "How about it, cupcake?"

Tears threatened, the child's thin shoulders shaking.

"What's wrong, baby? I thought you'd like the idea of going to the pet shop with Rowena."

"I do, Daddy. So much…but…I was bad. I don't…deserve it."

"Oh, sweetheart—" Cash leaned down to pick her up, but Charlie backed away. Rowena saw Cash's eyes flicker with confusion and a sliver of hurt as Charlie wrapped her arms tight around her middle. What on earth was going on here?

Rowena knew there was no place on earth the little girl would rather be right now than in her father's arms.

"I thought…I thought you'd lose your job because all the policemen had to come to our house and Mr. Google couldn't watch us 'cause his leg got broke." The child's fears spilled out in a rush. "And maybe Mac and me couldn't go to school. And then I'd have to flunk fourth grade."

"Yeah," Mac said from her window. "And all 'cause you broke Mr. Google, right, Charlie?"

Charlie nodded. Her mouth wobbled as she fought not to cry. Rowena saw Cash's hands fist. "Mr. Google is going to be fine—"

Rowena caught his eye, gave her head the tiniest shake. Cash went quiet. It humbled Rowena, his first fragile offering of trust.

Rowena hunkered down in front of Charlie.

"Want to know a secret? I break lots of things, too," she confided, drowning in Charlie's sad green eyes.

"So does Clancy," Charlie said, looking from Rowena to her father; Cash so tall, so strong, as lost and alone in his way as his little girl was. "Maybe that's why me and Clancy love each other so much. We match, Clancy and me. We break stuff but we don't mean to." Her chest rose and fell under the weight of a sigh far too heavy for such a little girl. "But it's too late. Sorry doesn't matter."

"Of course it matters that you're sorry, sweetheart," Cash insisted, looking bewildered.

Charlie shook her head. "That's not what Mommy says."

"What did your mommy say, cupcake?"

"I know!" Mac piped up from her window. "Last time Mommy came, Charlie stepped on the bracelet Mommy was letting me play with and Mommy said, *Once you break something you can't ever fix it, Charlotte Rose, so don't be saying you're sorry to me, young lady. 'Cause sorry's just a big fat lie.*"

If Rowena, a virtual stranger, heard Lisa Lawless's unforgiving tone in the little girl's voice, Cash did, too. His jaw clenched so tight it seemed ready to snap.

Charlie cringed at the memory of the harsh words, her thin cheeks coloring in embarrassment at having yet another of her "sins" exposed. Rowena wished she could grab the cold woman who was the child's mother and shake Lisa Lawless until that cream suit of hers looked as if she'd slept in it. She wished she could parade Lisa's mistakes in front of the world, denying her absolution.

Once you break something you can't ever fix it...

Charlie believed that. And so did Cash.

"Listen, cupcake," Cash tried to soothe. "Sometimes when grownups get mad, they say things they don't mean. I'm sure your mother—"

"Mommy meaned it all right," Mac said. "That's why she went away. 'Cause she broked my legs and couldn't fix it. I told her she could come back. 'Cause I don't think sorry's a big fat lie. But I don't think she believed me."

Was Mac right? Rowena wondered. Did Lisa Lawless hold herself to the same harsh standard she did her eldest daughter? Did Cash's ex-wife blame herself for Mac's injuries? Was that why she'd left—because it was too hard to piece together her little girl's life after the child had been hurt so badly? Too hard to face her husband when she'd been the one behind the wheel?

Lives, broken to pieces like the teapots in the box in Rowena's back room. All those jewel-like fragments Miss Marigold had tried to throw away. Just like Lisa Lawless had thrown away her family.

"How would you like to do something magic?" Rowena reached out, cupped Charlie's face in her hand.

"Magic? Like talking to Clancy?" She chewed at her bottom lip. "I don't know. That didn't turn out very well. I listened, just like you told me to. He told me he came all the way to my house to find me, and he promised he'd live in my playhouse and never let Daddy see him. Like—well, like the invisible bunny in that old movie Daddy showed us. The picture that only has black and white. What was that movie's name, Daddy?"

"*Harvey*," Cash said, actually sounding a little embarrassed at being caught watching something like that. "It's an old black and white with Jimmy Stewart."

"I know," Rowena said softly. "That's one of my favorite movies."

"Me, too," Charlie agreed. "But the rabbit was better at staying invisible than Clancy was." Charlie's brow wrinkled up as if she were thinking hard. "Getting invisible is a very tricky thing."

So is healing broken hearts, Rowena thought, looking from the little girl to Cash.

But tricky or not, she had to try.

CHAPTER EIGHT

ORANGES AND PINKS SMEARED the horizon like one of Charlie's watercolor skies, a single bead of light running along the edge of town. Cash climbed out of his SUV, every muscle in his body aching from two days without sleep.

But he wouldn't be able to hit the sack any time soon. He had breakfast to make, the girls to get to school, and then a trip to the grocery store to stock up Vinny's cupboards. Mr. Google wouldn't be up to carting bulging bags of salami and stinky cheese to his apartment anytime soon.

Mounting the stairs, Cash rubbed his eyes with one hand, wondering if he should try Charlie's sure-fire method for staying awake when she had friends stay overnight. He smiled, remembering the night he'd caught Charlie and Hope Stone in the bathroom at two in the morning, splashing their faces with ice-cold water.

How long had it been since Hope had been underfoot at the house almost as often as his own kids? Cash's smile faded. Too long. One more piece of everyday life that had gone missing in the years since everything had fallen apart.

Cash unlocked the door and opened it quietly, not wanting to wake Rowena. But when he slipped into the living room, no blond-haired gypsy slept on the couch. The blankets and pillows Cash had set out for her still sat folded just where he'd put them before he'd left for work.

He tried to quell a twinge of uneasiness—but he made his living by paying attention to things that looked suspicious. Still, suspicious didn't always mean something was wrong. He glanced into the kitchen—empty, except for…what was that delicious smell?

Coffee?

He flicked on the light. There it was, right on the counter. The carafe was full, looked steaming hot, promising the caffeine he needed to kick start his morning. Rowena must have made it before she went to sleep and set the timer. But how had she known how badly he needed a cup of joe when he got home?

It surprised him, tugged at something inside him he didn't want to name, that she'd taken the trouble on his behalf.

He'd check on the girls first, then pour himself a mug full. Reenergized just at the prospect, he went down the hall, peering first in Charlie's room, then in Mac's. The girls' beds hadn't been slept in either. Alarm quickened his pace to his bedroom. But what would they be doing in there? Cash pushed wide the door and went still.

Rowena lay in the middle of his bed, her yellow sweatsuit like a drop of sun that had spilled through the window. Picture books littered the floor, and it looked like the stuffed animals had made a jailbreak from the toy box. The fugitives scattered the bed. Mac and Charlie snuggled against Rowena like kittens, as if they were trying to burrow as deep into all that womanly warmth and softness as they could.

Cash didn't blame them. They'd missed so much—his girls—even before Lisa had left them, from the sound of Charlie's revelation after school yesterday.

Sorry doesn't matter…

Anger and bitterness gnawed inside him. How could Lisa have said that to their little girl? Charlie, with her tender heart and her desperate need to please. Charlie, who had always tried so hard to get things right even before the accident. And now...

"Cash?"

He started at the low, husky sound, a sleepy feminine voice. Rowena, looking abashed as she carefully disentangled herself from the girls and eased herself up to a sitting position. She looked so damned beautiful, her hair all tousled, pillow creases in her cheek, her shirt rumpled where Mac's head had lain.

"Go back to sleep." He squeezed the words from a throat suddenly too tight.

She shook her head, then oh so carefully started to climb over Mac. The blankets snagged around her legs and Cash reached over to set them loose. He didn't expect to touch bare skin, where her sweat pants had ridden up. He gritted his teeth at the smoothness of her ankle, her perfectly shaped bare feet.

The instant he got the blanket loose he leaned over and grabbed Rowena under her arms, lifting her over Mac's sleeping form.

What'd you do that for? a voice inside his head asked him. *So I could touch her.* The truth unnerved him. Yet he let his hands linger as he set her on her feet. What else could he do, since her shirt had ridden up in the process and his left palm melded against bare skin? The cove a mere finger's width away from where her breast began.

He couldn't help himself. His thumb skimmed up just a smidgen. Touched pillowy softness where a bra should have been.

Cash heard Rowena's breath catch, and for an instant he almost slid his hand up to cup her, then he glanced back at the bed. Was he so desperate he'd feel up a woman with his kids in the room? He drew away from Rowena, scowling. He covered the girls back up, then left the room. Rowena followed him. He could imagine those breasts he'd almost touched bouncing subtly against the soft cotton.

"Charlie was having trouble sleeping, so I said I'd lie down with her a little while," she explained. "Then Mac felt left out. Your bed was the only one big enough for all three of us to fit in." She swept her hair back from her face with one hand. "But you probably wanted to lie down this morning until it was time for the kids to get up. I just wasn't thinking."

"Don't apologize to me." The words jabbed him again, reminding him of Lisa, and the contrast between her and the woman standing in his kitchen this morning.

"Charlie still feels bad about what happened to Mr. Google. She just needed some snuggle time, you know? Instead of lying in her bed all alone, beating herself up."

"Yeah, and we know where she got that habit, don't we? From her *mother*. One more little present Lisa gave Charlie before she left the kid behind."

"You seemed as surprised by it as I was."

"How could I not have seen that? Not have known?"

"You were working hard. You couldn't be with them every second."

"No. But if anybody should have known about Lisa's talent for holding grudges, it was me. I bet she could have told you every mistake I ever made with her, including the first time I—" *Nailed her against the elevator wall.*

He winced, remembering how Lisa had pushed the stop button, then leaned back against the elevator doors, arching her back so her nipples pushed against her silk blouse. She'd smelled expensive, classy, way out of his league.

I've never done anything like this before. She'd flashed him that smoky come-hither look, hiking her already short skirt up so he could see shapely thighs, a flash of red panties. *Be bad with me, Cash...*

He'd known she and her rich girlfriends had come to the bar slumming, aware that it was frequented by sailors and marines on leave. But he didn't care. It was his first day off in months and he was drunk, not only from the tequila shots he'd been throwing back with his buddies, but with the freedom of having his discharge papers in his pocket and knowing he'd never have to go to war again.

"It must have been hard for you." Rowena's voice jarred him, and for a moment he wondered if she'd read his mind. Yeah, he'd been hard all right, and dumb as a rock. He gave a snort of self-disgust.

"I mean, to have your wife hold things against you that way," Rowena explained hastily.

"Yeah, well." He walked to the coffee machine and pulled a mug down from the cabinet. What else was there to say? he thought as he poured himself a cup. Lisa was a master at revisionist history. Somehow later, the whole elevator scene became his fault instead of hers.

But then, maybe Lisa was right. He'd been more than willing to bury memories of bullets tearing into human flesh by fulfilling one of those *Penthouse* moments any red-blooded twenty-two-year-old male fantasized about. Especially since fantasies were the only kind of sex he'd been having while deployed for the past nine months.

When the condom had torn he should've ignored her urging just to pull out before he came. He knew better than to take that kind of risk, but he'd done it all the same.

When he'd awakened the next morning with a throbbing headache, he figured she must've enjoyed their interlude in the elevator, too, because she'd given him her number. The next night, they'd done a repeat performance—this time in the ladies' room at a different bar.

He'd taken her back to the hotel room he and one of his

marine buddies shared. By the end of the week he had a room of his own and Lisa's one night of slumming had turned into weeks, then two months.

"You know what gets me?" Cash surprised himself by saying. Part of him knew it was strange to be having a personal conversation with his babysitter first thing in the morning, but something in Rowena's open expression made him continue in spite of that.

"What?"

"If she wanted to hold crap against me, then fine. I'm a big boy. I can take care of myself. But to do that to Charlie...my little girl..." Fury boiled to the surface. "How could Lisa do that to her?"

"I don't know."

"A mom is supposed to build kids up, you know? Be there, no matter what. When I was a kid, I got in plenty of trouble. I could probably have even given you a run for your money in that department."

"Good to know."

"My mom—she was about five feet tall, ninety pounds soaking wet. She had this temper, you know? Fired off when she was mad like nobody's business. She could still scare the devil out of my brothers and me when we were a foot and a half taller than she was."

He saw a smile tick up the corner of Rowena's mouth. "Hell on wheels with a wooden spoon, huh?"

"She never hit us once. She never had to. She'd be the first one to lay into us over whatever trouble we'd gotten in. Take away ball games, television, whatever punishment she thought would work. Time out was the worst. Sitting on the kitchen stairs, watching out the back window, seeing the rest of those lucky sons of bitches playing ball." He chuckled at the memory. "We begged her just to spank us and get it over with like all the other moms."

"I know what you mean. My mom was the queen of 'I'm so disappointed in you.' Wow, does that ever mess with a kid's mind."

Cash studied her face for a long moment. "You know what the best part about my mom was?"

"What?"

"After we'd served our sentence, she'd come over and sit on the step with us. She'd give us this bone-cracking hug and say, 'if you're not making mistakes, you're not living. And living's what God put you here to do.' It was like a lead weight rolled off my chest when my mom would say that."

"She sounds wonderful. Your girls must adore her."

"She died a few months after Charlie was born. Breast cancer." But even sick as she was, she'd wanted what was best for all six of her boys. The last bit of advice she'd given Cash was to move the new granddaughter she'd adored far away from her. It was the only way to get Lisa's family to give them the space they needed to build a life of their own. As usual, his mom's plan had worked. Until the accident had brought Lisa's sister swooping in.

"You know what I miss most about my mom? I'd feel so— I don't know, so *clean* when she'd hug me and say everything was all right. She'd forget whatever bad thing I'd done. Never brought it up again. At least not to hurt us. Sometimes, when we got older, she'd retell one of the stories and laugh."

Come to think of it, something in Rowena's face reminded him of Rose Lawless. The fresh-scrubbed look of her, the eyes that sparkled, the warm, ready smile and the fierce way she protected any creature she loved. He'd seen it with that devil dog of hers. And with his daughter. He'd thought she was just trying to foist the dog off on the nearest mark. But obviously that wasn't the case since she'd refused to sell Destroyer to Mac's teacher. And why? Because keeping the dog herself meant Charlie could visit it, even if she could never have it for her own.

Even if the dog caused mayhem anywhere he went. Even if Cash raged at Rowena and argued with her and hated the dog on sight.

"You showed that dog of yours more compassion than my ex-wife showed our kids," Cash said. "My mom was so…so kind. Loved us, you know? But Charlie—what did Charlie get for her apologies? 'It's too late'? The feeling the black marks under her name would stay there forever, tallied up by her own mother?"

"But Charlie has you."

"Yeah. She has me. Poor kid."

Rowena closed the space between them, laid her hand on his arm. "You're a good father, Cash."

"Even if I won't let Charlie have that dog?"

"Well…" Her eyes sparkled beneath those thick gold-tipped lashes. "The truth is I haven't given up on you yet."

He should have been aggravated. Instead he took her hand in his and turned it over, looking down into her palm. "At least you're honest."

"I have to be. I'm a rotten liar. My sister Ariel says it's one of my worst faults. When Mom came through town I told her I got the black eye from stepping on a rake."

"Like in *The Three Stooges*?"

"Something like that."

"I'm thinking your mother didn't buy it?"

"It's tough to fool a doctor."

"She must have been proud of you when you explained. I mean, you thought you were rescuing a defenseless little girl."

"My mom isn't exactly thrilled about rescues that aren't of the medical sort, so I figured telling her I barged into a stranger's house and attacked a guy who carries a gun wouldn't exactly make her visit go any smoother. The consensus of my sisters is that the unfortunate rake incident was the lamest excuse I've come up with yet, in a lifetime of lame excuses. Next time I decide to fib so Mom won't worry about me, I'm supposed to clear my story with them first."

She looked so abashed that Cash actually smiled. "I could help you out in that department if they aren't available. You wouldn't believe the number of excuses I hear in my line of work. *I didn't see the stop sign. I just forgot I had the candy bar in my hand when I walked out of the Quick Stop. We weren't really having sex in the car. My girlfriend just lost her contact lens and we thought it might have fallen and gotten caught in her clothes.*"

Rowena ran her hands over her shirt as if patting herself down for the missing lens. "I'll keep that one on file just in case. But I think my mother would be relieved to come bail me out of jail for something normal instead of the weird kinds of trouble I get into. Do you go to jail for getting caught parking?"

"Not on my shift. I suppose legally I could take them in for indecent exposure or lewd acts in a public park or disorderly conduct, but I just send them home with a warning. Vinny used to say it wasn't fair to ruin some high school kid's night just because we were jealous they were getting lai—well, you get the gist." God. He must be even more tired than he thought, talking to a pretty, sleep-mussed woman about a subject as dangerous as that one.

"It's been a long time then? For you?" Rowena asked a trifle shyly.

Cash's gaze collided with hers. "What?"

"Since you…" She fretted that plump pink lower lip, and Cash tamped down a surge of heat behind the fly of his pants.

"Since I had sex?" He intended to startle her with his blunt answer, then tell her it was none of her business. It wasn't, after all. And yet, there was something about her straightforward question that tugged at his defenses. She looked so empathetic, her head cocked to one side and her eyes so green and soft and warm that he surprised himself.

"There hasn't been anyone since Lisa left," he admitted.

"Oh."

She didn't ask for him to elaborate. He had no idea why he did it anyway. "My girls have been hurt enough. Bringing some new woman into their lives just so I can have casual sex hardly seems fair."

Not to mention that sex had a dangerous way of tearing down walls, leaving a man vulnerable, tempting him to take risks. If he hadn't understood how costly those risks could be when he was a horny kid just back from Kuwait, he sure as hell understood them now. Every time he saw his daughters' faces when their mom bothered to call them on the phone.

"Of course—" he saluted her with his coffee "—most days I'm too damned busy to care about sex at all."

"I never even think about it myself. Well, *almost* never." She flushed, dropped her gaze to the floor. She looked so flustered he knew exactly what had flashed into her mind. That hot, heavy moment when they'd stared at each other through the picture window. When he'd been naked and she'd been breathless, and they'd both been excruciatingly aware of possibilities.

Eve stumbling across Adam in the garden the very first time. Not sure what to do, on the brink of unraveling the mysteries together.

She'd stirred feelings in him he hadn't had since before his stint in Kuwait, when he'd been clean himself, a kid who believed in honor and valor, determined to prove himself in battle. But he wasn't that kid anymore. He never would be.

And yet, she'd reminded him what it felt like to be a man, not just a father.

She's your kids' babysitter, he told himself sternly. *You can't afford to screw that up to get her in bed.*

Which would be damned well impossible, considering where his little girls were sleeping at the moment.

That's what you need to be remembering...how peaceful the girls looked snuggled up to her, their stuffed animals and books scattered around them.

"So, what about you?" he asked.

She'd said she hadn't been having sex, but for all he knew her boyfriend could live far away, be in the military or a dozen other places that would keep him out of reach.

"Have you got some guy out there who doesn't mind dog hair on everything he owns?" He hoped so. It would make the next six weeks a whole lot easier if she did.

Regret flickered in her eyes. He almost let her off the hook, but curiosity pushed him. "Come on. I answered your question about my nonexistent sex life. The least you can do is tell me about your boyfriend."

"He was my fiancé."

Whoa. "You're engaged?"

"I was. Past tense. Before I came here." Distress etched her features.

"Want to talk about it?"

"Oh, yeah. That would be big fun." She rolled her eyes, and he thought that was the end of it. But after a moment she spoke. "There's one undeniable truth about me you probably need to know, Cash."

"What's that?"

"When I screw up, I screw up big. I've known Daniel forever—since we were kids. Our parents were friends. My sisters played with his sisters. When he asked me on a date the folks practically set off fireworks. It was the first thing I'd ever done that made my family that happy."

"Don't tell me. He was really a jerk?" Cash wanted him to be a jerk. He wasn't sure why.

"No. Dan was exactly the opposite. He was a pediatrician at my mom's hospital. No one but Mom and I knew, but he was helping pay for prescriptions out of pocket for kids whose parents fell between the cracks."

"That's too bad." Cash scrambled to make sense out of what he'd said. "I don't mean it was bad he was helping with expenses. After Mac's medical bills—well, all I can say is thank God I had decent insurance. But losing a jerk would have been a lot easier on you than losing a guy who, well, didn't let anyone fall through the cracks."

"Isn't that the truth?" She gave him a wan smile. "Dan was everything my mom ever wanted for me. Brilliant, kind, responsible, well-off. And…" She hesitated. "He loved me."

Terrific, Cash thought. But he could hear the pain and regret in her voice.

"In fact, I figured they'd ditch me and adopt him when I called the wedding off."

"You called it off?" Cash asked. She'd dumped Prince Fucking Charming?

"Yep. I called it off and almost got arrested in the process."

He almost smiled. "What offense was it this time?"

"I'd spent forever addressing invitations. Mom called me every day to see if I'd put them in the mail. You're supposed to zing the things off six weeks before the date, but my sister Ariel talked me into doing this thing with sealing wax and ribbons and I got too busy to finish…well, never mind. Suffice it to say five weeks before the wedding I couldn't stand Mom's ragging anymore. I finished the annoying little suckers and ran them down to the corner mailbox and dumped the envelopes in. I expected this huge sense of relief once it was done. Planned to run straight back home and call Mom, get her off my case, you know? But the instant those envelopes left my hands, I knew…"

She poured her own cup of coffee, looked out at his tree. Cash stood silent, waiting.

"I knew I'd made a terrible mistake."

Cash could imagine how she felt. He knew what it was like, looking at the person you were supposed to marry and seeing a train wreck. But then in his case nobody—not his family and certainly not Lisa's—was overjoyed at the match. It would be a whole different ball game if the fiancé you were dumping was Mr. Perfect, a family friend everybody else adored.

"It must have been hard for you," he said. "Breaking things off."

Setting down her cup, she hugged herself, rubbing her upper arms. "It ended up being a whole lot worse than it had to be. I sat by the box two hours until my mailman came. He'd known me for years. I begged him to give the letters back. I mean, my return address was on every one of them and there was that stupid wax seal with our initials woven together. Besides, wedding invitation envelopes are stuffed to the gills with all kinds of crap, so it's not like you can mistake them for anything else."

He could see her frustration rise, even now.

"But would the guy hand the invitations over?" she asked in disgust. "No. Neither rain nor sleet nor begging and tears would keep him from his appointed rounds. He said if I didn't quit following the mail truck he'd call the police!"

Cash could imagine, all too well, Rowena doggedly pursuing the mail carrier.

"Know what made me maddest of all?" she demanded.

"What?"

"He kept those invitations just to spite me. I'm absolutely sure it made his day to stick it to me that way."

Cash shrugged. "The man had a job to do."

"No. That wasn't the reason. You want to know why he

wouldn't give those invitations back? The man hated a dog I was fostering."

Another out-of-control dog? Maybe Cash could see where the mailman was coming from. "Did your dog bite him?"

"I'd never keep a dog that bit! The mailman was just steamed about that package Lulu chewed up."

"Your dog stole a piece of mail?"

"He left it on Mrs. Gully's porch," she bristled. "It was a windy day and it blew into my yard. The blasted thing was stuffed with oatmeal cookies! It wasn't Lulu's fault she ate them. Wouldn't you?"

Homemade cookies? Cash remembered when one of his marine buddies had gotten a care package from home. They'd all descended on whatever baked goods it held like a horde of Army Ants. Maybe it wasn't so hard to see how Lulu had been tempted into a life of crime.

But Rowena was still too focused on a past injustice to bother exploring his train of thought. "Too bad I didn't know what a jerk the mailman was going to be," she muttered. "I would've borrowed a neighbor kid and seen if I could lower him head-first into the mail slot. He could've gotten those invitations back."

Again Cash felt the urge to smile. "Then you really would have been arrested. Added child endangerment to the federal charge of tampering with the mail."

"Jail would've been a relief under the circumstances. I would rather have been locked up than have to face my mother and his parents and Dan himself. Even after the whole panic attack over the invitations, I still couldn't call the wedding off. My sisters tried to convince me it was just a case of pre-wedding jitters. My mother said it was only natural. Two weeks before the wedding, I knew for certain they were wrong."

"It's a good thing you didn't settle," Cash surprised himself by reassuring her. He hated the shadow of guilt that still haunted her eyes, and the tinge of self-doubt. "You've got a lot to offer a man. You deserve to find love. The kind most people only imagine."

Rowena gave him a wobbly smile. Her eyes filled with gratitude. "I couldn't go through with the ceremony," she said. "It didn't matter how kind Dan was, or how successful, or that my family worshipped him. You can't marry someone you don't love."

Cash winced at the conviction in her voice. "You can if they're pregnant." The words slipped out before he could stop them. But what the hell? They were telling their deep dark secrets this morning. Might as well get that one out in the open, as well.

"Lisa was…pregnant?"

Cash took a deep drink of his coffee, welcoming the burn in his throat. "The fact that Charlie was on the way was not good news," he said. "Especially to Lisa's family."

"But surely once she was born—Charlie is so precious. They must've seen that."

"What they saw was that I'd ruined Lisa's life. They had some guy from the yacht club picked out for her. Barry something-or-other. An up-and-coming executive in her daddy's company."

He felt it again, the sweat on his palms as he faced Lisa's father, the man's sneer, his sarcasm, the way he'd tried to make Cash feel small. Now Cash wondered how he'd behave himself if it was his little girl some smart-ass kid knocked up. He'd probably break the guy's jaw.

"I don't blame him now, for being angry. I was fresh out of the marines. A construction worker's kid. No education. No job. No money. A real catch. Your parents would have been thrilled if you'd backed out of a wedding to me."

"How did *you* feel about the baby?"

"The baby? I was scared shitless. I remember going to tell my mom. The look on her face when I admitted what I'd done. I told her I wasn't ready…I couldn't be a father. She sat there, quiet for a long time, listening to me. Then she looked me straight in the eye and said I was going to be a father, whether I was ready or not. The only thing left for me to decide was— what kind of a man I wanted to be."

Suddenly he felt warmth, Rowena's hand on his forearm. "She'd be so proud if she could see you now."

"I had five brothers—you know, this house full of boys. Every time we left the house for a date she'd catch us at the door and say 'keep your pants zipped.' Didn't matter who else was in the house—somebody else's girlfriend, Mrs. Crosly from across the street, even the parish priest. Used to embarrass us to death." He covered Rowena's hand with his own. "Too bad I didn't listen."

She pulled her hand free then cupped his cheek, her palm soft against the stubble of his beard. He felt her touch down to his soul. "But then there wouldn't be a Charlie or Mac," she said, her face mirroring his pain, his regret, offering comfort and wisdom that surprised him. "I barely know your girls, but already I can't imagine a world without them." Her thumb skimmed his cheekbone, feather light. "They're beautiful, Cash."

Cash's voice roughened with love, awe and a faint trace of fear that he'd fail them. "They are beautiful, aren't they?"

She smiled, an angel's smile. His gaze held hers, an eternity spinning out between them, mouths mere inches apart. He could feel her breath, sense her heartbeat, see so deep into her eyes that he was drowning in them.

"Beautiful…" he echoed the word, but this time it was Rowena he was seeing, the fresh cream of her face, the pink on her cheeks, her lips parted just a little. Her tongue swept out to moisten them. Cash's own mouth went dry.

"Listen, Rowena," he began. "I want…" *Want to thank you for taking care of my kids. Want to tell you how good it was to know you didn't leave them alone, Charlie with her guilt, Mac with her dreams of dancing*. It should have been easy to finish the sentence, but only two words kept echoing in his mind.

I want…I want…I want…

"Me, too." Such a small voice. Such a brave confession. She peered up at him with eyes wide and green and far more innocent than he deserved.

Don't do it…

He tried to warn himself. But he wanted too badly, needed too deeply, for just this one moment, not to feel alone.

Sunshine. Light. Hope.

Rowena was everything missing from his life. This one moment all he could ever have.

How could he resist stealing just one taste? Cash threaded his hands back through her tousled golden hair, tipped her face up and lowered his mouth to hers.

She gasped. In surprise? In pleasure? He was too lost in sensation to know for sure. He was sinking fast, diving deep. His pulse raced as he explored her mouth tentatively, trying to gauge her reaction. He skimmed his tongue over her lips, teasing them, learning their shape, their texture. He groped for sanity, but she melted against him, running her hands over his shoulders, along his throat, then back to cup his nape. He trailed kisses down to the hollow at the edge of her jaw, where he'd felt her pulse leap when he'd touched her before.

Still warm, her throat smelled of clean cotton sheets and faint traces of yesterday morning's perfume and he sucked there just a heartbeat before he kissed his way back to her mouth and slipped his tongue inside.

She tasted like summer as her curves fitted against him, her small breasts against his chest, her hips and thighs against his.

He hardened where he pressed against her, his pulse racing at sweetness beyond anything he'd ever known.

He felt her hesitate, her fingers stealing up to his face in shy exploration that nearly undid him.

And he wanted to find the edge of her top and pull it over her head, strip off every stitch of clothing between them and take her to bed.

Bed. Where his children were sleeping. Bed. Where he'd promised himself he'd sleep alone. He went still, reluctant to surrender her mouth. Knowing once he did, he'd never taste it again.

Breaking away from her cost more than he'd admit, even to himself. "I can't do this," he ground out.

"What?" Her eyes were still heavy-lidded, her cheeks pink.

"I can't do *this*." He waved his hand toward her sleep-mussed form. "I can't kiss you. Touch you. It's a bad idea."

"Is it?" Bewildered, she pressed the back of her hand to her mouth.

Cash stalked away from her, putting the kitchen table between him and the scent of her, the taste. "You're here for my kids. And from what I saw in that bedroom, you're good for them. You can't know what that did to me…seeing you there with all their stuff scattered around…seeing them sleeping…" His jaw worked. "I won't do anything to jeopardize that."

"No. Of—of course not." Color flooded her cheeks and he hated the stricken expression he'd put there. Shame…she should never feel shame for the way she'd kissed him. Not with just her body, with skill, with practiced technique. She'd kissed him with her heart, no games between them.

She lowered her lashes, hiding those incredible eyes. "Cash, I—I'm sorry."

"*You're* sorry?" Cash gave a ragged laugh. "What for? *I'm* the one who kissed *you*."

And would have liked to do a whole lot more.

"I don't know what I was thinking," he said. But that was a lie. He'd been thinking how beautiful she was, how perfect she looked in there with his girls. He'd wanted to pretend...

Pretend what? That he'd chosen a woman warm and real, like Rowena, instead of the one who'd left his daughters behind. Given his children a mother who'd chased away nightmares and soothed guilty consciences and let them scatter books and toys in their wake.

A woman worlds different from Lisa, who'd fled to her wealthy sister's Chicago loft when things got too hard, too difficult, too heartbreaking.

Images flashed into his mind. Rowena bursting into the Sheriff's office to ransom Destroyer any way she could. Rowena charging into Cash's living room, so fierce, so fiery, hurling herself at him to protect a little girl she'd barely met. Rowena facing him after the disaster with Vinny, doing her best to straighten things out. Promising to help Cash, take up the slack until Vinny got well.

Rowena, unflinching, fiercely determined to protect anyone she cared about. Who'd somehow decided she cared about Charlie. About Mac. And...he hardly dared think it. About him?

No. She was filling in for Vinny out of guilt over the destruction her dog had left behind the night before. And she was helping with the girls because...because she'd seen how lost Charlie was, how lonely. She'd heard Mac crying, felt the kick in the gut Cash felt every time he put his child in her wheelchair.

This wasn't about him. Only a selfish bastard would let it be. No matter how long it had been since he'd gotten laid or how good it felt to taste a woman's mouth, feel her hands, make her gasp and melt.

Rowena Brown wasn't for him. It was too late to question his decisions, too late to start over. Too late to do anything but keep his head above water, make it up to his girls for his past mistakes and help Mac learn to walk again. He didn't have room for anything else—in his schedule or in his heart.

"This won't happen again," he promised.

"No." Rowena sounded as certain as he was, every bit as resolved. But he couldn't miss the wistfulness in her eyes.

Don't look at me like that, he wanted to say. Then, *don't turn away...*

"What, um, time do you want me to take the girls to school?"

"I'll do it today. I have to stop by Vinny's anyway."

"Okay. If you're sure."

"I'm sure." He was sure, all right. Sure he needed to get her out of the house. Take a cold shower. Sweep together whatever brain cells he had left. He'd been right—the minute she'd stepped in his house, he'd lost his mind.

She hastened to where her jacket hung on the back of a kitchen chair, grabbing it up along with that giant red rug she called a purse.

"I'd better go take care of Clancy. And then there's the store. I'm supposed to get a shipment of dog toys in."

He shot her an ironic grin. "The excitement never ends. You'd better go, then."

"I'll pick the girls up after school and take them to the shop like we planned."

"Great."

She was out the door and halfway down the driveway when he stopped her.

"Hey, Trouble," he called out the back door.

She wheeled around as if he'd shot her with a rubber band. "What?"

"You forgot your shoes."

She jostled her coat and bag, looking down at her feet as if she didn't believe him.

He knew the instant she saw her bare toes. Humiliation washed her face bright red. She started back toward him, stumbled, stubbing her toe. He heard her gasp of pain.

"It was that kiss," she complained. "It…rattled me…"

The kiss had rattled his cages, too. Cages where he'd kept impulse and risk and faith locked up far too long.

He carried her shoes out to her. But she was stranded between the back door and her car with her arms full. Still burning with embarrassment, she looked way too cute for his comfort.

That kiss had just been momentary insanity, he assured himself. Look at her—all flustered and blushing and shy. She looked like a kid who'd been caught by her parents making out on the porch swing. Let her keep stumbling toward her car like that, she'd stub the rest of her toes.

He tried not to remember just how sexy her toes had looked, how silky her ankle had felt when he'd helped her get untangled from the covers on his bed.

"Give me your foot," he said, crouching down on his haunches.

"What?"

"Your foot." He cupped her calf with his palm and tugged. She leaned on him, struggling for balance, but after surviving two toddlers he'd gotten fast at slipping shoes on moving targets. He secured it in place, then double-knotted the laces like he did Mac's every morning.

"The other one," he ordered, beginning the process all over. It took barely a minute, but somehow it made him feel better. More centered. More himself.

Humor—how many times had he and his brothers used it to deflect emotions that got too strong? A surefire weapon against tears or sentimental garbage or even anger.

"I've heard of kissing the socks off somebody." Cash slanted her an ornery look. "But the shoes?"

Rowena grumbled something, nudging him with her knee, almost knocking him to his butt on the driveway. Cash caught himself with one hand then straightened, stood as Rowena climbed in her car. He blocked her door before she could close it.

"What did you say?"

"I said you're not that good," Rowena fired back, regaining some of her own.

He sobered, amusement fading. "You need to remember that, Rowena," he said, hiding his sudden pain. "I'm not good at all."

She looked up into his eyes. "I don't believe that."

For an instant he wanted to cling to the faith in her long-lashed eyes. But he knew better than to make that mistake. He shook his head, touched her cheek.

"You've got no credibility at all, Rowena Brown," he said, tenderly tucking a strand of hair behind her ear. "You believe in that demon dog of yours, too."

He let his fingers fall away from everything soft and warm in her, then closed her door with a soft thud and stepped back from the car. She started the engine and he watched her pull away.

He looked to the sky one more time, Charlie's watercolor blues and pinks. He remembered the gold of Rowena's hair and the green of her eyes.

Then he turned and walked into the house, and the gray he couldn't leave behind.

CHAPTER NINE

ROWENA TRAPPED the telephone receiver between her cheek and shoulder as she bagged some of the purchases the Delaney family had gathered for Sparky, the beagle mix they were taking home for their son's sixth birthday. The match had been a flawless one, as simple as Charlie's match to Clancy had been difficult. Within half an hour, the Delaneys had been raving about what a gift Rowena had, and promising to tell all their friends.

It gratified her, their confidence in her, one more step towards belonging in this close-knit town. She glanced over at the family, hoping they'd give her an excuse to cut short her lecture from Bryony, but Billy, his mom and dad were still in the throes of agony, trying to pick out the perfect pet bed.

Charlie and Mac were no help, either, the two girls engrossed in the after-school play that had become the highlight of their day during the past two weeks.

"Rowena Maeve Brown, are you even listening to me?" Bryony's aggravated voice jarred her from her thoughts. Rowena could hear the hospital noise in the background, could picture Bryony in her tidy white lab coat, her no-nonsense glasses perched on the end of her nose as she scowled at whatever poor intern happened to be in the vicinity.

"I wasn't listening before," Rowena confessed. "But I promise I'll listen now."

"No wonder you drive Mom and Ariel crazy. They call up your shop and some strange man answers the phone and says he's watching the store while you're off running errands for this deputy guy."

"I was taking his daughter MacKenzie to physical therapy."

"Don't you dare use that oh-so-calm tone with me, as if it makes perfect sense!" Bryony snapped. "This Lawless person tries to have your dog put to sleep. He gives you a black eye. And then his kid—who you've only talked to a couple of times—smuggles *your* dog into *his* house and his babysitter breaks a leg. So now you have to fill in for him?"

"That about covers it."

"And this makes sense *how?* You don't owe him a thing, Row. So why are you doing this?"

"Just because…" Rowena glanced at the girls, her heart warming at Charlie's solemn smiles and the muffled sound of Mac's laughter. She wished Cash could hear it. "There's something about him."

"Him and every other stray you pick up along the way," Bryony scoffed. "You barely know this guy. You've got a new business to run, contacts to make, stuff to design. When you dropped out of vet school, you told us it was because you were the only one who can do…whatever it is that you do. That hocus-pocus animal stuff. Now all of a sudden, that doesn't matter and this babysitter guy is watching your shop? You're lucky the whole family doesn't descend on you to find out what the blazes is going on."

"Don't." Just imagining that little family reunion was the stuff of nightmares. "The last thing I need is for you and Ariel and Mom to come here and make things even more complicated. It's my shop. It's my life. It's my choice if I want to do this. And I do. It's important."

"Important how?" Bryony demanded. "How do you know?"

"I feel it." Rowena held the phone a few inches from her ear and braced herself for her practical sister's reaction.

"You feel it. You feel it. Terrific. Good old intuition. Cuchullain's pipe, charming the heart out of any wounded beast. If Great Auntie Maeve wasn't already dead I'd wring her neck myself! Why you took that batty old woman's predictions as gospel I'll never know. At least Ariel and I had the sense to know she was loopy. You don't see us planning our lives around some old junk that probably belongs in a flea market."

Rowena's own brow knitted. "Maybe you'd be happier if you did." She did worry about her sisters. Bryony, so driven, determined to outshine even their mother's legacy, and Ariel, who fainted at the sight of blood, trying to tough it through her surgical rotation.

"My life is just fine, thank you very much!" Bryony sputtered. "You're the one in crisis at the moment. This Lawless guy isn't a dog you've picked up or a cat on the side of the road, Rowena. He's a man."

As if her sister needed to point that out—especially after that camera-worthy moment where Rowena had seen him fresh from his shower and wearing nothing but steam.

"And by the way," Bryony lectured on, "he didn't find those kids of his under a cabbage leaf somewhere. Where's their mother? His wife?"

"Ex-wife." Rowena tensed, remembering the elegant woman in the Easter picture who had denied Charlie forgiveness. "She's somewhere in Chicago."

"She left her kids? Then there must be something really, really wrong there, Row. A mother doesn't leave her children for no reason. Are you sure this man didn't beat her up? Or maybe he slept around."

"No!" Rowena protested, repulsed. "There's no way Cash—"

"You don't know that for sure. Creeps don't go around with neon signs flashing on their heads."

"But when he's with his girls…"

"In front of you. For whatever time that is. Even a psychopath can hold it together for a few hours at a time."

"Bry, you're being ridiculous."

"Am I? You don't know anything about this man except what he wants you to. His wife might be in hiding for all you know. Admit it."

"Okay. I don't know why she left. I only know what I see. But what I see is enough. This little girl…her eyes draw me in." She hesitated, Cash Lawless's hard-edged features whispering through her mind. "And his do, too."

She could hear Bryony muttering something under her breath. Understood her sister well enough to know she was trying to gather patience.

"Rowena, I know what a big deal it was for you, calling off the wedding. Like your own personal declaration of independence from family rule and all. But you've made your point. You don't have to run out and pick the man most likely to make Mom's hair turn white."

"Bryony, I'm not picking any man at all," she warned. "And even if I was, what's wrong with—"

"What's wrong with this guy? Let's see. For all we know he could be—"

"Let's stick to facts, not fiction."

"Fine, then. He's divorced. He's got two kids from a previous marriage, one in a wheelchair, and he's a cop. You know their divorce rates are incredibly high. Not to mention the danger he's in every time he walks out the door. He could be beaten up, shot at, killed."

Rowena winced at the picture Bryony's words painted. Cash hurt or worse. His daughters having to live without him.

"Row, I just want you to consider what you're getting into here."

"I'm not marrying him, Bryony. I'm just babysitting his children for a few weeks."

"If you really want to calm my fears, tell me he looks like Barney Fife on those old Andy Griffith reruns Dad used to watch. Or that he's about five feet tall, two hundred pounds."

Rowena's mind flashed back to that moment she'd seen Cash bending over the bed, his face rugged, his square jaw roughened with a night's worth of stubble, his eyes full of secrets he didn't want to share.

But he'd shared them with her in the kitchen with an honesty that disarmed her. Let her glimpse past the hard façade he showed the world, that desperate need he had to hold things together. He let her see dreams he'd surrendered, responsibilities he'd honored. The sacrifice of a kid determined to do what was right.

His mother's words ran through her head. *You're going to be a father, ready or not...the only thing left for you to decide is what kind of man you want to be...*

And yet, was it possible Bryony was right? From the first moment Rowena had met Cash Lawless, she'd sensed he was wound so tight he was doomed to snap. She thought of the woman in the photograph and couldn't help wondering what happened when he did.

Had the sacrifices made him bitter towards his wife? Just how fast could bitter turn to downright ugly? Being a good father was different from being a decent husband. Bryony *had* reminded her of one thing it would be good for her to remember: that as unconscionable as Lisa Lawless's decision to abandon her daughters might look on the outside, she had her own version of the story to tell.

Not that Rowena would ever hear it.

"Rowena?" Bryony's voice sharpened and Rowena knew

her attention had been wandering again. She closed her eyes, determined to focus. "I'm waiting for you to tell me he looks like Don Knotts," Bryony prodded.

Rowena remembered the beautiful shape of Cash's hands, the way he'd cradled his daughter, the way he'd touched Rowena's cheek. "To tell you the truth, I—I really haven't noticed what he looks like," she hedged, but the CIA could have used Bryony as a lie detector in a pinch.

"Oh, shit. Don't tell me he's gorgeous."

"Okay. I won't."

Bryony swore darkly. She'd always had a far richer vocabulary than the rest of them. In fact, she could probably give Elvis the parrot a run for his money. "Terrific," she finally said. "Just terrific. So this guy is a lost puppy dog who looks like Brad Pitt?"

Cash like the polished, handsome star? The comparison was laughable. "Cash is nothing like that. He's…real."

"Real what? Real dangerous? Real hot? Real sexy? Real hazardous to my sanity?"

"Real as in genuine. And there's no point in any of you getting all worried. We've already decided we're not having sex."

"You what?" Bryony almost choked. She went into such a coughing jag that Rowena wondered if she should call in the paramedics. But then, Bryony was in the middle of a hospital ward. Surely somebody would know how to perform the Heimlich maneuver before she turned blue and keeled over. Rowena heard a gulping sound on the other end of the phone, as if her sister had taken a drink of the diet cola she always had on hand. "You what?" Bryony croaked again.

"After Cash kissed me, we talked about having a physical relationship and decided it would be a bad idea." So why were her breasts tingling? Why did she keep wondering just what the sex they weren't going to have might have been like?

"Brilliant." Bryony cleared her throat then paused again, apparently gulping down another mouthful of soda. "Finally, something about the man I can actually approve of. Because I'd damn well bet *you* weren't the one who put the brakes on. Not my sister, the natural woman, Ms. There's-Healing-Power-In-Touch Brown."

"I'm watching his children, Bryony," Rowena snapped, offended. "If things got weird after Cash and I had sex…"

"Ms. Brown?"

Rowena started, suddenly aware the Delaney family was standing near her counter. Her cheeks burned.

"Listen Bryony, I have to go. I've got customers to horrify… I mean, wait on."

"Rowena—"

"Bye." She hung up the phone, pasted a smile on her face. "I'm sorry about that," she told Mrs. Delaney, but the woman's eyes were alive with curiosity and something more. No question she'd picked up at least a few words from Rowena's end of the conversation.

Cash…sex…

Luckily, the woman's little boy didn't have eyes or ears for anything but the dog in his arms. Billy Delaney was in heaven.

So was Sparky. The beagle had gotten the world's best dog toy for his breed. There was nothing a beagle liked better than having his very own boy.

"Listen, Bill," Ms. Delaney said to her husband. "Why don't you and Billy take Sparky across the street to the playground, see if he needs a potty break before the car ride home."

"Oh, Sparky's completely housebroken," Rowena began, but Mrs. Delaney shooed the three males in her life out the shop door.

"Ms…Brown, isn't it?"

"Please call me Rowena."

"Rowena, then. I couldn't help but overhear a bit of your conversation."

Rowena wished she'd installed a trap door in the shop floor so she could sink right through it at the moment. "I'm so sorry. I know it was inappropriate. I don't think Billy heard."

"I sent him outside because I think there's something *you* might need to hear."

"And what is that?"

"Lisa Lawless isn't some monster, no matter what that man tells you."

Rowena started in surprise at the woman's quick defense. "Actually, it's none of my business. I'm just helping him out—"

"Yes, well, since Lisa left, it seems everyone in town has cast her as the wicked witch. I suppose it's easy enough, seeing Cash pushing MacKenzie around in that wheelchair. Just don't forget Lisa spent twenty-four hours a day with those girls for six years of their life."

"Mrs. Delaney, I—"

"She had dreams, too. She was injured in that car wreck, too. Why don't you ask Cash about that?"

"I won't be asking Cash about anything."

"Except whether or not you're going to have sex?"

Rowena bristled at the cutting edge to the woman's voice. "That was a private conversation."

Mrs. Delaney flushed, but she met Rowena's gaze with defiance. "I'm just giving you a friendly warning. Like I'd hope someone would give me if I were in your situation. Be careful where Cash Lawless is concerned. He's a hard man, and a stubborn one. Lisa hated it in Whitewater. She begged him to leave, for all the good it did her. I'm just saying that if Lisa left her girls here, well, maybe that was the only way she could survive."

The woman swept up the bags of dog supplies and headed out the door.

Rowena gaped after her, Bryony's words of caution blending with Mrs. Delaney's defense…of a woman who couldn't explain her own side of the story.

If there *was* any good reason why a mother would desert her children when they needed her most.

Rowena peered over at the playroom and chewed at her bottom lip. MacKenzie, at least, was oblivious to everything but playing whatever pretend game struck her fancy at the moment— games starring none other than Clancy the Magnificent.

But Charlie…Charlie's too-old eyes met Rowena's as if somehow she'd heard the whole thing.

Impossible, Rowena knew. And yet, there were times in her own childhood when she'd wanted to plug up her ears because people were thinking too loud. Their emotions so strong they might as well have been screaming.

Rowena forced a reassuring smile onto her face, her affection for the two children pressing hard inside her chest. Her gaze caught Charlie's, held, and she wondered what the little girl had heard.

If not with her ears, with her heart.

THE SHOP WAS QUIET, the girls tired, when Mac rolled up in her wheelchair, Charlie close behind. "I want a story," Mac insisted, part of the ritual Rowena was beginning to cherish. The child didn't even bother bringing books for her to read aloud anymore. Not since the time she'd forgotten them at home and discovered the treasure trove of tales Rowena could spin out by heart. Stories Maeve MacKinnon had brought with her during the most magical summers of Rowena's life.

"Tell me a fairy godmother story," Mac clamored, but Charlie only looked at Rowena steadily.

"I keep telling Mac there aren't really fairy godmothers. They're only make believe."

Rowena laughed. "I wouldn't be letting an *Irish* fairy godmother hear you saying that. They're not quite the sparkly cartoon Cinderella kind."

"Then what kind are they?" Mac demanded, wicked delight flashing in her eyes.

And yet, it was Charlie's doubt that drew the tale from Rowena tonight, a story she'd never told to anyone before. "I was just seven years old the first time my fairy godmother came to town, and from that day on, nothing in my whole life was ever the same."

Charlie's eyes bulged a little, as if to say 'get real!' Rowena only smiled.

"Close your eyes," she said to the girls, "and imagine. The story I'm about to tell you is absolutely true. Cross my heart."

Mac closed her eyes, and after a grimace, Charlie did, too. Rowena smiled and let time spin backward, remembering....

AS FAR AS fairy godmothers went, Maeve MacKinnon was a big disappointment, Rowena thought, eyeing the strange woman on the sofa. She didn't look like a fairy godmother. At least not the kind Rowena had been imagining for weeks. Ones with sparkly wings and magic wands that filled her *Big Green Book of Fairy Stories* with magic and three wishes and such.

But that's who Daddy said Maeve was when they'd gotten the postcard with baby sheep jumping all over it: Rowena's very own fairy godmother, coming to visit from a far away place called Ireland.

Rowena had to believe him, 'cause Daddy never lied, whether you wanted to know the truth or not.

In fact, after the way he'd acted when Rowena sneaked her tooth under a pillow one night, she'd been pretty sure doctors didn't allow any fairies near their family at all.

But there one sat—her hat balanced on her bushy gray hair like a giant grape pizza. Some poor, furry animal that looked as if it had been squashed by a truck draped around her neck. Paws the size of Skitters the Cat's seemed to sink into Maeve's gigantic bosoms so the animal wouldn't slide into the purple bag perched, wide open, on the old woman's lap.

Don't get too close, Weenie, Rowena's younger sister warned as they'd trooped into the room an hour before. *A kid could get swallowed up by that bag and never come out again.*

Rowena shivered, the grownup voices around her sounding like the teacher in Charlie Brown cartoons, blah, blah, blah, with no words poking out.

Rowena's bottom slid a little and she jammed her fingers between her skritchy skirt and the blue satin seat so she wouldn't slide off the couch in the living room where nobody lived except the naked plaster angel who always looked cold.

Daddy wouldn't let me get gobbled by the fairy's bag, Rowena reassured herself. And yet, the picture in *Hansel and Gretel* kept popping into her head. The one with the witch biting the head off a kid she'd turned smack into gingerbread. Rowena shivered. From where she sat, Maeve definitely looked like the head-biting kind.

"And won't you look at the eyes on that one," Maeve said, gazing at Rowena so hard it felt like fingers were pressing on her. "I'd give a wish to anyone who'd tell me what's racing around inside her little head."

Everyone laughed.

"She's full of questions," Daddy said, smiling. "Trouble is she usually doesn't like the answers I give her."

"Then maybe she'd like to try asking me something instead," Maeve suggested.

Rowena slid off the couch and crossed the room. She sucked in a deep breath. "I was wondering what kind you are."

"What kind of what, child?"

"Daddy says you're a fairy godmother," Rowena puzzled earnestly. "But you don't look like the kind that grants wishes. You look more like a witch who'd shove Hansel in an oven."

Bryony gasped, Daddy stammering in horror. Arry choked on a laugh and Mom started protesting. "I'm so sorry, Aunt Maeve. Rowena's been spouting this nonsense ever since the letter came. Rowena Maeve Brown, you apologize this instant."

"Not a word I'll hear, not from any of you," Maeve insisted, shooting the rest of the Browns a quelling glance. "This is between the child and me." She cocked her head to one side, staring at Rowena as if she could peel the skin right off her. Rowena's heart played hopscotch in her chest.

"What would you say if I told you that you three girls are the last souls alive with my family's blood streaming through your veins? And I've crossed the wide ocean to pass treasures into your keeping?"

"Treasures?" Bryony echoed, her eyes lighting up. "Like the necklace Mom wore for her wedding? I get those because I'm the oldest."

Ariel bounded up from her seat. "I'm the littlest so I get the silver cup we got to drink from when we were babies."

"I see. And what will you get, Rowena?"

"I don't know yet. But maybe it will be wonderful. Maybe the fairies will leave something in the garden, or—"

"Rowena, we've had this conversation before," Mom warned, her face getting all pink and embarrassed. But she kept her voice patient. "She's a fanciful child, Maeve. Always dreaming. We've told her a dozen times there are no such things as fairies."

Rowena should have sat down, all ashamed. Scooted back up on the satin cushion and stapled her mouth shut for good. But something in that strange big bag kept calling her. She dug up all the brave inside her and looked into the old woman's eyes. "Are you a fairy?"

"No. But I've a fine lot of them back in Ireland for my friends." Maeve confided, her eyes dancing. "In fact, I was just waiting for them to give me a sign as to which of the three of you should choose their treasure first."

"I'll go first!" Ariel burst out. "The littlest always goes first!"

"Ah, patience. That's what you need."

"I'm oldest," Bryony began, tossing her hair as if no one, not even fairies, could fail to pick someone so perfect.

"No, it will be Rowena who will take her pick of treasure," Maeve said. "We'll see if she chooses wisely."

Into the bag Maeve reached. She drew out a bundle wrapped in raggedy velvet.

Slowly, she folded back the cloth, the girls jostling to see the treasures she showed.

A pair of earrings with pearls like teardrops. A dagger with a crooked blade. A slim silver straw with holes poked through.

"Touch them," Maeve urged gently. "See what speaks to you."

Bryony gasped, touching one earring with the tip of her finger. "You don't want these, Rowena. You'd just lose them."

"And the dagger—you'd cut yourself." Ariel stroked the battered sheath.

"She chooses first," Maeve warned. "And I'll sweep the lot back in my bag and sink it in the sea if I feel you've swayed her."

Rowena's sisters snatched their fingers back, looking dismayed.

Rowena edged nearer, astonished. "I always go last," she said softly.

"Not this time." Maeve smiled, and Rowena thought maybe she was just a bit sparkly after all. "Now tell me. What would you take for your own, little bird?"

"I know what the knife does. And those…" She pointed at the earrings and she could feel Bryony go still, scared that Rowena would choose them.

Rowena ran her fingertips along the hollow silver stick. "But this…what is this?"

"'Tis not a very valuable thing, like the jewelry, is it? Nor a very bold thing like the dagger. 'Tis just a pipe that makes fairy music. *If* you believe in that sort of thing."

Rowena glanced nervously at her father, her mother, her sisters. Then she turned back to Maeve.

The woman's wrinkly face glowed bright as Christmas bulbs. "This pipe has a secret," she confided. "My grandda and his grandda before him told a wondrous tale. Of finding this in a fairy ring. 'Tis Cuchullain's magic pipe, they say."

"Cu—who?"

"Cuchullain was the greatest warrior Ireland ever knew."

"But what would a warrior want a pipe for?"

"Let me tell you of his story and you'll understand. When Cuchullain was a lad, legend says, he came late to a warrior's home. The watchdog set upon him, trying to tear him to bits, and the boy had to kill the beast or die."

"Poor, poor dog!" Rowena's eyes sparkled with tears.

"That's what Cuchullain thought, too. Wasn't the dog's fault, you understand. It was just doing the job God gave it, guarding its master's door. Cuchullain grieved in his heart until a fairy took pity on him. A beautiful lady appeared, and gave him this magic pipe that sings so sweet it can charm the heart of any wounded creature all the world over."

"Don't encourage Rowena in that." Mom sighed. "She's already dragging home every stray she comes across!"

"Mom, let her have it," Bryony said, still worried about the earrings. "Maeve said we couldn't sway her."

"Would you try it, Rowena?" Maeve asked.

Rowena lifted the pipe to her lips and blew. A squawk came out.

Ariel smashed her hands to her ears. Daddy groaned. Bryony giggled. Rowena's cheeks burned.

"The music won't come out all magic at first," Maeve said. "Even fairy music takes practice. And I'll come back to visit you every summer so you can learn."

Rowena looked down at the whistle in her hand. It seemed so small, so plain. She knew that neither of her sisters wanted it. She rolled the small length of metal over in her hand. It felt smooth. As if it belonged there. And yet...

"Daddy doesn't believe in fairies," she said. "Bryony and Ariel and Mom don't either."

"Hmm." Maeve nodded her head, looking old and wise and mysterious, just like the kind of person a wandering princess might find in the woods. "Then I suppose there's only one question left, Rowena-my-heart."

"What's that?" Rowena asked, peering into Maeve's eyes.

"What do *you* believe?"

HER LIFE HAD CHANGED that day, in ways no one else understood. In ways that still permeated her every waking moment. She'd even come to Whitewater, believing in Maeve MacKinnon's special gifts. *You go off to Whitewater,* the old woman had urged, patting Rowena's hand. *He is waiting. Your soul mate. The one who's been looking for you since before you were born...*

Rowena felt a tug on her hand, drawing her out of the past, memories both painful and sweet. "So did you pick the magic whistle?" Mac asked, her eyes wide, even Charlie looking intrigued.

"I did."

"Can me an' Charlie see it?"

Rowena went to her desk, slipped the whistle out. The silver chain it dangled on draped over her hand.

"It's awful little," Mac said, obviously disappointed. "And it's not very shiny. Too bad you didn't pick something else."

"Mac," Charlie objected. "You didn't really believe all that stuff was true, did you?"

"Well, Rowena said it was magic."

"If it's magic, how come she leaves it in that drawer?" Charlie turned penetrating eyes to Rowena. "How come you don't wear it all the time?"

"I guess I'm scared I'd lose it," Rowena said, but that wasn't the whole truth. She'd taken it off as a teenager, when her sisters would give her no peace. And yet, though she hadn't worn the thing for years, she'd carried it with her, to college, to vet school, her secret talisman. Even when she'd moved to Whitewater with Auntie Maeve's blessing, Rowena hadn't consigned it to one of the neatly labeled boxes she'd filled with the other bits of her childhood too precious to throw away. She'd kept the whistle here in the shop for luck.

"Even though I don't wear it, I keep it handy where all the animals are. That way before I leave at night I can play it if I need to. It brings them to me, calms them down, puts them to sleep."

"Sort of like a lullaby?" Mac asked.

"That's right. Lullabies dogs and cats understand."

"Oh." Mac considered. "We don't do lullabies at my house. My daddy sings real bad."

Rowena chuckled, trying to imagine Cash singing off-key. "Well, the songs I played on the whistle sounded bad at first, too. But I practiced, so now I do better."

"Show me," Mac demanded.

Rowena raised the whistle, moistened her lips. Then softly, she blew into the mouthpiece. A haunting melody drifted on the air. Even Charlie stilled at the sound. Mac stared, wonder-struck. From where he was lying on a cool spot of tile, Clancy lifted his head, cocked it to one side. He climbed to his feet and padded toward them. The girls stared, stunned, as the big dog laid his muzzle on Rowena's lap.

"Look at that, Charlie!" Mac exclaimed. "He just came right to her. Like a spell. Rowena, is that what fairies really sound like?"

"So my fairy godmother told me."

Charlie regarded Rowena, the dog and the silver whistle.

"Clancy just came because he likes the whistling sound," she argued. "Jimmy Wong whistles for his dog, too. It doesn't mean it's magic."

"Is so! You're just going to ruin the whole story," Mac complained. "And the magic's going to go away forever."

"No, it isn't," Rowena said, wanting to reach out to Charlie, banish at least some of her disillusionment. "That's one of the big secrets about magic that no one ever tells you. You don't have to believe in it all the time. You can think it's gone, be so sure it's not real, but the magic will still be there, waiting for you when you're ready. It'll reappear for you the instant you get brave enough to look for it again."

Charlie seemed to consider. She touched the whistle with one small finger. "I know that's not true," she said stubbornly, then her voice dropped so low Rowena barely heard her confess, "But I wish it was."

CHAPTER TEN

"NEVER TRUST A SAILOR," Elvis the parrot warned with a suspicious squawk as Rowena scooped up a tray of fruit and parrot mix and crossed to the African Gray's cage. She smoothed the feathers on the bird's breast.

"Does that apply to any man in uniform?" she inquired dryly, remembering Mrs. Delaney's warning, Bryony's fears. "How about trusting a deputy?"

"Don't ask me, I'm just a bird." Elvis stretched out his beak to nab a green grape and cocked his head.

She pushed aside the niggling doubts that had troubled her since the day Bryony called, then laughed out loud, knowing the minute she had time she'd have to call Vinny and tell him Elvis had demonstrated another phrase the ex-cop had added to the bird's repertoire. Along with "Jeepers, creepers, Miss Marigold's got some peepers."

All things considered, Rowena owed Mr. Google a steak dinner.

Not out of guilt, but out of gratitude.

Too bad she couldn't cook.

The "peeper" gem had actually lured Rowena's neighbor into the shop, Vinny had announced with pardonable pride the day before.

It had taken him almost two weeks to pull it off. He'd struck up little conversations with her, told her how pretty her flowers were. Asked her to come in the shop because he'd been teaching the bird new tricks.

He'd been balanced on crutches as he took one of the dogs out and told the tea shop owner how heavenly her pies smelled from his side of the fence, him being a bachelor and all.

She'd brought him a lattice-crusted piece of cherry pie with the sole purpose of warning him off. *That girl's not right in the head, talking to animals the way she does.*

Vinny had told Miss Marigold there were days even he would like somebody to talk to. Even if that somebody couldn't talk back. He'd bet Miss Marigold sometimes felt the same way, too.

As if on cue, Elvis had piped up, and Vinny had explained he'd taught the bird himself, because Miss Marigold had such pretty eyes. The woman had blushed as if she were sixteen. In fact, if Rowena's matchmaking skills had included people as well as animals, she might have predicted neither Vinny nor Miss Marigold were going to be quite so lonely anymore.

Rowena smiled, warmed by the possibility. Whatever happened between the two older people in the future, at least there was some hope that Miss Marigold wouldn't bar the door when Rowena and the girls finished the surprise.

They'd been working on it together, the kids in tough leather gloves, Rowena's hands bare as they sorted through the colorful pieces of broken china, arranging them in flower shapes and hearts and stars. But when Mac recognized kitty pieces, she'd insisted they make animals. Without so much as a protest, Charlie had swept the table clean of her own painstaking work. And her blind acceptance of Mac's dictates made Rowena ache for her. No doubt about it. In this corner of the kingdom, Mac-Kenzie Lawless was queen.

Rowena empathized with the little girl. There was so much Mac couldn't do. And yet…Charlie was the one who got lost so often. In the rush to therapy. The complications of loading Mac and her wheelchair onto her special schoolbus while Charlie wandered alone to the regular bus stop at the neighborhood corner.

Rowena wondered how Charlie felt about it. Not that the child would say. Rowena had probed gently, but Charlie had closed up tight, her eyes on the floor so no one could see the sad in them. She'd just do what her sister wanted with a stoic determination that drove the color and laughter of childhood out of her eyes.

Even in the playroom, they played whatever struck Mac's fancy at the moment. Though Charlie seemed content enough, as long as the games starred Clancy.

It didn't seem possible that only two and a half weeks had gone by, their lives settling into a familiar rhythm: Vinny minding the shop while Rowena drove the kids hither and yon. Cash, on day shift now, home around dinnertime.

Instead of warning her off, Mrs. Delaney and Bryony had roused even more protective feelings toward Cash and his girls. She'd felt the same sensation she did when she'd first held the broken teapots in her hands and tried to figure out how to mend them.

Impossible, she'd thought at first, and yet, even if they couldn't be whole and perfect again, maybe the fragments could make something new, something just as beautiful.

Rowena had suspected Cash was a good father the day she'd surprised him during Mac's therapy. But as time slipped by, she'd peered deeper than the pictures on the wall. She'd caught Cash dancing Mac around the room in his arms, the ballet video from the little girl's last dance recital playing on the television. She'd heard him reading about Dangerous Fish with Charlie. And on the nights Cash was working, he'd call right at bedtime to tell his girls he loved them.

Little things, and yet, they haunted Rowena long after she left the gray house every day. Like the vulnerability she sometimes caught in the curl of Cash's lips, the heat in his eyes when he didn't think she knew he was looking at her. His hands—such strong, patient hands, hands that lifted Mac to the top of the sliding board when her own legs wouldn't climb the ladder. Hands that helped Charlie make Lego castles and tucked his children in at night.

Hands he had buried in Rowena's hair when he'd pulled her mouth to his.

Rowena shivered at the memory of those moments he'd let himself want her and she'd wanted him back. Time so brief, yet so powerful it seared itself into her very soul. Until every brush of hands, every smile he gave her, every time their gazes met, held, reminded her of that stunning moment Cash's mouth had captured hers. And the fact that he slept alone.

Two years' worth of loneliness had lodged in his kiss, had bled Rowena's heart raw. He'd shaken her to the core, his mouth so hot, the roughness in his palms so arousing, his hands unsteady with emotion as if he knew even then that anything more between them was impossible.

Maybe it was true, what Bryony had said. That Rowena believed so deeply in the healing power of touch that she would never have called a halt to the sharp-edged desire that had sprung up between her and the man she'd begun to admire. And yet, frustrating and contrary as it was, part of the reason she respected Cash Lawless so much was the fact that he'd drawn the line between them.

She belonged to his girls in Cash's mind. He'd sacrificed his own needs for theirs, as he had for the past two years. And, Rowena knew, even longer.

He'd made that choice, a man of honor. Sacrificed dreams Rowena sensed no one else would ever know. He'd looked his mistakes square in the face and done his best to make things right—for everyone but himself.

So every night he went to bed in that stark, cheerless room, where the empty spaces were visible and the nights were solitary.

And why was he alone? Mrs. Delaney had said Cash was hard—and Rowena herself had seen that steely quality in him the first time they'd met. A sensation that he was stronger, somehow more powerful than anyone around him. The kind of man weaker people might break themselves against, pounding against his unshakeable will.

Was that what had happened to his wife?

She hated it here...she begged him to leave Whitewater...

Rowena shivered. She knew how it felt to be trapped in a place she didn't belong. That panicky sensation in her chest when she couldn't breathe. *How can you blame Lisa Lawless,* a voice inside her mocked, *when you ran away yourself?*

But I didn't leave my own children behind....

The bell jangled, and Rowena looked up to see Cash striding toward her. Guilt flooded through her at the way she'd been dissecting his life in her head. And if she had any instinct at all, the raking over of gossip wouldn't stop there. Her heart flipped, then thudded at the memory of Mrs. Delaney's sharp eyes at the whole sex conversation. Doubtless the one word she'd missed was the most important one—as in *no* sex. Rowena hadn't lived in Whitewater long, but she was sure that Enquiring Minds in the town would want to know.

"Cash." Rowena tried to quash the flutter in her voice. "You're supposed to be at work."

"I had to stop by the school to drop off Mac's permission slip for the field trip tomorrow. I stuck it in my pocket instead of her bookbag."

"I hate when that happens."

"I don't. Especially when it gives me an excuse to stop by and see the girls. How are they doing?"

"They're in the playroom. Charlie was supposed to be doing some work on her science project—you know, the one about the animal world? She's doing it on dogs."

"Big surprise there," Cash grumbled.

"Anyway, she worked for a while and then got distracted. Mac needed her help for a game." She led him past the bird cages and a stack of sacks of dog food to where he could get a clear look.

Cash stiffened the instant he saw Clancy. The dog rolled on its back, while Charlie slid over his body like a slide. "Won't the dog bite them?" Cash asked as he watched Mac try to scrabble around the dog's massive bulk.

"Bite them? Are you kidding? Look at him." Rowena pointed to Clancy's face. The dog's eyes twinkled, his mouth lolling open in the canine version of a grin. "He's having as much fun as they are."

Cash couldn't deny it. He stared, silent, astonished.

"But then," Rowena explained, "they *are* at Disney World."

"Disney World?" Cash echoed, bewildered.

"The girls told me all about it on the way home the other night. Clancy is their personal version of Space Mountain. Before the tidal wave hits, that is."

"Tidal wave?" Cash repeated, as if that would help him understand what the devil she was talking about.

Rowena laughed and he felt his heart squeeze. "Never mind," she told him. "The important thing is the girls are having a ball. Apparently Clancy's the roller coaster and the kids are those little cart thingies that ride over the bumps."

Cash turned back to the view through the glass window. "How long have they been playing like that?"

"Practically since they got off school. It was Clancy's turn in the playroom at three o'clock and they wanted to go in there with him. I hope you don't mind."

Rowena kept talking, but Cash didn't hear her. He stared at Mac, scarce daring to breathe, half afraid to believe his eyes.

"Cash?"

Rowena touched him, jarring him to look at her. Her face creased with worry.

"Cash, is something wrong?"

Cash stared down at her, stunned. "She's pushing with her legs."

"What?"

"Mac. Look at her. She's pushing with her legs. Hard."

Rowena looked through the window. Cash felt her watching in as much astonishment as he was as the little girl scrambled around the big dog. Mac was pulling mostly with her arms, but that wasn't all. In her eagerness and excitement, she was digging her toes into the floor, as well. Cash clutched onto the image, tight.

"Remember when you broke into the house because you thought I was hurting her?" he breathed. "*That's* what I was trying to get her to do."

He heard Rowena gasp softly, knew she remembered all right. Mac's sobs as Cash pushed her to work her weakened muscles. *Hurts, Daddy...why do you always hurt me...* The words were razors, still cutting him.

"*My* turn, Charlie!" Mac cried in outrage. "You can't get two turns when I only get one. It's no fair!"

"Hurry up, then," Charlie urged. "Daddy's coming and he won't like it if we're in here." Cash felt a twinge, the girls so sure he'd quash their fun.

"Rowena said we could play with Clancy!" Mac thrust out her lower lip, but she shoved even harder with the toes of her pink tennis shoes, stubbornly determined not to give up her fun.

Her elfin face crumpled, hints of pain mingling with the determination in her face. "I got lots more rides to go on. I won't go 'way from Disney World. Daddy can't make me!"

Rowena tugged at Cash's arm and he glanced at her, seeing apologies and uncertainties in her eyes. Without a word, he turned back to stare at the little blur of motion that was his MacKenzie, amazement in his eyes. "My God, Rowena," he breathed. "Look at her."

Rowena squeezed his hand. He wrapped his fingers tight around hers, holding on.

"It's wonderful, Cash. Isn't it?" Rowena asked.

"Pretty wonderful." He watched his daughters, his throat too tight to speak. His ears thirsty for the sound of childish laughter. When he could finally squeeze out the words he said, "There's just one problem with this."

"I know," Rowena confessed, abashed. "You don't want the girls getting attached to him. I let them play with the other animals, too. It's just, Clancy is their favorite."

"That's not the problem," Cash growled. She looked up at him, so serious, so concerned.

"Then what is?"

"How in the Sam hell am I going to fit that dog in my house?"

"Your…house?" Her jaw fell open, her eyes saucer wide. And the sight of her, so filled with wonder and hope, made Cash feel a little less tarnished, a little less old. "Cash, do you mean…?"

"You heard me," he said with a mock severity that drew a glad cry from her. She flung herself at him, all but knocking him over as she hugged him with all her might. And she felt so good he couldn't help but catch some of her delight and crush her against him. He buried his nose in her hair, drinking in the lemony scent of her shampoo, feeling the generosity of her spirit, the way she hugged with every vulnerability in her exposed. He stiffened, started to pull away, but she wouldn't let go.

"You won't be sorry!" she vowed rashly. "You won't!"

"Easy, there," he said, putting her back on her feet. "Everybody on Main Street is going to see."

Why did her cheeks suddenly turn even pinker, her eyes avoiding his?

"You think I care?" she enthused. "Most of the people around here already think I'm crazy."

"Well, now they'll think I'm even crazier than you," he said with wry humor. "Everybody on the force knows I hate that damned dog. He's too big. Too messy. Too prone to get into trouble. And if he knocks Mac over, I swear I'll…"

"He won't." Rowena promised in such a rush Cash couldn't help but smile. "Look at how careful he is with her. He knows he has to be gentle."

"A trial run—that's all this is," Cash warned. "He's out on probation. One screw-up and it's back to juvie hall—or in this case, back to your pet shop. Got it?"

Rowena nodded. "Yes, sir, Your Honor. And the court thanks the judge for his leniency."

The corner of Cash's mouth curled up. "Where'd you pick that up? Not bad law jargon for a civilian."

"I'm hooked on *Law and Order* reruns. In fact, Brisco and McCoy kept me from getting arrested. That's how I knew about that whole 'tampering with the mailbox is illegal' thing. Oh, Cash—"

He held up his hand to stop her. "Listen, Rowena, I don't want the kids to know I'm actually considering letting them keep that monster. I don't want them hurt if things don't work out."

"Oh, everything will be wonderful! I know it will." Rowena

beamed. "I felt it from the instant I saw Charlie and Clancy together. It's never been stronger—that feeling I get when I find a perfect match."

Cash shifted, suddenly uncomfortable. "Hold on there a minute. None of that woo-woo psychic garbage. It's not admissible in court and I don't want my kids exposed to…"

He stopped, not sure how to finish.

"A crazy woman?"

"I don't want them believing in things that are just fantasy. It hurts too much when they find out it's not real."

"But it is real. What I do. My gift. It is real, Cash." She wanted him to believe in her. He could see it in her eyes.

"My kids have to deal in plain hard facts, Rowena. It's not what I'd have chosen for them, but…you know, for months after Lisa left, Mac insisted she'd been stolen by the Big Bad Wolf and that's why she didn't come back. But it kept the hard truth from cutting her. She'd insist that even in fairy tales wolves don't have telephones."

"No opposable thumbs," Rowena agreed, her eyes still shining. "It'd be too hard to hold the receiver. I never could figure out how the wolf managed to tie granny's bonnet under its chin in the illustrations."

"I'm serious." He felt like a killjoy, and yet he couldn't leave his girls open to any more pain. Reality was hard enough to handle without the added grief of pretty fantasies tumbling down.

"What about Santa Claus and the Easter Bunny and the Tooth Fairy?" Rowena asked. "The girls believe in those, don't they?"

"There's nothing I can do to protect them from those little myths crumbling. But the rest—well, if I let them start believing in impossible things, they're sure to latch on to the hope that in spite of everything, someday Lisa's coming back. I don't want them to go through that. Losing her again. It was bad enough the first time."

"I'd never do anything to hurt your children, Cash. But hope isn't the enemy. It's what keeps people trying. Gets them through the dark times, the hard ones. Isn't that what drives you every night when you coax Mac through her therapy?"

"No. Not hope." He looked at her then, knew the truth was stark in his eyes. "Desperation."

Mac's laughter echoed from behind the glass door. He turned back to his daughters, went into the playroom.

"Daddy!" Charlie skittered to one side of Clancy, as if trying to put a little distance between her and the fun. Because she didn't want to displease her daddy. The truth burned Cash, saddened him.

Completely the opposite of her sister, Mac glared at him, a crabby angel. "Listen, Daddy. Rowena's the boss of us here. We get to play with the doggy. Got it, dude?"

Cash tried to look stern, knowing he couldn't encourage Mac's defiance, and yet thanking God the girl had some of his stubbornness. He knew that was what would help her to walk.

"How about we make a deal, girls?"

"That depends," Mac said, still glowering. "You don't like Space Mountain and we do."

He turned to Charlie. "Rowena was telling me you're doing a research project on dogs, cupcake. Is that true?"

"Not just any dogs," Mac elaborated, stretching her arms over Clancy's bulk as if to demonstrate. "Giant-gantic bear dogs. An' Charlie gets to take him to school for her zibbet."

"*Ex*hibit," Charlie corrected, still peering up at him uneasily.

But Mac was already racing blissfully ahead. "An' then Rowena's bringing him to my room so all the kids can see him. 'Cause I'm doing a scientist reporter, too."

"She's just being a copycat, Daddy," Charlie said.

"Am not a copycat!"

"Are so! You're too little to do reports. You can't even write, so how're you going to do a report?"

"Pictures, dork face!"

"Whoa! Where'd that come from?" Cash gave his daughters a stern look.

"Kari calls her brother that all the time. She says her mommy doesn't even care."

"Well, I do care. No calling your sister names, got it?"

"Then tell her she gots to share." Mac pouted. "Clancy gets to come to my class, too. It's not fair. She gets all the fun stuff."

"You looked like you were having some fun yourself when I came in."

"Yep. Daddy, did you know doggies drool just like babies? An' if you hold onto his fur really tight you get whole bunches of it on your hands?"

"Really? I guess there are lots of things about dogs I'm going to have to learn if you two are going to get good grades on these reports of yours."

"You don't have to help me this time, Daddy," Charlie said earnestly. "Rowena's got lots of books."

"Yeah, an' we gots lots of dog to zibbet when our reporters are all done."

"I can see that," Cash agreed. "But you'll need to get to know what a dog is really like. Accuracy is really important in a report like this one."

"What's accur-sassy, Daddy?" Mac asked.

"It means you'll want to spend as much time as possible around your subject, so you get your facts straight. How about we move Space Mountain to our house for a few weeks?"

"Space Mountain? You mean...Clancy?" Charlie fairly trembled with delight. "Really, Daddy?"

"Just for a few weeks. Until your report's done. Fair enough?"

Charlie nodded. She knelt down, cupped Clancy's giant head between her small palms. "Oh, boy! Did you hear that, Clancy?"

Cash could almost swear the damn dog nodded.

"Hold on there," he said, his grudge against the dog needling him. "I forgot to tell the three of you—I've got one condition."

Rowena, Charlie and Mac looked up at him expectantly. He knew at the moment they'd promise him anything, even putting a leash around the moon. Yes. It was a perfect time to strike.

He folded his arms across his chest, giving them his toughest cop stare. "It's my house. It's my dog. At least for the next few weeks. Right?" He looked from one anxious face to another.

"Absolutely," Rowena agreed.

"Absolutely," the girls chorused.

"Good," Cash said, feeling downright smug. "Then his name's Destroyer."

He heard Rowena start to protest, heard Charlie pipe up.

"But, Daddy, he'll get all mixed up. And won't know to come when we call."

"Destroyer!" Cash barked out the name.

The dog sprang to his paws, loped over to Cash and sat down, looking up at him expectantly. Head dipped down in submission, the dog swiped Cash's pants leg with his tongue, leaving a mark on his uniform pants.

Cash stifled a groan. "I'd better stop on the way home and buy a lint roller."

"I sell them here," Rowena offered. "How about if I donate a case of them to the cause?"

He lifted his eyebrows. "A case?"

"And what size bag does your vacuum cleaner take?" Her eyes danced. Cash couldn't remember the last time he'd seen such pure joy in anyone, or felt that strange fizzy feeling in his chest. It made him edgy. Made him want to check the sky before a piece of it fell on his head, like the chicken in that storybook. Smart bird, that Chicken Little.

"Hey, Daddy?" Mac scooted over to him. Pulled on his pantleg. He bent down to pick her up. "Know what?"

"What?"

"I love Charlie, even if she is a dork face."

"MacKenzie." He drew out her name in warning.

"Don't *bad girl* me, Daddy, I'm saying a good thing. I sure am glad I'm not Tyler James' little sister right now."

Cash laughed at the expression on her face. "Why's that, kitten?"

"If you got to live with your zibbet to get to know it, that'll be a really bad thing for her."

"How come?"

Mac gave a delicious shiver, hugging him tight. "Tyler's zibbeting crocodiles."

Cash looked at Rowena and laughed until his side hurt, his eyes stung, laughed in a way he thought he'd never laugh again.

Charlie rose to hug his legs. "You're the best daddy in the whole wide world."

No he wasn't, Cash thought, his eyes burning in a different way as he caught Rowena's hope-filled gaze. He wasn't the best daddy in the world.

He only wanted to be.

ROWENA LEANED AGAINST the playground fence, one more in the cluster of parents and grandparents, babysitters and such, all waiting for the kids to spill out of the newly adorned double doors. Giant pumpkin banners taped in all the school windows spelled out "Harvest Fair October 9 and 10, Jubilee Park. Family Fun For Everyone!"

As if anyone could miss the dates, Rowena thought wryly.

The town was peppered with the signs. Even her own shop displayed one—half-torn by a cat named Shakespeare who objected to sharing even the sunniest window with anything in such a gaudy color.

Rowena smiled as she saw the first kids rush down the steps, glimpsed Mac's teacher at a separate door, holding it open while Charlie pushed her sister's wheelchair down the ramp.

"Hey, what's the deal with all the pumpkins?" Rowena called out as she went to meet the girls. She couldn't wait to hear their versions of Whitewater Pumpkin Mania.

"That's 'cause it's time for the Harvest Fair," Mac enthused, bouncing a little in her seat. "There's a ferris wheel and pony rides and you can eat all the candy you want."

"Wow." Rowena moved behind the chair and took over, pushing it.

"Everybody in the whole world comes to the fair. Daddies and mommies and kids."

"Not *everyone* in the world," Charlie said.

"Well, it's family fun for everyone. Not family fun for just a few people," Mac argued. "My teacher says so."

"Mac, that's just what the sign says," Charlie explained. "It's like a commercial." But her sister didn't bother to argue.

"Are you one of the everybodies going to have fun at the fair, Rowena?" Mac asked.

"I don't know. It'll be all brand-new to me."

Mac gasped as if she could hardly fathom such a fun-deprived childhood. "Didn't you *ever* go to a fair before?"

"Can't say I have. There aren't a lot of country fairs where I come from."

"Where's that?"

"Forest Park."

"You came from a forest? Like the one Hansel and Gretel got lost in?"

"Actually there weren't any forests at all. Just lots of buildings up near Chicago."

"Oh." MacKenzie scratched her nose and looked away. "That's where my mommy lives. She won't be coming to the fair."

"But Daddy will," Charlie chimed in, her small features brightening. "I counted on the calendar on the refrigerator three whole times just to make sure it's his weekend off."

Rowena grinned. "Three times, huh?"

"Just to make sure."

Rowena couldn't resist giving the little girl a quick hug, and was surprised when Charlie hugged her back—just a brief squeeze, and yet as telling as if the child had whooped with delight, Public Displays of Affection with grownups being high on the "definitely not cool" list for the fourth-grade crowd. Rowena laughed, steering the wheelchair toward the break in the fence. As she neared it, she was startled to see a brown County Sheriff vehicle pull up.

Cash. She could see him through the window of the tan SUV, his chiseled face, his dark hair, his eyes obscured by a pair of gold-rimmed aviator sunglasses. Had she gotten the day wrong? She was sure she'd been scheduled to pick the girls up from school today. Did Mac have a doctor's appointment scheduled or had something come up? She hoped she hadn't zoned out and made a mistake. She'd tried to be so meticulous with her babysitting duties, not wanting the girls ever to be waiting on the playground, alone.

Cash parked and climbed out of the vehicle, looking sexy as all get-out in his uniform. Khaki pants encased his long muscular legs, his shirt crisp, his badge gleaming. The deep brown tie made his throat look even stronger, his jaw squarer, his skin a richer tan. All that was missing was his smile. But Rowena bet he'd flash one of those blinding white knee-melters when he heard just how excited his girls were that he'd be taking them to the fair.

"Good afternoon, Deputy," Rowena greeted him. "Don't tell me you're here to bust that ring of hardened criminals who keep sticking gum underneath the school desks."

"Actually it's the ones who spit gum in the water fountains that drive me crazy."

Was that a joke? The man had definite possibilities. Maybe his sense of humor was only hiding instead of missing altogether.

"I just happened to be in the area," Cash went on. "I like to make my presence known when school lets out. Slows traffic down."

"You might want to check and see if there's an 'excessive signage' ordinance somewhere. This town's beginning to look like a movie set for *Attack of the Killer Pumpkins*."

"You ain't seen nothin' yet." Cash drawled, the corner of his mouth ticking up. "This will be pumpkin central for the next few weeks."

"So this Harvest Fair is a big deal in Whitewater, huh?"

"The biggest, right Daddy?" Mac flung her arms wide in excitement. "Even puppies can come. Hey, Charlie! This year we've got a puppy we can bring!"

"No," Cash warned. "Not Destroyer. No way. No how."

Rowena made a face at him. "Why are you looking at me when you say that?"

Cash pulled off his sunglasses, his brow stern. "I mean it."

"Spoilsport." Rowena teased. "Oh, well. At least you and the munchkins are going to have a good time. Charlie's over the moon."

"Yeah, Daddy!" Charlie's eyes sparkled with rare excitement. "I even checked to make sure it's your weekend off."

Cash's jaw worked. He didn't meet his daughter's gaze. "About that weekend, Charlie. There's a little snag."

"Wh—what?" Charlie stammered. Rowena could almost see the little girl shrinking into herself.

"I have to work some, uh, overtime."

"Overtime?" Rowena protested. "But you can't! This Harvest Fair thing is so important to the girls…and it's supposed to be your weekend off! Charlie counted it out three times. Surely you can switch and work some other weekend."

"I volunteered for this one."

Rowena's chin almost hit the floor. "You *chose* to work the weekend of the fair?"

"Oh, *man!*" Mac wailed, whacking her little hand down on the arm of the wheelchair. "That's bad, Daddy. Real bad!"

Cash tugged at his collar as if his tie had suddenly grown too tight. "Listen. I talked to Hope's mom and dad. They're going to take you to the fair with them. You girls love spending time with Hope and her family, right, Charlie?" He turned to his oldest daughter. "Hope's your best friend."

Charlie toed a crack in the asphalt. "Sort of."

Uh-oh, Rowena thought, warning bells ringing in her head. A "sort of" best friend meant trouble in elementary school. "Something wrong between you and Hope, honey?" Rowena probed gently.

"Hope says Charlie doesn't play very good anymore," Mac informed anyone in about a ten-yard radius.

"Mac!" Charlie protested, giving her sister a poke. Mac squawked but Charlie was already glancing around the playground, obviously fearful that a classmate might have overheard. Rowena saw a few people glancing their way. Her heart sank.

If even Mac knew what Hope had said, other children around school must, too. Her friend's words must have hurt Charlie. Badly.

Charlie doesn't play very good anymore…

No, Rowena thought. The problem was that Charlie didn't play *at all*.

"I thought you'd be excited about going to the fair with your friend," Cash insisted. "Mrs. Stone even said you girls could have a slumber party the night before."

"Do you have to work Friday night, too?" Charlie asked, her bottom lip quivering just a little. "It's not on the calendar, Daddy."

"No, cupcake. I don't have to work Friday night. But wouldn't you like to stay at Hope's?"

"You're supposed to be off," Charlie surprised Rowena by asserting. "Friday and Saturday and Sunday." Charlie folded her arms tight against her middle.

Cash looked even more uncomfortable. He hunkered down so he could meet Charlie's eyes. "The work I have to do the day of the fair is really important, Charlie. Try to understand."

"Understanding's hard when you have to do it all the time," Charlie mumbled.

"What?" Cash asked.

"I said...Mommy won't be there. We'd be broken anyway."

"Broken?" Cash repeated, confused.

"That's what our kind of home is. If there's only a mommy or a daddy but not both it's broken."

"Charlie—" Cash's tone grew tight. Rowena could see Charlie stiffen. She laid a hand on the little girl's shoulder.

"Listen, Charlie. How about you take your sister over by that tree over there? Your daddy and I need to talk for a minute. Grownup stuff."

"Okay." Charlie did as she was told, her brief mutiny over. Her quick surrender bothered Rowena.

She turned toward Cash, making sure sharp kiddo eyes couldn't read her lips or hear what she was saying. "Overtime? You can't do this to them, Cash. Charlie and Mac will already be without their mother at this big family shindig. It's hardly fair for their father to blow them off, too."

Rowena could hear the iron bars crashing down all around him, cutting her off, shutting him down. It shouldn't have surprised her. It happened any time a subject veered too close to mothers in general and Lisa in particular.

"I'm not going to discuss this with you," he said in that deputy deadpan tone she hated, as if she were some perp he needed to talk down from a ledge.

"Didn't you hear Charlie?" Rowena insisted, her temper boiling. "She counted out the days on the calendar, Cash. Three times. That's how much it mattered to her to make sure you would be off."

"My job that day is important."

"So are your little girls! But you're ditching them to work voluntary overtime? I never would have believed it of you."

His cool cracked. "Believe it," he snarled. "Mac's medical bills aren't free, you know!"

That little comment shut Rowena down for a moment. How *did* a single father—a deputy in a small county like this one—afford the astronomical medical bills Mac's condition would generate?

And yet, even knowing that grim reality, Rowena was surprised by how gut-deep disappointed she felt. Disappointed in him as a man, as a father. Not that she had any right to be. It wasn't as if they had a personal relationship. She was just the temporary babysitter, after all. A necessary evil who made Cash edgy on the best of days. But this time *he* was the one who'd tripped one of *her* major hot buttons for a change.

Rowena couldn't count how many times she and her sisters had been shunted off to an au pair while the doctors Brown busied themselves with volunteer work or community leadership instead of spending time with their daughters.

Rowena stalked away a few paces, then turned back to confront him, not giving a damn about the other adults on the playground eyeing them with blatant curiosity. "You know what, Cash?" she said, still careful that the girls at least couldn't hear her. "One of the things I admired most about you was the way you put your girls' welfare first, even when it meant denying your own needs. Even the most elemental, primitive instincts like the ones I see simmering in your eyes whenever you look at me."

"Damn it, Rowena—"

"Don't deny it. I know you feel it, too. This…this thing… between us you want to pretend away."

She chafed her arms remembering how many times in the past month her skin had felt on fire, ignited by nothing more than the hot lick of Cash's gaze fixed on her across his kitchen table in the morning. She'd felt mesmerized by the passion he repressed in himself so ruthlessly. Been tempted to cross the boundary he'd drawn between them, prove that it couldn't be as powerful as her imagination had made it—that heart-searing arousal that had jolted her to the core that first morning when he kissed her.

The feeling that between one heartbeat and the next her entire world could change. But he wouldn't accept that anymore than he seemed willing to face the truth that his girls would need him badly come fair day, a day on which their mother's absence would already highlight the deep, dark void in their lives.

"That 'thing' between you and I is just lust, Rowena, pure and simple," Cash sneered. "I don't have time for sex."

"Fine. If you want to make your personal life as joyless as possible, that's your decision. A stupid decision, but yours to make nonetheless. But those girls—*those girls*—*damned* well better be more important than your *work*."

His eyes turned flinty, the eyes of a man who could pull the trigger if he needed to. "Mac and Charlie are the most important things in the world to me."

"Then prove it. Do whatever you have to do to make this weekend perfect for them. A day they get to spend with their father! The girls aren't going to want you around forever, you know. You've got just so much time to make memories at places like this Harvest Fair, and then they're gone. Your children are *gone*, Cash. And all you'll have left is your empty gray house and your police radio and your gun to hold on to."

Rowena spun around and stalked off toward the girls. Anger pulsed through her. Anger and shame. What had she been thinking? Blowing up at him about the way he made her feel? The way her body wanted him, even though he'd never let her in. Into his life, into his heart, into the wounded places that still left him bleeding. Like the creatures she'd rescued, holed up somewhere, alone with their pain.

Cash wasn't an animal, she reminded herself. Not one of her injured strays. He was a man. And a father.

She only hoped she'd managed to say something in the last few minutes to remind him of both.

CHAPTER ELEVEN

THE DAY OF THE HARVEST FAIR dawned crisp as a Granny Smith picked fresh from Webster's Apple Grove. Even the weather seemed to taunt Rowena, because she would be one of the few Whitewater residents who would spend the day inside rather than discovering exactly what all the fuss about the festival was about.

She stuck another can of Salmon Delight cat food on the metal shelf labeled "Shakespeare's Favorite"—in hopes of piquing the curiosity of customers who might be interested in adopting the world's haughtiest cat. The feline in question watched Destroyer like an enemy spy from his perch atop a kitty condo made out of real tree branches and carpet-covered platforms.

Beyond the pet shop window, the entire town of Whitewater was decked out in pumpkin, wheat and red colored buntings, the streets that were usually bustling with weekend traffic deserted now.

It wasn't that Rowena hadn't been warned by Mac that *every*body in Whitewater went to the Harvest Fair. *Even* the puppy dogs. But at least one human and one morose-looking mutt would be missing out on the fun today.

Poor Clancy—Destroyer, or whatever his name was at the moment—had been dropped off on her doorstep at the ungodly hour of six in the morning. Cash had handed the leash over with a sarcastic sneer, repeating—almost verbatim—the doomsayer litany he'd used to con her into watching Destroyer the day before. *With Destroyer in the hands of a trained professional for the day, maybe Cash wouldn't have to pay a fortune in damages when the furry menace chewed the legs off a merry-go-round horse or raided the corn dog stand.*

Cash was so darn funny Rowena forgot to laugh.

It wasn't like her to feel so…sour and cranky. But today she couldn't help it and it was all Cash Lawless's fault. He'd been immoveable as the bluffs above the river when it came to working fair weekend. And nothing, not Rowena's arguments, Mac's whining or Charlie's big, sad eyes had budged him. If anything, they'd made him dig in deeper, until even Rowena had to admit it was hopeless to keep hammering at the man. But she'd felt so let down by him, as if…

"I know. I'm being ridiculous," she told the Newfoundland, who looked even more droopy than she felt. "It's not as if Cash and Mac and Charlie belong to me."

The dog stared at the pet shop door, and she could almost hear him grumble, *Maybe they don't belong to you, lady, but they do belong to me.* His worried expression almost made Rowena laugh.

"All right, already. They're your kids now," she soothed, rubbing behind his silky ears. "But even I have to admit it would be just a little too much to expect the Stones to handle two extra kids, a wheelchair *and* a dog the size of Manhattan. Your girls will be back to get you tonight, buddy."

He turned his gaze up to hers, deep creases above his eyes, as if to say "by that time anything could have happened to them." He whined, then took hold of Rowena's forearm with his mouth the way he would to drag her to safety in a water rescue. But this time he tugged her toward the door.

"Everybody in the world is not at the Harvest Fair," she argued aloud. "Just everybody in town—except us."

And exactly why was that? Rowena frowned. From the first time she'd read about the celebration in the pamphlet Aunt Maeve had given her about the town, she'd been eager to experience it. A large part of the flavor of this place she'd decided to call home. Truth to tell, the image of all that Halloween enthusiasm had made her feel she could belong here, where such whimsy and warmth held sway.

She'd even thought about putting together some kind of concession where she'd do a doggy biscuit hunt to raise money for the local animal shelter. But the time she'd spent away from Open Arms was beginning to tell. A quiet Saturday to sort and shelve and catch up on the jillion and one things that had been swallowed up by taking care of Charlie and Mac *should* have been more important to her than having fun.

It wasn't as if she'd be missed. Few people in town would notice the crazy lady from the pet shop wasn't wandering through the booths, although some of her success stories might. Mac's teacher was now the proud owner of Pickles, a ten-month-old Newfoundland puppy Rowena had found for her. Sparky the beagle and Billy were attached at the hip now and five other new Whitewater pet owners were singing Rowena's praises. But Rowena still had that feeling she'd had so often as a kid. As if no one saw her—the screw-up between her over-achieving sisters.

You're my little dandelion between two roses, her father once teased, ruffling Rowena's yellow hair. Everyone else in the family had laughed when she'd told him dandelions were her favorite flowers. They'd thought she was either too naive or too thick to understand what he'd meant, but even then she'd known the truth.

She didn't fit. She wasn't right. Rowena Brown, the family ugly duckling who'd never turn into a swan.

She tried not to let the memory hurt her again. She'd promised she never would. Once she moved here, once she settled in, she'd finally feel…what? Like a dandelion nicely settled in a yard where no one ever put down weed killer?

She grimaced. Who would have guessed she'd feel as adrift here as she'd been everywhere else in her life? She'd hoped for so much more when she'd taken the drastic step of moving here. Believed she'd finally find that piece she was missing, the one that made her feel so restless, so flawed. As if she wasn't finished yet.

Destroyer—would she ever get used to that name?—pawed at the crack of sunlight at the bottom of the shop door.

"I know, I know," she muttered to the dog. "There's a great big party out there and we're missing it."

Destroyer gave her a look that seemed to say "You're the one with opposable thumbs. So turn the damned doorknob already."

"Cash said you couldn't go. No way. No how. And that's a direct quote." But maybe Cash didn't get a vote today. He'd blown the fair off. It wasn't as if he'd be around to complain. And even if he did, he could just deal. If the girls couldn't share the fair with their father, they should at least be able to enjoy it with their dog.

Rowena's lips firmed. She looked from Destroyer to the cat to the half-stocked shelf in indecision. Then she picked up a can of cat food and popped open the top. She perched the can on the top level of the kitty condo where Shakespeare was looking suddenly alert.

"Maybe you two are right," she told the animals. "I sure won't find whatever it is I'm looking for if I stay shut up in this shop shelving cat food. If I want to be part of this town, I'm going to have to make an effort to see more of it than Cash Lawless's bedroom." She stopped with a squeak of surprise. "I mean, *living room.* Kitchen. House in general."

She was trying to throw the dog off the scent, hide where her imagination had been spending far too much time of late.

But since Destroyer was neutered, she doubted he'd understand her dilemma.

"What say we close the place up and go see what this whole Harvest Fair deal is about, puppy? Eat a few funnel cakes, chomp a corn dog or two. See how Charlie is doing without her daddy around. Bet she'll be thrilled to see you!"

Rowena scrawled "Gone to Harvest Fair" on a piece of cardboard and propped it in the front window. Leaving her purse tucked safely under her desk, she pocketed a little money, then locked up and headed out the back door with Destroyer on a leash. She glimpsed Miss Marigold watering a patch of fading geraniums and wondered how long it would take for each of six concrete tabletops to dry. She'd been setting them permanently in one mosaic at a time.

"There isn't a soul in the shops today," Rowena called to her. "Aren't you going to the fair?"

The woman took one look at Destroyer and fled. Apparently the truce Vinny had struck between Miss Marigold and the pet shop in general didn't extend to Destroyer in particular. Rowena sighed and headed on foot toward the park a mile away.

The brisk walk was glorious, a cool wind ruffling her hair and the handkerchief hem of her gauzy aqua blouse.

She could hear the excited buzz of the fair blocks away, the tinny clamor of carnival-style music, the distant racket of a crowd. The whole atmosphere felt charged with delight. Rowena might have felt happy, too, if it weren't for Charlie's eyes haunting her. Charlie's secret sadness.

Hope says Charlie doesn't play very good anymore. Mac's words echoed in Rowena's memory. It was a clear insight and a painful one.

But today would be different, Rowena resolved, reaching down to adjust Destroyer's collar. Charlie would have fun at the Harvest Fair. Rowena was going to do her best to find the child and make absolutely sure of it, if Hope Stone and her family weren't up to the task.

Rowena rounded a cluster of houses and saw the spacious town square, fenced in for the weekend and frilled out in all its finery. The wide expanse of grass had been transformed into a patchwork of tents and traveling carnival rides. One of the neon lights on the small ferris wheel blinked on and off. A merry-go-round chugged in a circle to calliope music. A pair of kids with pumpkins and scary monsters painted on their cheeks rushed past her, but Destroyer barely noticed them, his obedience training beginning to fray around the edges as he neared the park.

Rowena checked in her jeans pocket for the Ziploc bags she kept in case one of the shop dogs left a little reminder of their presence someplace. As usual, she was a good girl scout. Prepared.

She paid at one of the entrances in the temporary fence and had her hand stamped, then she and Destroyer headed in. It was the kind of fair she'd read about in storybooks—homespun, the tents a little faded and down at the heels if looking at it with a grownup's critical gaze. But to the kids scrambling hither and yon, Rowena knew it seemed like fairy land.

She kept an eye out for Charlie and Mac as she wandered, and was embarrassed to admit that when she did finally spy them, it was because she'd allowed herself a moment to ogle one of the best-looking men she'd ever seen.

The guy looked like a throwback to another era, his long black hair tied at his nape with some kind of Celtic-inspired silver interlacing, his eyes piercing, his movements surprisingly graceful for such a large man. She'd seen him in her shop once with his daughter. A comical little button of a girl with a take-no-prisoners aura who said she wanted a kitten for Christmas.

Hadn't Charlie said something about her best friend wanting the prettiest kitten in the world for her birthday?

Rowena strained up on tiptoe, and sure enough, there was the pink glitter of MacKenzie's wheelchair. Keeping Destroyer at heel, she made her way in that direction.

The kids were sitting at a craft booth, making something out of dry pasta. A petite woman with short dark hair and an elegant, catlike face balanced Mac on her lap while the little girl tried to thread rigatoni onto the ends of her tiara. The woman was already wearing a brightly painted dry noodle necklace while Charlie and the girl Rowena recognized as Mr. Celtic Fantasy Man's daughter finished stringing things on bright colored yarn.

Rowena sucked in a breath to call to the girls, but before she could do it, Destroyer emitted a Newfie-sized woof of joy. Charlie's head jerked up, her mouth round with disbelief before delight set in.

"Destroyer!" She leaped up, pasta necklace in hand. Before Hope's mom could stop her, Charlie bolted out of the booth and raced toward Rowena. Destroyer tried to muscle his way toward his girl, but Rowena made him sit, wait for her. By the time Charlie reached them, worry had settled back between the child's brows.

"You're not supposed to be here," Charlie said as if the dog had made a jail break and gotten to the park on his own. Charlie glanced up at Rowena. "Daddy's not going to like this. He said Destroyer being at the Harvest Fair is just asking for trouble."

"Well, your daddy's at work, isn't he? I'm in charge." Rowena tugged on one of the French braids Hope's mom must have put in Charlie's hair that morning. "Your puppy missed you and so did I."

Rowena was surprised just how much. She didn't want to think what it would be like a few weeks from now when her time with the children was over.

"I missed you, too, boy," Charlie told the dog earnestly. "I made him a necklace, but it smells like food, you know. He'd probably just eat it." Charlie looked up at Rowena and fingered the craft she'd made. "It's not very pretty and it's just made out of noodles and stuff. Hope gave hers to her mom."

Rowena's heart hitched at the wistfulness in Charlie's voice. Wanting to drive it back, Rowena slid the palm of her hand under the necklace, angling it so the sunlight made the glitter sparkle. "Charlie, this is beautiful," she said with a warm smile. "Just look at how it shines."

"The glitter comes off pretty quick. But maybe you could wear it instead of Destroyer, Rowena. Only if you want to."

"I'd love to. You put it on me." Rowena knelt down and Charlie carefully slid the loop of yarn over her head. When Charlie surveyed her handiwork and actually smiled, it hurt Rowena's heart.

"So you're the great Bear Tamer we've been hearing so much about," a gruff voice said nearby. Rowena looked up to see the Celtic sex god looming over her with a wicked grin that could melt any red-blooded woman's knees. Did they put something in the water around here that produced such a crop of gorgeous men?

"That was quite a controversy you stirred up over at the playground," he continued with a wink.

"Daddy, that was over ages ago!" his daughter complained, giving him a nudge with her elbow. "So it's not a bear. All right, already! Me and Charlie got that all straightened out."

Charlie leaned over and whispered in Rowena's ear. "You've got to bow to him."

"Huh?" Okay, maybe the guy *did* look like some High King. But he was standing in the middle of Illinois, for crissakes. Wasn't bowing to the man a little over the top?

Still, it seemed important to Charlie, so Rowena climbed to her feet and did as the little girl asked.

"Bo Stone," Charlie introduced, "this is Rowena."

"Yeah!" Mac put in her two cents' worth. "She's lots prettier than Mr. Google, huh?"

The man's eyes twinkled. "Lots."

Rowena extended her hand a little sheepishly. "Nice to meet you, Bo."

"I'm Jake. *Bo* is the word for teacher in Korean. My Tae Kwon Do students have to call me that and bow when they see me, right, kiddo?" He shot Charlie one of those charming winks. "Charlie here was champion board breaker in her class."

"Hope was real good, too," Charlie added hastily.

"We both miss having Charlie in the dojo—classroom. We can't wait until she comes back. The girls used to have a great time together when they were sparring partners."

Rowena remembered the photograph in Cash's hallway, Charlie adorable in her little karate suit. She'd bet breaking boards had helped the child channel some of her stress. The poor kid would probably have to decimate a whole lumber yard to mellow out now.

Charlie shifted from one foot to the other, uncomfortable. "I'm real busy, Bo Stone, so I can't come to class right now. Mac's got therapy and I got schoolwork and stuff."

"Well, try to keep in practice so when you come back you'll be in shape. I don't want you to turn into a fluffy on me, got it?"

"A fluffy?" Rowena's eyes narrowed in confusion.

"Never mind, it's a long story. A family thing." The wispy-haired woman handed Mac off to her husband. He set the child up on his shoulders. "I'm Deirdre Stone. I hear you're on the lookout for the perfect Christmas kitten for someone who shall remain nameless."

"See," Charlie reminded Rowena. "I told you people only want the cute ones."

"Well, I'll keep my eye out, but I still say beauty is in the eye of the beholder."

"My older daughter, Emma, sent Hope a calendar from Scotland with all kinds of cat breeds dressed in medieval clothes on it. The Persian princess seems to be the current favorite."

Rowena chuckled as Jake nabbed the kids and herded them over to the fish pond game. Armed with cane poles and all jazzed up on sugar, kids tossed the lines over a curtained pond where volunteers clipped prizes onto clothespin "hooks."

Destroyer, with his girls in sight, settled down to watch them with such a relieved aura Deirdre laughed out loud.

"You'd think he was a mother hen, the way he watches those girls."

"Newfies are natural babysitters."

"So are you, from what I hear." Deirdre appraised her with frank blue eyes.

Rowena thought of Cash and made a face. "You're obviously not talking to the right person."

"Who better to judge than MacKenzie and Charlie? Don't get me wrong. Cash is a wonderful father and Vinny is great, but the girls are so hungry to have a woman around it's hard to watch them sometimes."

"I know." Rowena remembered a dozen little things the girls had said or done that hinted at the loss in their lives, the absence of a mother.

"I kept hoping that Cash might hook up with someone. He's still so young, and with his looks I know a dozen women in town who would love to strike up a relationship with him."

"Mac's teacher for one." The sour words slipped out before Rowena could stop them.

Deirdre laughed. "Make that a dozen and one. Jake even tried to set him up once or twice with women from the self-defense classes he teaches, but Cash's whole world is his girls now."

"Except for today, when he can't be bothered to—" Rowena checked herself, wary of letting her irritation show. The last thing she wanted to do was make Deirdre Stone uncomfortable. Especially since Rowena felt an instinctive tug toward her, as if she and the woman could become friends.

But Deirdre's intelligent blue eyes sharpened. "Be bothered to what?"

"Don't get me wrong. I think it's wonderful that you and Jake were willing to take care of the girls today. But they should be with their father."

Deirdre gave her a funny look. "That could prove inconvenient."

"I know. He's working. Overtime. But he volunteered for it. And the girls—Charlie, especially—need him on a day like this."

Mischief danced across Deirdre's animated face. "Maybe we could...uh, take the girls over to, um, say hello to him."

Rowena could have sworn Deirdre was the blunt, outspoken type. So why did she seem to be fighting to keep her voice level at the moment?

"You mean Cash is here?" Rowena glanced over to where Charlie and Hope huddled over their brand-new secret decoder rings.

"Jake?" Deirdre hollered to her handsome husband. "Let's take Rowena and the girls over to see Cash."

"You mean at the—oof!" Jake winced as Deirdre ran the wheelchair she'd just retrieved over his foot.

"My daddy's in the drunk tank." Mac waggled her head in disapproval.

That was the overtime he'd volunteered for? Rowena's outrage grew. The man was wrangling the town drunks instead of spending the day with his daughters?

Gripping Destroyer's lead so hard her knuckles turned white, she followed Deirdre and Jake Stone through the crowd. It thickened in front of one particular booth, hoots and hollers erupting all around.

"Three balls for a dollar!" A soccer mom hawked as she pointed to the contraption above. "Dunk the deputy!"

"Dunk?" Rowena choked as her gaze locked on Cash. He sat on a seat about four feet above a giant tank of water. A metal arm with a bull's eye painted on a disk operated the mechanism that would plunge Cash into the tub. "That's a dunk tank, not a drunk tank." Her cheeks burned. Wow, had she ever misjudged Cash Lawless this time. She couldn't help but grin, she was so glad he was here.

"Didn't Cash tell you he volunteered...?" Jake asked, his surprised exclamation drowned out by Cash's taunts.

"My grandmother can pitch harder than you can, Potter!" Cash shouted as a portly man in a Hawaiian shirt fired off his last softball, missing the target completely. "I'm getting downright bored up here. Who wants to take a crack at me next?"

"Talk about your dream opportunity!" Rowena shot a pointed glance at Deirdre Stone. "Would you mind holding the dog for a minute?"

"Not a bit." Deirdre grabbed the leash and Rowena shoved her way to the front of the line.

She loved the stunned expression on Cash's face when he saw her lay her money down. But he retreated to his banter moments later.

"Shouldn't you head over to the merry-go-round, honey? You don't look like the fast-pitch type. You don't want to hurt yourself, throwing a big bad baseball or anything."

"That's a risk I'll have to take." Rowena scooped up the first baseball and winged it at the target. The ball fell short, plopping into the tank. He laughed out loud, mocking her.

"Hey, Charlie, want to give the little lady a hand? My hair's turning gray up here."

Who would have guessed Cash Lawless had such a sense of humor? Rowena could hardly believe how good he was at goading her. She threw a second ball. Then a third. He leaned back in his little seat and put his folded hands behind his head, pretending to snore. But all it did was accentuate the breadth of his chest, the muscled planes Rowena had felt against her own far too briefly.

Rowena dug into her pocket, regretting her decision to leave her purse at the shop. Five dollars disappeared, then ten, and still Cash perched on the seat, laughing at her.

"Give it up, darlin', you're hopeless."

He echoed the taunts of kids in her gym classes decades ago. Rowena channeled all that old anger, all that old frustration.

She scrounged for pocket change, but before she could piece together enough to buy three more balls, Jake slapped a five-dollar bill down for her.

"Hey!" Cash crabbed. "You're supposed to be on my side, Stone."

"Money's for a good cause, isn't it, buddy?"

"Well, you're just throwing good money after bad, Jake. The lady couldn't hit the broad side of a barn."

Rowena gripped the softball, felt the weave under her fingers and fired the ball at the target with all her might. The loud clang of leather hitting the bull's eye surprised everybody. A whoop rose from the crowd as Cash plunged down into the tank, his mouth hanging open in shock.

He came up coughing and sputtering while the crowd around him hollered with glee. Rowena wheeled to give Deirdre a high five, but a mountain of black fur almost knocked her on her backside, Destroyer shooting past her as if he'd been fired out of a cannon.

Destroyer!

Rowena dove for the dog's leash as it tore from Deirdre's grasp. The leather yanked taut, all but dislocating Rowena's left arm as it jerked her into the vendor's table, softballs bouncing wildly onto the ground. Rowena yelled at the charging dog— sit, stay, come—any command she could think of, but the Newfie bounded up onto the table and launched himself like a canine version of Superman into the tank of water where Cash was struggling to get his feet back under him.

Destroyer landed on Cash, shoving him back under the water, the tank barely large enough to hold the two of them as Rowena rushed around the table, trying to get hold of the lead. But the dog was in full rescue mode, trying to grip Cash's arm, haul him to the surface.

Rowena boosted herself on the edge of the tub, grabbing the sopping wet dog around the neck, but before she could muscle Destroyer out of the tank, the dog made another dive for his "victim." Rowena yelped as the metal rim of the tub raked her stomach, Destroyer hauling her with him into the tank.

She went in the cold water headfirst, colliding with Cash in a tangle of arms, legs and paws. Her lungs were exploding as she tried to surface, but there was no room to turn herself around. She seemed to be stuck forever when suddenly a roaring splash sounded in her ears, the metal gong sound of something striking the tub's exterior. Pain raked her chest as something—probably Destroyer—clawed at it. Then suddenly hard hands closed around her waist, pulling her upward.

Air. It hit her in a wave—the autumn crispness she'd enjoyed before suddenly chilling her to the bone. She tried to suck in oxygen, but her nose was still full of water. She snorted, choked until someone whacked her on the back.

Cash. He held her up, the two of them, chest deep in the water, the dog struggling in Jake Stone's powerful grasp. The crowd cheered wildly, her head still spinning.

"D-damn…dog…" Cash swore, thumping her back again to clear her lungs.

"He was…trying to…save you!" Rowena choked out.

"Save me? He almost drowned me! And you, too!"

Rowena tried to get the water out of her ears. The man almost sounded shaken.

"Daddy?" Mac seemed to take it somewhat in stride, but Charlie sounded on the verge of tears. "Daddy! You okay?"

"I'm fine, Charlie," he called to his daughter, then he turned his searching eyes on Rowena. "How about you?" he asked, smoothing her hair back from her face, where it was clinging like a mass of seaweed. "Did that demon dog hurt you?"

Rowena felt a little sick. Were they back to Destroyer the incorrigible already?

"It's not the dog's fault," she said, her teeth starting to chatter. "I st-started his water rescue training…last summer. He was…just doing what…I taught him." A shiver rocked her. "I'm f-freezing! What are you? Crazy? Who would…volunteer for this?"

"I would. Where's your car?"

"I w-walked. Thought it w-would wear Clancy out b-before we got here so he'd behave."

"You mean Destroyer," Cash teased, but his eyes were warm. He helped her out of the tank to the crowd's shouts of approval, then climbed out himself, his athlete's body perfectly outlined by his wet jeans and sweatshirt. For once Rowena was too tired to argue with him.

"Hey, Lola," he called to the soccer mom. "I'll be back in about fifteen minutes. Once I get this lady and the dog here settled."

Jake Stone chuckled. "Take your time, Lawless. I'm soaked already. I might as well take a turn in the wet seat."

Cash saluted him with a grateful wave, then grabbed the

Newfie's leash. The dog knew the instant the alpha took control. If Destroyer could have, he would have saluted.

"I—I brought the dog here," Rowena argued. "I can get him h-home."

"I'll help Rowena, Daddy," Charlie volunteered, still looking shaken.

"No way, cupcake. You go have fun with Hope. I've got this crisis covered."

Reluctantly, Charlie let herself be herded away by Deirdre.

Rowena had always felt a little awkward, strange, the new person in town. But as she and Cash and the sopping-wet dog wound their way through the crowd, she knew they made a spectacle few citizens of Whitewater would ever forget.

People clapped, yelled out teasing remarks—not just to Cash but to Rowena, as well. Kids called out to her about the pets she'd matched them with, wondering if guinea pigs could swim like the big dog, or if kitties liked the water.

It warmed Rowena to see how much people cared about Cash, respected him. And as the story of her plunge in the tank spread, their good-natured jokes gave her a sweet taste of what it would feel like once she belonged here like Cash did. A welcome she wanted now more than ever.

When they reached Cash's SUV, she was surprised to see him flip the back hatch open.

"Get in, dog," he ordered, grabbing his spare jacket and wrapping it around Rowena's shoulders. Destroyer did as he was told, and Cash closed the door with a bang.

"You can't mean...you'll never get the wet dog smell out of your car," she warned.

"Guess I'll just have to deal. Occupational hazard when you take a dip in the dunk tank."

"Wh-what kind of occupation is that anyway? Working overtime, my foot!"

"This is the first year I've been able to take on that concession. I'll be manning it from now on if I have my way."

"Why? It's cold! It's miserable! And I only went in the water once."

"It's my way of paying back. Remember when I told you Mac's medical bills weren't free?"

"How could I forget? You about bit my head off *and* you made me feel guilty at the same time. That was pretty rotten of you."

"Yeah, well. You saw a fine example of my temper the first time you met me. You could have stayed out of my way."

"Destroyer's the one who…who…got so attached to you and your kids. He just dragged me along for the ride."

She was right, Cash thought wryly. In spite of Destroyer's latest infraction, he was probably going to be stuck with the dog forever. He should be loading Rowena into the car, too. Driving her home, then rushing back to the dunk tank. But he found himself lingering.

"You know the proceeds from the Harvest Fair go to help the community," he said. "Sometimes scholarships for local kids, sometimes help for families whose homes have been hit by fire. Right after the accident, the committee donated a huge chunk of money to Mac's medical fund."

"Mac's…"

Did she have any idea how hard it was for him to admit it? That he hadn't been able to afford everything his daughter needed when she was so badly injured. The hospitals, the specialists. The surgeries. The wheelchair and God knew what else.

"It can get cold this late in the season, so it's always been hard for the committee to convince somebody to get wet. I figure it's the least I can do."

"Wh-why didn't you tell me? When I got so mad at you?"

Cash looked down. "I'm not proud of the fact I couldn't provide everything my daughter needed. It's still hard for me. Besides, it seemed…"

Safer to keep you angry, smarter to drive that look out of your eyes, like I'm some kind of hero when I'm not.

He never said the words, but he could tell she understood them. Maybe there was something to all that intuition garbage of hers after all.

She peered up at him, those eyes that made him ache, made him want to feel warm again when he'd been cold for so long. "Why tell me now?" she asked softly.

"Because…" He lowered his gaze, searching for the words to explain. Not knowing if he could ever find them. His muscles clenched when he saw the angry red welts the frantic dog had clawed into her skin from collarbone to breast.

"Sonofabitch!" Cash swore, touching one of the nasty scratches. "Now I am mad at the dog."

"It's nothing. Really," she brushed his concern off. But when she glimpsed her chest, dismay flooded her features. Her blouse was ruined, Cash noted, the cloth stained with glitter and tempera paint from—what the hell was that thing around her neck?

Her eyes filled with tears.

"The dog hurt you!" Cash exclaimed, feeling like he'd been punched. "Why didn't you say something?"

"N-no. That's not it." Her voice quavered as tears escaped, running down her cheeks. "It's…my necklace."

Cash watched as she scooped the sodden mess off her shirt as if it were some kind of treasure. Pasta strung on yarn.

"Ch-Charlie gave this to me and it's ruined."

Cash stared down at her, stunned. Tears. Over a necklace Lisa would never even have put on in case it stained her blouse.

Cash couldn't help himself. He cupped Rowena's cheek,

swept away the tears with the pad of his thumb. "I'll have her make you another one."

"I know…it's silly." Her voice cracked and so did the hard wall he'd built around himself. "I want…this one and it's all wet."

Cash glanced around, saw how alone they were. He pressed his cheek against hers and closed his eyes. They were different, so different. His face a little roughened eight hours after his last shave, her skin too soft, too tender. Just like Rowena's heart.

Yearning surged from deep inside. And for an instant he wanted something from this woman, far more important than sex—and far more dangerous.

He wanted to comfort her and be comforted himself. To drive back the shadows and share…share the truth about fears and doubts and mistakes he'd never wanted to confess.

He kissed her where her tears had run, tasted the salt of her, the unbearable sweetness. Her breath hitched and Cash trailed his mouth to the corner of hers.

"Rowena." He whispered her name deep inside where even his conscience couldn't hear it. "Rowena…Rowena…"

"Hey! Hey, you!" A woman's shout cut in. Cash glimpsed a blonde stranger charging toward them, the jacket of her business suit flapping, her heels clicking militantly on the pavement. He started to draw Rowena into a protective embrace, wanting to shield her tears, save her dignity. But the stranger grabbed his arm and wrenched him away, her eyes ablaze with righteous indignation behind intimidating black glasses.

"Look at me when I'm talking to you, mister!" she railed, her blue eyes flashing. "Who the hell are you and what did you do to make my baby sister cry?"

CHAPTER TWELVE

"BRYONY?" Rowena exclaimed, and Cash could see stunned recognition registering as she stared at the woman who looked ready to take Cash apart with a pitchfork. "Cash, this—this is my big sister."

Rowena's sister? Cash thought in astonishment. This Bryony person didn't look as if she was even from the same planet as Rowena. Understated, expensively tailored clothing accented posture a marine would envy, silver blond hair was twisted into submission and caught back in a tortoiseshell clip. The woman could be a poster child for the young urban professional.

Black framed glasses did their best to hide anything feminine or vulnerable about her eyes. She needn't have bothered with them at present. She had roughly the expression of the most cutthroat criminal-defense attorney Cash had ever faced in a courtroom.

"I told Mom and Ariel something was wrong, Rowena!" The woman shifted her black leather briefcase-style purse higher up on her shoulder. "I could tell when I talked to you on the phone last week. And now, here you are crying. And I'd bet my medical license that *he's* the reason why!"

Cash stiffened under the weight of the woman's glare. Truth was, he hadn't made Rowena cry this time, but he'd been plenty hard on her before. Even the possibility that he'd brought tears to those warm green eyes in the past made him sting with regret.

"Maybe we'd all better settle down and take a deep breath," he said in his calmest deputy voice. "I'm Cash Lawless."

"Of course you are," Bryony bit out in a tone that could give a man frostbite. "The deputy with the kids who tried to steal Rowena's dog."

Cash felt his temper rise, fought it back. He could understand the impulse to protect someone you loved. "Stealing is a pretty harsh charge, Dr. Brown. My daughter's nine years old. She found the dog running loose and she brought it home."

"Then you have my sympathy, Deputy Lawless, because your child is bound to run you a merry chase. She sounds just like my sister—always finding *some*body to save."

Cash knew what Bryony Brown was implying, comparing his little girls to Rowena's strays. He wanted to grab the woman by the arms and shake her.

"Bryony, stop it!" Rowena stepped between them as if she'd read his thoughts. Her face shone, beet-red. "This isn't what it looks like!"

"It never is." Cynicism dripped from Bryony Brown's words. "So how about if you and I get out of here so you can tell me all about it."

Rowena dug in with a stubbornness that would have done Mac proud. "Bryony, you're way out of line here."

"*I'm* out of line? It's a simple question, Row. Explain what you're doing in the middle of this parking lot, soaking wet, crying your eyes out with this guy while the rest of the world is at Pumpkin Hell."

"Harvest Fair," Cash corrected, bristling at the woman's scorn for his town, his child. Bryony had a look reminiscent of Lisa's sister—a high-ticket item who knew her price tag wasn't one his salary could afford. An interfering sort who thought she knew best and was going to make sure younger sister saw things her way.

"I was crying because I broke something…precious." Rowena's voice quavered, pushing a sliver of something unexpected into the shell closing back around the place she'd opened in him moments before. "Cash was just…comforting me."

"Such a great guy."

"He is!" Rowena exclaimed, her eyes flashing. "And anyway, it's none of your business what the two of us were doing! You're not even supposed to be here."

"Neither are you!" Bryony challenged. "Shouldn't you be at your shop? The pet shop that was going to be the be-all end-all of your existence?"

"I never claimed that." Rowena's chin tipped up. "You and Mom did. I said the shop would make it possible for me to work with last-chance pets and—"

"And heal the world." Bryony turned back to Cash, exasperation pulling down the corners of her mouth. "But could Rowena do it the way Browns have healed for decades? No. Not with a scalpel in an operating room. Rowena is going to fix everything with some rusty old piece of junk a batty old woman—"

"*Enough,*" Cash snapped in his hardest deputy voice.

Bryony went rigid, blinking in astonishment behind her glasses lenses. It was nice to know he could even cut doctors off in the middle of a tirade.

"I appreciate that you're upset, Dr. Brown. You're worried about your sister. But causing a scene here, in the middle of a parking lot, is no way to handle this."

Bryony opened her mouth, shut it. Cash sensed it wasn't something she did very often when she had an opinion. She swallowed. The strand of gumball-sized pearls at her throat rippled, reminding him of the necklace he'd bought Lisa when MacKenzie was born, the pearls beautiful, perfect, but much smaller than she was used to. Lisa hadn't bothered to take them with her when she left. He'd put them in their velvet box, tucked it away to give Mac someday.

"You're right."

Bryony Brown's words blindsided him. Her lipsticked mouth pursed, as if admitting that to him cost her, big time. One thing he and Rowena's sister had in common, Cash thought. Neither of them liked to admit they'd made a mistake.

"I didn't come here to yell at you," Bryony said. "I came here to see my sister. Make sure she's okay. We're all...worried about her."

I'll just bet you are. Cash's life depended on being able to gauge what people were thinking. And Bryony Brown made no attempt to hide her opinion of him, his town, his kids.

A deputy? Divorced? With two kids, one in a wheelchair? Oh, yeah. He knew exactly what Dr. Bryony Brown thought of him.

And yet, the idea of leaving Rowena to be lectured by her far tougher sister when she was still broken up by the ruined necklace bothered him in spite of his badly singed pride.

"Rowena," he said, turning to look at her, the drying tracks of tears on her cheeks, the smears of paint from her ruined necklace on her blouse. God help him, he'd never seen her look more beautiful. "Do you want me to take you home?"

"No. I'll go with my sister."

Unexpected bitterness welled up in Cash. It wasn't fair to Rowena, but he couldn't help it—her words the same ones Lisa had used when she broke his daughters' hearts.

"Fine." The ugliness in him leaked through just enough to draw Bryony's incisive gaze.

Rowena's eyes pulled at him, pleading. As if she sensed in

him all that poison, knew somehow her sister had cut some of it loose. "You need to get back to the dunk tank. It's important, Cash. What you're doing here."

She stretched up on tiptoe, kissed him on the cheek. In front of her sister. In front of the whole freaking parking lot. "I'll see you on Monday."

Not if your sister has anything to do with it.

"I will," she insisted, again seeming to read his mind. "Do you want me to take Cla—Destroyer?" She pointed to the Newfie worriedly smearing up Cash's back window with tennis-ball-sized nose prints.

"Take that—that wet dog in my car?" Bryony's eyes went round. Too bad Cash was wound too tight inside to enjoy it. "I thought it belonged to him…his kids. It'd never fit."

"Destroyer does belong to them. But I'm babysitting. The dog. While they're all at the fair."

It was tempting to hand the sopping wet Newfie over, let Destroyer become Rowena's uptight sister's problem for a while. But Cash had seen enough interactions between Lisa and Joan over the seven years he'd been married. Sometimes he'd almost felt sorry for Lisa. Seemed as if the younger sister always paid for any rebellion.

"It's not a problem," Cash said. "I'll run the dog home quick and put him in the backyard to dry. Jake said he'd cover for me until I get back."

Rowena gave him back his jacket. She looked up at him, so earnest. "The Stones are nice people, Cash. I like them."

"That's a big surprise!" Bryony grumbled under her breath. "You like everybody."

"Not everybody," Rowena said with an edge to her voice Cash couldn't help but admire. She turned to her intimidating sister. "Right now, Bryony Brown, I don't like you at all."

Dropping that little bombshell, Rowena spun on her heel and

walked away, toward a gunmetal-gray Porsche with two seats and enough engine to haul ass.

Maybe it would be better if Rowena did just that, Cash thought. Hauled ass, out of his life, out of his head, out of the hot dreams he'd been having at night, alone in his bed. Dreams he knew would be different after today. He looked down at his hand, saw the green smear of tempera paint and glitter Charlie's water-soaked necklace had left there.

I broke something precious... Rowena's words rippled through him. He couldn't help feeling that he had, too. He'd decided that first night he'd kissed her that he'd never give the feelings he had for Rowena a chance to grow. And yet, for just a moment, when she'd been weeping over that necklace, he'd almost...

Almost made the biggest mistake imaginable.

Get involved with another woman whose family would look down on him? Take the chance that they'd be cold to his children, as well?

No. He wasn't going to risk letting that kind of rejection back into his daughters' lives. They'd already suffered enough.

But he wanted her.

Rowena.

He wanted to take her to bed with him. To laugh with her. To soak up just a little of the colors she trailed wherever she went.

He wanted...

But he'd done without things he'd wanted before.

You've always been my strong one, his mother had often told him. *Strong like the rock of Cashel I named you for...*

He could do this, Cash told himself firmly. He could get through the next few weeks with Rowena.

And then he could walk away.

ROWENA STALKED toward the car, her temper blazing as she thought of how deeply her sister's barbs must have cut Cash, the echoes from his past Bryony must have awakened. Not that Bryony could have known that, and yet far too often, Bryony made snap judgment calls, too used to being right ever to consider she might be wrong.

"You were way out of line back there," Rowena said as she plopped her wet butt down on Bryony's leather seat, feeling a petty sense of getting her own back as her sister gave a gasp of displeasure.

"I'm out of line?" Bryony arched one dark brow up. "I drive three hours to see you because I'm worried about you—and with good reason if that little scene with the deputy was any example of what you've been up to since you moved here."

"You have no idea what happened."

"You were crying. And he was looking at you like— like—"

"Like what?"

"Like he…God, Rowena! A man stuck with two kids on his own? You've got to know he'd have to be after the first woman he could find who'd take some of the load off his shoulders. You might as well have walked into town with a target painted on your ass."

"And you all wondered why I moved so far away from home."

"Okay, so maybe that's not the—the most P.C. way of putting it. But admit it. On some level, you know I'm right."

"Actually, Cash decided after the divorce that he wouldn't date, wouldn't risk bringing another woman into his daughters' lives."

"And of course, men always tell the truth."

"Cash does. Bry, I'm sorry Richard hurt you. And I'm sorry you wasted your day off driving down here on some hare-brained scheme to rescue me from…whatever you think you're rescuing me from."

"Being used. Being hurt. Getting trapped in a situation that—that... I don't care what the man told you. The way he was looking at you back there scares the pants off me."

Rowena felt a shiver run down her spine at the memory of those moments when Cash had stared down at her, his eyes vulnerable, his mouth so close. Then closer still, brushing her cheek, the corner of her mouth. Warmth, heat, emotions cruising far too close to the surface. Cash's voice, whispering her name as if it were a prayer.

But he'd only been offering comfort, only been grateful that she'd cherished the gift his daughter had given her.

"Rowena, you know I love you. And I admire the way you're always so willing to rush into things, take risks I never would. But this thing with Deputy Lawless is just asking for heartache."

"What thing is that?"

"You care about him. You always want to give love so—so freely. It never occurs to you that most people take time to count the cost and the benefits before they make a leap like that. I don't want Lawless to figure out just how much easier you'd make his life and decide that that would be enough to base a marriage on."

"You're delusional! Talk about overreacting! Considering what Cash's first wife did to him and to his children, I doubt he'd ever marry anyone else."

"I feel sorry for whoever he did marry."

"You've met him for what? All of three minutes—while you were having a fit, by the way. You don't know anything about him."

"Don't I? I saw that anger of his running so close to the surface. I know just how dangerous that can be."

Rowena turned her gaze out the window, remembering the boyfriend who had broken her sister's arm three years ago.

Knowing how ashamed Bryony had been. Even so, she didn't want Bryony to know she'd struck a nerve. "You attacked him, Bry. For no reason. What did you expect?"

"Are you trying to tell me that he's the Good Humor man the rest of the time?"

"Not a lot to laugh about with his daughter in a wheelchair. But he's been learning."

"From you, right?"

Rowena knew the answer must be on her face. Bryony sighed, a rare chink showing in her armor, old sadness in her face.

"Oh, sweetheart," she said, the endearment so rare it was too precious to entirely dismiss. "I've spent years treating patients. I've seen all kinds of families go through tragedies like this one. I know just what kind of man Cash Lawless is. The kind of man who's angry, who blames—"

"Bryony, stop." Rowena said, gentler this time. Quieter. "I know you're scared for me. But Cash has been brutally honest. The boundaries between us are absolutely clear."

"But—"

"I'm not going to listen another minute."

Bryony gave her the once-over, with far too serious eyes. Eyes that reminded Rowena of Cash. Eyes far too good at hiding pain. "That's okay. You don't have to listen anymore," Bryony said at last.

"What?" Rowena said, surprised at her sister's capitulation.

"You're nothing if not fair, Row. Even though you're pissed off at me for interfering, you'll consider what I've said."

There was no sense in arguing with her. Not when she was right.

"What say we go to your house? Get you out of those clothes. I'm afraid you'll catch your death of cold."

Oh, Bry, Rowena thought, reaching over to squeeze her

sister's hand, Bryony, so closed off, so determined to be strong. Cool and capable on the outside. Never letting anyone see deeper. *I'm afraid you'll do the same thing...*

SOMEBODY ON THE STREET outside slammed a car door. Cash glanced up at the clock as Destroyer gave a low woof from Charlie's room, just in case "the boss" had missed the potential intruder. It was ten o'clock—not late by Fair day standards. Cash figured the local teenagers still had plenty of night left to celebrate, so even quiet little Whitewater had the potential of seeing more action than usual tonight.

At least there was no chance either of the girls would wake up, Cash thought, sinking even deeper in his easy chair. Both kids had fallen asleep in the car on the way home. He'd carried them in, both sticky and smelling of cotton candy and mustard and face paint and fun. He figured he'd have to wash them and the sheets come morning. But he didn't mind. They'd be jabbering all day about their adventures. He'd barely have to talk at all. Good thing, since shouting at people from the tank had left his throat a little sore.

While Rowena had left another kind of ache. In his heart.

Cash snagged his half-empty bottle of Budweiser from the table beside him and took a drink. But tonight the beer did nothing to help him relax. He kept remembering the sight of Rowena's back as she walked away from him.

And the kicked-in-the-gut feeling that had taken him completely by surprise.

He grabbed the remote and switched off the news, then rubbed his face with one hand. Better go take a hot shower, drive back the chill that had grown so much worse in the hours he'd spent in the dunk tank after Rowena had left.

A quiet rap made him turn toward the front door. His heart skipped a beat. The kids were safe in bed, Vinny was still without wheels. The only person he knew who would show up on his doorstep this late was Rowena.

Doubtless trying to "fix" things, the way she had the day after Vinny had broken his leg. Cash winced, remembering Bryony Brown's exasperated remark that Rowena was always finding somebody to save.

Cash clung to that bitter thought, trying to arm himself against Rowena's lost-fairy eyes, her generosity of heart, her sensitivity that seemed able to find any wound, no matter how old or how deeply buried. Even so, his heart skipped a beat at the thought of her on his doorstep.

Cash looked through the peephole, then went still. After a moment, he turned the lock and opened the door. "Dr. Brown."

"Deputy Lawless," Rowena's sister greeted him. "I was hoping I could have a word with you before I left town."

The idea of letting the woman into his home grated Cash's nerves. He could remember far too well the way Joan's aristocratic nose had wrinkled in distaste the few times she'd walked through his door. He blocked the opening pointedly with his big body. "Not necessary," he told her. "You made your point in the parking lot."

She actually looked a little chagrined. The ice in her eyes thawed a bit, revealing something darker beneath. Something Cash understood. "I'm afraid I made a rather bad job of it this afternoon," Bryony confessed. "I hate seeing Rowena cry."

What could Cash say to that? He stepped back, opened the door wide enough for Rowena's sister to come in.

"I'm sorry it's so late. But I didn't want the children to be up. I knew this would be awkward."

"They're out for the night."

"That's good." She rolled her shoulders a little as if working out the kinks. "It always amazes me, how children sleep. So easily. As if…" Her features grew puzzled. A little wistful. "Well, I didn't come here to talk about my insomnia, did I?"

"What did you come here for?"

"To talk to you about my sister."

Cash waited a few seconds, silent, seeing that the doctor was gathering her thoughts.

"I know Rowena seems so…strong. Fearless, the way she plunges heart-first into life."

"Fearless, or crazy," Cash said, surprising himself at his honesty. "I envy her that. I hate to think what will happen when she finally gets hurt. It's inevitable, I guess. Even so…I hope to hell I won't be around to see when it happens."

"So you really don't have any…well, designs on my sister?"

"No." At least, not anything real. But in his fantasies… have mercy…

"When I saw you with Rowena, before you knew anyone else was there—I could have sworn—"

"I'm no man for Rowena, Dr. Brown."

The doctor turned her back to him, and yet, not before he'd seen the echo of his sentiments in her face, and an intimate knowledge of exactly how scorched a spirit could be. Something deeper than Lisa's sister had experienced, and far sadder.

"Thank you for…putting my mind at ease," Dr. Brown said. "After the way I behaved earlier, you could just as easily have let me stew about it."

"You're welcome."

"I guess I'd better hit the road."

Cash's brows lifted in surprise. "You're not going to drive back to the city now, are you?"

Bryony lifted one elegant shoulder. "Might as well. I don't sleep much anyway."

Another foible they both understood. "Maybe it comes with our jobs, eh?" Cash observed. "Cops and doctors. We're always waiting to see what disaster hits next."

"Knowing something always will." Bryony sucked in a deep

breath, let it out. "Rowena doesn't, Deputy. Doesn't know. Doesn't wait."

"It's hard to believe."

"But it's not because of the reasons you might think. Because she's naive. Or—or chooses to pretend away heartache. Rowena has cried far too many times in the past. It used to drive our mother crazy. Rowena would get herself bitten by some dog or scratched by a cat or hurt by some kid in school everyone else stayed away from. Mom would take Rowena in for stitches or sit up all night talking to her and she'd say to me *maybe this time she'll learn, Bryony...please, God, let Rowena learn.* Rowena never did."

Cash couldn't count the number of times he'd leaned over his own daughters' beds, pleading with God—to protect them, heal them, keep them safe.

"When Rowena moved here, I guess we all hoped...maybe a fresh start would do her good after all she'd been through."

"Calling off the wedding, you mean."

Surprise filled Bryony's gaze, her uneasiness about the closeness between Cash and her sister obviously deepening again.

"Rowena told me all about it," Cash explained. "She said... you can't marry someone you don't love. It took a lot of guts for her to do what she did, upset your family, publicly break this guy's heart."

"Break *his* heart? Is that what she told you?"

"Yeah." Cash's brow knit with confusion. "She said the family wanted her to marry him. But the moment the invitations hit the bottom of the mailbox, she knew it was all a big mistake."

"Not because she wanted out. Because she guessed *Dan* did. She didn't tell us that, at first. And he never said a word. He never would have had the courage to call off the wedding, face the two sets of parents. Duty, obligation, mean everything to Dan's family. And to our own."

"But…that doesn't make any sense."

"That's what we all said. Until three months later Dan eloped with his lab technician."

Cash imagined Rowena hearing the news, and he wanted to beat Dan senseless. "That asshole," Cash snarled aloud. Heat spilled up his neck. He could almost feel his mom taking him by the ear. *A man has no business swearing in front of a woman.*

"Sorry," he said gruffly.

"Don't be. I've called him plenty worse. To his face." Her features went grim with satisfaction.

Considering the ass-chewing the doctor had given Cash when she just suspected her sister was being taken advantage of, Cash could imagine Bryony Brown's reaction when Rowena had been humiliated for real. Cash wished he could have added his two cents to her tirade.

What the hell kind of idiot would fall for some other woman when Rowena Brown loved him? But he swallowed the words before he could say them aloud.

Instead he fisted his hands. "That must have hurt Rowena."

"It hurt her plenty. But by the time Dan showed his true colors she'd worked through most of it alone. *I'm happy for them.* That's what my sister said when she heard the news. Her gutless wonder of a fiancé had let her take the heat for calling off the wedding. Left her open to gossip—*Rowena, the flighty Brown sister. Nadine must be so disappointed. Imagine having to send back all the gifts, cancel the reception…contact all the guests.*" Bryony pressed her hand to her stomach, and Cash guessed it was as knotted up as his own.

"What I'm trying to tell you, Deputy, is that Rowena *has* been hurt by life. Badly. She just…doesn't care." Bryony frowned and gave her head a brisk shake. "No. That's not it.

She dives right back in, in spite of it all." She fell silent a moment, hugged her arms around her middle, as if instinctively trying to protect herself from a blow. "Why does she do that?"

The woman looked at Cash as if he had the answer. He was the last man on earth who would understand why anyone would take such a risk. When they'd already been betrayed. Bitten. Again and again, from what Bryony Brown said. And yet even if he didn't understand how Rowena could do it, he knew her well enough to understand *why*.

"Hope," he said, the word feeling strange on his tongue.

"What?"

"Rowena told me she believed in hope. That my girls needed to believe in it, too."

"What do you think?"

He shrugged. "For months after their mother left my girls kept hoping she'd come back. And after every one of Mac's surgeries I kept hoping she'd dance. Hope can eat you like acid from the inside out."

"I know." Her mouth softened with a grief and a sensitivity that surprised him, Dr. Brown reminding him for the first time of Rowena. And he wondered what had made Bryony Brown slam bars down around whatever was soft inside her. Like Cash had. Bars neither of them could afford to knock down.

"I don't want Rowena hurt," Bryony said, looking him square in the eye. And he could see just how much she loved her sister. Just how much she feared for her.

"Neither do I."

She searched his face. Something she saw there must have satisfied her. "I guess I'd better go. At least I won't have to worry about falling asleep at the wheel."

Cash grimaced as he opened the front door for Rowena's sister. "I won't, either."

Bryony hesitated a long moment and fingered the pearls

at her throat. "When it comes to real life, Rowena's completely hopeless," she confessed. "I know that. But…sometimes I envy her."

Cash met Bryony's eyes in complete understanding. "Sometimes I do, too."

HE COULDN'T STOP THINKING how much as he walked toward her shop the next day. Jake had taken the three girls to the movies, giving Cash the chance to put Destroyer in the giant-sized kennel Rowena had sold him. Cash wasn't taking any chances with the hellhound during the trip to the drugstore he was taking Vinny on so Mr. Google could get his meds.

From what Cash could tell, the crusty ex-cop didn't need to be manning the counter on a weekend. After all, Rowena was there. But it seemed as if Vinny was finding more and more reasons to be in the vicinity of a certain tea shop owner, flirting as shamelessly as any high school quarterback with his first cheerleader.

Cash couldn't help but grin as he entered Open Arms. Trust Vinny to make the best of a bad situation. He might be on crutches, but he'd found a lady friend to make him smile.

Speaking of a killer smile, Cash thought, Rowena's was absolutely glowing as she polished something that sparkled under the fluorescent lights.

Tables. Five of them marched in a row down the center of the store, the mosaic kind Lisa had shown him in her upscale garden magazines. The concrete tops perched on wrought-iron legs, matching chairs flanking each one of them. What the blazes was the woman doing now?

"Nice touch," Cash teased. "Planning on opening a kitty coffee shop?" He swallowed in an effort to soothe the rawness in his throat.

"No. They're for Miss Marigold. What do you think?"

Cash crossed to take a closer look. He could make out curved handles and tea spouts, shards that now made beautiful designs. "Did you do that yourself?"

"The girls helped."

"No. The designs, I mean. You're good. Real good."

"I've never been very good at throwing things away. You should hear my sister." She paused, looked a little shy. "About Bryony, Cash—"

Cash actually smiled and he could see surprise and confusion cloud Rowena's face. Better not tell her about her sister's late-night visit. Or the little chat they'd had. "Actually, your sister and I are a lot alike. She loves you... Not that I...well, you know."

Rowena's gaze snapped up to his. Asking questions he couldn't answer. Searching for feelings that wouldn't be there. No. Couldn't be.

He cleared his throat. "I mean, I'd be all stoked up, too, if I thought somebody was messing with someone I...like my brothers or Mac or Charlie."

Or you, he added silently.

Was that disappointment that darted into those incredible spring-colored eyes? Just a heartbeat, and then it was gone. Replaced by a furrow of concern between her brows.

"You sound hoarse."

He rubbed his throat, self-conscious. "It's no big deal."

But she ignored him, reaching up, laying her soft, feminine hand on his forehead to see if it was hot. The touch felt strange, and Cash wondered how long it had been since anyone cared enough about him to do such a thing. Maybe *cared* wasn't the right word. Felt...intimate enough...

To gauge his temperature? *Hell, Lawless. You act as if she stuck her hand down your pants.*

He winced at his own crudeness, and yet, he needed to

muster whatever defenses he could against the sweet, seeking spell Rowena's touch cast upon him.

"You don't have a fever," she said, obviously relieved.

"Just yelled too much, I guess."

"I've got the perfect thing to make it feel better."

"That's not necessary." Cash tried not to regret when her hand fell away. "I've already put you to enough trouble."

"How about if we make a trade? Even things up a bit?" she said. "I'll give you my magic potion, and you can make those tables disappear from my shop and reappear in Miss Marigold's garden."

"I'm happy to help," he said. "But you don't have to—"

"I want to." She walked over to a table behind the counter where she had an electric kettle. Turning it on, she dug through a bunch of little envelopes that held teabags.

"I don't drink tea," he said.

"Today you do." She fussed with the cup, squeezing in— was that fresh lemon juice? And then honey out of a little clear plastic bear. She pressed the concoction into his hand. Cash eyed it suspiciously.

Vinny limped out from the back room on his crutches. "I tried to piece that paperwork together for you, sweet cheeks, but it's a—"

"Disaster. Yeah. I know. I'm terrible at that kind of stuff." Rowena made a face. "Oh, well. It makes a good excuse for you to charm Miss Marigold out of another cherry pie."

"So that's why you look like you're putting on a few pounds," Cash teased his friend.

Vinny shot him a grin. "Hey, there, junior! Look what the cat dragged in."

Good call, Cash thought. The junk in the cup smelled just like a donation from that snooty cat eyeballing him from some kind of kitty jungle gym.

"Cash has a sore throat." Rowena appealed to Vinny. "I made him some tea with lemon and honey, but he doesn't want to drink it."

"Great stuff," Vinny said, giving him the stern eye. "My grandma swore by it. Go ahead. Drink it up. Rowena made it for you special."

What could Cash do with Rowena gazing up at him so hopefully and his ornery ex-partner looking like he'd pour the junk down Cash's throat if he didn't take it like a man?

Hell, Cash didn't need much of a shove if drinking this mess would make Rowena's eyes light up. He grimaced inwardly, feeling a little bit guilty at the direction his runaway thoughts led him.

Truth was, he'd like to light Rowena up in every way a man could imagine. He'd already had it bad for the woman before Fair day. And the necklace deal—that had almost been more than he could take.

But Rowena's sister...damn, her sister had told him things about Rowena that had made him burn with anger, made him want to bundle her up and keep her safe. Protect her from the world, but most of all from himself.

Considering how hard that had been to swallow, how bad could a few swigs of cat-piss tea be?

Cash slugged the liquid back in a burning gulp. Once he got it down, he came up sputtering.

"That stuff tastes like hell!" he complained.

"I know. But it'll make you all better." She was teasing him, lights dancing in her eyes.

If he were a different man, he would have scooped her into his arms. Pretended to turn her over his knee. If she belonged to him he'd tickle her until she laughed and he could show her just how much better she'd made him feel.

But she wasn't his to hold, to protect. She wasn't his to love.

"You know, Rowena," Vinny teased, "you're taking such good care of the bullheaded cuss and his girls they don't even need me around anymore."

Either the time with Miss Marigold had gone to Vinny's head or Rowena's influence was at work, because it sounded for all the world as if Cash's ex-partner was matchmaking. Cash didn't know whether to scowl or smile.

Rowena flushed. "You know that's not true, Vinny," she insisted.

"Hell, I don't know," Cash said. "She's plenty bossy, but she sure makes better coffee than you."

"I make mine taste that way on purpose to try to get you to cut back on the caffeine. Maybe Rowena will have better luck reforming you." The old man's eyes twinkled. "She's a hell of a lot sweeter than I am."

"That's for sure," Cash said, but it was the taste of her he was remembering, her mouth under his. "I'll get those tables over to the garden before morning," he added, his voice rough, but not from the shouting.

He wished he could move other things out of the way as easily.

Like the heavy weight lodged in the region of his heart.

CHAPTER THIRTEEN

ROWENA WOULD NEVER be able to show her face at the local Cub Foods again.

She stared down at the daunting challenge of Cash's stove, still dazed at how fast her day had gone from bad to worse. It had seemed like such a minor snag when the frozen homemade dinners Mr. Google had prepared in case of emergency had finally run out.

Rowena had even teased Cash when he'd scrupulously saved them for the nights she was in charge of feeding the kids. After all, women the world over fed kids every day, Rowena had reasoned. And she'd managed to reach the ripe old age of twenty-seven without starving. How hard could it be to fill up two much smaller stomachs, as long as she went into battle prepared?

She'd had her arsenal of kid friendly recipes that Mr. Google had downloaded off the Internet for her. She'd tucked the shopping list torn from the magnetic pad stuck to Cash's refrigerator door into her purse—even if the military precision of the goods penned there *did* give her the willies.

A list. To shop from.

Talk about killing the whole adventure angle of the trip. She preferred a free-spirited stroll through the grocery store, choosing whatever happened to look good to her at the time. She'd gorge on fresh pineapple one week until she had canker sores. Then it would be tuna from a can—the leftovers from that meal sending the kitties she was fostering into spasms of joy.

More often still, Rowena settled for takeout, or whatever people-food happened to be sharing her refrigerator with the tins of stinky cat food. But she supposed you couldn't expect a nine-year-old and a five-year-old to eat leftover pad thai straight out of the takeout carton, no matter how hungry they were.

The one thing she'd learned for certain during her stint at the Lawless household was that hungry kids equaled cranky kids, and tonight she had already mediated her quota of sisterly arguments.

Especially battles over who got to sit in which car seat, the one nearest to where Destroyer was riding now deemed prime real estate by the sisters. "You promised you'd let me sit wherever I wanted forever and ever," Mac had whined. "Cross your heart and hope to die."

"When was that?" Rowena asked as she heaved the wheelchair into the rear compartment with Destroyer.

"When I woke up in the hospital after they glued my legs back together. The doctors said they put them together just like puzzle pieces. I got a big scar. You wanna see?"

"You showed me when you took your bath, remember?" Rowena had reminded her. "Look, Mac. The accident happened a long time ago. How about we give your big sister a break?"

Charlie had looked pretty stunned when Rowena had ruled in her favor. But maybe it was because Charlie had an idea what the rest of the afternoon was going to be like. Rowena, Charlie and Destroyer had paid for her decision the rest of the ride. Whining turned into wailing, the trip to the grocery store a visit to hell Rowena would never forget.

When they'd finally gotten back to Cash's house, Rowena

had been tempted to kiss the kitchen floor. Now she'd even resorted to sitting the disgruntled Mac in front of the television, hoping that watching an episode of *Dora the Explorer* with Destroyer would buy half an hour. Rowena needed at least that long to hunt down the army of gremlins taking dentist drills to the inside of her head.

Rubbing her temple, Rowena glanced over at Charlie. The child sat at the kitchen table, its surface covered with poster board, markers and pictures cut from a stack of old dog magazines Rowena had resurrected from her basement. Charlie looked as if she could use an aspirin or two, herself. The extra-strength orange chewable kind designed specifically for those times when your little sister was driving you nuts.

Rowena dug out the contents of the grocery sack she'd lugged in fifteen minutes before and lined her purchases up for inspection. Macaroni—check. Butter—check. Milk—check. Hot dogs—check. Corn—uh-oh. Where the heck was the corn?

She rummaged once again through the sack as if the thing had a false bottom, like one of the antique writing desks Ariel liked to collect. But Rowena still came up empty. She could have sworn she'd put it on that conveyor belt thing at the checkout line. Rowena frowned. The kid behind the counter had looked a little shifty. He'd probably left the corn out of her sack on purpose, his fiendish revenge for the damage Mac had done to his eardrums.

Rowena opened the cupboard door where the canned goods were usually kept. Empty. But then she had known it would be. Cash had meant to stock up at the store the night before, but one of the other deputies had called in sick. He had ended up working a double shift instead. Rowena had told him not to worry about it. She'd just make a trip to the grocery store with the girls. How big a deal could it be?

Bryony would have warned Rowena scoffing like that was

tempting fate. There were times even her interfering older sister had a point.

Rowena closed the cupboard and leaned her forehead against it, trying to resist the urge to thump her head against the panel a few times.

"Is something wrong, Rowena?"

She turned toward the table to find Charlie regarding her with solemn eyes, her silver wire glasses a little crooked on her nose. "I don't suppose your dad would consider olives a vegetable?" She was sure she'd seen a half-empty bottle of them on the refrigerator door.

"I don't know," Charlie answered, considering. "But they wouldn't taste very good with macaroni and cheese. I thought you told Mac we were having corn. It's her favorite."

Forget the dentist drills. The gremlins had moved on to jackhammers. She was more than willing to tussle things out with MacKenzie when necessary. At least anytime except right now, when she was still reeling from her first experience of a full-fledged tantrum.

But in this case, nixing the corn and substituting something else wasn't an option. There was really no help for it. Another trip to the grocery store was a downright necessity. Who knew? Maybe she and the girls could beat some kind of record, being banned from two different grocery stores in one day.

"Better head in and tell your sister she's got a choice. It's either olives, or an emergency trip to the store."

"An emergency?" Charlie fretted her bottom lip.

"Believe me, if it wasn't, I wouldn't be setting foot out of this house tonight."

Charlie mused for a long moment. "I could get you some," she offered finally.

"Corn?" Rowena brightened. "Is there some neighbor you borrow things from?"

"No." Charlie carefully capped her purple marker. "I can get some from me. Only you've got to promise you'll put it back."

Rowena shook her head, trying to process the girl's offer through the throbbing in her head. "You have corn stashed somewhere?"

Fine lines of worry etched between Charlie's brows. "You *will* put it back, won't you?"

She seemed so concerned Rowena made an *X* on her chest with one finger, just as she and Bryony and Ariel had when they were kids. "Cross my heart."

The familiar vow seemed to calm the little girl's doubts. Charlie climbed out of the kitchen chair. "You can come with me to get it if you want to. As long as you promise not to tell anybody else where it is."

Charlie slipped her hand into Rowena's. Her fingers felt small, warm with a trust that nudged Rowena's heart. She suspected Charlie would head off to her bedroom. Ariel had kept Oreos in a shoe box in her closet until an army of big black ants had demanded she share. But instead of heading deeper into the house, Charlie went to the back door and led Rowena out into the fenced backyard.

"You don't have a secret garden where you're growing sweet corn out here, do you?" Rowena teased, but Charlie wasn't laughing.

The child led Rowena to the bottom of the oak tree. "You gotta climb up. You know how to climb?"

"It's been a while."

Charlie bit one ragged nail. "Maybe we better not risk it. I don't want to break you like I broke Mr. Google."

"That was just a freak accident, honey. You didn't break anybody." But she could tell Charlie wasn't buying it. "I'll be really careful," she promised instead.

Charlie scrambled like a little monkey up the ladder nailed

to the trunk, then watched with a worried frown as Rowena followed suit.

Rowena pulled herself onto the platform, saw the framing that would have made two walls. She looked around. "Wow. What a great tree house."

"It's not a tree house," Charlie said. "It was just s'posed to be one. It was going to be a fort, with towers and flags and even bars on one of the windows, like a jail. And Daddy was going to make a slide so I could get down real fast if the bad guys took it over."

"Really?"

"Yeah. We were going to play cops and robbers, Daddy and me. But now, well, this place isn't for fun anymore." She was hovering on the edge of saying something, sharing secrets, trusting. Rowena could feel it. It should have been so easy for a child of Charlie's age, so natural. And yet Rowena sensed the gravity in the little girl's decision to bring someone up the makeshift ladder to a place that was no longer meant for fun.

"What is your tree house for now, sweetie?"

"Emergencies. They talked all about it on television. You need a disaster kit just in case your house gets bombed."

Rowena did a double take. "Bombed?"

"I saw it on the news. These houses all smashed up. The man said it was a bomb."

Rowena stroked the child's hair. "It was an awful, terrible thing that happened. But those bombs fell in a country far away. It's not going to happen to you." Charlie didn't seem comforted. Instead she crammed herself back deeper into the corner of the unfinished framing.

"Those houses fell down on soldiers, you know. And policemen just like my daddy."

"Oh, Charlie."

"It's okay," Charlie insisted. "If anything happens I'm all

ready to save him now. See?" From the cover of leaves she pulled out a green plastic tub. "Mommy used to put pretend flowers and stuff in it, but she doesn't want anything in our house anymore. Not her flowers. Or Daddy. Or Mac and me."

"You don't know that, sweetheart."

"Daddy said she got a divorce."

"That's between your daddy and mommy. It doesn't have anything to do with you."

"That's a lie." Charlie regarded her doubtfully. "We're the ones that don't have a mommy anymore."

Rowena could hardly argue with that. She swallowed hard. "Will you show me what's inside your box?"

Charlie popped open the tub's lid, rummaging around. Rowena looked inside the container herself, her heart aching. She knew where all Cash's bandages had gone. Boxes and boxes of them crowded against a stockpile of canned goods. A flashlight complete with extra batteries lay atop an old blanket. The stethoscope from a toy doctor kit nestled up in a corner. A cupcake was starting to mold against its cellophane wrapper.

Charlie held up a shrink-wrapped rawhide dog bone that had been stowed amongst her provisions. "I put this in when we brought Clancy—I mean Destroyer—home. I guess the regular old bandages will work on dogs, too, if you can make them stick to all that hair. I asked Mr. Google if I can have his cast after the doctor takes it off. He thinks I want to show it to my class, but I really want to put it up here, just in case. I don't know how to make casts."

"Sweetheart, if somebody needs a cast we'll take them to the doctor."

Charlie selected a can of corn from among the foodstuffs and bottled water she had stored there. She handed the corn to Rowena. "Mac's got lots of doctors. They didn't make her well. Maybe I'd have a better chance if I tried it myself. I've been getting books about doctors. It's okay I took them. They say 'free take one' on that rack thing they're in."

She grabbed a pamphlet from her stash and put it in Rowena's hand. "They've got lots of stuff to read. Books with pictures of brains and your spinal cord. It's like a snake that goes all the way down your back and has these little spiky things sticking out. And if somebody breaks it you can't move your arms or legs or anything. Did you ever feel your head to see if it's hard enough not to let your brain get broken?"

"Nope. I never have. But my dad used to say I've got the hardest head in the family, so I figure I'm okay." Rowena tapped her fist lightly on Charlie's head in hopes of teasing a smile from her. "I bet you're safe, too."

"I'm not so sure about that."

"Oh, sweetheart. I wish…" Rowena's voice trailed off. What could she say to this worried little soul? *I wish I could make everything better for you? I wish I could fix your little sister and make your daddy smile again the way he did in that picture with you. I wish you would never have to think of things like tidal waves and car accidents and mommies who leave you behind.* But there were things Rowena couldn't fix, couldn't change, no matter how much she wished she could.

"Rowena?" Charlie slipped a small hand into hers, curled those warm fingers tight around Rowena's. "Know what?"

"What, honey?"

"I wish I had leg braces instead of Mac."

Rowena's throat felt tight. "It's wonderful you love your sister that much."

A tiny crease dented Charlie's brow as if she were trying to puzzle out what Rowena said.

"That you'd take Mac's pain away if you could," Rowena explained.

"That's not what I meant," Charlie said. "It's just that if I were hurt like Mac, my daddy would see me again. See, 'cause when your sister gets braces, you get invisible."

Rowena swallowed hard. She pictured Cash's tormented features, his exhaustion, his battle, trying to will his child to walk. She remembered the pictures she'd seen on the wall—Charlie, obviously Daddy's girl—building tree houses, hanging from jungle gyms, camping out in the make-believe wilderness of the backyard.

"Your daddy loves you, Charlie," Rowena said, knowing it was true.

"Well…you never know," Charlie said, and Rowena knew the little girl must be thinking of her mother.

"Rowena?" Charlie scooted over, as close to Rowena as she could. The little girl leaned up against her. She looked so small it broke Rowena's heart. "You know what scares me most?"

Rowena tucked Charlie safe in the curve of her arm. "What?"

Big eyes peered up at her. "Someday I'll get so invisible nobody will ever see me again."

"WE'VE GOT A PROBLEM," Cash warned as he walked into the kitchen, slinging his dark brown jacket on the back of the nearest chair. That change alone, from the king of organization, should have set warning bells ringing in Rowena's head.

"Some rescheduling snafu?" Rowena asked as he set down the thermos he took to work every day filled with coffee. "Don't tell me some other poor deputy caught chicken pox from his kids."

At least that was one danger Cash wasn't in. When she asked if he'd had the disease he'd laughed and said with five brothers there was no escape. His mother had battled itchy sores and boys spoiling for a fight for almost two months by the time the house in Chicago had been pox-free.

"No. Looks like Rasmussen was the only lucky SOB to get that. We all got together at the office and sent him a Teddy Bear gram. This person dressed up in a bear suit delivers a bouquet of sugar cookies and sings the chicken pox song. I keep hoping it'll distract everybody from the fact I brought that damned dog home. It's somebody else's turn to get the devil tormented out of them."

If only another round of teasing was all Rowena had in store for him, her task would be a whole lot easier. She squirmed inwardly at the memory of Charlie's revelation in the tree house an hour before.

As problems went, she figured she had a far bigger one to discuss than he did. But she wasn't going to hit the guy with it the moment he walked through the door. Feed him first, her instinct said, then talk to him about the little girls who were playing out in the backyard.

"If complications from chicken pox are out of the running for trouble of the day, what's the deal? You've got a problem besides burned macaroni and cheese and hot dogs that exploded in the microwave?" She dished up a scoop of her latest creation. "Don't worry. I scraped most of the black stuff off the bottom of the pan. I think I owe you a new one, though." She indicated the pot soaking in the sink. "I was just about ready to blow taps."

"A military funeral, huh?" Cash eyed it and grimaced. "You should have seen the casualties around here when I first started cooking. I even managed to set the oven on fire that first Christmas Eve. It had been so long since I'd cooked anything in the oven, a mouse had stored dry cereal under a panel inside it. When I turned the damned thing on the whole house filled with smoke."

"Okay. You win. That's a way better cooking disaster story than mine. Of course, this is only my first attempt. I still might beat the pants off you." Rowena cringed. Oops. Way wrong thing to say.

He looked flustered himself, as if he were considering the same thing she was. He hooked his thumb behind his belt buckle, as if to make sure it was fastened up tight.

It was. No chance of an instant replay of the shower scene here. Too bad it wasn't on a tape where she could just hit Rewind. *For pity's sake, Rowena! You said you weren't having sex with the man!* Bryony's scolding ran through her mind.

I said I wasn't having sex with him. I didn't say I wasn't thinking about it.

"So what's this problem?" she asked, trying not to notice the way the muscles of his forearms rippled as he unbuttoned his cuffs and rolled them to his elbows one at a time.

"The school called." Cash grabbed a scraper and raked it across the burned patch on the bottom of the pot.

"What's wrong?" Rowena was almost afraid to ask. Had Charlie confided her secret to her teacher? Rowena knew Charlie felt disconnected even from her own best friend. No matter how the subject of Charlie's troubles was broached to Cash, Rowena knew it would devastate him.

For an instant she hoped she wouldn't have to be the one to tell him about the tree house, Charlie's fears—fears seen through a child's eyes, and yet heartbreakingly real.

How did you tell a man who was fighting to keep his head above water that his best wasn't good enough? And no matter how Rowena couched the words, that was exactly what she'd be telling him.

She swallowed hard. "Is it Charlie?"

Cash abandoned the pot and turned to look at her, his big hands glistening wet. "How did you know?"

I found all those bandages you're missing. And by the way, did you notice that Charlie's invisible?

"Chalk another one up to intuition."

Cash frowned. "I thought we agreed none of that psycho-garbage around here."

"It's not psycho, it's psychic, really. And I'm not, I'm simply good at—never mind. Just tell me what's up."

Cash grabbed a towel and dried off his hands. "The kids' bus driver called me at work. Destroyer got loose and was at the bus stop today."

"That's impossible." Rowena crossed to the back door and peered out to where Charlie and the dog were curled up at the foot of the tree, a book on the child's lap. "He was fenced in out back the whole time. I let him out before we left the house this morning. I sent Charlie off to her stop and then waited for Mac's bus with her. Once I got her loaded on, I came back in the house and let him in. Really, Cash. He was right here by the back door, waiting for me to load him in the van to head to the shop." She tried to untangle the mystery. "Maybe there's another Newfoundland in the neighborhood."

"Trust me. I would have noticed."

"Well, it wasn't Clanc—I mean, Destroyer!" Dread pulled at Rowena, Cash's warning the day he'd agreed to take the dog home resonating inside her. *The first sign of trouble and back he goes...* She could only imagine what that loss would do to Charlie. "Destroyer." She all but spat the word. "That's a terrible name! Talk about your self-fulfilling prophecies! Ask Charlie! She'll tell you it wasn't him at the bus stop."

"Charlie gave this mystery dog of yours a big kiss before she got on the bus."

"But—but he was in the back yard," Rowena insisted helplessly. "I swear it!"

"The bus driver said that dog's been out there every school-day for the past week. Just sits there with the kids, watching until he pulls up. And when the kids load onto the bus, it's like the dog's counting them."

Was that a smile cracking Cash's face? Rowena wondered in amazement. "Somehow I wouldn't have thought you'd find this funny," she said.

The watts on his smile spiked up, making Rowena's heart flutter. She turned her back to him to hide her reaction to it.

"It's something the bus driver said," Cash crossed to the door, flattened one hand against it. A shiver of awareness rippled through Rowena as she felt the heat of him, caught the subtle scent of him as he leaned close to look over her shoulder into the yard. "When the driver tried to shoo the dog away, Destroyer gave him this long-suffering look as if to say 'I know you're supposed to be in charge here, but after all, you're only human. I'd rather keep track of the kids myself.'"

"Cash, really," Rowena argued. "You've got a chainlink fence out back. What's the dog going to do? Pole vault over it?"

"I don't know." Cash's warm breath stirred the wisps of hair clinging to her neck, and she wondered what it would be like if he lowered his mouth to that tender skin. "All I can tell you is that Destroyer gives me that very same look every night when I tuck the girls in bed."

Rowena closed her eyes, imagining Cash pulling the covers up to his daughters' chins, kissing their foreheads. A ritual he'd performed alone for so long. It made her feel better somehow, knowing that now he had someone else to share that time with. She turned to look into Cash's face, saw the sudden vulnerability in the curve of his mouth. He was so close, and yet, so very far away.

"Destroyer loves the girls," Rowena said, feeling a little breathless.

"He does. At least that's one thing we have in common."

Cash lifted a strand of Rowena's hair, ran it between his fingertips. He peered down at the golden strands as if they held the secrets of the world, his nostrils flaring slightly.

Rowena sucked in a steadying breath, knowing that all she had to do was tip her head just a little to kiss those fingers. Would that make it easier to tell him what he needed to know? Cushion the painful truth she had to tell him?

No. No matter how much she believed in the healing power of touch, Cash would see it as something darker, a betrayal that held the potential of hurting his girls. And how could she blame him? In a few more weeks, her time in the Lawless house would be over. Clancy—alias Destroyer—would hopefully be part of the family. She'd have fixed things as much as her gift allowed her to. And then, she'd do exactly what her gift required of her. Walk away to find the next creature she could love to a brighter future.

"Cash, there's something you need to know," she began, trying to tame the catch in her voice. "It's about Charlie."

His questioning gaze caught hers. "Charlie?"

The sharp ring of the telephone made them spring apart as if they'd been struck by lightning.

Rowena rubbed her neck, as if to obliterate the trails of heat his breath had left on her skin.

"It's probably someone trying to sell you siding," she said with false brightness. "I'll get it. You go see the girls."

"But what about—"

"It'll keep." She all but shoved him out the door, glad for a reprieve, time to catch her breath, sort out the emotions racketing inside her, time to form her words in a way that would do the least harm.

She heard the Newfie's deep woof of greeting, Charlie's more solemn hello and Mac's shriek of delight.

Rowena snagged the phone, put it to her ear. "Lawless residence."

No answer.

"Hello?" Rowena said.

"Where's Cash?" a woman's voice, sultry and cultured, demanded without preamble.

"Who wants to know?"

"Just tell him it's Lisa."

His ex-wife? Rowena tensed. Hadn't she guessed as much the moment she'd heard the woman's voice? So this was the woman who had abandoned Mac and Charlie for the past two years, who had divorced Cash.

The woman Mrs. Delaney had defended, saying that leaving might have been the only way Lisa Lawless could survive.

"Who are you?" Lisa Lawless demanded.

Rowena felt her temper prickle, and yet—it couldn't be comfortable, hearing a female voice in your ex-husband's house, no matter what the circumstances of the divorce. And it wouldn't do any good to alienate the woman within the first two minutes of opening her mouth.

"I'm the babysitter," Rowena explained.

"You don't sound like Vinny to me."

"I'm not. I'm just filling in."

Rowena looked outside to where father and daughters were playing now. Cash with Mac on his shoulders, Charlie, her book placed neatly on the picnic table, was now pumping her legs in the swing. In spite of the girls' obvious pleasure, Rowena could see the stiffness in Cash, knew he was trying to puzzle out what she'd been about to tell him.

"I'd like to talk to Cashel now," Lisa said impatiently.

"Cashel? Uh, right. Cash." Rowena asked her to hold, went to the door and opened it. She fought to keep her voice steady as she called out. "Cash, the phone. It's for you."

He loped in, Mac, rosy-cheeked, hanging onto his ears. Cash growled like a wolf and faked gobbling up her little arm. "Hey, kid. I need one of my ears." He gestured with the phone. Mac let go, and Rowena gently grabbed her by the waist.

"No!" Mac protested, wriggling in frustration. "I don't want to get down! Tyler James's crocodiles will eat me."

"It's okay," Cash told Rowena. "Just leave her where she is. This will only take a minute."

Rowena angled herself so only he could see her. "It's Lisa." Rowena mouthed the name, hauling Mac into her arms as Cash's face turned grim. "Come on, sweetie," she said aloud. "We need to figure out something for dessert."

"Can we make my daddy a cupcake?" Mac asked, distracted for the moment by the prospect of pink frosting and confetti cake.

Rowena heard a voice, unintelligible through the phone receiver. Cash's mouth pressed in a thin line.

"How about if we go outside and ask your sister?" Rowena carried Mac through the back door and put her back in the wheelchair. Charlie gave her a probing look, as if she knew something wasn't right when Rowena left the girls to discuss the merits of pink frosting over chocolate fudge.

By the time Rowena entered the kitchen again, Cash was somewhere deeper in the house, his voice so harsh it didn't seem possible it could belong to the man who had pushed one daughter in the swing and protected the other from imaginary crocodiles moments before.

Rowena peered around the corner into the living room. Empty. She crept in and looked down the hall. His bedroom door was closed tight.

Common courtesy demanded that she head back out to the yard. She had no right to eavesdrop on such a private conversation. And yet, Cash suddenly seemed a stranger, so hard, so angry. Almost…frightening.

Rowena nibbled at her index finger, wavering as Mrs.

Delaney's warning haunted her, Bryony's fears digging at Rowena's nerves.

For all you know she could be in hiding…he could have been abusing her…maybe leaving here was the only way Lisa could survive…

His voice rose through the door, almost audible. Rowena bit down a little harder on her finger and edged farther down the hallway. The floorboard creaked, but she didn't worry. She doubted if she banged two pot lids together he'd hear it.

"Go to hell, Lisa. You can't just waltz back in here and… you're their mother? You think I don't know that? I blame myself for that every day."

Rowena heard him pacing, could sense how caged he felt. "*You* left *them,* remember?" Cash snarled. "Sure, sure. I may be a rotten sonofabitch. But at least I'm here… Now you want to talk? After two years? You called, you visited. Hell, Mac and Charlie talk to my brother who's serving in Germany more often than they talk to you."

He paused and Rowena knew Lisa was talking. When Cash replied his bitterness seared her.

"You would prefer we settle this between us? You don't want to go through a lawyer? Are you threatening me?"

Rowena jumped at a crash against the bedroom wall, knew it was Cash's fist slamming into the panel.

"Don't you *dare* take that tone as if I'm the one who…unreasonable? I'll show you unreasonable if you… Maybe I've got something special planned for the weekend. Maybe we're going to Disney World over Thanksgiving break—they're in school, for cripes sake. You want me to yank them out for a week just because it's convenient for you?"

Rowena pressed her hand to her galloping heart. Was he refusing to let Lisa see the girls? Making it as difficult as possible for her? Was that what was really going on here?

Bitterness and anger could make good people do bad things. Was Cash behaving this way because Lisa had deserted his girls? Or was this ugliness the side of him Lisa had seen every day?

Bile rose in Rowena's throat. She knew now what Charlie must have seen, must have heard, must have sensed. Knew what had put the soul-weary look in the sensitive little girl's eyes.

Reeling from all she'd heard, Rowena started to back away from Cash's room, but her left shoulder swept against the wall behind her. Rowena whirled around. It was too late. Picture frames fell. Glass shattered, a horrific sound. Cash flung open the bedroom door, the phone in one hand, his face dark with rage.

"What the hell?" he swore. But he knew what had happened. "Lisa, I have to go." He didn't wait for an answer, just hung up the portable phone.

"I was just…I…" Rowena's throat closed.

"You were listening at the door to a private conversation?"

"Actually, I didn't have to get that close. I could pretty much hear you in the hall."

"You had no right to listen!" Cash roared.

"I know," Rowena said quietly. "And you have no right to keep Lisa away from those girls."

"Don't you dare defend her! She deserted them! And now she wants to act like it was no big deal? She's *ready* to have them back in her life? *Ready?* Well, I'm not ready to have her tear everything up again! I've already wiped up too many tears, dealt with too many nightmares."

"Cash—"

"You know when she left, Charlie started wetting the bed? She was too scared to sleep. And Mac… Christ, do you have any idea what it was like when she'd wake up crying that she wanted her mommy and I couldn't give even that small comfort to her?"

"You can give it to her now."

"It's too late! Lisa doesn't deserve those girls."

"Maybe not. But Mac and Charlie deserve the chance to know their mother hasn't forgotten them."

"They don't miss her. They don't even mention her anymore. I'm not going to let her rip my children apart again. What if she decides…"

"Decides what?"

Cash wheeled back to his bedroom, threw the phone onto the bed. When he turned back to Rowena his eyes burned black fire. "There was something different in Lisa's voice. Something dangerous…I feel it in my gut."

"Maybe different is better this time. It would be good for the girls to know their mother hasn't forgotten them. Cash, you're a loving father, but you're not their mother."

"You don't think I know that?"

"Give it a chance."

"The last time I took a chance with Lisa, it wrecked our lives. And my girls are still paying for that mistake."

"It's just a week."

"What if she wants more?" Cash challenged. "What if she wants to keep them?"

"You'll deal with that if it happens. But in the meantime, Charlie and Mac will have two parents instead of a gaping hole where their mother should be. I know you're doing the best you can, but there are problems with the girls, Cash. That's what I was trying to tell you earlier."

"Then tell me, for God's sake. What problems?"

"Things that worry me. Especially where Charlie is concerned. You'll know how scared she is, too, when you see what she's got up in her tree house—this tub full of bandages and

cans of food and everything she can think of in case some
building falls on you."

"What?"

"She's seen bombed-out buildings on the news. She told me
soldiers and policemen got killed there. She's got pamphlets
on brain damage from the doctor's office, and she's worried her
brain's going to break and she won't be able to walk, and she's
scared that when you take her to Disney World, there'll be a
tidal wave."

"Kids get scared," Cash said, but Rowena could see the
unease in his face. "Monsters in the closet, that kind of stuff."

"These aren't imaginary fears. They're real ones. Every
time she moves, she's scared something terrible is going to
happen to her, to you, to Mac. It makes me sick, thinking how
scared she must feel inside."

"I thought getting that dog was supposed to make everything
perfect for her, wasn't it?" His lip curled, mocking her.

"You didn't get the dog for Charlie," Rowena snapped.

"The hell I didn't! He's here, isn't he?"

"You brought Destroyer home because of Mac."

Cash's cheeks darkened and she knew her words had struck
someplace raw. He swore bitterly. "Maybe I should have let you
talk to Lisa on the phone. The two of you could have made a
list of everything I'm doing wrong."

"Cash, I'm on your side here. But Charlie's not stupid. She
wanted Destroyer to keep her company when you were busy
with Mac's therapy, but even I've noticed that you do everything possible to keep the dog inside with you."

"You've heard what those sessions are like when things go
badly! So I keep the dog inside to distract Mac so she doesn't
melt down. If that's a crime, then send me to jail."

Rowena's fists knotted in frustration, empathy, anger. All
overlaid by her need to make him understand. "*I* know why you

do it. *I* understand the reasons. Maybe when Charlie's older she will, too. But right now she feels…"

Rowena hesitated, hating the anger in Cash's face, hating the fact she was about to cut him even deeper.

"She feels what? Just say it. Why not? You've said every other goddamned thing you wanted to."

"She told me she wished she had braces instead of Mac."

"It doesn't take a genius to figure that one out! Charlie doesn't want her sister hurting. Neither do I! Do you know how many times I've wished I was the one who'd come out of that crash with my legs broken? They could've sawed my legs off without anesthetic and I'd have laughed the whole time if I could have saved Mac that pain!"

"At first that's what I thought Charlie meant, too. But it wasn't. She said she wished she'd gotten hurt because— because when your sister gets braces you get invisible."

"Invisible?" Cash scoffed. "It's just some crazy kid game she's got in her head. Like when she was three and I'd stick the tip of my thumb between two fingers and pretend that I'd stolen her nose. She's squawk until I gave it back."

"It's not a game," Rowena insisted. "Charlie's losing herself, Cash. She knows it. She doesn't know how to make it stop."

"Losing herself?" Cash spat. "She's nine years old! Not some wacko teenager with an identity crisis. This garbage is just more of that psychobabble bullshit you've been feeding me since the first day I met you."

"It's not—"

"First that dog is her destiny, now Charlie's invisible. What are you going to lay on me tomorrow? That I should let Mac quit trying to walk because she's tired of doing her exercises? Or maybe I should just tell Lisa to move back in and share Charlie's bedroom. That way we wouldn't have to involve a goddamned lawyer."

"Cash, I know how you feel—"

"No, you don't. You don't have the first idea how I feel. And you never will."

"I want to understand. If we could just talk this out—"

"There's not a damned thing to say. Just because I was desperate enough to take you up on your offer to help babysit my kids doesn't mean I've given you leave to butt into the rest of my life, Rowena."

"Well, somebody's got to tell you what's happening with that little girl! Cash, she—"

"Go home." Cold, hard, his voice lashed her. She reached out to touch him. He jerked free. "I said go home."

"At least let me help you clean up the glass." She started to bend down to pick up the shards that scattered the photographs strewn across the floor. Cash caught her arm, pulled her up.

"Don't touch it," he growled. "It's my mess. All of this. It's mine."

The back door banged, Charlie calling as she came through the kitchen. "Daddy, Mac's crying. She says the alligators bit her and she's supposed to make cupcakes." Charlie entered the living room, looked down the hall.

Her face paled at the wreckage. "My picture!" she cried, diving toward the glass-strewn floor, in spite of the obvious tension between the two grownups.

"Charlie, stop it!" Cash snarled, scooping her up more roughly than Rowena had ever seen him. "You're going to cut yourself."

"But my picture! Daddy, my tree house picture!"

"It's just a piece of paper, damn it! It's not worth cutting yourself over."

Rowena watched him carry his daughter out to the kitchen, heard the back door slam. She picked up the image of the tree house and laid it on the kitchen table before she scooped up her purse and keys and slipped out of the house.

She'd done what little she could, and yet she knew it wouldn't matter.

It was too late.

Cash and Charlie were already bleeding.

CHAPTER FOURTEEN

CASH DUMPED the last dustpan full of glass shards into an old cardboard box he'd tape up and put out with the garbage on Tuesday. He only wished he could do the same thing with the emotions inside him—sweep up the sharp edges and stow them away where they couldn't cut anymore.

But Lisa's call had ripped everything wide open, poison pouring out—his rage, his scorn, his hate…

Hate.

There it was. The stark truth. He hated Lisa.

The woman who'd borne him two children. The woman who'd shared his bed for six years. The woman he'd tried so damn hard to make himself love, as if you could love someone the way you were supposed to just by force of will.

He hated her for leaving him with all the wreckage to clean up when he was so damned tired he couldn't even see straight. When his girls needed so much and he had so little left to give them.

Like now, when the two of them were waiting out in the backyard, Mac with her therapy yet to get through, Charlie with her eyes so wide and worried.

Charlie's scared of everything… Rowena's words raked at his fury. *She feels invisible…. You didn't get the dog for Charlie, you got it because of Mac….*

The damn dog is here, isn't he? Cash argued in his head.

What did it matter why he'd finally caved in and brought the animal home? As for being invisible, there were times Cash would pay his last red cent to disappear himself. Just sink into oblivion, where there weren't small hands always reaching for him, little faces forever turning to him, wanting answers he couldn't give.

Times like this minute, when he had to go out to his kids and couldn't let Mac and Charlie see what he was feeling. If Charlie had been scared before, she must be downright terrified now, after the scene in the hallway. He'd even scared himself.

Cash hunkered down to put the dustpan in its place. But he didn't rise again once he released its stubby handle. His head rocked back until it rested against the mudroom wall and he rubbed his face with both hands. Instinctively he reached for the one influence he'd depended on his whole life to help beat back his temper when it raged out of control.

"Mom...I'm tired," he whispered aloud. "I'm so tired..."

It was as if he could feel the touch of Rose Lawless' work-reddened hands, her no-nonsense voice. *I know you are, son. But you've always been my strong one...strong and stubborn as the Rock of Cashel I named you for. And your babies need you.*

How many times had she told him how strong he was? That nothing on earth could defeat him? She'd believed in him as no one else ever had. Or ever would again.

The knowledge dug into his chest. She'd hate that her loss still hurt him so. Knowing that single truth helped Cash straighten.

He squared his shoulders and headed for the backyard. Somehow Charlie had wrestled her sister into the swing and was pushing Mac. Cash wondered if Charlie had done it for the same reason he had so many times before: so Mac couldn't see the worry in her face. Destroyer sat on guard beside the empty wheelchair, the dog's eyes following the children with that expression the bus driver had described. Strange, Cash thought, there was something of his own mother's steadfastness in the Newfoundland's gaze.

Of course, Rose Lawless would've been horrified at the comparison. She'd as soon let a pig inside her house as a dog. It was still a wonder to Cash how neat she'd kept that house with six boys tramping in and out.

"How about we head inside?" he called to his girls.

Mac craned herself around, her swing wavering so wildly she almost took out her sister. "Where's Rowena?" Mac cried, petulantly. "We been waiting forever an' ever."

"Rowena had to go home." The real question now was whether or not she'd ever set foot in the house again. Not to mention what he'd do tomorrow if she didn't.

"I'm *starving* for cupcakes," Mac said as Cash grabbed the swing's chain and pulled it to a stop. He plucked her from the seat and settled her on his hip. "Rowena promised we could make pink frosting and everything."

"I'm more of a chocolate frosting man myself."

"That's the whole problem of it, Daddy. You're a boy. Boys like chocolate. Girls like pink."

"I like chocolate," Charlie said, falling into the usual routine and taking hold of the handles of Mac's chair. Cash's heart hitched as he noticed for the first time how small Charlie looked, pushing the weight of the wheelchair along behind him.

"You always like everything Daddy likes." Mac dismissed her. "I like what Rowena likes better."

"Mac!" Charlie hissed. "You're gonna hurt Daddy's feelings."

"Am not. I'm just saying it's nice having a girl around here for a change."

Cash forced a chuckle. "Hey, from where I'm sitting it looks like I'm already outnumbered around here two to one."

"I don't mean *little* girls," Mac explained. "I mean a grownup girl. It's like having a mommy even if I *am* just borrowing her the way A.J. used to borrow my crayons."

"Used to?" Cash said as he opened the back door with one hand, holding it so Charlie could push the chair up the ramp he'd built there two years before. "Don't tell me A.J. finally got a box of his own?"

"Nope. I just won't share with him ever again."

Lovers' quarrel? Cash wondered, exhausted at the thought of handling yet another complication. A.J. VanDuren had been sweet on Mac since they started the early intervention program for kids with special challenges a year ago. Last Valentine's Day he'd given her a boy's idea of the most awesome present ever: a plastic heart full of edible green slime crawling with gummy worms. "You and A.J. have a fight or something?"

Mac's small chin jutted out with pure Lawless stubbornness. "He said you can't borrow a mommy, but I can so."

Borrow a mommy... Cash felt as if the kid had sucker punched him. He hesitated, busying himself with getting the girls, Destroyer and the chair back inside.

"Rowena's borrowed, isn't she, Daddy?" Mac insisted.

"Rowena's not a mommy, Mac," Charlie said in that serious tone of hers. "At least not a kid kind of mommy. Maybe a dog one."

Mac didn't like that answer. She kicked at her sister with one foot. "I didn't ask you. I asked Daddy."

"Rowena is just babysitting for a little while," Cash said, trying not to betray his unease. "Mr. Google will back soon." In fact, it was a damn shame Cash couldn't arrange a miraculous recovery for the guy or his ex-partner would be back on the job tomorrow.

Mac frowned. "A.J. says that families are supposed to have a mom and daddy or they're broken. He even says all the books in school are proof he's right, 'cause they've got mommies and daddies in every one. A.J. is a poopy-face."

Cash didn't bother to correct her. At the moment he wasn't too fond of A.J. himself.

"There are lots of different kinds of families," he said carefully. "Some have just a mommy, some a daddy or maybe just a grandma or grandpa. As long as they love each other, that's what really matters. Not whether your family is just like everybody else's."

"But you had a mommy. Didn't you, Daddy?" Mac demanded.

"Of course he did," Charlie said, rolling her eyes.

"You've seen the picture of me in my marine uniform. That lady standing next to me is my mother. Your Grandma Rose."

"She's in heaven," Mac said. "But my mommy isn't in heaven, is she?"

"She's in Chicago!" Charlie exclaimed, glancing nervously up at Cash. "I told you and told you a jillion times, Mac! Remember?"

Cash's stomach sank. Charlie had been telling Mac that Lisa was in Chicago? Then Mac must have been asking.

He remembered snapping at Rowena, telling her that his kids barely even remembered their mother anymore. That they never even mentioned Lisa's name...

It looked like he'd been wrong about that. Like so many other things.

Mac scrunched up her face. "It must be a long way to Chicago. Even farther than the moon."

"Chicago's not farther than the moon!" Charlie argued with the dignity of her years. "The moon's in outer space, so far you'd have to take a rocket ship to get there. Besides, they don't just take anybody up to the moon, you know. You've got to be an astronaut."

"Is Mommy an astronaut, Daddy?" Mac asked as he pulled out the barstool-high chair he used to boost Mac up so she could "help" at the kitchen counter.

"No, sweetheart. She's not."

"Well, Chicago *is* real far away though, right, Daddy?"

Not nearly far enough, Cash thought, looking into Mac's curious blue eyes. "I can show you where it is on the map if you want," Cash offered, trying to avoid answering the question his daughter was really asking. How far away did a mommy have to be if she almost never came to see her children?

"I don't want maps," Mac complained. "I want Rowena to play with."

"What am I, kid? Chopped liver?" Cash gave her a head a gentle knuckle rub. But she still hurt his heart. "Suddenly your old dad's not good enough?"

"'Course you are, Daddy!" Charlie exclaimed, poking her sister none too gently. "Tell him, Mac. Right now."

"Ouch! Stop pinching me!" Mac yelped, and yet something in the glare Charlie gave her must have surpassed even that indignity.

"Charlie, no pinching—" he started to warn. But Mac jumped right in.

"I'm not trying to be mean, Daddy, really. It's just, you're here all the time, but Rowena...Rowena's way different."

God, yes, Rowena was different in about a hundred ways Cash couldn't forget, no matter how hard he tried. She was soft to his hard, warm when he felt so cold. She was brave enough to be vulnerable, a kind of courage he could never again possess. "Different how?" he asked, his voice sounding strange even to his own ears.

"She jingles all the time."

Cash thought of the bracelets Rowena wore on her slender wrists, the music they made, even when she was in the other room. He couldn't help the way his spirits lifted at the sound, knowing she would soon appear.

"She smells good, too," Mac added.

"Daddy doesn't smell bad!" Charlie defended.

"I didn't say he smelled bad. He just doesn't smell pretty."

"That's a good thing for a deputy, right?" Cash tried to joke. "If I smelled like flowers the bad guys would probably laugh in my face."

"Rowena doesn't smell like flowers, silly. She smells like… like…"

"Lemonade," Cash supplied. Charlie's gaze snapped up to his. He felt his cheeks warm under his daughter's searching stare, thought of how Rowena's hair had felt in his hand, the way the scent of her had filled him with longings he dared not allow. Needs obliterated when he'd raged at her in the hallway. And by his duty to the girls he loved more than life.

"That's right, Daddy!" Mac piped up in delight. "She *does* smell like lemonade. See, Charlie? Even Daddy says Rowena smells better than he does! And Rowena gets to use all the colors in her crayon box. I wish we could."

"Back to crayons again?" Cash tried to decipher what Mac was trying to tell him. "What do you mean, kitten?"

"She's got orange and pink and yellow and blue and purple in her shop. We just get to use gray."

"Are you talking about the house?"

Mac nodded.

"I thought…" Cash stopped himself. What had he been thinking? He'd kept the house just the way Lisa had left it. Thought he'd been doing what was right for the girls' sake. They'd been forced to endure so many other changes.

"I thought you liked the house just the way it was. The

way…" Obviously avoiding saying Lisa's name to the girls didn't mean they weren't thinking about her. "The way your mom left it."

"I don't remember Mommy that much anymore. But Charlie does. She tells me 'bout her sometimes."

Cash's throat felt tight as he glimpsed Charlie's face, pinched with guilt.

"I only talk about Mommy when she makes me, Daddy," Charlie apologized. "I won't ever again if you don't want me to."

Charlie knew, Cash realized with a sick lurch in his stomach. Charlie knew talking about Lisa upset him. All these months his daughter had been trying to shield him—from his own rage, from MacKenzie's questions, from the woman who'd painted the house gray and left empty places at the kitchen table, on the walls, in their lives.

Charlie was protecting him… Damn it, he cursed in self-disgust. He was the one who was supposed to be protecting her!

"Daddy?"

He felt a tug at his sleeve, looked down into Charlie's worried face. "Are you mad at me?"

"No, sweetheart," he said. "I'm the one who made the mistake."

For the rest of the evening he tried to lose himself in a whirlwind of cake mix speckled with broken egg shells. Spatulas he let the girls lick clean of batter. He worked through Mac's exercises, Destroyer watching by his side. He felt Charlie's loneliness emanating from the gray room where the little girl had gone with her book. And he fought the truths Rowena had put into his head, the needs his little girls' questions had finally driven home.

They wanted their mother. Even though she'd deserted them. Had rarely called them. Didn't deserve them.

It didn't matter that Lisa was nothing like Cash's own mom had been, or Rowena with her jingling bracelets and her laughter and all the colors of the rainbow. Rowena was right. Lisa was the only mother Charlie and Mac would ever have.

It was well past midnight when he went into Mac's room, expecting her to be asleep. Instead, she was lying bare-legged with her feet up by her headboard, while she stared out her window at the sky.

"What are you doing, you goofball?" Cash said, kneeling down beside the bed. "Your head's supposed to be on your pillow."

Mac rolled over toward him and sighed sleepily. "I got some questions. But a moon is real hard to talk to."

Cash's throat constricted as he tucked Mac's ballerina bear tighter into her arms. "You could talk to me."

"It's girl stuff, Daddy. You wouldn't understand."

She was right, Cash knew.

Girl stuff… Those feminine secrets that had daunted him for two long years.

How many times had he thought about them himself on nights when he couldn't sleep? He'd imagined trying to explain to Charlie how her body would soon be changing. About boys and tampons and how deathly important it was that she protect herself. He'd imagined trying to help her understand how precious she was. Worth waiting for. Worth far more than the backseat of a Buick or a wall-shaker in an elevator frozen between two floors.

Worthy of a man far better than Cash had ever been.

Girl stuff…

Rowena was right. He might love his girls with every cell in his body. Might be willing to fight for them, die for them. But he'd never be their mother.

"I love you, Mac. You know that, don't you?"

"Yeah. I love you, too. 'Cept when you make me do therapy sometimes."

Cash smiled in spite of his pain. No pulling punches with that kid.

Cash scooped Mac up and turned her around. He tucked her legs under the sheets, covering up scars he couldn't change.

"You're going to get cold lying that way," he explained. "Your legs are supposed to be under the blanket. Not on top of it."

"I s'pose," Mac allowed. He leaned over her and kissed her forehead, wondering why love had to hurt so much.

"Mac?"

"Humm?"

"I'd move heaven and earth for you and your sister."

Tonight he had to move something far harder.

The boulder of hate weighing down his own heart.

Cash went to his room, picked up the phone and punched in Lisa's number. He ground his teeth as it rang, hoping the answering machine would pick up and he could just leave a message. Wouldn't have to say the words to her.

But just when he thought he might be in luck for once in his life, he heard the bounces and bleeps of Lisa fumbling with the receiver.

"Hello?"

"It's Cash."

"Cash?" He could hear her pushing herself upright in bed. She'd have that bewildered look Mac sometimes did when he woke her from a sound sleep. One more of the marks that he'd tried to deny she'd left on his daughters.

"You can take the girls for the weekend."

"Great! That's…great," Lisa said, and he could hear the relief in her, and something else. An undercurrent of fear? "But it's…it's two o'clock in the morning. Couldn't this have waited?"

"I was afraid I'd change my mind." He wished the words back the instant he said them. Exposing the truth to an enemy was a chance he didn't want to take.

"Cash, I really do appreciate you letting me take them. And…everything else you've done for the girls."

"You want to show your appreciation, Lisa?" he growled. "Bring them back in decent emotional condition. I don't want to have to patch up your messes again."

"Cash…" Was that a quaver in her voice? Or just the last threads of sleepiness? "The last thing I want to do is hurt them."

"Somehow I don't find that very reassuring. You said the same thing when you called to tell me you weren't coming home."

"Cash, I—"

"They have a four-day weekend coming up soon. You can get them Thursday night, bring them back before Tuesday morning."

"That would be…wonderful. Thank you."

What the hell was he supposed to say to that? You're welcome? She wasn't welcome. Not to his kids, not back into his life. He let the silence stretch between them until she broke it.

"I'll pick them up as soon as they're off school. Make sure to pack their swimsuits. My new condo has an indoor swimming pool."

He should have been glad about that. Mac would get some exercise. Her muscles wouldn't get stiff. "I'll pack 'em."

"And I thought I'd take them to Brookfield Zoo. Do you think they'd like that?"

Cash pushed back a surge of bitterness. When was the last time he'd had the time or energy to take the girls someplace like that? Somewhere special Mac and Charlie would remember?

"Yeah. They'd like it."

By the time he finally hung up the phone, he felt so drained he sank down on his bed and threw his arm over his eyes. He tried not to remember how natural Rowena had looked cuddled with the girls on his pillows that first morning. How safe, how comforted, how at peace his children had seemed for that tiny space in time.

The way a child should feel with a mother. How would they be with Lisa? He'd never know.

Cash swallowed a lump in his throat, his jaw clenching hard.

Let it go, he told himself.

It was done. All the arrangements were made. He'd explained to her about Mac's chair, booster carseats and such. Every question was asked and its answer filed away—except for the one that really mattered.

Had he just made the biggest mistake of his life?

CHAPTER FIFTEEN

IT WAS HARD TO STAY ANGRY at a woman who kept plying him with coffee first thing in the morning, Cash realized as he leveled a bleary eye at Rowena. Especially when he had figured she'd never set foot in his kitchen again.

Tiny turquoise stones embroidered around the V-neck blouse she wore shimmered against her creamy throat, the notch in the fabric revealing just the barest hint of cleavage. No question about it, Cash thought grimly. He was definitely underdressed.

His police academy sweats were cut off above the knee. His hunter-green terrycloth bathrobe hung open because its belt had come up missing after being put to use in one of the girls' games. Cool air tickled the fine mat of hair on the rectangle of skin left exposed as he crossed to the counter and grabbed a steaming mug. He tried to ignore the strange sensation beneath his ribs when she lifted her own cup to those soft pink lips he'd kissed and her bracelets jangled softly.

"What are you? A glutton for punishment?" he grumbled, tugging his robe a little tighter over his bare chest. "You aren't supposed to be here."

She eyed him a little warily, and yet there was the tenacity of a bulldog in the tilt of her chin. "I promised I'd help you with the girls until Vinny gets well. He's not well yet, is he?"

"No," he said a little too vehemently. Then more quietly,

"No. But we didn't exactly part on the best of terms yesterday. In fact, I was mad as hell."

"Not much question where MacKenzie gets her temper. After her little meltdown in the grocery store, you're just not that scary, Deputy."

Really? he wanted to say. *I managed to scare myself.*

"You had plenty of reason to be angry last night. What with Lisa calling after all this time. She—she hasn't been trying to talk to the girls, see them, has she, Cash? You haven't been keeping her away?"

Cash wondered why the disappointment hovering about Rowena's lips bothered him so much. Even if he *had* been keeping the girls from Lisa, he would have been doing it for their own protection, he reasoned, feeling a little surly. But he hadn't been.

"The last time Lisa saw them was around Christmas. She buzzed in for the day, stayed about an hour and dumped off a couple of extravagant presents. She gave Mac this whole elaborate stage thing with dolls you could make dance, except you have to be able to stand up to make them work. The only part of it Mac can play with is that ballerina bear she takes to bed."

Bitterness curled his lip. "The kid can't dance anymore. She can't even walk, and she gives her goddamned ballerina dolls. Mac hitched her way over to the VCR on her bottom the way she does, to play one of her old dance recitals, and Lisa just—just split. Ran out the door like the house was on fire."

Cash's throat convulsed. "That was big fun, that Christmas. Trying to explain why Mommy wasn't staying for the afternoon like she'd promised. Lisa hasn't asked to see the girls since."

What the devil was Rowena looking at him like that for? As if she were still waiting...for an answer, he realized.

"No," he said bluntly. "I haven't kept Lisa out of Mac and Charlie's lives. Now...well, I wish to God I could."

"But you can't."

"I thought we'd agreed you weren't going to interfere in my life."

"I know, I know. One more of my fatal flaws, at least according to my sisters. *Just keep your nose in your own business, Rowena. Your own life isn't exactly going perfectly, now, is it?*"

Cash pulled out the kitchen chair across from her and sank down, cradling the mug of coffee between his two hands. Warmth seeped into him, but he wasn't sure why, whether it was the smell of the coffee, the heat from the pottery or the fact that Rowena's cup nestled mere inches from his own.

"There's one of life's more aggravating mysteries for you." She grimaced, a little sheepish. "How come it's so much easier to see how other people should manage their lives than it is to fix your own?" She peeped at him from beneath a fan of gold-tipped lashes, and Cash sensed a very real ache beneath her humor.

It was a relief to be able to change the subject from his world to hers, at least for a little while. "Your life needs fixing?"

"Depends on who you ask. I mean, I've got my pet shop. I love my work. I think it's important."

There was a time Cash would have had to fight to keep from sneering at her assertion. But now he couldn't help but think of Charlie at the bus stop, kissing Destroyer goodbye. "So that's all good news, right?"

She smiled. "It is." Then why did she look a little wistful? "I guess I never realized before what doing a good job means for me."

"What's that?"

"If I do what I'm supposed to do, I'm always letting go. Maybe I didn't notice that so much until I watched you with your girls, Cash. You hang on tight."

"Too tight sometimes." Cash shifted the cup around in his

hands, staring into the dark brew. "After you left yesterday, I found out I was wrong about the girls not missing their mother. Charlie's just been trying to hide it from me. *She's* the one who's been fielding Mac's tough questions about Lisa. When Mac blurted it out, Charlie was afraid I'd be mad at her. Mad at her," Cash repeated again, shaking his head. "Just because my kid was talking about her own mother."

Cash heard a soft tinkle of bracelets as Rowena moved to cup her hands over his, cocooning him in her touch. She ran her fingertip over his knuckle in a caress so tender he had to swallow hard before he could speak.

"I didn't know they still missed her. I didn't *want* to know," he corrected with brutal honesty. "If you hadn't said the things you did to me yesterday, Rowena, I wouldn't have been listening any more carefully than I have been for the past two years."

"You're a wonderful listener. Those girls are lucky to have you. They adore you and I don't blame them."

Something about her words pulled Cash's gaze to hers, those eyes drawing him in. And for a heartbeat he wanted her to mean what she'd said in a way far different than she ever could. He wondered what it would be like to be the man Rowena Brown adored, all of her big, generous heart wide open to him.

He took a sip from his cup, using that as an excuse to break the contact between them. But when her hands fell away he felt the chill of it clear down to his core.

"I called Lisa last night. She's taking the girls for a few days in a week and a half."

"Oh, Cash!" Rowena's eyes glowed with pride in him. "It will be so good for them."

"I hope so. It will be good for you, too."

"How's that?"

"Last night when I couldn't sleep I made a few calculations.

Between Lisa taking the kids for four days and Vinny's convalescence almost over, if I add in some of the vacation time I have coming at work, you can be off the hook come Monday."

"What?"

"I could probably even manage without you the rest of this week. You remember Charlie's best friend Hope Stone?"

"Jake and Deirdre's daughter."

He wasn't surprised that Rowena remembered their names. "When I asked Deirdre to watch the kids at the fair, she said it was no trouble. She offered to keep the kids a few more nights if I needed help. I just never took her up on it."

"Oh."

Why didn't Rowena sound more relieved? She tilted her head, and he could see her delicate throat work. "That's—you really shouldn't have. I mean, I don't mind watching the girls. In fact…"

"They like having you here, too." His voice dropped low. "Maybe too much."

Rowena's mouth opened, closed. "I understand."

"Rowena, I'll never be able to repay you for what you've done for my family during the time you've been here. You've opened my eyes."

And my heart…?

"Cash, you really didn't believe I was coming back this morning, did you?" Damn if she didn't look genuinely stunned. "You thought I'd leave you stranded with two girls to get to school, a babysitter with a broken leg, cupboards that would do Mother Hubbard proud and your job to do?"

How could he tell her the truth? The thing that scared him most of all? Imagining what it would be like when she *was* gone, the music of her bracelets silenced, the scent of her hair, summer-fresh on his pillow, fading, all the colors in the crayon box tucked away. Knowing that the longer he postponed the inevitable moment she left the gray house behind, the harder it was going to be for everyone when she disappeared for good.

He told himself he was trying to shield his daughters from that hurt. And yet deep inside he knew the truth: she was burrowing her way into even *his* hard heart. With her courage, her fierce protectiveness, her ability to see into the dark places inside him and not run the other way.

If she stayed much longer, he didn't know if he could resist her. He just wasn't that strong. And he'd meant what he'd said to her sister that night after the Harvest Fair. He was no man for a woman as full of light and life as Rowena Brown.

"Have you told the girls I'm leaving yet?" Rowena's query brought him back to his kitchen and the last time he'd see her sitting across from him at the table.

"No."

"Maybe they could still come to the shop sometimes until you get off work. Really, Cash, I love having them there. They're no trouble—at least, not unless they both want to sit in the seat by Destroyer or we run out of corn for supper."

Her humor made him ache. Her eyes pleaded.

"I'm not sure prolonging this is a good idea."

Rowena's face fell. She nibbled at her bottom lip and he could tell that he'd hurt her.

"It's not that you haven't done a wonderful job with Mac and Charlie. You've been…" A scene flashed into his head, Rowena in his bed, his children cuddled around her, their toys in disarray. How many times in the weeks since had he imagined what it would have been like to lie down on top of the covers that blanketed them, stretch his arm across them and gather them close while they dreamed dreams too sweet for him ever to understand.

What would it be like to belong in that picture? But he knew he never could.

"It's okay," Rowena said. "It's your decision to make. You don't have to explain."

"Yes, I do. I won't have you thinking you did something wrong. I'm the problem. I want you too much. And…I can't have you."

Her eyes pierced right through him, to where his chest felt too small. "Why can't you?"

"My life is too complicated. I barely have time to shower some days let alone— A relationship takes time and energy and I don't have either by the end of the day."

"Who said it had to be a relationship? Couldn't it just be… something we both wanted? A…soft place where you could catch your breath? Give yourself something you need for just a little while? You're a man, Cash. Not just a father. And at the moment, you're running on empty. You have to fill yourself up or soon you'll really have nothing left to give."

"Rowena, you don't understand."

"Don't I? What kind of example are you setting for the girls right now? That life's hard and difficult? That you have to fight through it every moment? That it's wrong to take care of yourself even a little? There will always be responsibilities, Cash, duties that you're responsible for. What about joy?"

"Exactly where would you suggest I find that? Someplace between Mac's wheelchair and Charlie being tossed out by her mother like last week's garbage?"

"You have to find joy yourself or you can never teach it to them. And they need that, Cash, more than they need anything else. Or how can they survive? More important, why would they want to?"

He stood, stalked to the back door, looking at the tree house, half-finished, abandoned like his children were. His voice turned gravelly in his throat. "Rowena, I'm doing the best I can."

"You have to do better."

He swung around, wanting anger, wanting to bite down on the bullet and keep his head down, charging into combat mode. The mode he understood. Was good at. Survival. But survival wasn't living. It wasn't playing cops and robbers with Charlie or having Mac stand on top of his feet while he taught her to waltz. It wasn't laughter or light or Rowena's mouth under his, so eager, so spontaneous, so full of promise.

Even before Lisa's betrayal had left him bitter he'd have been no kind of man for Rowena. He'd already been hard inside, a soldier, without the tiniest bit of whimsy in his soul.

Cash heard footsteps behind him. Felt Rowena's hands. She slid them up his back, his muscles tensing beneath her fingers as they traced up the ridge of his spine, then spread across the breadth of his shoulders. He hardened beneath his sweats as she kissed him just beneath his shoulder blade. She slipped her arms around him. Her hands slid beneath the robe, her palms burning prints on his bare skin as she pressed her body tight against his back, holding onto him.

He could feel every inch of her through the soft cotton, her breasts flattening against him, the slight swell of her belly, her thighs against the back of his legs. Her hair teased his bare neck, the silky wisps trailing across his skin arousing him more fiercely than he'd ever been before.

And he wondered what it would be like. To be clean. To be whole. To be hers. Her man. Her lover...

He turned in the circle of her arms, meaning to pull away from her, put distance between himself and sweet temptation. But she wouldn't let him. She just burrowed closer, hung on tighter, melding the front of her to him, until his erection lay heavy against her stomach and her hands splayed across his bare chest, fingertips skimming his nipples, making him burn for the flick of her tongue on his skin, the sweet suction of her mouth taking sips of his throat, his jaw, his mouth.

Why didn't he push her away? Because some part of him had imagined this for far too long, the warm cove between her thighs cradling his hardness, his hands cupping her butt and lifting her up…lowering her down onto him inch by inch.

To feel the warm in her, taste the sweet in her, her body hot underneath him, wanting him so badly she cried out his name. Making love to him with so much passion he'd get to keep just a little of her with him when she was gone.

And now she was going. He was sending her away. And part of him was glad. That fierce, primal part he couldn't deny. Because now, with the girls sound asleep in their rooms and no future encounters to tempt him, he could kiss her, just kiss her. Touch her one time, before it was too late.

Cash buried his hands in her hair, tipped her face up to his and took what he'd been craving. His tongue swept the seam between her lips, opened it and slipped inside. Arousal speared through him as he caught her soft moan. His name…his name sounding so different on her tongue, like the man he wanted to be.

She tugged him into the laundry room, bumped the door closed with her hip, then melted back into his arms.

Cash wanted so much more for her. More than desperate kisses among baskets of clothes he still needed to wash. He wanted a bed big enough to hold everything he felt for her. He wanted nights on end to discover every mystery of her body. He wanted her laughing and free and full of sunshine.

If anyone deserved all that was good in life it was Rowena. No dark. No grinding, weary hours of physical therapy. No wheelchairs to lug out of cars or nights when the dark inside her lover went so deep even she couldn't find any light.

Cash eased his hands down to her waist, meaning to push

her gently away, but her mouth was on his throat, warm and moist and full of desire. Her lips trailed downward, pressing kisses to his chest, nuzzling against him, until she touched his nipple with her tongue.

Cash's breath hissed between his teeth, his shaft throbbing, his whole body on fire. Her hair teased his skin, her fingers making him hotter than he'd ever been, scaring the hell out of him, opening a well of need in him so great it stunned him.

His hands found the hem of her shirt, slid beneath it. The velvety skin of her stomach brushed his as he shoved the fabric up to find her breasts. He slid the thin lace of her bra aside and cupped her, ran his thumb over the pointed crest, knew by how tight it was that she wanted him almost as much as he wanted her. He bent her back over his braced arm as his mouth took nips and his tongue sips of her collarbone, the hollow of her throat, and then he drew her into his mouth.

She gasped as he suckled her, seducing her, memorizing the taste of her on his tongue.

She moved her hand between their hips and found him through the worn material of his sweats. Then she insinuated her fingers beneath the elastic band, touching him with exquisite delicacy, astonishing wonder. "How—how can you…believe this…is wrong, Cash?" she breathed as she curled her hand around him, ran her thumb over the tip. "What we feel for each other."

Wrong. This was wrong. On so many levels he couldn't even begin to explain. Cash swore under his breath, dragging every ounce of will he had to the surface, breaking the contact of her skin on his one agonizing inch at a time.

He circled her arms with his hands to keep the space between them, rested his forehead against hers as he tried to remember how to breathe.

"You need to go, Rowena," he said hoarsely. "Surely you have to see."

"I see that I care about you, Cash."

Bryony Brown's exasperated voice echoed in his mind. *What a surprise...*

"There are times when I think I could..."

"Could what?"

"Fall in love with you. If you'd let me."

Cash's heart beat faster despite the logic he knew he had to hold on to. "I won't, Rowena. Let you. I'd only..." Cash arched his head back, closed his eyes. "I'd only bring you down. I couldn't ever forgive myself if I did."

"But what if this is destiny? You and me together. Loving each other. Loving the girls. What if—"

"Your sister said you've never been wise about creatures you try to heal. I'm going to be wise for you." Cash cradled her cheek with one hand, ran his thumb across the place where her tears had run over the ruin of the necklace Charlie had given her. Then he touched her lips, the lips that hadn't hesitated to tell him truths that hurt, made him angry. At last, he lifted her hand and pressed her palm against his.

Her hand seemed so small, delicate compared to his.

"What if I don't want to be wise?" she asked. "What if I'm willing to risk everything by loving you?"

"Then you're braver than I can ever be. We have to end this, Rowena. Now. Before it gets any more painful. For the girls. For you. For me. The longer we wait, the harder it will be for all of us. Help me do what I know is right."

He felt a tearing away in her, a sadness, a surrender.

"Can I say goodbye to the girls? I have something for Charlie."

"Sure."

Rowena ran her fingers through her hair to straighten where he'd mussed it. He had to open the door, go back to the kitchen. She was waiting, hoping that he would change his mind.

But they'd barely stepped out of the other room before they heard Charlie's call, shrill, almost…alarmed.

They rushed together down the hall and saw Charlie, round-eyed in her red-and-white candy-striped pajamas, Destroyer at her side, peering up at her with a worried expression. No doubt about it, Cash thought. The dog sensed as much as he did that something was amiss. As for any lingering traces of the arousal Rowena had stirred up in the laundry room, the sight of Cash's daughter doused them more effectively than another dip in the dunk tank.

"Daddy…Mac…Mac says she got her bear down all by herself," Charlie accused.

"And this bothers you?" Cash drew it out into a question, mentally bracing himself for the daily task of mediating yet another argument between his girls.

Charlie twined her fingers in the ruff of thick fur at the back of Destroyer's neck. "I told Mac it was real bad to lie. You *always* give her bear to her when she goes to bed, don't you?"

Cash scanned for verbal booby traps. "Ballerina Bear is a big favorite at the moment." He headed for MacKenzie's bedroom to try to figure out exactly what had tripped Charlie's aggravation wire.

"That's what I told her! But Mac said she slept with her Dora the Explorer doll last night."

Cash filed back through his memory, trying to remember any variation in the usual bedtime ritual. "Mac's right. I tucked her in with Dora. And that little monkey guy Dora hangs out with. I stuck the bear up on the shelf."

"But that's impossible!" Charlie wailed, rushing into Mac's room ahead of him, the dog at her side. "Just look!" She pointed and sure enough, the ballerina bear wasn't on the shelf where he'd put it. The fluffy stuffed animal was tucked securely in the crook of Mac's arm.

Cash stared, bemused. "Mac, how did you get your bear?"

"My doggy helped me," Mac insisted, sticking her tongue out at her big sister.

Cash didn't stop to correct her. He looked from the dog's tongue-lolling grin to the belligerent jut of his youngest daughter's chin. "Destroyer fetched it?"

Rowena hugged Cash from behind. "I *told* you he's a smart dog!" she exclaimed.

Mac scowled at them, disgruntled. "Destroyer didn't fetch it. *I* did." She jabbed her little thumb at the cartoon bunny decorating her ruffled nightgown. "My doggy just helped."

"But how…?" Cash struggled to get his mind around what she'd claimed.

"By bein' my magic carpet ride. I told you an' told you, an' Charlie, too. Aren't your brains turned on this early?"

Cash was grateful for Rowena's hand against his back, her voice, so filled with an innate optimism he didn't dare share. "Can you show us, sweetie?" Rowena asked.

Mac heaved a sigh that could have shaken the rooftops. "I suppose. But you have to put my dolly back on the shelf first." She thrust the bear at Rowena with such a long-suffering attitude Cash almost managed to smile. But his face felt too stiff to do anything but hold his breath and watch.

Rowena did as the child told her, settling the ballerina bear back on its perch atop the white painted shelf he'd built the year Mac was born. There was no way Mac could reach the toy there, Cash reasoned, trying to guard himself, keep himself from being disappointed. It was just a little too high. A little too far.

And yet…Rowena's enthusiasm threatened to seep into his very bones. It scared him. Fucking terrified him. Daring to hope that much.

"C'mere Destroyer," Mac commanded.

The Newfie left Charlie's side and padded over to Mac's bed, putting his big body between the child and the shelf. Soulful canine eyes peered into Mac's face, as if in complete communion.

Cash held his breath as MacKenzie grabbed big handfuls of the dog's fur and slowly, laboriously pulled herself up onto her feet.

Her feet…for a few precious seconds all of her weight was on her own legs. And they held—sonofabitch!—those thin, scarred, mended little legs held!

Then it was over. She leaned across Destroyer until her tummy was pressed to the dog's back. She held on tight with one hand and reached her other arm across to her doll.

For a moment the stuffed bear twisted, started to fall, but Mac got hold of a piece of tutu. She hauled the doll into her arm, stood for a heartbeat, then plopped her nightgown-clad bottom back down onto the bed.

"Mac, you—you were standing up," Cash breathed. "You were."

Red-faced with exertion and more than a little breathless, she scowled at the three dumbstruck people before her.

"I was getting my doll all by myself. 'Cause you always take too damned long."

Cash didn't even mention the bad word. Let the kid swear today. She could say anything she wanted as long as she kept doing that miraculous thing…spending a few precious seconds standing on her own two feet.

Mac shoved her doll aside and put her hands on her hips, shooting the stare of death across the room. "You got something to say to me, buster? Like you're sorry."

"Sorry?" Cash exclaimed. "I'm not sorry. I'm elated. I'm so—so proud, kitten."

"Of me and not Charlie, right?" Mac insisted, driving her

point home like a ruthless little pirate. "'Cause Charlie called me a big fat liar."

"I did not!" Charlie protested. "Not the big fat part, anyway."

"Maybe I'll take the doggy for walks," Mac said as Cash swept her up into his arms, hugged her tight. "Maybe Destroyer'll like me best. Maybe…"

"She can't do that!" Charlie burst out, her face pale. "Tell her, Daddy! He's my dog, isn't he?"

"He's everybody's dog now," Cash said. "Mine, too. We're keeping him."

"Forever?" Charlie gasped, her dread of moments before transforming into amazement, joy. "Really, truly, Daddy?"

"Forever," Cash said, rumpling Charlie's sleep-tousled hair. "Now, we'd better get you girls ready so I can take you to school."

Lines appeared in Charlie's brow. "You're taking us? But I looked at the calendar. I thought Rowena…"

Cash grinned at her. "The hell with the calendar! Today's a special day. I decided to take some vacation, spend time with you. We'll work real hard on therapy, right, Mac? Maybe by next year you really will be taking your dog for a walk."

"My dog," Charlie whispered.

"Yeah, cupcake, your dog, too."

"Listen, I need to get back to the pet shop," Rowena said. "Vinny could use the time off."

"Aren't you going to take vacation with us?" Mac asked, dangling her bear upside down by one furry leg.

Cash looked at Rowena, suddenly remembering, an unexpected ache taking a bite out of his joy. This was goodbye. "No, sweetheart," he said. "Rowena's got stuff of her own to do. She can't stick around here forever."

"Oh," Mac said, puzzled. "Is it like, we have to pick one like on game shows? The puppy or the trip to Disney World? Except Rowena's not Disney World."

"She was never ours to keep. She was just helping out. We don't need her help anymore."

Talk about a big fat liar, Cash thought. He needed Rowena. And badly. He just couldn't have her.

But this breakthrough with Mac—it would change everything. He'd need to channel even more of his energy into making his little girl stronger. What was that strange fluttering sensation in his chest? Hope?

"We can still come to the shop sometimes, can't we?" Charlie asked, looking more than ever like a lost little soul.

"You have to buy dog food, don't you?" Rowena asked, and Cash could see how fragile her smile was. "Destroyer eats a lot."

Charlie nodded.

"He poops a lot, too," Mac said. "You should see how big—"

"Hey, there, Princess." Cash cut her off, laying his hand gently across her mouth. "We don't discuss that subject in front of company. Got it?"

Mac nodded and pulled his hand away.

Charlie chewed on her bottom lip, her eyes locked on Rowena. He hated the loss in his little girl's face. He searched for something to drive it away. Latched onto the night before.

"Listen, I've got some news for you," he said, feeling a little uneasy even as he said the words. "It's about your mom."

"Our mom?" Mac bounced in his arms. "Is she sending me toys, Daddy?"

"No. Well, I don't know about that." But it was a pretty good bet Lisa would come through the door with a bag bigger than the one Santa carried, Cash thought. "What I do know is this— you know you've got four days off next week?"

"Yeah," Charlie said warily. "My teacher says we should use it to work on our projects."

"You're going to have to do that some other time, kiddo.

Because you and Mac are going to spend your vacation time in Chicago with your mommy."

Mac squealed in delight, even Charlie's features lit up.

"Really! Really, truly, Daddy?" Charlie asked, breathlessly.

"That's what she says. She's picking you up on Thursday."

"Hey, Charlie! Remember what Mommy said? They got the biggest toy stores in the world in Chicago! Bigger than our house! Bigger than Toys 'R Us. Bigger than the uni-verse!"

Rowena listened to Mac's crows of delight, saw the anticipation in Charlie's far quieter response. Searched Cash's face, so glad he'd taken the chance, letting Lisa take the children for a little while.

She hoped he'd rest, hoped he'd recharge in his time alone. Catch his second wind. But it seemed Mac's triumph, standing for those moments, had surged energy back into him, restoring his depleted resources.

All that was left was for her to go.

Her throat ached with loss as she backed out of the room, not wanting to ruin the girls' delight, trying not to mind that she was already forgotten, replaced by their anticipation and excitement at the thought of seeing their mother.

That was how it should be. And yet…

No matter how many times she said goodbye to someone she'd loved, be it animals or now, little girls, she was always surprised just how much it hurt.

As she paused in the kitchen to fetch her purse and keys, her gaze snagged on the paper bag she'd left on the counter. Grabbing up a stray marker, she wrote Charlie's name on it.

She capped the pen and headed for the door.

"Rowena?"

She turned at the sound of Charlie's voice.

"You disappeared," the little girl said. "You didn't say goodbye."

"You were all so excited about your mom coming I didn't want to bother you. And you get to spend time with your daddy, too. Aren't you a lucky girl?"

"No. Not very," Charlie said, pushing her glasses up her nose.

Rowena crossed to where Charlie stood, lifting the child up in her arms. "I've got a feeling your luck is about to change. Now that Destroyer is permanently on guard."

"Like your luck did when you got your magic whistle?"

"Just like that." She squeezed Charlie tight, drinking in the warm, little-girl smells of baby shampoo and strawberry soap and freshly washed linens. She wasn't going to cry, give Charlie one more thing to worry about.

"I'm glad you came out here, because I've got something for you," Rowena said. She settled the little girl on her hip and Charlie let her, winding her arms around Rowena's neck as she carried the child to the counter.

"What is it?" Charlie asked as Rowena handed over the paper sack.

"See for yourself."

The paper rustled as Charlie opened the bag.

"Corn," Charlie said as she gave Rowena a little smile. "You remembered."

"I promised you I'd put it back, didn't I?"

Charlie nodded.

"There's something else in there, too. Dig a little deeper."

Frowning in concentration, Charlie rummaged around in the sack until she came up with something shiny, metal.

"It's a can opener for your survival kit," Rowena said, her voice breaking. "You've got to have some way to open all those cans. Just in case."

Charlie ran her fingertips over the simple tool as if it were made of gold. "You know, I got lots of stuff up there," she said.

"For me and Mac and Daddy and Mr. Google. If there's ever a tornado or a flood or the world blows up or something, I bet I'd have enough food so you could come be safe with us, too."

"I'll count on that," Rowena said. She wanted to hug Charlie, tight, but if she did she feared she'd cry. Better try to keep this parting light. No matter how much it hurt. She set the child back down on her feet, Charlie's practical navy-blue slippers so different from Mac's flowered ones that it hurt Rowena's heart.

"See you later, alligator," she said, touching the little girl's nose.

"After a while, crocodile."

The last thing Rowena saw when she glanced back was Charlie, in her striped pajamas, climbing up into her tree house, the shiny new opener in her hand.

CHAPTER SIXTEEN

THE DOG WAS WHINING AGAIN, looking up at Cash with eyes that could have conned Scrooge out of his last stinking nickel. Okay, so the girls had only been gone a little while. Cash left off cleaning his service revolver at the coffee table in the living room and glanced at his wristwatch. Nine hours, twenty-six minutes and...who the hell could keep track of how many seconds anyway, the little hand seemed to flash around so fast? Then why did this day seem to be crawling by so slowly it was almost going backwards?

Destroyer paced into Mac's room and brought out ballerina bear, drooling all over a mouthful of purple tutu. The dog dropped it at Cash's feet, adding one more toy to the pile of the girls' stuff that the animal had been amassing in the living room. One of Charlie's neon-orange rollerblades lay on its side, the pocket of her baseball mitt held three of those scrunched-up hair bands she used to put her hair in a ponytail. A fugitive sock that had dodged the laundry draped over every stuffed animal that had been within the dog's reach.

Did tutus wash? Cash mused as he looked down at the bear. It looked as if he was going to find out before Mac got home.

"Mac's not here," he griped at the dog. "Charlie's not here. They're gone. This is our big break, dog. We can do whatever the hell we want to. Fix the garage door, watch all those cop dramas that are too violent for the girls. Man stuff, you know?

We can go have a beer with the guys or play a little pool with Jake, or…sit in this miserable gray house and listen to how quiet the place is."

Destroyer laid his head on Cash's knee and heaved a sigh so heavy the gun parts rattled against the tabletop. Could a dog die of a broken heart in four days? Hadn't one of Cash's brothers had a book about some mutt that had pined its way into the grave before its boy came home from the war?

Yeah, Cash recalled. It was Donovan, making one more attempt to convince their mom to let him get a dog for his birthday. Mom hadn't budged. She already had too much work to do, too much house to clean, too many kids to keep track of and too much laundry to hang out on the line. All the reasons Cash had told Rowena he couldn't manage a dog.

But if Destroyer weren't here now, Mac wouldn't have wrestled her way to her feet last week. Charlie wouldn't be smiling more often. And right now, he'd be all alone.

Alone with the images of his children clasped in Lisa's arms. Alone with the memory of the girls' absolute delight as they scrambled for her attention. Haunted by the way they hadn't looked back at him as she drove them away.

Cash knew they hadn't looked. He'd watched for it. Waited. So sure Charlie, at least, wouldn't fail him. He'd felt like hell when even she finally vanished from sight without so much as a careless wave.

They'd forgiven their mother everything. Forgotten that she'd ditched them at Christmas. How she hadn't come to see them. They'd been willing to start all over, give her another chance, even if he hadn't.

More nerve-racking still, Lisa had seemed different, too. More together. Stronger. Something stubborn in the way she'd scooped them into her arms, saying how much she'd missed them. Things were going to be different, now.

Different? What the devil does that mean? Cash had asked himself that question a hundred times since they'd left. He liked things fine the way they were. His girls in his house with their mother three hundred odd miles away doing…whatever it was Lisa was doing now that she "had her own life to live."

That's what she'd said she wanted when she walked out on the three of them. Her own life.

She damned well couldn't have his.

She wouldn't want it, he reasoned, trying to ease his nerves. Nothing had changed. Mac needed her therapy sessions more than ever and Lisa didn't have the stomach for it. She hated small-town living and the kids were rooted right here: their schools, their friends.

Their father.

He picked up Mac's bear, his jaw clenching against the fear scratching inside him. That he might lose his little girls.

No. Hauling that wheelchair around for four days should remind Lisa how hard it could be. She'd probably overload the kids on sugar and let them stay up too late, playing mommy wonderful. He couldn't help but hope she did. That way, Mac was bound to have a temper fit. That kid erupted like Mount St. Helens when she was up too late. And Charlie—she'd be asking all those impossible questions of hers, far too smart to be satisfied with the usual off-the-cuff answers grownups wanted to give.

He wondered how Charlie was doing with her mom. If she'd spent the past hours scared of making a mistake and bringing Lisa's disapproval down on her.

Cash frowned. Charlie had accidentally stepped on Lisa's taupe designer shoes when she'd flung herself into her mother's arms. *Sorry,* his little girl had exclaimed, stirring up Cash's memory of what Mac had told him the day of Charlie's covert operation in the pet shop. That to Lisa, sorry didn't matter. By the time you said it, it was too late to matter.

Cash hoped his ex-wife would take a page out of her own rule book. And not…not what? Try to rearrange things? Try to be a real mother to the girls?

Cash could almost hear Rowena's voice scolding him. *Isn't that exactly what you should want? What's best for them?*

"So, I'm a selfish bastard where my kids are concerned," he muttered. "There you have it. One more ugly truth about Cash Lawless. I want to keep them to myself. Want to protect them from being hurt. I want Lisa to suffer for what she did to them."

And he wanted to see Rowena.

Cash closed his eyes, leaned his head back and kneaded the muscles at the back of his neck. He'd spent the past week in withdrawal. Trying to get her off his mind, out of his dreams, his fantasies. But those hot kisses behind the laundry room door and the way her hand had felt encircling him weren't on his mind the most. No. He wanted to see her across his kitchen table in the morning, wanted to talk to her—about how much he missed his kids. About how angry he was at Lisa.

About all that poison inside him that made him unfit to love any woman ever again.

He missed Rowena's company, her smart-ass comments, the jangling of her bracelets and the way she cut to the chase, saying what needed to be said, not counting the cost.

I'm doing the best I can… he'd defended himself, feeling at the end of his rope.

You have to do better.

If anybody else had said that to Cash he would have exploded. But he'd listened to Rowena. Tried…

Destroyer pawed at him, then lifted his mammoth head and uttered a mournful howl that would have done a banshee proud.

The damned dog was driving him crazy.

What was Cash supposed to do to shut Destroyer up? When it came right down to it, he didn't know a damned thing about dogs. Except for the fact that he should have taken Rowena up on that little vacuum cleaner bag deal she'd offered. And that this dog in particular was a mess when his kids were gone.

What about you, boss? The dog seemed to complain. *You're just a party waiting to happen.*

"Well, we've got to figure something out," Cash groused. "Otherwise we're both going to lose our minds." Cash hunkered down and scratched behind the Newfie's ear. "And I don't know about you, but I don't have a lot of extra brain cells to lose."

Cash's foot dislodged a Frisbee from somewhere in Destroyer's pile of girl paraphernalia. The plastic saucer rolled a little way, then settled on the floor.

A toy. That was the answer. Get the dog a new toy. A bone. Something to distract him, just like Cash distracted his kids when the girls got restless. There *had* to be some kind of plaything that would distract the mutt for a little while. And distract Cash, too. He'd load Destroyer in the SUV, drive down to Rowena's shop and...

She'd make them both feel better.

Dangerous stuff, thinking like that, a voice whispered in Cash's ear as he deftly reassembled his revolver and locked it in its metal box on the highest shelf in the house. Dangerous or not, he was too far gone to care.

He nabbed the leash from a coat hook near the back door and snapped the lead onto Destroyer's collar. "Let's get the hell out of this fucking tomb of a house," he told the dog. Destroyer's tail drooped as much as his spirits.

They'd both perk up once they saw Rowena, Cash promised himself. In fact, just thinking about seeing her managed to cheer him up.

What was that old adage his mom had repeated over and over again? You're never finished learning. About life. About yourself.

Whoever would have imagined she was right again? He thought back to when he was a kid growing up in that tiny house overflowing with brothers. All those times he'd wished the whole tribe would get lost so he could just take a leisurely shower. Or lately, when his life had been so busy with his girls that he'd longed to sack out in front of the television and watch what *he* wanted to watch—no more singing sponges who lived in pineapples or cartoon girls with their pet monkeys.

All those times he'd considered just how good it would feel—to do exactly *what* he wanted, *when* he wanted, he'd missed one minor point.

Cash hated being alone.

CLOSED.

Cash's mood plunged as he glimpsed the sign in the shop window. He checked his watch again. Okay. So the shop closed at nine and it was almost ten o'clock. But the light was on back in the office, so surely Rowena must be inside. Maybe working on the paperwork Vinny said had taken a backseat during the weeks Rowena had been helping out with the girls.

Cash could have turned around, loaded his morose dog back in the car and headed home. Seen how many more of the kids' toys Destroyer could add to the pile. Instead he knocked on the door, first softly, then more loudly, hoping she'd hear.

It took barely a minute for Rowena to appear. Backlit for a moment by the office lights, she looked ethereal, like one of the fairy princesses in the books Mac liked to read. Her hair long and loose and gold, a violet blouse flowing to mid thigh, a subtle shimmer of gold threads at throat and cuff. Only her jeans, ripped at the knee, ruined the picture. She flicked on the shop lights and rushed to the door, a trio of puppies gamboling behind her. The kind with the pushed-in faces and tails that curled like a pig's.

As she opened the door she looked flushed and worried and almost as glad to see him as he was to see her.

"Cash! How are you?"

The puppies leaped on Destroyer, trying to lure him into a game. The Newfoundland ignored them, and let out a pitiful whimper. He lay down and rolled over on his back, feet in the air, as if to say, "he let that stranger take my kids right out from under my nose! It's killing me."

"That bad, huh?" Rowena hunkered down to scratch the Newfie's belly.

"He's been like this for hours. It's driving me insane."

Rowena scooped up two of the puppies and popped them in the nearest exercise pen. Cash grabbed the third and did the same thing.

Destroyer was already miserable. Being tortured by those little menaces was over the line.

"You've got to do something with this dog," Cash said, trying to pry his cuff from between needlelike puppy teeth. The dog let go and chased after the nearest curly tail. "From the minute Lisa picked up the girls, Destroyer's been pacing, carrying around the girls' toys. He's got a whole pile of them in the living room now."

"Oh, dear."

"That's not the worst of it. He whines. He howls."

"He misses them."

Yeah, like he'd needed to drive all the way over here to pick up that newsflash. "I miss them, too. But I'm not being a great big baby about it."

The woman actually smiled, her eyes twinkling. "You're jealous, huh?"

"Jealous?"

"I bet you wish you could whine and howl right along with him."

"I do not!" Cash snapped, then he grimaced. "But…I guess I can see where he's coming from. It's too quiet at home. That house is like a tomb. I was hoping you'd have some kind of dog toy or bone or…I don't know, something to take our minds off…*his* mind off…"

"Four days is a long time, huh?"

Cash gave a wry chuckle. "And getting longer by the minute."

"Come on in. I'll make you a cup of tea."

"No!" he said so quickly she laughed. "God, Rowena. Anything but that."

"There may be beer in the fridge in back. How about one of those?"

"Got anything for him?" Cash said, nudging his lump of a dog. "Like a doggy tranquilizer or something?"

"I've got another rescue I'm trying to socialize. Their mom." She leaned over to pet the nearest pug's wiggly hind end. "She could use a break from these little pirates. Motherhood isn't all it's cracked up to be, is it, Lucy?"

Cash could tell the moment Rowena realized what she'd said and how it might affect him.

"Lucy's been nursing them and they've been biting her nipples."

Nipples…now that was a word to get a man's attention, Cash thought, trying to keep his gaze from straying to the swells beneath Rowena's neckline.

"Lucy adores her babies," Rowena tried to explain, "but she's sore and…well, how would you like it if somebody was teething on your tender parts?"

That depends on whose mouth is involved. Cash reined himself in. That train of thought was going to end in nothing but trouble.

"What I'm trying to say is that Destroyer can play with her in the play area, and you and I can—" She hesitated, and Cash remembered what they'd gotten up to the last time they'd been in a small, closed-in room together. Her breasts under his hands, his mouth finding the pearl-like tip. Need surged through him, and he turned his gaze away from her tempting curves, her slim waist, her legs, long and willowy in those jeans ripped out at the knee.

What was to stop them tonight? From finishing what they'd started? They were two consenting adults who wanted each other. People had casual sex all the time, the devil on Cash's shoulder tempted. Rowena had said so herself. Asked him why they couldn't just give each other what they needed, a soft place to forget for just a little while.

He needed to forget more than ever tonight.

But generous as she'd be, Cash knew Rowena better now. His talk with her sister Bryony had dashed any illusions away. He didn't want to hurt Rowena. Use her to get the physical release his body craved. Sometimes it was wrong to take a gift, even when it was offered.

"Maybe I'd better go," he said, his hand tightening on Destroyer's lead. "I don't know why I came here."

"To find something to distract you. And Destroyer. I've... missed you, Cash." Her mouth looked so pink, so vulnerable, so tender. Needing to be kissed.

He'd known she'd miss the girls when she left the gray house. That had been a given, the way she'd mothered them during the time Vinny had been gone. But Rowena missed *him*. Cash.

Not the man he really was. The man she hoped he could be. But then, how often had Rowena been wrong in the past? Been bitten. More times than her sister could count. If Cash had had any delusions left about himself and his own inner darkness, his reaction to Lisa taking the girls was warning enough.

"Don't look at me like that, Rowena," he warned. "Your

sister was right. I am a user. I used you to watch my kids. I'm using you right now. Looking for something…"

"Using has nothing to do with it. But neither you nor Bryony will ever see that if you don't open yourselves up just a little. I care about you, Cash. And I know you care about me. More than you want to."

"Rowena—"

"People help each other. That's what they do. That's how they get through times like these. Not because they have to, but because…I want to."

"You give too much. Too fast."

"And you don't trust yourself to give at all."

Rowena was right on target with that one. He'd quit trusting anything too good, too perfect, too easy long ago. And it would be easy—damned easy—to fall in love with her.

"I need to go before you do something stupid." He said it so tenderly she smiled. He figured if he'd said that to her sister, the good doctor would have rearranged his face, like he deserved. Rowena laid her fingertips against his cheek.

"Don't worry, Cash. I won't jump your bones—at least, not unless you ask me to. But I think I *have* managed to come up with something to take your mind off the girls being gone. And see that the kids have a wonderful surprise when they come home."

"What's that?"

"You could finish the tree house."

"No." He could see his harsh refusal cut her, but what else could he say? It was too hard knowing Mac couldn't climb it. Too bitter. The symbol of everything he'd lost when the car carrying his family was crushed.

"Well, then…what if we painted your whole house?"

She was serious. Dead serious.

"We could pick colors the girls would love. You could do

their bedrooms, the exterior. All of it. In four days, you could have it done if you worked like a crazy person."

"Three and a half days. I promised Potter I'd work part of his shift on Saturday so he could take his wife out for their anniversary. Fifteen years."

"That's something to celebrate."

"It's a goddamned miracle these days," Cash scoffed.

"You know there are marriages that work. Jake and Deirdre Stone seem happy."

Happy? The two of them were almost nauseating, they were still so much in love. Even before Lisa left Cash had envied his friend, wondering what it would be like to have a woman look at him like that.

Well, now you know, a voice whispered inside his head. And it had only made things harder, knowing he didn't deserve her.

"Paint. We were talking about paint. And how long it would take me to put it up."

Rowena frowned, and Cash could see her mentally tallying up the time she thought it would take in her head. "If you're filling in for Potter, you may need a little help. How about if I come over after the shop is closed? And Sunday's my regular day off."

"You want to paint my house on your day off?"

"Vinny would jump at an excuse to work a few hours in the shop so that he could flirt with Miss Marigold. He's almost convinced the woman she's in love."

"Miss Marigold in love with Vinny?" Cash exclaimed.

"She's not in love with Vinny—at least not yet! Though I have to admit, I keep hoping. And Vinny certainly seems to like flirting with her. But I meant she's in love with Elvis."

Cash shook his head. "That sweet old lady is an Elvis junkie? Please don't tell me she's got some blue suede shoes tucked in the back of her closet."

"Not Elvis, Elvis. The parrot, Elvis. And let me tell you, it would be a load off my mind to get that bird settled someplace where his swearing wouldn't singe the ears of small children."

"Whitewater's notoriously proper Miss Marigold…and a swearing parrot? That seems like a match made in hell."

"Wrong again, Deputy Lawless. He's charmed the bi-focals off her."

Cash glanced over toward Elvis's cage. "But aren't those birds expensive? Like, close to two thousand dollars? How could she ever afford it?"

"I'd give him to her. To make up for all the damage Destroyer did."

She meant it. Cash did a double-take. "You're not going to make much money if you're giving away fifteen hundred dollars in merchandise. And the cage—that has to cost more on top of it. Besides, you made her those tables out of the broken teapots. I'd say you squared up that debt already."

He'd settled the heavy suckers inside Miss Marigold's fenced back garden himself. He knew just how fantastic they looked. The sun glinting off the colors, setting the porcelain shapes aglow.

"She loves the tables, Cash," Rowena said. "They made her so happy she cried. But they can't talk to her at night. She's still lonely. It would be so good to know she had company."

Cash shook his head. Vinny was right. Rowena might not be the best businesswoman in the county, but when it came to understanding how to get people through their pain, she had a gift. A real gift. He'd always be grateful that she'd weaseled Destroyer through his front door.

"You're good at this, you know?" he admitted. "Figuring out what people need. Dogs. Parrots. Colors."

A pretty flush spread across her cheeks at his praise. "Just think of the girls' faces when they come home! Oh, Cash. Little girls don't belong in gray houses. Those rooms feel so sad. Like they are. And you."

He straightened, defensive. As if she'd insulted him to the core. "I'm not sad. I'm mad as hell."

"And lonely for your girls."

Lonely.

A marine wasn't allowed to get lonely. He was trained to get angry, get tough, be strong. Channel his emotions into fuel to fight whatever life threw at him. A cop was supposed to do the same. And yet…

Cash hated to think of the weekend stretching out before him, days of wondering what his girls were doing, if they were okay. He couldn't stop feeling all messed up inside, knowing a better man would hope they'd have a great time. When the biggest part of him was afraid that maybe they would. If that happened, it would make things…different.

At least if he were painting the house, he'd fall into bed at night and sleep like the dead. Or if he couldn't sleep, he could just keep slapping up paint, keep his mind on something besides the fear he couldn't admit to anyone. Not Rowena. Not even Vinny.

That he could lose his daughters' love. He'd seen it happen before, kids caught in some kind of wrestling match between their parents, their loyalties, their love the prize in broken homes.

But he was the one who was broken. A selfish, sick sonofabitch wanting to keep them all to himself. And yet he didn't know how to stop feeling the way he did. Lisa had hurt them so badly in the past. How else could he be sure Mac and Charlie were safe?

If Rowena knew the truth, she wouldn't look at him with those eyes of hers, filled with…

Christ, Cash, don't even think it! The words she'd said, so honest, so brave.

I think I could fall in love with you if you let me.

He couldn't. He wouldn't.

"Cash?"

"Huh?" Cash let Rowena pull him up, out of the dark.

"What colors?"

"Colors?"

"For the house. What are the girls' favorite colors?"

"Mac's is pink. Charlie's purple."

"What's yours?" She smiled at him.

"What does my favorite color have to do with anything?"

"Your bedroom's that awful gray, too." She gave a theatrical shudder. "I only slept there one night and it gave me bad dreams."

Cash hadn't dreamed at all there for a long time. Until Rowena. Maybe he needed to keep the room gray, to remind himself who he was. "There's no point in painting mine," he said sharply. "I'll have enough to do without it."

"I wish you would…"

"Leave it, Rowena. It's like the tree house. Some things hurt too much to change."

She looked as if she wanted to argue with him, but she stopped herself. "Oh, well," she said, lifting her delicate shoulders. "It's your house. What about the living room?"

"Green." He surprised himself, saying it so fast.

"See! You do have a favorite color after all," she said, triumphant.

Cash looked at her, wondering if she knew, if she'd guessed.

Somehow, since he'd met her the boring blue that had been his color pick since he'd been a kid in grade school had changed for good.

Into the spring-warmed green of Rowena's eyes.

"HEY, LAWLESS, there's a rumor going around the squad room that you started painting your fingernails pink." The dispatcher's good-natured ribbing came through a brief burst of static in Cash's earpiece as he cruised along in his squad.

"Mayo here was wondering where you're getting your manicures done."

Cash held his hand up to the glow from the nearest streetlight, noting that in spite of scrubbing up before work, his nail beds were indeed stained pink. "I just finished painting Mac's room," he explained.

"Likely story." Darrell chuckled, not sounding the least bit tired, while Cash felt the way he had his first week of basic training. Beat to hell, but still enjoying it somehow. He'd blasted through Charlie's room, the kitchen and the wall that faced the street on the exterior. A warm yellow that reminded him of sunshine. He'd even started on the living room before he'd left for work, figuring he could finish the other three sides of the exterior later. He was going for high impact here, his goal to knock the girls' socks off, not attack the job in his usual logical way.

"Well, the consensus around here is that pink's your color, buddy," Darrell joked. "We're thinking of petitioning the county to see if you can wear a necktie to match."

"And the county lets you yahoos carry guns."

"Somebody's got to keep the citizens of Whitewater safe. Vinny watching the kids while you're painting?"

"No. They're with Lisa this weekend."

A beat of silence. Cash knew Darrell was kicking himself. In spite of the dispatcher's crusty exterior and endless teasing, the guy had a notoriously soft heart.

"No wonder you're painting."

"Yeah, well. They'll be back Monday night."

He just wished he knew what kind of shape his kids would be in when they walked through the door.

Cash didn't even want to think what his instincts were telling him. That gut-level cop sense had been buzzing inside him all night. His nerves twitchy, as if he could feel a storm coming.

Or was the tension knotting him up inside just knowing that one word from him would bring Rowena over to his house. To his bed.

And that a night making love with her really might drive back the vise of dread clamped around him.

The dispatcher buzzed back on. "Got a little action for you. Bev Keller just called in a 10-14 at the boathouse near Jubilee Point."

Prowlers? Cash thumbed his speaker on to say he was on his way, then turned his car around and headed in the direction of the river, glad of a little action to help take his mind off things.

He passed a car full of kids in a blue Mustang as he turned down the lane to the abandoned boathouse, and figured either the party was over or Bev had warned them she was calling in a complaint. He considered stopping them, just to make sure whoever was driving hadn't been chugging beer. But at that moment he glimpsed something orange flickering against the night sky.

Fire.

He called in for the fire crew as he sped down the dead end lane. "I'll secure the area," he said. "Make sure they didn't leave anybody behind."

He pulled to a stop, climbed out of his car. Looked as if a bonfire had gone out of control. A scattering of beer cans and a bottle of cheap wine littered the ground near some lawn chairs the partiers hadn't taken the time to stow in their trunk.

The kids had probably seen the fire, been scared shitless, and gotten the hell out of Dodge, Cash figured.

Even so, he'd better check, make sure nobody was inside. He knew for a fact the town drunk, Les Dickers, sometimes brought his mangy old Lab here to sleep off his latest bender so he could stay clear of his wife. The woman had a left hook that would do Evander Holyfield proud.

Cash started toward the building, the heat hitting him like a wall. It was already almost unbearable, the old place ready to go up like tinder. At least there was no sign of Les's rusted-out dump truck.

Cash started to circle around the building when he froze, paralyzed for a moment by a chilling sound.

Shrieking? Crying? Some creature terrified. In pain.

Something streaked past Cash, low to the ground. A cat. But it wasn't running out of the building. It was running in.

What the hell? Seconds later, the creature rushed back out, fur smoldering, a tiny mewling kitten in its mouth.

Sonofabitch! Cash saw the cat drop its burden with three other crying babies and turn back to the blazing structure. The damn crazy animal. She was going to be burned alive!

He should have snatched the cat up, shoved her and the kittens in the car to keep them safe, but something in the mother's desperation as she fought to save her babies hooked Cash right in the chest.

This was crazy…the voice of reason warned him. It was just a stray cat. And the firefighters were already coming with their air packs and their gear. He could hear the sirens in the distance on Jubilee road.

And yet…by the time they got here it would be too late.

Cash glimpsed a flash of tail as the mother cat raced back into the fire.

He covered his mouth with his jacket and plunged in behind her.

CHAPTER SEVENTEEN

SOMEONE WAS KNOCKING.

Rowena heard the pugs let out a snuffly chorus of barks from their crate in her small kitchen. She struggled upright in bed and shoved the hair out of her eyes. Who in the world would be knocking at her door at this hour?

Her heart leaped underneath the thin layer of her night-gown. There was only one person in town that might seek her out at this time of night. Cash.

Another knock sent the pugs into a cacophony of barking, determined to sound the alarm. Rowena's bare feet hit the floor and she hurried down the stairs, barely taking time to flick on the porch light.

When she did, her pulse raced at the sight of broad shoulders she'd stroked in her dreams. Cash's face was turned away from her, but she knew there could only be one reason why he'd come to her now.

And her whole body burned with the need to feel his hands on her, his mouth on her, loving her in the only way he knew how. The mere fact that he'd allowed himself that much seemed like richness beyond Rowena's imagining.

She flung open the door, intending to throw herself into his arms and kiss away any lingering doubts he might have. But when Cash turned toward her, her stomach dropped to the floor.

"Oh, my God, what happened?" she gasped, staring at his soot-blackened face, his uniform filthy with ash, stinking of smoke.

"There was a fire at the old boathouse."

He looked so haunted, every nerve stripped raw. The whites of his eyes shone stark, only accenting his torment.

"You mean the one where Les and his dog hide out?"

Her question seemed to puzzle him, finally penetrate the haze clouding his usually laserlike gaze. "How do you know that?"

"He comes into the shop. I save dog food for him— Oh, God, Cash, tell me he's all right."

"He's fine as far as I know. Wasn't there tonight. But these were."

He thrust a bundle toward her, his uniform jacket. She hadn't even noticed he'd been holding it, bunched up in his arms.

Heedless of her nightgown, Rowena took it from his hands. Her heart twisted as she heard a weak meow. She folded the material back to find a mass of tiny kittens and what looked to be their badly scorched mother.

The stench of burned fur assailed her nostrils, but Rowena only turned and rushed up the stairs to her kitchen, Cash right behind her.

The light stung her eyes, the harsh glow driving the last vestiges of sleep away as she went to her kitchen table. One sweep of her hand knocked whatever was atop it away— unopened mail, an empty pizza container and a bag of stuff from the drugstore she hadn't had a chance to unpack.

She laid his jacket right on top of the cheery orange tablecloth and unwrapped the bundle Cash had brought her. The kittens struggled pathetically to get as close to their mama as they could, but the mother cat was fighting a battle of her own. One ear singed off, patches of fur burned away. Rowena scanned the cat's skinny body with the eyes of the vet she'd almost become.

"I didn't know where else to go," Cash said. "We've got to do something for her."

Rowena ran to the sink, got a bowl she filled with cool water. "There's still some of my medical stuff in my bathroom," Rowena told him. "Grab it while I try to find out how bad this is."

Cash stared at her, confused. He'd never once been in her apartment. "That way," Rowena directed him with a wave of her hand. She heard him rush through her bedroom. He was back before she could even take a breath.

"How bad is she?"

Even in spite of the adrenaline rushing into Rowena's veins she was struck by the fierce emotion in Cash's voice. Surprised by it.

"These burns are pretty bad. She's going to have some nasty scars. And I can't tell how much smoke she inhaled. It's hard to tell."

A black kitten with white paws tried to climb up on its mom. The mother cat let out a yelp of pain, but instead of pulling away she bent over and licked her baby's muzzle, nudging it toward one swollen teat.

"Will she make it?"

"Four of the kittens look good, but the other two and the mother—I don't know, Cash. They need IVs, to get them stabilized. We need a vet."

"I tried Dr. Wilcox on my cell. He wasn't there. You've got to help them." His voice was hoarse with smoke, ragged. "Jesus Christ, Rowena. She went after them into the fire. Six times. Trying to save her babies. We've got to help her."

He turned his eyes to hers, and it was as if she could see into his very soul. To the darkest places, where his agony lived in secret. Cash's cell phone rang, piercing the sound of the kittens' frightened yowling. He flipped it open, all cop again, efficient, ready to handle the crisis as he saw the caller ID. "It's the vet," he said, sounding relieved.

Rowena didn't hear anything more. She ran into her bedroom and yanked on the first clothes she could put her hands on. Yesterday's jeans and a T-shirt so baggy it would hide the fact she didn't have time to bother with a bra. She jammed her feet into her sneakers, meaning to head back to the kitchen. At the last second, she glimpsed her blue plastic laundry basket where she'd left it earlier, half filled with clean clothes she hadn't gotten around to putting away.

She grabbed the basket up, carrying it out with her. Cash had already gathered the animals up in his ruined jacket.

"They'll be more comfortable in this," she said, rumpling the clothes with one hand to make them softer, then scooping the kittens and their mother into the makeshift nest.

"Let's get out of here." She grabbed her keys off the hook near the door and ran after Cash as he carried the basket to his squad car.

She climbed into the passenger seat and held the basket full of traumatized cats on her lap while Cash drove like the cop he was—skillfully, fast, every cell of his body seeming focused on getting them help as soon as possible.

The whole interior of the car stank of smoke and burnt hair, and Rowena noticed Cash's jacket had blackened patches in spots. She searched his face, saw soot marks and sweat running down his throat. His shirt, torn, his elbow stained where he'd cut himself. Rowena stared at Cash's hands on the wheel, the light dusting of hair burned off them, his knuckles red, one split.

"You went in after her," Rowena breathed, knowing it was true. Cash turned back to her, his soul laid bare.

"What else could I do?"

TRUST ROWENA TO NAME the mother cat before they'd left the vet's office, Cash thought as he turned down Rowena's street and glanced at the tousled, soot-stained woman in the seat beside him. Once the storm of emergency care was over, she'd named all the traumatized animals, as if that simple gift would make them seem more important to the vet techs who'd be caring for them, make the kittens cling to life more tenaciously themselves.

The gesture had touched Cash, watching Rowena pen each name onto the cardboard sign on the cage where the little family had been put together. The vet had considered splitting up the babies from the mother to give the newly christened Cinderella a rest, but Rowena wouldn't hear of it. She didn't want Cinder to wake up and be terrified her babies were gone.

Cash was damned glad Rowena had stepped in when she did. He doubted he could have taken it, watching the babies being pulled away. He knew just how the cat felt.

The guys down at the Sheriff's office would think he'd gone crazy. It was just a cat. A stray at that. Probably had a dozen kinds of worms, carrying all sorts of diseases and dropping another litter every five minutes. And yet, as Cash had pitched in, working side by side with Rowena and Dr. Wilcox to get everyone stabilized as soon as possible, he'd been haunted by the primal courage of Cinderella racing into the flames. Haunted by his own personal nightmares now two and a half years old.

Triage…it was part of a deputy's job to handle things until the EMTs arrived on an accident scene. Trying to stop dangerous bleeding. Get victims out of cars before they caught fire. Keep the injured from moving until medics got there with the neck braces or back boards so often necessary before they could whisk the victims off to the emergency room.

How many times had Cash watched the ambulance's flashing red lights disappearing toward Whitewater General Hospital? Only once had he climbed into his car and followed them. Raced after the EMTs into rooms filled with the biting smell of antiseptic. Witnessed the rush of medical staff starting drips, cutting away clothes, washing off blood so they could see the wounds beneath.

He pulled to a stop in front of Rowena's place, his hands gripping the wheel to keep them from shaking. His head swam with images he'd tried to block from his mind, leaving him dizzy. Sick to his stomach. Wondering how in the hell he was going to make it home.

Home where the rooms still reminded him of the days after Lisa's wreck, and horror all the paint in the world could never blot from his mind.

He waited for Rowena to climb out of the vehicle, but she only sat there, watching him. "Now that we've got Cinder and family tended to, it's time to take a look at you, Deputy Lawless."

Cash knew what she was doing—using his official title to put distance between them, make him feel more at ease after the raw places he'd revealed to her.

"I'm fine," he insisted.

"Actually, you've got some pretty nasty-looking scorch marks on the back of your shirt. I want to see what's underneath them."

"I'm used to taking care of myself."

"I know. But this time you'll just have to resign yourself to letting me check you over. Burns are a great entry point for infection, in case you weren't listening when Dr. Wilcox gave us Cinderella's prognosis. You might be able to dress the burns on your knuckles, but your back is way out of your reach."

"It doesn't hurt." Not compared to the gaping wound in his chest.

"That doesn't mean you aren't burned there. Adrenaline

dulls your pain sensitivity. Upstairs. I mean it, Cash. Better surrender now, and save what's left of your pride."

What was left? Not much, Cash thought. Not when he was coward enough to feel grateful to her for giving him a slight reprieve from being in his house, alone.

He switched off the engine. Grabbing the laundry basket full of all-but-ruined clothes, he followed her to the door. She took the basket from him and stashed it behind a bush outside, to keep from bringing the stench from smoke and seared fur into the apartment.

She might as well have not bothered, considering that every layer of clothing he wore was saturated with the very same smells.

He climbed the stairs after her, his eyes feeling parched and itchy. Once in the kitchen, she turned on the overhead light then wheeled to face him.

"All right, let's see what we've got here." She reached for the buttons that marched down the front of his uniform shirt. Cash knew he should do it himself, and yet, his own hands felt too large, too awkward, too heavy with mistakes they'd made at an accident scene long ago.

Her knuckles brushed the hollow of his throat, then lower, down to the middle of his chest, his stomach, hesitating where his equipment belt cinched his waist, the wide leather strap weighted down with his gun, his nightstick, his flashlight, whatever he might need on a call. She carefully laid it all aside, then pulled out his shirttails and eased the scorched cloth off him.

Cash winced when she came to his injured elbow, the dried blood gluing the shirt to the wound. Regret shaped her mouth as she pulled the fabric loose then dropped the garment to the floor. Grabbing a clean kitchen towel, she dabbed at the newly opened cut until the wound quit seeping. Her gaze shifted. He saw her moisten her lips as she peered at his naked chest.

Grabbing up a washcloth and filling another bowl with

water, she returned and began cleansing the cut, dabbing away the dirt and blood. She ran a fingertip over his tattoo, obviously trying to distract him.

"U.S.M.C.—I wondered what this said. That day I charged into your house I barely got a glimpse."

"My buddies and I got them on our last liberty before we left for Kuwait."

"You were in Desert Storm?"

"Yeah."

"How…was it?"

He grimaced. "It was hot as hell."

"Tonight can't have been much better for you," she said, turning his burning arm in her cool hands. "You're a mess. It would take an hour to clean all the soot and such off you this way. I can't see what part's dirt, what part's burn. Do you think you could take a shower? That would clean away the worst of the grime so I could see what I'm doing."

He couldn't argue with that. She took him to her bathroom, started water running then gathered an armload of sky-blue towels from the closet. Cash tried to take them from her, fumbled, knocking something from the rim of her sink—a rubber-ducky-shaped soap dish that bounced when it hit the floor.

Cash stared down at his hands as if they weren't attached. They'd been tired from all the painting he'd been doing. Now, after the fire, they felt practically useless.

"Sorry," he said. "It's like my hands aren't working right."

"No problem." Rowena grabbed the smirking duck and dumped it into the sink. "Pretty much everything around here gets knocked off at some point. If I had anything breakable around here the critters would all think their names were 'no' or 'stop that!'"

He fumbled with the fastenings of his pants, knowing he was supposed to be heading for the shower. His knuckle split, bled.

"Let me help." She said it so simply. Cash clenched his jaw as she unbuttoned his fly, unzipped it, her fingers brushing him through the front of his briefs.

She caught her lower lip between her teeth and Cash knew he should take over. How difficult could it be to hook his thumbs in the waistband and shove the ash-stained pants down his legs? But he couldn't make himself move.

She folded her jean-clad legs under her and untied his boots. And Cash let her. Let her work the stiff leather off his feet and divest him of first one sock, then the other. She hooked her fingers in his pants pockets and then drew them down his legs. His change and keys jangled as his pants hit the floor. He kicked his bare feet free of the material and he was standing in Rowena's bathroom wearing nothing but navy blue briefs. Wisps of her hair feathered against his thigh, her hands still touching him, her finger tracing a three-inch scar near his left knee.

She didn't even ask how he'd gotten it, but the story beat its way into his mouth.

He walked to the window, with its blurred glass to keep people from looking in.

"Do you have any idea how sharp metal can be when a car gets twisted in an accident?" he asked quietly. "The sheets crumple like tinfoil, but so much sharper. Even before the firefighters use the jaws of life to tear the passenger compartment open. Charlie was right when she described it. Like—like teeth, these horrible, metal teeth I had to fight my way through to reach her."

Cash felt a crushing weight on his chest, as if he couldn't breathe. But not because of the smoke that had seared his lungs hours before. Instead, it was a different stench, the sickly sweet, metallic smell of blood.

"The people at the department called you to the scene the minute they knew your family was involved?" Rowena asked.

"No. I was first responder. All I knew was that a car had been hit by a semi. They don't have to tell you that there are going to be serious injuries in a case like that. You know. I didn't realize that my kids were in that car until I drove over the hill and saw…"

He wrestled open the stubborn old window, trying to draw oxygen into his lungs as he peered out into the darkness.

He heard the rustling sounds of Rowena getting to her feet, felt her slip her arms around his waist. She laid her cheek against his back, her silky hair feathering against his waist, her warm arms around him.

"The car had rolled, landed on its roof down in the middle of the highway. I still don't know how any of them survived it. When I got to them, the kids were screaming. I could see Lisa's arm was broken, her sleeve soaked with leaking gasoline. She was wild with panic, begging me to get them out."

She'd been terrified for the girls, Cash remembered. Strange, that was the closest to his wife he had ever felt.

"I knew…knew I should leave them where they were, just…wait for the EMTs. There could have been spinal injuries. God knew what. But the engine was smoking. Gasoline had spilled everywhere. One spark and the whole car would have blown up. Charlie was closest. I grabbed her, handed her out to some Good Samaritan who'd stopped to help. The semi driver cut Lisa out of her seat belt while I went in for Mac. She took the worst of it. Her legs…her little legs were trapped."

Rowena held him even tighter, and he could feel the warm wetness of tears on his skin.

"I reached in where they were caught, tried to work Mac free, but I couldn't get her out. The car's engine was smoking. I thought…thought she was going to burn to death if I didn't get her out of there. I braced myself against the car, grabbed her tight and…I pulled."

Bile rose in Cash's throat. "I did that to Mac. Made all those scars and breaks so bad when I pulled her out."

"Cash, her legs were broken from the wreck. You're not responsible."

"Four more minutes. That's all it took before the firefighters got there. With the tools they needed to stabilize Mac's legs and get her out the right way."

"You thought the car was going to explode."

"But it didn't. You know what keeps me up at night, Rowena? What if I'm the reason my little girl never walks again?"

"MacKenzie *is* going to walk again, Cash. You saw her pull up on Destroyer yourself. But the real reason she's going to get back on her feet is because of you. Every day you will your strength into that little girl. Every day you believe so hard that Mac has to believe herself."

"And that will change what? It won't wash me clean of everything I've done wrong. When I ran into the fire after that cat, all I could think of was that cat is a better mother than the one I gave my children. And what kind of father am I? I hate their mother. I hate her."

"Almost as much as you hate yourself?"

Cash started as Rowena's blunt words sliced deep, rang true. How long had she known?

"Maybe if you could forgive, you could start over. All that hate isn't doing those babies of yours any good, Cash. It can only hurt them."

"Sometimes I feel like all that poison is the only emotion that's keeping me standing. I see you and…I try to remember what it was like to be…clean. Whole."

Rowena turned him to face her. "All you have to do to heal is let in some light. Take care…not only of your daughters, but of yourself. You can't ignore wounds and you can't hide them.

You have to be willing to let someone else see them, touch them."

Irritation nudged him. "What the hell do you call what I'm doing now?"

She stood on tiptoe and kissed him, her mouth soft, tender on his. "I call it a start."

She turned toward the shower, opened the door, guided him in. Water streamed down over him when she turned the nozzle on. He closed his eyes and leaned his head back, let the spray drum against his face, beat his bare shoulders, water soaking through his briefs. He heard the shower door click shut then heard the hollow knock of something against the shower's interior wall.

Rowena had come with him, followed him through the fire of memories into the water she'd offered to cool him.

"Bend down so I can reach your hair," she said. Cash opened his eyes and memorized the look of her, her face dewy with droplets, her clothes getting wet. Then he did as she asked, surprised at the sudden freedom of letting someone take care of him just a little. She washed his hair, her fingers feeling like heaven massaging his scalp. Then she rubbed soap between her hands, the scent of oranges battering back the thick, choking odor of sweat and smoke.

Lather foamed between her slender fingers and she set the soap aside, began rubbing her slick palms against his left hand. Between his fingers, up his arm, kneading the tight, aching muscles. She lingered over the cut on his elbow, and he welcomed the sting of soap on raw skin. It made him feel as if she really were searing it away somehow, the grime he'd felt gone forever.

She worked up to his shoulder, then onto his soot-smeared chest. Slow, deliberate circles she drew on his skin, so careful to cleanse away every bit of sweat or dirt, as if she'd take forever if he needed her to.

Forever with Rowena and the hot, soothing water, her hands gathering what was broken inside him until even he could feel her piecing him back together again. There was no place on his body she didn't touch. No place in the darkness of his soul she couldn't reach.

He'd expected her to recoil from all that ugliness he'd revealed, but she never did. She didn't love him in spite of all his flaws. She loved him because of them. Because she knew how he'd survived each day. Because she'd seen him at his worst and at his best and she knew what kind of man he wanted to be, even if he never could achieve it.

He could feel in the very marrow of his bones how much magic she deserved. All the impossible wonder in those love songs he heard sometimes. But she wanted *him*. He hardened against the clinging wet cotton of his briefs, knew she had to guess how close he was to the breaking point.

But she hadn't kissed him. Not once. Hadn't even shed her clothes. She just stood in the shower with him, patiently washing away stains no one else could see. Her T-shirt clung to her breasts, her aureoles visible through the almost transparent cloth, her feet bare as she knelt down to wash his legs. He knew she had to notice his erection, but there was no seduction in her touch, no temptress trying to break through his control.

Her words in the squad came back to him, her promise she wouldn't jump his bones unless he asked her to. Her efforts to respect the boundaries he'd drawn humbled him. Her emotional courage awed him. And he knew Rowena would always do what she promised, say what she meant, be exactly who she was, no matter how much darkness battered her.

She carried her own light.

He whispered her name hoarsely, admitting something he'd never imagined saying to anyone again, let alone to a woman.

"I need you."

Not *want*—in spite of the way his body clamored for release. Not *desire*—because that was too fleeting. She filled up the hole in his chest. She thawed the hard in his heart. She spurred in him the courage to try…

Her gaze caught his, warm as spring sun, starting a greening inside Cash that drove back winter gray. He could feel life unfurling inside him, opening up to possibilities that should have terrified him. Did terrify him.

She stood up, catching the hem of her wet shirt as she rose, pulling it over her head, dropping it to the shower floor.

What the hell could he say? She was beautiful? That didn't begin to describe what he saw in the perfection of her breasts, the tips of her nipples already pearled and eager for his mouth.

She fumbled with her jeans, and he helped her take the sodden denim off. Then he gathered her to him, felt her naked thighs against his, her breasts bare against his chest, his hard-on burning through the layer of cotton, eager to push past the last barrier between them.

She pulled back just a little. Cash saw her glance at his damp briefs, but instead of going for the elastic waistband, she hesitated. And Cash loved her for it—for the surprising shyness in her, a refreshing kind of innocence that amazed him. He stripped the underwear away himself, man enough to be pleased at the way her eyes widened as she saw him up close for the first time.

Water and rivulets of soap suds streamed down him, washing him all over. He kissed her, long and deep, sweet, life-giving kisses that dragged him up to the surface again from where he'd been buried. Her hands cupped his face, stroked back his wet hair, her touch feathering down his throat, then spreading, splay-fingered down his back.

His breath caught just a little as one of her fingernails

scratched a sore patch. She turned him around and kissed near the place on his skin, her fingertips and eyes searching for any wound, any scar. But Cash doubted at the moment that he'd be aware of even the most excruciating pain, as long as Rowena kept using her gift upon him, healing him with those determined, tender hands.

"It's just a scrape," she whispered, sounding relieved. "I'll put some antiseptic on it when we get out."

"Later," Cash said. "It's your turn." He took up the orange-scented soap to wash her body now, but far differently than she'd touched his—stroking into her flesh needs he'd ignored, bringing to the task all the passion of a man who'd not touched a woman's body in so long.

A man who'd never known what it felt like to bury himself in the sensation of loving his woman with both body and soul.

When he was finished, he turned off the shower and shoved open the glass door, grabbing one of the towels from the stack she'd laid out for him earlier.

They dried each other, hands and towels slipping over bodies they were learning by heart. In spite of the passion rising between them, she insisted on spreading ointment on his back, his elbow, and his split knuckle, then bandaging them. Only when she was satisfied they wouldn't get infected did she let him take her hand and lead her to the bed.

Rowena sat down and he eased her backwards into mounds of pillows colored orange and purple, red and gold. Her skin— pale and exquisite as Miss Marigold's finest porcelain—stood out in stark relief against the vibrant flowers blooming on her sheets. He stroked her damp hair away from her face and kissed her temple, her cheek, her throat, pausing when he felt the subtle bump of an old scar on her collarbone.

How had she gotten it? he wondered, tracing the shape of it

with his thumb. If it had been during one of the attacks Bryony told him of, no wonder Rowena's family feared for her. It chilled him to think how close the animal had gotten to her throat.

The thought pushed hard at the arousal pulsing through him, but couldn't drag caution back up from where he'd abandoned it a short time ago. It was too late to turn back now. Need for her, primal, thick, beat inside him, instincts denied so long threatening to rage out of control.

He couldn't let them. Wouldn't let them. Not this time. Their first time. He braced his weight on one elbow, swearing to himself he was going to take this slow, give her all the pleasure he could. A small payment for the risk she had taken, welcoming him to her bed.

He kissed the small round scar, drowning in her scents, her taste, textures uniquely Rowena's own. Savoring stirring the response in her he'd craved for so long. She was on fire for him, he could feel it, as she trailed her fingers across his skin, her bare legs restless, tangling with his.

She didn't say a thing, as if she was afraid she'd break the spell—that he might draw back, reconsider the risks, pull away from her and leave her with her emotions wide open to him, all defenses stripped away.

But he was too far gone to be wise now. He'd denied himself too much. And the hunger in him for Rowena was so fierce there was no way he could keep from spending this night in her arms.

Cash teased the corner of her mouth with his tongue, losing himself in the blade-edged torture of self-restraint, penetrating her lips the way he'd soon be burying himself in her body.

She moaned when she opened her mouth and let him inside. He sank into the moment, savoring her, stroking her, his palm on the swell of her stomach, his little finger circling her navel, dipping inside.

Rowena kissed him with an eagerness, a sweetness, that shook Cash to his bones, disarming him with her gasps of pleasure and unrestrained moans of delight. He palmed her breast, the globe so dainty against his far rougher hand, her nipple blushed and taut with arousal as he bent to draw it into his mouth. He flicked the hardened bud with his tongue, swirled around the tip once, twice, while she arched her back, begging for the sensations he could give her. He sucked her in, pulled her deep, teased her with the gentlest brush of his teeth while she cried out, her fingers tightening against his waist as if to keep him from ever pulling away.

As if he could now that he had her, naked, wanting him. Cash dragged his mouth across the place where her heart was pounding, to the other crest in need of his care. But his own needs were clamoring, as well, his hips flexing, instinctively pushing his hardness against her hip. She moved just a little, and the brush of downy curls against him beckoned him toward his goal, threatening to unleash the beast in him that wanted to take, screamed for release.

He fought it back and slid his hand down Rowena's belly, sifting through the soft hair at the crux of her thighs. "Open for me," he urged her as he dipped his fingers lower, found her silky center. She did as he asked, parting her legs for him, just a little.

Cash bit back a groan as he slid his longest finger down, found the tiny bead he knew could make her writhe under his touch, cry out his name.

And he wanted to hear her say it, wanted to pierce her so deep she'd never forget this night. The first night he'd buried himself inside her.

"Cash...I've needed you...for so long...wanted this." Rowena kissed wherever she could reach, his chest, his nipple, the heat of her breath ratcheting the temperature up inside him, leaving him gasping.

She didn't say she loved him. She didn't have to. She pressed that truth into his skin, breathed it into his mouth, murmured it to his soul as she trailed her fingers down, feather-light, tentative, until she touched him, traced him. He felt so heavy, so hot in her grasp he feared he'd explode. The torturous seeking of her fingers made Cash grit his teeth as pleasure threatened to throw him over the brink. He nudged her legs apart with his knee and eased himself into the cove between her thighs.

His whole body raged with the need to drive his shaft home, bury himself to the hilt in her, spill himself inside her. He imagined how damned different it would be to hear Rowena tell him the news that his baby was growing inside her.

A baby who would be bathed in love from the moment Rowena knew it existed. What the hell was wrong with him? Some throwback to cavemen days when impregnating a woman was number one on the evolutionary scale. He still didn't know where this relationship between them was leading. And he wouldn't take advantage of the way Rowena gave her heart. Too completely to guard herself.

"Protection," he said, more gruffly than he intended. "I don't want to make you pregnant."

But that was a lie, selfish sonofabitch that he was. Some part of Cash *wanted* to say the hell with being safe. Wanted to lay his cheek on her stomach and feel a new life they'd created together kicking inside her. As if he didn't already have more than he could handle with the babies he'd fathered without thinking the consequences through.

"The drawer in the night table," Rowena directed him.

Cash rummaged around, found the unopened box. He tore the packaging open, sheathed himself, the muscles in his arms rigid, his heart racing as he wedged his hips between her slender legs. He found the damp heat of her with the blunt tip of his sex.

He tried to close his eyes, not able to bear the way she was looking up at him, with love so naked it terrified him. But he needed her too badly. He couldn't even pull his own emotional barriers down to deflect the impact she had on him.

Gritting his teeth against the agonizing pleasure, he thrust his hips forward, felt her body glove him as he sank into her, inch by inch.

Rowena gasped when he'd buried himself to the hilt, her fingers clutching his hips as if to hold him, tight inside her. But he wanted more. Wanted to hear her cry out, shattering with pleasure beneath him.

He drew out, then thrust home, burying himself deeply inside her with far more than just his body, hard as it was. He drove into her, wanting to stay where they were forever, wanting to lose himself in her so he'd never have to face the man he hated again. The man he'd seen in the mirror every morning for the past two years. What would it be like to look at his face and find the man he saw reflected back to him in Rowena's eyes?

But Cash wasn't that man. He never could be. All he could give Rowena was right now. Physical pleasure so intense it made him feel as if he were speeding, out of control. And Rowena was hurtling along with him.

She met him, thrust for thrust, cry for cry, as generous with her loving as she was with everything else. And he could feel the climax he was building in her. Feel her limbs shaking, her head tossing. She reached for it, knew that he could give it to her. And he wanted her to have everything she'd ever dreamed of in a lover. Wanted her to fly.

As he neared his own release, he reached between them, found her, stroked her, his fingers keeping rhythm with his hips, his voice hoarse as he urged her to come.

Rowena clutched him tight as Cash caught her breast in his

mouth, sucked hard, drawing her in. Letting her inside even thought he wasn't sure he wanted to.

His thumb pressed hard on the nubbin of flesh as he drove himself deep one last time. Rowena cried out in release, her whole body shaking, and Cash could feel the sensation rushing through her again and again and again.

Every muscle in Cash's frame went rigid, and he gave a hoarse cry of triumph as he found his own release.

It poured through him, driving back loneliness for a miraculous instant. Battering back self-doubt. He collapsed on top of Rowena, burying his face in her neck, his breath ragged, his body sated in a way he'd never known.

He damned well didn't cry. An ex-marine would rather be hung. It was sweat, pure and simple, that made Rowena's skin feel damp beneath his face.

She stroked his hair, his shoulders, kissed his ear, the only place she could reach.

"Rowena?" he murmured against her.

"What, Cash?"

He lifted his face, looked down at her, her kiss-reddened lips, tumbled hair, the thickly lashed eyelids that seemed suddenly far too heavy.

He searched for the words, but how could he tell her what she'd given him tonight?

She feathered her fingertips over his lips. "It's all right. You can tell me. Anything."

Anything…secrets like Charlie had shared with her, fears like the animals she'd healed revealed when she was near them. Charming out the pain, drawing out the things that stung or burned or scarred. Washing it all away the way his mother had bleached white the sheets she'd hung out on the line.

He could imagine how anyone else would react if he blurted that homespun comparison out. But Rowena would understand things he was trying to say, words that didn't even begin to measure up to the feelings clamoring to the surface inside him.

"Rowena," he whispered, tracing her cheek. "I feel...*clean*."

Her eyes glistened with tears, and for a moment she stayed silent, then she smiled an angel's smile that belonged to him alone.

"I hoped that you would."

"You hope too much," he warned, knowing he couldn't live with himself if he didn't tell her the truth. "I don't have... whatever it is inside you that gives you that kind of strength. Even now, after making love with you, I can't be sure I ever will."

She smoothed the lines etched in his forehead from burdens he'd carried alone, and he felt her touch down to his very soul. "When it comes to hope I've got enough for all of us."

CHAPTER EIGHTEEN

EARLY MORNING SUNSHINE streamed across the mussed-up bed, Cash's chiseled masculine body deliciously out of place against the splashy sunflower-print sheets. Rowena perched on the corner of the bed, her back against the footboard, her arms clasped loosely around her knees. The nightgown she'd slipped on when she'd sneaked out to start the coffeemaker drifted over her bare feet.

She should have been amused at the contrast of Cash's honed muscle and long limbs awash in sunflowers, and yet, something about the sight of him sleeping so soundly made her throat feel tight.

When was the last time this fiercely responsible man had relaxed the way he was right now? Flat on his stomach, his arms bent, hands folded under his temple. He looked so young with his profile softened in sleep, his lips parted, thick, dark lashes heavy on his cheek. And as Rowena gazed down at him, she could see shades of his little girls. Charlie's nose was exactly like his; so was MacKenzie's stubborn little chin.

Rowena hugged her knees tighter to her chest, the harrowing tale Cash had told her last night flashing back in her mind, the images he'd colored so vivid it was as if she had been there with him, trying to wrest his children from the gnarled metal that held them trapped.

Cash, whose job forced him to see other cars explode, see

other victims of crashes burn. Cash, faced in those few crucial moments with the terrible choice between putting pressure on Mac's broken legs or letting her lie there while the pool of gasoline kept spreading and the odds that a spark from the engine could touch it off grew more perilous by the second.

Cash had made love to her twice more during the night. And Rowena had sensed it was as if Cash were hoarding the feelings, the sensations in his memory, as if he didn't trust in any kind of future where he could be happy.

He'd been so hungry for her that it made her ache to think how long he'd been alone. Not just the two years after the accident, but longer still. When he was trying to make a life with a wife he'd never loved the way a man like Cash was designed to love a woman: tenaciously, with that steadfastness so deeply ingrained in his very nature.

It was as if he'd been starved for touch, like the creatures she'd worked with for so long. And yet, in spite of how wonderful their lovemaking had been, Rowena sensed the minute he woke this morning, Cash would begin counting the cost. Figuring in his children, everything they needed. Knowing how little time, how few the resources he had left.

"Hey."

Rowena suddenly realized he was watching her with one dark eye. "Good morning," she said with a smile.

Cash rolled to his side and stretched, the toned muscles of his chest rippling as he ran his hand back through his hair. Rowena wished she could just reach for him, drive his shadows away, but she knew better than to try. Tension was already curling around him. And regret?

Rowena tried not to let that possibility sting her. "I talked to Dr. Wilcox, and Cinder and her babies made it through the night. They're not out of the woods yet, but they're a pack of fighters, just like the hero who saved them."

She saw him wince. "I'm no hero," he said.

"You're my hero. For so many reasons. But I know you're not ready to hear that."

Cash frowned. Rowena felt her stomach sink. "Rowena, last night was amazing. But…"

"Why did I figure 'but' would be one of the first words out of your mouth this morning?"

"You deserve to hear the truth." Cash's jaw worked. "Things are complicated. I'm still not sure what I'm doing here. I should be home trying to figure out how the hell I'm going to deal with whatever is happening with my kids. Who knows how Lisa coming back into the girls' lives might affect them? And Mac needs to work harder than ever trying to walk. I've got to keep focused, Rowena. There's not much left of me at the day's end as it is. I can't plan any kind of future…anything."

Rowena couldn't deny his words hurt. At least she'd braced herself for them.

She nestled in beside him, comforting herself with the warmth of him, the strength of him so close, at least for now. "Cash, you want to know what I love about dogs?"

"Dogs?" He frowned, an incredulous cast to his far too serious face.

Good, Rowena thought. She'd managed to throw him off balance.

"We just had sex."

"Made love," she corrected gently. "You made love to me, Cash. I'll never forget the way you touched me, kissed me."

Cash swore under his breath, looking pleased, looking uneasy. "If it was even a tenth as incredible for you as it was for me, I'd be grateful. But that doesn't change what's real. We don't know where the hell this thing between us is going and you're talking about dogs? Rowena, what the devil do dogs have to do with how damned messy life can get?"

"A lot, if we humans are smart enough to learn from them," she said, drawing a pattern on his chest, the rough mat of hair abrading her palm. "Dogs love every minute of every day. They don't worry about what might happen tomorrow or regret what happened yesterday. They embrace the moment. Feel grateful just to *be*."

"Lucky bastards," Cash muttered.

"Why can't you and I follow their example for at least a little while? Not ruin what happened last night by coming up with the jillion and one reasons we shouldn't have done it, or all the ways it's too hard or too difficult to make work."

"Ignoring the problems aren't going to make them go away," he warned.

"There's no doubt about that," Rowena said, stopping to consider. "They'll all still be right there when we have to face them. But today will already be gone. So let's keep today simple. I made some coffee. We can stick it in travel mugs and head to your house to let Destroyer out. He's probably worried sick about you by now."

"You think?" Cash asked, surprised that the possibility warmed him.

"Oh yeah." Rowena smiled. "Come on, Deputy, let's get some caffeine in you. We're both going to need it if we're going to get the house back in order before the girls get home."

"What?"

"It's Sunday. My day off, remember? I want to spend it painting with you."

"Rowena, you don't have to—"

"I want to. For strictly selfish motives. That way, we'll have more time to just…be…when tonight comes."

"Be? Hell!" Cash grimaced. "I know my own limits. If you're anyplace near me tonight I won't be able to keep my hands off you!"

"I'm counting on it," Rowena said, and kissed him just above his heart.

THE PAINTING WAS DONE. Cash knew he should be setting the rest of the house in shipshape order, but damned if he could make himself do it. Not with Rowena looking so irresistible, paint-spattered and rosy-cheeked, her eyes sparkling.

He'd ordered pizza when they'd been so famished they couldn't hold a paint roller or brush. They'd shared the pie on the only horizontal surface in the house that wasn't stacked neck-deep in stuff. When Rowena had dripped a bit of sauce on her chin, he hadn't been able to resist licking it off. Her mouth tasted even better. They'd taken another trip to the shower and ended up back in bed. Too tired to move, Rowena had teased, but apparently not too tired to make love.

Cash couldn't help it, trying to squeeze in every moment he could with Rowena underneath him. She'd grown more relaxed every time they came together, and he'd grown more desperate. He could feel his real life breathing down his neck. Knew that once the girls came home everything would be different. Moments like these, with Rowena naked in his bed, in his arms, would be almost impossible.

And yet, he tried to be in the moment. It's not as if he didn't have plenty of reminders about how dogs handled life. He now had not only Destroyer, but Lucy and her pups in his backyard, the arrangement only logical while Rowena and he worked.

The puppies at least gave the Newfie some kind of baby to fret over after his lonely night. Cash had felt like a real jerk when the dog leapt all over him in a frenzy of relief the minute he'd unlatched the cage. Destroyer still looked pensive, and determinedly carried Charlie's rollerblade around with him, but at least the dog wasn't howling anymore.

Rowena purred, rubbing herself sleepily against Cash, burrowing into him like a cat, and he felt himself start to harden, wanting her again. Tempted to drive her even higher than before, he kissed her throat, her breasts, blazing a path down her belly. He started inching lower, encouraged by her soft moan, when the pack of dogs fired off louder than a goddamn Fourth of July fireworks display.

Cash glanced at the clock—almost ten. Then he sat up in bed, his cop instinct driving him to go to the window, look out into the backyard. All the pugs were plastered to the fence by the driveway, barking wildly. But the only glimpse Cash caught of Destroyer was a flash of giant fuzzy butt bailing over the top of the fence.

Cash threw Rowena his robe, then jammed his legs into his jeans as he headed out to see what the devil was going on. But before he could reach the front door, it burst open in a blur of bounding, joyous dog and Charlie's worried face.

Charlie?

Cash barely had time to process the fact it was her before Lisa swept in, pushing Mac in her wheelchair. He froze, sensing Rowena right behind him, knowing the instant Lisa realized they'd been in bed together. It didn't take a genius to figure out what they'd been up to. Cash could only pray Charlie was too young to sort it out.

"You aren't supposed to be here until tomorrow night," Cash accused.

"Daddy, I was getting all worried, and—and the house is all torn up." Alarm spread across Charlie's face. "Rowena's here. Rowena, did you come 'cause there was a disaster?"

Cash half-expected Rowena to jump in, but she only moved to stand beside him, letting him handle this his way. He'd sworn he'd never let this happen to his girls. Never let them stumble in on him with a woman.

"I told Rowena she could come here in case of emergency," Charlie explained. "Did you have a tornado, Daddy?"

"No. I was just doing some painting. Rowena, uh, helped."

He could see what Lisa thought of the bright new colors by the arch of her elegant brow.

"Rowena, this is Lisa," Cash said, feeling awkward as hell. "Lisa, Rowena Brown."

"Were you trying to trick us by painting the house all new?" Mac frowned.

"Trick you?" Cash echoed.

"Like that bad woodsman daddy in Hansel and Gretel." Mac scowled. "What if you lost us and we couldn't find home ever again?"

"No danger of that, kitten. Your mom knows where to find me." He wished to hell she didn't; he and the girls, off somewhere in witness protection. Except that he shouldn't hide them from their mother. He only wanted to. "And even if your mom didn't, I'd come and get you. I could never ever be without my girls."

Did Lisa's expression change when he said that? Cash's gut clenched like a fist.

He turned toward his ex-wife. "So what are you doing here? Now? You could have telephoned."

"The line was busy. Probably because someone knocked it off the hook." Lisa pointed to the phone dangling off its cradle.

"My cell—"

"I don't know why you didn't hear it. Unless it's set on vibrate."

She didn't add, *Hard to feel that when you're not wearing any pants.* But Cash was thinking the very same thing.

Damn. As if this whole "return of the prodigal mother" scene weren't difficult enough. He'd had to indulge himself, not only have sex with Rowena, but have her sleep here in his house.

His daughters' home.

And the way the girls were eyeing Rowena's present state of undress, there was no doubt the two of them would come up with plenty of questions.

"I came here early because what I have to say just couldn't

wait," Lisa said, glancing with barely veiled hostility from Rowena to Cash. "We had a good time together, didn't we, girls? Made some wonderful new friends."

"What kind of friends?" Cash asked, suspicious, knowing he didn't have much room to criticize at the moment.

"Good friends, yessiree," Mac claimed. "I went to this doctor. Do you know they've got the best doctor in the world in Chicago, Daddy? He can make me walk in two snips of a lamb's tail."

Cash's glare snapped to Lisa's face. She looked a little guilty, even under all that perfect makeup. Outrage pulsed through him. "You took my daughter to a doctor in Chicago without my consent?"

"MacKenzie is my daughter, too. When I moved to Chicago I arranged for copies of all her medical records to be sent to me."

It had been part of the divorce settlement. Seemed harmless enough at the time. He'd never imagined she'd try to hijack control of Mac's treatment.

"I've been keeping track of her progress, Cash and…we need to get a few things settled."

Her attitude irritated the hell out of him.

"Maybe your, ah, babysitter, could take the girls someplace so we can talk."

The look Lisa shot Rowena, so full of superiority, burned Cash, badly. Rowena knew him well enough to gauge his control was about to snap.

"It's okay," Rowena soothed. "You want to see your rooms, girls? Your daddy painted them, too."

But Charlie hung back from Rowena, looking reluctant.

"Maybe we could go out back and get Destroyer's new friends," Rowena tried to tempt her. "There are some pug puppies I'm working with."

"Oh, goodie!" Mac enthused, rolling her wheelchair into the

kitchen. Cash knew she'd made it outside on her own when he heard the familiar bang of the screen door closing behind her.

Cash's sense of foreboding worsened when Charlie didn't add her delight to her sister's. Charlie leveled a probing stare on Rowena. "You can't go outside without clothes on."

Cash winced inwardly as Rowena's cheeks flooded with color. "I'll go get some right now," she said, turning and fleeing back to the bedroom. It didn't take her ten seconds to come back out, her painting clothes on—one of his old Marine Corps T-shirts and those split-kneed jeans.

But Charlie didn't look relieved. Something was definitely wrong in the girls' world and Cash's oldest daughter was smart enough to know it. He could see the furrows in her brow, the dread in her eyes. She crossed over to him and leaned against his side as if she were silently asking him to protect her from whatever bad thing was making the grownups in the room seem like a pot about to boil over.

Charlie's fear made Cash resolve to hold his temper together for his children's sake as Rowena tried to herd the children out of the line of fire. But Charlie dug in by his side.

"Charlotte Rose, outside," Cash ordered as gently as he could. "Now."

Charlie started at his command and in that moment Cash knew how Benedict Arnold must have felt. Charlie's bottom lip quivered, but she did as she was bid. She skirted around Rowena as if she were afraid the woman was going to bite her, then she fled outside, Destroyer following right behind her.

"I'll just go watch them," Rowena said. "Take as long as you need."

Cash listened until he heard the hollow clunk, Rowena shutting the door solidly behind them, leaving him and Lisa alone. Good thinking on her part, closing Mac and Charlie off from the discussion their parents were about to have.

"Why don't we just cut to the chase? What exactly is this sudden transformation into a concerned mother?"

"I know I haven't exactly been mother of the year since I moved to Chicago, Cash—"

"That's for goddamned sure."

Lisa only seemed to steady herself and plunged on. "I'm not proud of the way I've behaved. But I've never stopped loving my girls."

He snorted in disgust. "You've got a funny way of showing it. You know, this weekend the old boathouse down in Jubilee park caught fire and I rescued a cat who had more mothering skills than you."

Pain filled Lisa's eyes. "We were always good at hurting each other, weren't we, Cashel?"

"And you were good at bailing any time there was any kind of conflict between us. Running away doesn't solve anything."

"Neither does being cruel. How does that make things better for our children?"

Cash stalked away from her, fisted one hand against the wall. He wanted to beat his knuckles against it until the plaster broke, his knuckles bled. Damned if Rowena hadn't said almost the same thing. Hate—that most corrosive emotion. One that two innocent kids shouldn't ever have to see do its ugly work, especially between their parents.

Cash went into the kitchen, needing room to pace. He knew Lisa had followed him. He could smell her expensive perfume. He clenched his jaw, reaching deep for the truth. "You abandoned them. They needed you."

"I wasn't any good to them. Not in the shape I was in."

Cash sucked in a breath, meaning to argue, but Lisa cut in.

"You know it's true. I was miserable even before the accident, Cash. And afterwards…I left because I was two steps away from taking a handful of those pain pills the doctors pre-scribed for me, wanting just…peace."

She'd contemplated suicide? Cash recoiled from the thought. He'd never loved Lisa the way he should have, but she'd been his wife for six years. The mother of his children. "Our life together was so terrible?" he asked.

"Yes. It was. I hated it here. You knew that. I didn't have anything for myself. A career. A purpose."

"You think I would have stood in your way? You could have done anything you wanted. I would have supported you."

"Yes. You would have. But there's one thing I needed you couldn't give. You couldn't love me, Cash. You never did."

What could he say to that? It was true. He compared what he'd felt for Lisa with the way his heart raced every time Rowena came into a room. The way he'd had sex with Lisa, as if there was still a wall between them, and no matter what, they couldn't seem to reach each other.

With Rowena, every nerve in his body seemed attuned to her, every wall crashed down, every sensation sharper, sweeter.

He didn't want to feel sorry for Lisa, or regret the pieces of himself he'd withheld from her. In the end, she hadn't loved him either. But in spite of all that, he couldn't help regretting all those barren years.

"We could spend all night talking about how we failed each other," Cash said. "But in the end, this is ancient history. What matters is now." More of Rowena's wisdom.

"That's what I want to negotiate with you. The future."

Negotiate? That sounded bad. Real bad.

"And so you appear out of the blue?" Cash challenged, the tension cinching tight again. "Take Mac to some doctor? Feed her some line about how he'd make her walk in no time?"

"John says…"

"John?" Cash sneered. "Well, if *John* says it."

"From the looks of things your social life is not exactly on hold either," she snapped. "I might as well just blurt out the whole thing. You're going to take it wrong any way I say it."

"Then get it over with."

"John is an orthopedic surgeon. I hired him to help me make sense of Mac's medical reports."

"So you didn't completely ignore Mac's condition," Cash said. "That doesn't give you the right to make medical decisions without my consent."

"And just because John is my fiancé doesn't change the fact that he's one of the top men in his field."

"You're getting married?" This interfering stranger—a goddamned doctor—was going to play stepfather to his girls? Panic jolted Cash, as if a steering wheel had just gotten yanked out of his hands and his life was careening out of control.

"The wedding is in June. He's worked on cutting edge treatments at the university hospital at Northwestern. He's been studying MacKenzie's case."

Resentment crushed Cash in his grip. "Dr. Malley is Mac's doctor. He's been with her through every surgery, every step of the way."

"Exactly which *steps* would those be, Cash? As far as I can see, MacKenzie hasn't taken any steps at all."

Cash slammed his fist into the wall. "Damn it, Lisa, Mac's starting to stand on her own now, and—"

"Losing your temper isn't going to change the truth. I know you've been doing the best you can, but this town is so far off the medical map that it might as well not exist."

"We're hardly using leeches and witch doctors around here."

"John measured MacKenzie this weekend and he's putting up handrails on every wall in our condo. So as soon as she's on her feet she'll be able to hold onto them, make her way around without that horrible wheelchair."

Cash didn't want to feel this sudden sense of inadequacy. Wanted to cling to hate, anger. "And who's going to go through Mac's exercises with her? Hold her hand while the doctors are pulling out stitches or poking where it hurts and she's scared and crying? You couldn't stomach it before. Why do you think you can do it now?"

Lisa couldn't meet his eyes. "John is going to hire someone to come to our home to help with the things that were too hard for me before."

"A stranger can do it better than her own father can?"

"A trained professional—"

"She has sessions with her physical therapist all the time right here. But nobody, Lisa, *nobody* else knows Mac the way I do."

Lisa sighed. "You always *have* felt like no one can possibly do things as well as you."

"And all of a sudden you can?"

"The whole city is handicapped accessible. She would have the best of everything. Every advantage money can buy. Museums. Culture. The finest schools in addition to superior medical care."

"So we're back to money again, are we? I can damned well support my own daughters! They've got a roof over their head. Plenty to eat. Clothes on their backs. But most of all they know when they need me I'll be right here."

Lisa fidgeted with the diamond ring on her finger. It was the size of a goddamned gumball. How had he missed seeing it?

"Cash, I've grown up a lot the last two years. When I left, those first few months it was a relief not to have to face the mess our marriage had become. A relief not to hear Mac screaming and not be able to stop her pain. I know you think I was weak, a coward, a terrible mother. I thought so, too. Then I started to miss the girls terribly."

"All you had to do was pick up the phone," Cash said, bitter. "You didn't."

"I was ashamed. Have you ever made a mistake that horrified you so much you could never forgive yourself?"

What the hell could he say? "You know I have."

"I started therapy with a really gifted psychologist. Wanted to sort through all the wrong turns I had taken, figure out how my life got so tangled up. She's the one who suggested I talk to John about Mac. It was hard, Cash, to be honest with myself, get all the ugliness out in the open. But in time I came to realize how much I love my children."

Cash gave a snort of dismissal.

"I know you think I don't deserve MacKenzie," Lisa said. "And maybe you're right. But maybe what we should both consider is what *she* deserves. And which one of us can best give it to her."

Cash reeled inwardly, trying to imagine Mac gone. Not waking her up every morning, seeing that grumpy face she always made. Not dressing her and buckling her into her wheelchair. No more battles, trying to get her to fight her way up to her feet. His life would be so much easier, a dark voice whispered. Not to have all that responsibility on his shoulders.

No. What his life would be was *unbearable*.

"We can fight this all out in court if we have to," Lisa said, "but I hope we don't have to put the girls through it."

Lisa? The voice of reason? Cash wanted to puke.

"All I'm asking you is this, Cash. Just think about it. I'm going to stay at March Winds tonight. Maybe we can meet for coffee tomorrow and discuss this further."

She was staying at the local B&B Deirdre Stone and her sister-in-law ran? Terrific. Cash wanted Lisa as far away from town as possible.

"If tomorrow is too soon, we can talk when I pick them up a week from Friday."

"What do you mean a week from Friday?"

"I'll be taking them on every one of my visitation days from now on. And their next summer vacation. John's lawyer says the court should award me at least two months."

Two months? Just these few days without his kids had left Cash ragged.

"Lisa...don't do this. Those girls are my life."

"I know," she said quietly. "That's why I plan to leave Charlotte with you when MacKenzie moves to Chicago."

"Separate the girls?" He tried to imagine the damage that would do. Cash flashed back to the years before the split. How Lisa had doted on MacKenzie. The baby she'd actually wanted, maybe hoped would fix their floundering marriage. He couldn't help but feel Lisa's rejection of their oldest child like a boot in the stomach.

"That's the arrangement I'd like to propose," Lisa said. "Believe it or not, Cash, I'm not trying to ruin your life. I want custody of MacKenzie so I can focus all my energy on her while she's learning to walk. The advantages I can give her..."

"And you're going to explain all this to Charlie how?"

"She spent most of the visit up in the loft bedroom because her sister couldn't follow her up the ladder."

"That's what kids do. Try to ditch younger siblings. I tried to ditch my little brothers all the time." Not that his mom had let him get away with it very often.

"Well, then think how happy she'll be when we sort this out. Her sister in Chicago, and her, here with you. Unless you don't want custody of Charlie."

Cash's rage broke free. "You're right, Lisa," he shouted in cutting sarcasm. "I don't want either of my kids. It's too much trouble. I want to do what you did and take two goddamn years off to do whatever the fuck I want to."

He spun around and kicked the kitchen chair. It careened across the floor, smashing into the stove with a hellacious clatter.

He didn't hear the tiny cry a dozen yards from the window Rowena had opened earlier to clear that new paint smell from the house. Didn't see Charlie drop the football she'd been tossing to Destroyer as her whole wide world fell apart.

CHAPTER NINETEEN

LISA WAS LONG GONE and the girls were finally sleeping when Cash loaded the dog crate in the back of Rowena's van, the pug puppies completely exhausted after their day in his backyard. Cash shut the hatchback, then noticed Destroyer's mangled football lying forgotten beside the fence. He picked up the dog's favorite toy and turned it in his hands, feeling chewed up and spit out himself after Lisa's little announcement.

"She wants custody of Mac," he told Rowena flatly.

"What?" Rowena paled, her eyes stark with disbelief, pain. Hell, she looked almost as rotten as he felt.

"She's got some specialist in the city who says he can get Mac on her feet faster than we can here. I can keep Charlie, as far as Lisa's concerned, but she's going to fight me for Mac. In court if necessary."

"Well, she can't have Mac!" Rowena protested, every bit as stricken as he was. "You're the one that child depends on, Cash. Every moment of every day. You're her rock."

"Am I?" Cash leaned his back against the car and stared up at the stars. Dawn was just starting to scrub them out. "Right now I feel like I'm anything but. What if this doctor of Lisa's is right? What if moving to Chicago would mean..." He hesitated, faced a possibility too painful. "You come from a family of doctors, Rowena. What if I'm just being a selfish bastard keeping her here and I'm denying my little girl her best chance?"

"Has she been to any of the university hospitals? Seen any specialists in the past?"

"Right after the accident they life-flighted her to Iowa City. She had two of her surgeries there. That's when we hooked up with Dr. Malley. Everyone said he was the best."

"What did he say?"

"He said people heal in their own time."

"I've seen that with animals, too." Rowena nodded, so earnest. "You try to rush them and it sets them back instead of pushing them forward."

"I push, Rowena."

"Sometimes. But mostly, you love her, encourage her. Believe in her."

Cash looked away. "I can't just dismiss this new prognosis as crap. No matter how much I want to."

"If you want to have this new doctor of Lisa's checked out, fine. I can call Bryony. She's tough to impress. But even if there *is* merit to what this doctor is suggesting, Mac moving in with Lisa isn't the only way to make that work. I can help you get her to the city for treatment. My mom would be thrilled if I were driving to Chicago more often."

"No, she wouldn't, if you were ferrying my kid there. And she'd have every reason not to be. You've already done too much for my family." He must have looked like hell. Rowena slid her hand down his arm, the shirt he'd grabbed after Lisa left rippling under her touch.

"That's my decision to make. I know all this upheaval is hard, Cash, but you're going to have to pull it together. Charlie suspects that something is going on. She barely even looked at the puppies. Or me."

Cash heard the hurt in Rowena's voice. Charlie *had* been wary of Rowena, that old, haunted look in his little girl's eyes. No—not the old expression at all. Something new pinched Charlie's pale face: shock, pain, as if Destroyer had suddenly wheeled around to bite her. She'd shut Rowena out completely and she didn't trust Cash at the moment either. He'd felt plenty rotten himself when Charlie had posted a KEEP OUT sign on her bedroom door an hour before. Even when he'd knocked, asking her to let him in, she'd stubbornly refused.

I got to think and I think better when I'm alone. Her muffled reply made him wince. The words could just as easily have come out of his mouth. He'd always been one to withdraw, sort things out. Maybe that's why the last two years were so hard. There had been no time, no safe place to do either.

He'd give Charlie some space, and they could talk more in the morning. By then, maybe he would have figured out what to say.

"I know Charlie's acting strange," he reasoned, "but she was just surprised to find you in my bathrobe. That's a lot for a nine-year-old to handle."

"Too much right now, with everything else going on." Rowena looked so wistful he reached for her. She slid into his arms, fitting against him as if she belonged there forever. "I think I should stay away for a while, Cash," she said, leaning her cheek against his chest. "Give the three of you time to sort this out."

"No." Cash held on tight. "Charlie will get used to us being together in time. Everyone in Whitewater is going to have to."

"What?"

"I realized one thing for certain tonight." He hesitated, the words feeling so important it was hard for him to say them aloud. He took her chin between his fingers and forced it up so she was looking right at him. "Rowena, I'm in love with you."

God, it felt good to say it out loud. Scary as hell, but good.

Cash held his breath, waiting. He knew she loved him, but he needed to hear her say it. Needed to know she was as far past the point of no return as he was. What would it feel like? To love a woman and know she loved you back?

Rowena looked so shaken it terrified him. "What's that thing lying on the grass?"

"What?" Cash drew back, confused, a little irritated. He'd just told her he loved her, and it was as if she hadn't even heard him. She was pulling out of his arms, opening the gate and hurrying toward some object that caught the light's beam with a metallic glimmer.

Cash followed her and scooped up the thing before she could reach it, in case it was something sharp—the lid of a tin can, a dangerous piece of metal. When he turned the object over in his hand, he frowned. "It's a weird thing for somebody to drop," he said, glancing up at her alarmingly pale face. "It's a can opener."

"It's Charlie's," Rowena whispered. "I gave it to her. I saw her climb up to the tree house and put it in her survival kit with my own eyes."

"She must be plenty mad," Cash said, "throwing it out like she did."

"Throwing it out when? She didn't go near the tree house tonight. And the can opener wasn't there when I came over to paint. Something's not right, Cash."

Foreboding closed in. Cash loped into the house, Rowena right behind him. His boot caught a bucket of paint as he rushed to Charlie's room. He didn't even bother to see if the can was sealed. He opened her bedroom door, the tape holding the Keep Out sign pulling loose in the draft from the wide open window, the piece of notebook paper drifting to the floor. Cash flicked on the overhead light.

What the hell? Adrenaline shot through his system. The covers were lumpy, but there wasn't a single wisp of Charlie's brown hair visible on the pillow. And the dog—he'd been glued to the kid since she got home. Now Destroyer was nowhere to be seen. Cash flung back the covers, revealing the stuffed animals Charlie had used to make it look as if she was still there.

But she wasn't. The bed was empty.

"There's a note," Rowena said, hurrying over to Charlie's desk. She handed him a piece of loose-leaf paper with "Daddy" printed on it in purple crayon.

Cash grabbed the letter, unfolded it and read aloud.

Dear Daddy,
I know it is real hard for you to take care of Mac and me all by yourself. Now Mommy wants Mac but she doesn't want me. It's O.K. It's better if I take care of myself. Don't worry. I got everything I need. Even my flashlight.
Yours Truly,
Charlotte Rose Lawless

His little girl was out there, somewhere in the night, alone?

Cash's blood ran cold as possibilities flashed through his mind. He'd seen the worst of them happen before. She could run in front of a car that couldn't see her in the dark. She could fall and get hurt. Some sick sonofabitch could get his hands on her.

And what had made her run?

Cash staggered back a step under the weight of Charlie's words, his eyes finding Rowena's heartbroken gaze. "How the hell did she know all this?" Cash asked. "The door was shut when Lisa and I were fighting. I know it was. But the things we said…this is too damned close to be a coincidence."

A breeze lifted the curtains. Rowena stared at it, her face ashen. "The windows," she said. "They were all open because of the paint. Charlie must have been close enough to overhear…"

How could she have avoided it? He'd been yelling his head

off, so angry, so scared, feeling gut shot over the possibility he might lose his children. Cash flinched, remembering how ugly things had gotten when he'd stormed into the kitchen, kicked the chair. "I said I didn't want the girls. I said it was too much trouble," he choked out.

"No, you would never—"

"I was being sarcastic, but Charlie didn't know that. She just heard that her mother didn't want her. And now she thinks I don't want her either. You warned me about letting all that hate for Lisa come out. Christ, Rowena. How long ago do you think she left? Where would she go?"

"Someplace she feels safe. I'll check the tree house. The play house. You search the inside. She couldn't have gotten far."

Cash clung to that as he whistled sharply for the dog. "Charlie!" he yelled as he ran through the house, flipping on lights, flinging open closet doors. Nothing.

Mac came awake grumbling, startled from her sleep. Cash rushed into her room, the blinding glare of lights leaving Mac blinking. "Mac," Cash said, scooping her up in his arms, "your sister's gone. Did she say anything to you? Where she was going?"

"Going?" Mac scrubbed at her eyes with one fist.

"Did Charlie tell you she was running away?" Cash demanded.

"Charlie runned away?" Big tears welled up in Mac's eyes. "Bad stuff happens when you run away. Monsters eat you an' witches steal you an' you never come back." She started to sob, kicking her legs. Any other time, Cash would have rejoiced at it—Mac's movements stronger than they'd ever been before. But now, with Charlie missing, the kicks only seemed to worsen the foreboding in his gut.

"I want my sister!" Mac wailed. "I want my sister!"

Rowena bolted into the room. "Charlie's backpack is gone, and a bunch of stuff from that box up in the tree house is missing."

"She's not in the house," Cash said.

"Then she's out there, somewhere." Rowena waved at the darkened window.

Cash beat back the rush of pure terror shooting through him. *Panic is deadly.* A distraction he couldn't afford. He grappled for the focus and calm that had gotten him through combat. But this was different. It wasn't his life that could be in danger. It was his little girl's.

Think! He told himself fiercely. *Damn it think how to find her!*

"Destroyer is with her," Rowena said.

Cash latched on to that. "Charlie might be able to hide, but that dog of hers is impossible to miss."

"That dog will guard her with his life, Cash."

And yet—there were dangers even a Newfoundland couldn't protect a child from. The fact that Destroyer was with Charlie didn't guarantee that either one of them were safe.

"We're going to find her," Rowena said. "Call Lisa. She can watch Mac while we search."

Cash recoiled from the idea of asking his ex-wife for anything. *Admit I lost my own kid?* For a heartbeat Cash resisted. Wouldn't that give Lisa plenty of ammo for a custody suit? But before he could weigh out the danger, he handed Mac to Rowena and grabbed up the phone.

What mattered was finding Charlie as fast as possible. And if Lisa were here, he and Rowena could split up, cover twice the ground. He hung up bare minutes later, having started the chain that would notify whoever necessary. Vinny, Lisa, the Stones. Whoever Charlie might seek out in her pain.

Lisa, sounding as panicked as Cash felt, wanted to join the search. He'd convinced her she could help most by coming to the house to calm Mac. Vinny was calling the Sheriff's department for good measure, the dispatcher asking whoever was on patrol to keep their eyes peeled.

"Daddy's real good at finding people," Mac said. "He finded me when the big truck hit me. Didn't you, Daddy?"

Cash's stomach sank, remembering. All the guilt, all the dread, the gnawing fear that he'd damaged his child instead of saving her.

"Your daddy is going to find Charlie, too," Rowena insisted, with so much faith in him it tamed the old memories, shoved them back where they belonged.

"I'm going to check out the way to Hope's house. And the park," Cash told her.

"Go!" Rowena urged. "I'll head out in the other direction as soon as Lisa gets here. If you find them, Cash, call right away."

"I will." He opened the door and set out at a dead run, self-blame heavy on his shoulders. If anything happened to Charlie it would be his fault. For losing his goddamned temper, letting all that hate for Lisa out. His little girl had heard it. His stomach churned at the knowledge. She'd never forget the things he'd said. The things her mommy and daddy had said to each other.

Let me tell her I'm sorry. Let me try to explain...

He prayed harder than he had since the accident two years ago. But he felt no more absolution now than he had then.

This time he hadn't twisted up his child's legs. This time he'd scarred something even harder to heal.

His little girl's heart.

ROWENA'S SWEATY FINGERS clamped around the handle of the flashlight she'd gotten from the mudroom, her lungs burning, her heart pounding. For almost an hour, she'd been searching, anyplace she could think of where a little girl might hide. She'd checked in with Cash on the cell phone, but neither he, Jake Stone nor anyone else who was searching had caught a glimpse of the lost little girl or the big dog. A fact that was beginning to tighten the grip of fears pooling all around them with the night's darkest shadows.

I've looked everywhere I can think of, Rowena thought miserably. *Where else could she be? Her favorite places. Her safe places. Somewhere all those books of hers would say could shield her from disaster...*

If only Charlie knew the one place she'd be safer than any other was her own daddy's arms.

But how could you find a child as good at disappearing as Charlie was? Fading into the background? It was as if the little girl finally *had* learned how to make herself invisible.

Rowena felt queasy with remorse. She was the one who had made such a disaster out of things. If she hadn't been fresh out of Cash's bed when the girls got home none of this would have happened. With the girls still in the house Cash would never have allowed himself to lose his temper. But with Rowena watching the kids at what he'd thought was a safe distance away, he'd let his anger get the better of him.

She hadn't kept Charlie safe.

Now the little girl was out there somewhere, scared, alone, believing that even Cash didn't want her.

The very thought was absurd. And yet, Charlie had seen far too many terrible things happen before. The accident that had destroyed the only life she'd ever known. Her sister walking one day, in a wheelchair the next. Her mother disappearing, then coming back just to reject her all over again. In Charlie's world days were spent waiting for the sky to fall on her head. No calamity was out of the realm of possibility.

But the whimsy other children took for granted was. The word *impossible* was reserved for make-believe or dreams come true or magic whistles Cuchullain once played.

From the moment Charlie had gone missing Rowena had sensed the little girl's desperate need for someone to prove that she was wrong. That she wasn't invisible, that it would matter if she disappeared, that her daddy loved her enough to come after her. That maybe, just maybe there was some bit of magic left in the world that seemed so big and scary and uncertain.

Rowena remembered Charlie's reaction to the whistle and her heart squeezed, the little girl dismissing the story with a wistfulness that showed just how much she wished it was true, that Cuchullain's fairy pipe could heal even the most wounded spirits. Even Destroyer's reaction to the haunting melody Rowena had played hadn't convinced the little girl. The dog suddenly enchanted, blissful, drawing nearer to Rowena as if by a spell that lit the way to someone who would love him.

The whistle... Rowena stopped. If Charlie wasn't willing to answer when called, maybe there was someone else who would.

She ran back to Cash's, got in the van and drove to her shop. She rushed in, flicking on the overhead light. Hurrying to her desk, she drew out the antique whistle on its silver chain. She slipped it around her neck then started for the door. Suddenly she froze, staring. A handful of kibbles scattered the counter she'd wiped clean before she locked up Saturday night. Right beside it sat a little pile of money.

Rowena heard a scuffle somewhere deeper in the pet shop. One of the other animals settling in for the night? No. It had to be...

Rowena lifted the whistle to her lips, praying that Auntie Maeve was right and the pipe held mystical powers. For no one in a thousand years had ever needed the power of healing promised by the old Irishwoman more than the little girl who had gone missing tonight.

Soft, sweet, Rowena piped the haunting tune Auntie Maeve had taught her, the one that Charlie hadn't believed could be magic.

Rowena walked through the shop, searching, wooing, calling out to Charlie with all the love in her heart. Until suddenly, a pile of boxes in a corner erupted, an earthquake in the guise of a giant black dog bursting from its midst. Destroyer trotted toward her, looking almost as glad to see Rowena as she was to see the dog.

Relief shot through Rowena as she saw the small figure behind him, huddled as deep into the shadowy corner as possible.

Charlie, so woebegone that tears stung Rowena's eyes. Destroyer sank to his stomach, his big head low, and inched toward Rowena as if to say he was sorry. He should have been able to stop Charlie from running away.

Rowena dropped the whistle, wanting to scoop Charlie up in her arms, but something in the child's face stopped her. An invisible wall, as palpable as the one Charlie's father had once built around him. The kind not even the most determined person could batter through. The prisoner had to give you the key.

Like Cash had tonight, before the world fell apart, Rowena thought, his emotion-roughened voice echoing through her. *I'm in love with you...*

Rowena shook the memory from her mind, guilt raking her again as she hunkered down in front of the little girl still reeling because the adults in her life had failed to protect her.

"Are you hurt, honey?" Rowena asked quietly. She wasn't about to ask if the child was okay. The answer to that was a Destroyer-sized *no.* If Charlie had been fine, she never would have fled the house.

"Where's my daddy?" Charlie asked, and Rowena could see the salty tracks of dried tears on her cheeks.

"He's been looking everywhere for you. How about if I call him right now?"

Charlie looked down at the toes of her shoes.

"He's so worried about you, honey. Please let me?"

Charlie shrugged. "I guess."

Rowena dug her phone out of her jeans pocket and dialed

Cash's cell, the emotion in the man's voice shattering as she told him Charlie was safe at the shop. He promised to rush right over. And what would he find when he got here? Rowena winced, taking in every detail of the bedraggled little girl before her.

Charlie's jacket sleeve was torn. The zipper on the backpack Rowena had once teased could make the trek up Mount Everest lay split wide open, empty of "all the stuff" Charlie needed to feel safe. Only one can of corn and a rawhide bone were left of all her tools and provisions.

Rowena tucked her phone away and hunkered down. "Where have you been all this time? People are looking for you everywhere. Your daddy and me. Mr. Stone and Mr. Google and all the deputies your daddy works with. We didn't see you anywhere."

"First I went to the old boathouse. Me and Hope went down there once with her uncle. My backpack ripped and stuff fell in the river. I tried to get it back, but Destroyer wouldn't let me."

"Thank God!" Rowena shuddered, thinking of the Mississippi, so unpredictable, with its treacherous currents.

"He grabbed my arm and pulled and pulled until all my stuff disappeared. But then I didn't have anything for him to eat. So I came here and got the key out of that little rock you keep it in. I left money on the counter for the food I took. I wasn't stealing."

"I know you weren't, honey."

"And then, I couldn't go back outside because I figured something out that's really bad."

That your father is sleeping with someone? That your mother doesn't want custody of you? That she wants to take your little sister away?

Rowena couldn't resist smoothing a tendril of hair back from where tears had glued it to Charlie's cheek. "What did you find out?"

Hollow-eyed, the little girl peered up at her, so empty of

hope Rowena couldn't bear it. "It doesn't matter how hard you work to get ready," Charlie said. "Even disaster kits don't matter. Bad stuff happens anyway."

Rowena searched for wisdom, wanting so badly to find the words to reach past the fears gripping this child she'd come to love. "It may seem that way sometimes," she reasoned. "But maybe the problem is counting on things like bottled water and extra flashlight batteries to keep you safe. Maybe it's magic you should be depending on instead."

"Magic's not real."

"Isn't it? The magic whistle called to me all the way across town tonight. It made me come here. It helped me find you, safe and sound." Instinct made Rowena draw the chain over her head, the whistle cupped in the palm of her hand. "You want to know what its secret is?" she asked as she tilted the silver tube to catch the light. It glimmered, drawing Charlie's gaze. "It's love, Charlie. That's the magic. And I want to give it to you."

Rowena slipped the necklace over Charlie's head. The little girl touched the tin whistle with her finger as if she wanted so badly to believe.

"I know the world looks scary sometimes," Rowena said, "and it's true you can't count on some things. But there are others you can depend on."

"Like what?"

"Someone who won't ever let you disappear, even if you try to run away or fall in the river. Someone who loves you with all their heart."

"Remember I told you people only love the cute ones. Like the puppies Mommy got rid of when they got too big. Like the kitty Hope's going to get. Like Mommy loves Mac because she's little and looks like a Christmas tree angel."

"Destroyer wouldn't ever leave you alone, would he? I knew it the instant I saw the two of you together. You were a perfect match."

As if in answer, the dog scooted over and laid his head in Charlie's lap.

"Your daddy would never leave you alone either," Rowena assured her.

Charlie picked at a tuft of Destroyer's fur. "But I'm alone lots of time after school when Daddy's busy with Mac. He's like—like a birthday cake cut up in so many pieces there almost isn't any left. That's why…"

Charlie chafed her bottom lip with her teeth, and Rowena could see the child teetering on the knife's edge of confessing her true feelings, terrified about the calamity such honesty could bring.

"Why what, sweetheart?" Rowena asked. "You can tell me."

Charlie's little voice got gruff, her eyes pleading for understanding. "I can't like you anymore, Rowena," she confided. "If my daddy gets in love with you, I'm scared there won't be any room left for me."

Rowena felt pain pierce her heart, the memory of Cash declaring he loved her still fresh, a little raw, a little too precious to touch. Something she'd longed for. Something this child would view with dismay.

"I try not to care he's so busy," Charlie went on, "but I want my daddy back the way he was before. I want my tree house to get done with a roof and a slide. And I want my mommy to love me as much as Mac. But nobody ever loves me best."

"Your puppy loves you best in the whole world."

"No. He and Mac get locked up in her room and I've got to share because she can't go play with other kids and…I want Daddy even more than I want my doggy. Does that make me bad?"

"Of course not!"

"I've already lost Mommy. And now Mac's going to go away. When I heard Daddy say he didn't want me either I just wanted to really get invisible. 'Cause maybe then it wouldn't hurt so bad. But it didn't matter. It still made my tummy feel all icky inside."

"Well, you don't have to get invisible, not ever again," Rowena promised.

"But I don't know what else to do."

"How about if we try something different?" Rowena suggested, fighting to keep her voice from breaking just like her heart. "This time I'll disappear instead."

"You would do that? For me?" Charlie's eyes clouded, so old, so sad.

Rowena nodded, her own chest aching. "Cross my heart."

Destroyer woofed as a car screeched to a halt at the curb, lights flashing, and Rowena knew Cash had caught a ride in the patrol car nearest wherever he'd been. He rushed into the shop, haggard, his face seeming to have aged ten years.

"Jesus Christ, Charlie!" he swore, scooping his little girl up in his arms. "I was so scared I lost you!"

He kissed her cheek fiercely as she buried her face in his neck.

"I'm sorry, baby," he soothed, hugging her tight. "I'm so damned sorry for everything you overheard between me and your mom. I was just angry, saying things I didn't mean. If I ever lost you..."

His voice cracked, and Rowena knew the images flashing through his mind, how close he'd come to losing Mac to the accident, how many ways Charlie could have disappeared into the night. "You're my whole life, Charlie."

Rowena loved him all the more, knowing that was true.

Charlie leaned back, cradled Cash's face between her hands. "You're *my* whole life, too, Daddy. I know you found Mac after the crash. But...tonight...want to know a secret? I was scared you'd give up because it was only me."

"Only you?"

Rowena saw his face contort with disbelief.

"Charlotte Rose Lawless, don't you know how special you are? You were my very first baby. The first baby whose smile made me…feel love so big my heart couldn't even hold it. From the minute you opened your eyes, I knew the most important thing in my world was being your daddy. And I knew I'd hold on to you with everything inside me and never, ever let you go. You were the most beautiful baby I'd ever seen."

Rowena saw Charlie frown, doubtful.

"But in the picture the hospital took my head was all pointy on top and I had a big red scratch on my face," Charlie said. "I think you got me confused with Mac."

"I do not, Charlie. I remember exactly how you looked the first time the nurse put you in my arms. You didn't even cry when you were born. You were so patient, Charlie. You looked up at me. And…I fell in love. I'm sorry I let you down. I'm sorry for everything. For not paying enough attention to you. For not noticing that you needed me. That you were feeling invisible. I'll do better from now on. I promise."

Charlie looked into his eyes, so earnest, so much like her father, Rowena felt her heart break, felt their hearts heal as Charlie promised.

"I'll do better, too. See, I've got magic now." She pulled the whistle up on its chain and showed it to him. "It came from a fairy godmother and it makes hurting stuff all better 'cause it's got love inside. Rowena said so."

Cash's gaze found Rowena's, and in that instant Rowena knew just how much she'd lost.

"Rowena can teach you everything there is to know about magic," Cash said, his heart in his eyes. "And love."

No, Rowena thought. Not everything.

Cash held on tight to those he loved.

She let go.

CHAPTER TWENTY

CASH SAT ACROSS the kitchen table from his ex-wife and tried to squeeze his heart back into his chest. He felt slashed wide open by the night's events, every nerve bare, every mistake he'd ever made lying right out in the open. He wished he'd been able to convince Rowena to stay, needing her near him. But she'd insisted they could talk later. His family needed time alone.

He'd let her go for the time being, secure in the knowledge she loved him, grateful, so grateful he'd been given this second chance. To build a life. To be a parent. To make a new family with a woman he loved, and show his little girls by example just how beautiful life could be.

And life would be beautiful here in this house now that Rowena had transformed it: turned its gray walls bright with color, banished the gray of dreams lost and brought hope back into the lives of Cash and his children. Made Charlie believe in magic again. Feel safe.

And Charlie did. He's seen it in his little girl's eyes when he'd held her on his lap in Rowena's van, as she'd dropped them off and he'd carried Charlie in to bed. His bed, not hers.

It was the only one big enough to fit the dual guardians who not only stubbornly insisted on keeping the runaway in sight, but had to be touching her at all times just to make sure she couldn't escape. It had moved Cash to the core, seeing De-stroyer plastered against one side of his daughter, keeping watch, while Mac snuggled in on the other side of her sister, her little hand holding tight to Charlie's pajama top just to make sure her slippery older sister didn't disappear again.

Even Lisa seemed subdued by what had happened. Cash was thankful his ex-wife had greeted their oldest daughter with tears and hugs, as relieved as Cash was to see Charlie safe. And yet, even that couldn't bridge the gap between two warring parents. Cash knew he had to do that himself.

"I lost my temper tonight," he admitted. "Let all that poison between us spill out. And Charlie paid the price."

"She always paid the price, didn't she, Cashel?" Lisa gripped her hands together, her voice shaking. "Somewhere deep inside I blamed her for the fact that we had to get married. And I was jealous when I saw the way you looked at her. But when Mac came along—it was so much easier for me to love her. God, what an ugly thing for a mother to admit. But tonight, while Charlie was missing I had to face the truth about myself. The reason I ran."

"Because it was too hard for you to see Mac in pain." He'd always known the reason. Lisa had told him long ago.

"No. That's what I told you. Told myself. Because it was easier than admitting the truth." Tears welled up in Lisa's eyes. "I left because I was terrified someday Charlie would look in my eyes and guess the truth. That if one of my girls had to be hurt so badly in that accident, I wished it had been her."

Lisa looked at him, and he could sense what she expected to see. Revulsion. Disgust. Hate. But in that moment what he felt was grateful. Cash realized he'd known how she felt the whole time. She'd been trying to protect Charlie, in her own way. One he never would have chosen. And yet, trying to protect a child, even in the most misguided way, was something he could understand.

"You didn't want Charlie hurt, Lisa," he said at last. "You wanted Mac well. We both wanted that."

"I kept thinking God was punishing me," Lisa confessed, twisting her engagement ring around her finger. "Because I loved MacKenzie too much and Charlie too little. I can't tell you how many hours I spent with my therapist, trying to believe I could make things better. But I didn't know until tonight how cruel I'd been. When I thought of Charlie alone out there in the dark, thinking I didn't want her...it hurt me so badly, Cash. Then I knew for the first time how much I loved her, too. If I could go back and change the way I held my heart back from her, I would. But all I can do is try for the rest of my life to show her just how much she means to me."

"There are plenty of things we'd both change, Lisa," Cash said. "Tonight Charlie could have been killed because you and I were too busy hurting each other to do what parents are supposed to do—love their children together even if they can't stay married to each other."

"We've never been good at working together. Everything in our marriage was a contest. Either you won or I did. Never both. What are we going to do now? About treatment in Chicago? About custody?" Lisa asked. "And how am I ever going to make it up to Charlie now that I've hurt her so badly?"

Cash lowered his face into his hands. He had plenty of his own fences to mend when it came to his little girl. But Rowena would help him figure out how to heal things in time. "We'll have to put our own needs aside. Think of what's best for the girls. Both of them."

"Even if that means moving them to Chicago?"

"I want Mac to walk as much as you do, Lisa. And I feel like she really is starting to make progress. She's pulling herself up, and—"

Cash stilled, hearing the creak of the bedroom door. A metallic thump he recognized as Mac's wheelchair whacking into the wall.

"It's the girls," he warned, getting to his feet. As if she didn't know. He saw Lisa fight to hide the misery in her face.

"Let me do it!" he heard Mac grouse as the wheelchair banged against something again.

"You're gonna scratch the wall," Charlie warned. "Daddy worked real hard to paint it."

"I don't care about any old paint! Even pink!" Mac insisted.

Cash headed through the living room, then down the hall to see what all the commotion was about. Not only had Mac wrestled her way into the wheelchair, she'd gotten Charlie to put on her leg braces and her sturdy-soled shoes. The kid was definitely dressed for battle and not planning to go back to bed anytime soon.

"You're supposed to be asleep," he said. But the only one who seemed to care about his opinion was the dog. Destroyer dropped down onto his belly and laid his head on his paws.

"Well, I'm not sleeping," Mac insisted with her best "off with their heads" regal glare. "I got important stuff to say and you an' Mommy got to listen."

Cash sighed. He knew he'd have to deal with whatever was on Mac's mind, but he'd be better prepared to face the kid's inevitable questions once he and Lisa finished sorting things out themselves.

"It's been a pretty tough night, kiddo," he said. "Can't it wait until tomorrow?"

"No way." Mac gripped the metal rail that spun her wheels and gave the chair a shove so hard one of the footplates banged into Cash's shin.

"Ouch! Hey, you! Watch it!"

"I'm going to run you right over if I got to!"

"It's that important, huh?"

It must've been. He dodged as she propelled the chair forward with another shove.

"I'm sorry, Daddy," Charlie said, looking miserable again. "I just didn't want her to get a bad surprise like I did. I was just trying to explain—"

"—why Charlie runned away," Mac blustered, hijacking the spotlight again with one of the direst expressions Cash had ever seen. *"Mommy maked her."*

Oh, God. Cash closed his eyes for a moment, surrendering to his youngest daughter's iron will. There was no way Mac would let this subject wait until tomorrow.

Mac all but ran over Cash's feet as she wheeled her chair into the kitchen. He hadn't realized avenging angels came in the guise of five-year-olds wearing Hello Kitty nightgowns, but Mac fit the bill perfectly. Cash, Charlie and the dog followed in her wake.

"Remember, I told you that Mommy and Daddy made a mistake," Cash began, but Mac wasn't hearing any of it.

"Mommy sure made a great big giant-gantic one." Mac leveled a baleful glare on Lisa. "Charlie says you're making me move to your house. But she's got to stay here."

Lisa flushed, struck speechless. Cash knew Mac's translation of the situation was making his ex-wife even more uncomfortable than she already was.

"Well, you're not the boss of me!" Mac crossed her arms over her chest. "Me an' Charlie got important stuff to do right here. We got to take care of our dog and go to school and Charlie's got to come get me at the playground door every day and tell me all the bad things Tyler James did in fourth grade. And me and Daddy got stuff to do, too."

"Your therapy? Maybe I could learn to do it," Lisa said, and Cash knew she meant it. She was willing to try. It surprised him. Warmed him toward her, just a little.

"Therapy stinks! It's *dancing* I got to do."

Cash felt the old knife twist in his chest. How many times

had he and Mac watched that old recital tape, her little body swaying to the music, her arms going through the ballet moves even though her legs couldn't hold her up.

Lisa was trying hard not to cry. "Dancing's not the only thing in the world. There are lots of other things you can do. I could buy you a piano. You could play the pretty music sitting down."

"What are you? Crazy?" Mac gaped at her in horror, as if she were Baryshnikov himself and someone had just suggested he turn in his tights to play Chopsticks. "I'm a dancer. And my daddy dances me whenever I want to. Round and round with my recital dress on."

"In Chicago you could see real dancers do ballet on a great big stage." Lisa tried to tempt her.

"I *am* a real dancer," Mac insisted, in high outrage. "I don't want to sit around and watch. And know what else?"

"I'm listening, MacKenzie," Lisa said, and for once Cash could see that Lisa was.

"I'm *keeping* my sister. 'Cause right now I like her lots better than either one of you!"

Cash saw Charlie's jaw drop. She stared at Mac, and he could see the conflict going on inside, that Charlie was still almost afraid to hope.

"And if you or Daddy even *try* to take us apart, you'll be sorry! Me an' Charlie won't live with either one of you."

Cash glanced at Charlie, saw something wonderful dawn in his little girl's face. Her eyes started to shine.

"Mac, kids have got to live with a mom or dad or I think we'd get arrested," Charlie said. "Besides. We don't have anyplace else to go."

"Oh, yes we do. The tree house! And we'd eat corn every single day and have a flashlight and everything."

Charlie scooted over to her sister, leaned against Mac's chair, looking as if she'd just won something precious.

"Kids, your mom isn't trying to be mean, talking about taking Mac to Chicago," Cash tried to explain. "She was trying to figure out what's best for you, just like I am. We both want the same thing, Mac. You back on your feet."

"I'm *already* on my feet," Mac asserted, thrusting out her chin. "My doggy helped me."

"He did," Charlie affirmed. "Daddy and I saw it, right, Daddy?"

"We did," Cash said, remembering the day she'd gotten her bear from the shelf and the sweet burst of hope he'd felt. She'd been standing now at therapy, too. A little longer every time. "You're so brave, Mac. So strong. I know you'll walk—"

"Walk, walk, walk. I'm sick of hearing 'bout it. If I do it right this minute will you promise to leave me alone? Will you, Mommy?"

"Sweetheart, you can't—"

"You better promise."

"I'd give anything if you'd walk," Lisa said. Cash knew that he would, too. Because walking was the first step toward dancing. And he wanted that for Mac now, more than ever before.

"C'mere, doggy," Mac ordered, regal as a queen. "Charlie, pull me. I'm stuck."

Charlie eyed her parents nervously, then did as she was bid.

Lisa started to protest, but Cash laid a hand on her arm, stopping her.

Mac clenched her little fist in Destroyer's plush fur and grabbed tight to her sister's arm. She scooted her bottom forward to the edge of the wheelchair's seat. "Fold up my feet thingies so I can reach the floor."

Charlie bent down to flip the footrests up at her command. "Like that?"

"Egg-zacly. That's what I like 'bout you, Charlie. You do everything just right. When I grow up, I'm going to be just like you."

Charlie's chest seemed to puff out just a little, her chin a little higher at Mac's praise. "You ready to try standing up?" she asked.

"I'm sick of trying. I'm just going to do it so everybody stops bugging me crazy."

Cash held his breath as Mac set her jaw and pulled, pulled herself hard, pulled herself up, her face turning red with exertion as she got her feet underneath her. She was balancing there on the stiff soles of her shoes, braced between the dog and her sister. Standing, stronger than she'd been since the day her legs had been crushed.

"MacKenzie!" Cash breathed in amazement. "Look at you!"

"You ain't…seen nothing yet." Mac's brow furrowed and she glared down at the floor as if it were an enemy soldier. Slowly, painfully she shifted all her weight to her left foot then slid her right forward three inches. Four. Readjusting her grip on the dog and her sister, she concentrated on shifting her weight again, this time sliding her left foot up to her right.

One step.

Cash held his breath as she fought for every inch.

Two steps.

Three.

Charlie nearly dropped the kid, she looked so stunned. "Mac, you—you're walking."

Mac held her ground, panting, her face glowing with triumph. "Yeah. So there. Me an' Destroyer been practicing. An' I'm not going to Chicago and I'm keeping my sister 'cause Charlie and our doggy are lots better at making me walk than any old doctor ever is. Right, Daddy?"

"I guess so!" Cash fell to his knees. He opened his arms.

Mac let go of her hand holds and reached for him, taking one last step on her own. Into a future far brighter. Into arms she knew would always be there to catch her if she fell. Charlie piled on, too, hugging them both. He wished Rowena was here to see this. His children together, his anger at Lisa tempered, on its way to being healed. Maybe Rowena was right in the end: love could fix what was broken now that he finally believed.

Lisa stood a little way off, crying, suddenly looking so alone. The woman who'd given him these two children. That alone was a gift beyond measure.

He promised himself that he'd try harder to work with her, reason with her, make her a part of their daughters' lives. Mac and Charlie would have Rowena—all her warmth, all her joy. But even then, they deserved the chance to know their real mother, too.

Cash held out his hand to Lisa, inviting her into the circle he and the girls made, a ring of healing. Hope. And she came, hugging Mac, hugging Charlie, her eyes thanking him.

"You did this, Cash," Lisa whispered to him. "Thank you."

Mac's mouth popped open. "What'd you mean, *he* did it?" she complained, pulled back in Cash's grasp. "*I* did it. An' Charlie an' Destroyer. And I'll tell you something else right now, Mister Daddy."

Cash laughed, standing up with his youngest daughter in his arms. "What's that, kitten?" He perched her on the edge of the kitchen table.

"You better get busy makin' our tree house. 'Cause maybe Charlie doesn't like either one of you anymore. An' maybe me an' her'll go out an' live there even when it rains!"

"I like Daddy," Charlie said, a little shyly, leaning against him. "I *love* Daddy." She hesitated, and Cash could feel how big a chance his daughter was about to take. "And I love Mommy, too. But its okay you don't want me, Mommy. I know it's 'cause it's my fault Mac's legs got all smashed."

"Your fault?" Cash asked, dumbstruck. "That's ridiculous, honey. It wasn't—"

"It was so. Remember how me an' Mac always used to fight over the good seat? The side where you could see people's yards?"

Cash remembered. "My brothers and I used to have the same fight. All kids do."

"On the day that truck hit us it was Mac's turn to sit in the good seat. But I wanted to see Jimmy Wong playing Frisbee with his dog. He took it to all kinds of contests and it'd jump way up in the air and catch everything Jimmy threw. I promised Mac could sit in the good seat the next two times if she'd trade that day."

"Charlie, you couldn't know Mac would get hurt," Cash insisted.

But Lisa cut in. "Charlie, I know it's easy to blame yourself when bad things happen to someone you love. I—I've blamed myself for not being quicker to hit the brakes. Not seeing the truck sooner."

"I blamed myself, too," Cash confessed to both of them. "Maybe if I hadn't been so desperate to get Mac out of the truck, the EMTs could have done a better job. I was so scared. All that gasoline spilled."

"You guys are crazy!" Mac said. "The truck man was the one that was bad. He didn't stop at the stoplight. 'Member, Charlie? Daddy said Mr. Google 'rested him."

It had been an arrest Vinny had been thrilled to make. Cash couldn't count the times his ex-partner had said that collar was the one that drove him to retire. He came far too close to putting the trucker's head through a wall.

Lisa gathered Charlie up into her arms. "Maybe it's time we all let the past go and focus on the future. I love you, Charlie. Maybe I didn't know how much until I thought I'd lost you. We'll start all over. Can we? Will you give me another chance?"

"I want to," Charlie confided. "But I'm scared."

"I'm scared, too," Lisa said. "I don't want to make any more mistakes with you. I've made so many."

"Destroyer made lots of mistakes, too, before he got to be our dog," Charlie said. "He even gave Daddy a black eye. But I still love him anyway."

"That's good news," Lisa said, trying to smile. "Maybe there's still hope for me."

"There's hope for all of us," Cash promised. Rowena had taught him that.

He knew it would take time for Charlie's wounds to mend, but at least they were all uncovered. Out in the light and air Rowena promised could heal them.

"Can Mac and I stay with Daddy?" Charlie asked.

"Will you visit me sometimes?" Lisa pleaded. "And let me visit you here? I've missed you. Both."

Charlie looked to her sister and Cash had to smile as Mac balanced her small legs on the Newfoundland's back, using Destroyer as a footstool. "Is that okay with you, Mac?" Charlie queried.

Mac paused to consider. "I guess so. On one condition." The kid might as well have been threatening to turn Little Rabbit FuFu into a Goon. "That you *never* make my sister sad again, Mommy. And Daddy finishes that tree house right away."

The tree house. A symbol of everything Cash had lost. And yet, now it seemed full of possibilities. For the first time since the accident he could imagine Mac climbing up the ladder. He could picture his children storing not disaster kits in the oak's broad branches, but rather, dreams. He could weave fantasies of taking Rowena up there when she was his wife, making love with her under the stars, maybe creating a new life, a baby of their own.

"You said you only had one condition, Mac," Charlie's earnest correction jarred him from picturing joys tomorrow might bring. "You gave two."

Mac plumped out her bottom lip. "I don't care. You ran

away too far this time an' we couldn't find you forever an' ever. You got to have a better place to hide next time so you don't scare me so bad."

"I'm not going to run away," Charlie promised solemnly. "Never again."

"Well, I s'pose that's good." Mac scratched her nose, obviously weighing her sister's promise. "But Daddy's got to finish the tree house anyway. I got to teach you how to play good again before it's too late."

AFTERNOON SUN MADE the shop window glisten like gold as Cash pulled his SUV up to the curb and parked. He fingered the small velvet box in his jacket pocket, nervous as hell, and maybe happier than he'd ever been.

He had so much to tell Rowena. So much to share. MacKenzie's first steps. The way she'd clung to Charlie and the dog. The way Charlie's face had lit up when Mac insisted that she was keeping her sister.

Even the tree house clause in Mac's negotiations would make Rowena laugh. But as much as any of these miracles, he hoped the last one he offered would bring joy to Rowena's heart.

Asking her to be his wife.

And yet, Cash couldn't help but sense Rowena was avoiding him. Not picking up the phone the past week. Not returning his calls. He knew she was trying to give him and the girls the space she thought they needed after the hell they'd gone through the night Charlie had gone missing. But what Rowena had to understand was this: the enchantment the Lawless family really needed most at the moment was *her.* The colorful paint didn't brighten the house nearly as much as Rowena's smiles. The dog didn't shower his girls with even half of Rowena's unconditional love. And not even Cuchullain's magic whistle could awaken in Cash an ounce of the enchantment he felt holding Rowena in his arms.

And she loved him right back.

What could possibly go wrong?

He drew in a deep breath and opened the door. Saw Rowena at the register ringing up what looked like a sack of parrot food as Miss Marigold counted money out of her old-fashioned beaded bag.

As Cash approached, the older woman turned and flashed him a smile beneath the brim of what looked like an old-fashioned Easter bonnet. "Bless my soul! If it isn't that handsome Deputy Lawless!"

Rowena started at the sound of his name. He'd hoped she'd look happy to see him. Instead she looked...ragged around the edges, the light in her eyes so different it sent a shiver of unease down his spine.

"Ma'am," he greeted Miss Marigold, trying to figure out what the devil was wrong. Who had put the sadness in Rowena's glen-green eyes.

"So you're back at the pet shop again," Miss Marigold said. "I'd never have guessed you were an animal lover after the words you said when you chased that awful monster of a dog out of my tea room! I declare, you near burned my ears raw, but I expect I'd be a lot less shockable these days than I once was, considering the company I've started to keep."

"Ms. Brown here has a gift for changing people's minds. Actually, my girls adopted Destroyer. Although I do confess I get tempted to swear at him when he misbehaves now and then."

Miss Marigold tittered and pressed her fingertips to her rather buck teeth. But Cash looked right past her to the golden-haired gypsy who'd snagged his heart. Why was it that even her bracelets didn't seem to jingle quite so merrily today?

"Rowena," he said, low, husky. Her name. It was just her name. And yet he infused it with all the love he felt for her. Why wouldn't she meet his gaze?

"Have you heard the news?" Miss Marigold asked him. "I've finally found a gentleman who appreciates my finer qualities. I always told my folks I was waiting for Cary Grant to sweep me off my feet, but I've decided to settle for Elvis."

"So Vinny sweet-talked you into the parrot at last?" Cash reached for his cop mask, hiding the mounting tension he felt.

"It's true, Vincent did introduce me to my feathery soul mate. But it was that rogue bird himself who won my heart. And in the end, I fell head over heels for Vincent, as well. I just couldn't help myself. Vincent claims that someday he's going to sweep me off to Vegas to get married in an Elvis chapel— in honor of the King who introduced us."

Cash grinned, happy for both of them. One more miracle Rowena had made happen. "You in an Elvis chapel?" he teased. "It's hard to picture."

"Well, young man, there's a lot about me you don't know. I haven't a drop of willpower at all when it comes to love."

"I understand completely." Cash tucked his hand in his pocket, his fingers skimming the velvet on the box. "Love—" he grimaced with a shake of his head "—sneaks right up and bites you in the—"

"Cash!" Rowena protested, and he hated how pale she seemed. "As you can see, I'm sort of busy."

"I can wait. Forever if I have to." As long as she'd let him drive the shadows from her eyes.

Miss Marigold's gaze sharpened. "Well, I declare! Elvis isn't the only one who's looking to 'love me tender.'"

"Miss Marigold," Rowena protested. "This isn't what— what it looks like."

"I may be an old maid, dearie, but my glasses work just fine.

I'll be getting back home. I've a tea party for six in two hours. And I'll wager it'll be an adventure. Elvis has a spicy vocabulary, Deputy, but I confess, I can't wait to hear what he'll say next."

She scooped up her purchases and started toward the door. "Hmm." Miss Marigold turned at the door, surveying Rowena. "You make a very striking couple, the two of you. You might want to consider taking on a man of your own, Ms. Brown. One without feathers or four paws."

Rowena flushed. "I don't think…"

"Just consider the possibility," Miss Marigold suggested. "I must warn you, dear, that being the town's maiden lady isn't all it's cracked up to be. It gets tiresome, being alone. I thank God for my two men every day. Well, my man and my parrot."

Cash went to the door and opened it for the older woman. The bell jangled as it shut.

He turned back to Rowena, a nagging weight in his chest. Something was very wrong. "You haven't been answering my calls."

"No. I've been busy. How—how are the girls?"

"Pretty damned amazing, actually. Charlie's smiling. Mac's taken four steps."

Finally a spark lit her eyes. "Really? Oh, Cash! Thank God!"

"*And* you. She held on to Charlie and that damned dog you foisted off on me. I wish you could have seen her, Rowena."

"You did. That's what matters."

He touched one of the brass dogtags decorating a miniature tree near the register. He could make out the familiar figure etched into the medal. St. Francis of Assisi. The patron saint of animals came complete with a hook ready to be attached to a beloved pet's collar. Cash would have to pick one up for Destroyer. Even Rose Lawless would have to approve of the dog now, looking down from her seat in heaven. Especially since before Rowena and that Newfoundland had come into Cash's life, his family would have fit far better under the jurisdiction of St. Jude, patron of hopeless causes.

"I took your advice about Lisa," he said. "We're working things out. We're not exactly sure what we *are* going to do yet, but we know what we're *not* going to do. Fight with each other, tear our girls apart."

"I'm glad."

"I still don't agree with the way Lisa handled things. But at least I understand what she was trying to do. She's worked hard on herself these past two years. And in her own way she loves the girls."

"I'm…happy for all of you."

She sounded so strange, so withdrawn, her eyes red, their lids heavy as if she hadn't slept. He'd had insomnia long enough himself to know what it meant: a troubled heart.

"If you're happy, why do you look like you want to cry?"

She said nothing. He saw her throat work.

"Rowena, I know everything has been changing, happening so fast. But there's one thing I'm absolutely sure of. You're the reason my daughter is walking. You're the reason Charlie has the dog who kept her safe when I couldn't be there. You gave her your magic whistle. I guess I want to give you something to take its place." He pulled the box out of his pocket. "This didn't come from a fairy godmother, but it's got all my love inside it. Maybe that will be enough."

He opened the box, the engagement ring he'd bought just that morning sparkling. He slipped it out, holding it in the palm of his hand. "I was so sure I'd blown my chance at this kind of loving. But I want to spend the rest of my life with you, making up for lost time. I've even imagined the two of us in the tree house when it's finished. Making love. Making more babies. Making…all the good things you promised life could be."

Anguish welled up in Rowena's eyes. "I can't. We can't."

Cash's chest felt too small. He struggled to quell the dread that gripped him. "What do you mean we can't? You love me. I love you."

"The two of us together would have been complicated before Charlie ran away. But now—it's impossible."

"You don't believe in impossible. That's what you told me."

"I believe in it now. Your girls have been through so much, Cash. And Charlie is so afraid of losing you. Marrying me and forcing them to accept a mother they don't want would be a mistake. I won't be the cause of more hurt in their lives."

Cash reeled in disbelief. "But you're the best thing that ever happened to them."

"Charlie doesn't think so."

"Give her a little time. Remember what it was like between the two of you before she ran away? If it wasn't for you she wouldn't have that dog she loves. I still wouldn't know she felt invisible. You helped my little girl see magic in the world again, Rowena. Don't take it away from her now."

"You're the magic in her world, Cash. You always were. She lost you after the accident and she just got you back. She's scared I'll take you away from her."

Charlie's small, lonely face rose in his memory, how lost she'd been, how brave. Giving her mother a second chance. Forgiving him for the things he'd said, the things he didn't mean. God, he didn't want to put any more fear in her eyes. And yet, he felt as if in losing Rowena he was surrendering a part of his soul.

Cash skimmed his thumb over the ring he'd bought with so much hope, never dreaming she'd turn it down. "But I need you, Rowena," he said, low. "Doesn't that matter at all?"

"It matters. But not enough to change anything. I know you, Cash. You don't know how to do anything but your best. Especially when it comes to your girls. If there were problems later because you married me, you'd never forgive yourself. And I couldn't bear that. I won't have you feel guilty for marrying me. I won't have you look back and resent me."

"I wouldn't. I couldn't," Cash rasped. "Good God, Rowena, I love you."

"I know. But you loved them first." She took his hand, closed his fingers gently over the ring, blocking out its shine. "I won't be changing my mind, Cash. I promised—"

She cut herself off, and he wondered what it was she was about to say. "You promised what?" he asked.

"I promised myself I'd disappear now that you and the girls are—are all healed." She smiled, a wobbly smile. "Giving up something you want with all your heart is the part in fairy tales that makes the magic stick. The miller's daughter giving up her baby so she could spin straw into gold. The Little Mermaid giving up her beautiful voice for a chance to love the prince. I have to give up you."

"What about happily ever after? That's the way the stories I read to Mac always end."

"The watered-down versions, maybe. But if you read the real ones, the old stories, you'd see that sometimes the prince has to love somebody else and the mermaid turns to foam."

"Damn it, Rowena, this isn't some fairy tale. This is real life. *Our* lives."

"I know. But it's not like the ending is any big surprise to me. It's what I always do, you know. Disappear once things are fixed."

She meant it. And the knowledge was killing him. He'd ended up hurting her the way Bryony had feared he would. Rowena had given too much and he'd taken it. All her hope.

All her heart. After everything she'd sacrificed to make his family whole it seemed so damned unfair to leave her all alone.

And yet, her resolve seemed so steely. Her fears all too real.

"You did fix us, Rowena," Cash said softly. "In so many ways." He cradled her cheek, wanting with all his soul to kiss her one last time. But she caught his wrists to stop him. Pain flared, hot in her eyes.

"God, Rowena," he pleaded. "I just wish you'd let me…let me try…"

"It's not worth the risk. You know that even better than I do. Go home, Cash. To your daughters. And if you love me, even a little, respect my decision."

It tore him apart to step away from her, walk out the door. He went back to his house. To the colors she'd chosen, the walls she'd painted, the children she'd healed.

To the lives that she'd changed forever.

The life she was so damned sure that Cash had to live without her.

I TOLD YOU SO was an ugly bunch of words, but tonight Rowena was just miserable enough to risk hearing them. She pulled off Michigan Avenue into her sister's parking garage. Even at four in the morning with her eyes nearly swollen shut, the spacious building Bryony lived in looked gorgeous, elegant, soaring with confidence and all the other things Rowena knew she could never be.

She rushed up to the doorman who'd known two generations of Browns. He took one look at her and buzzed her in, his leathery face worried as he let Bryony know she was on her way to the apartment on the twenty-seventh floor.

"Dr. Brown just got in," Michael said, rushing to push the elevator button for her as if he was afraid she'd miss it. "An emergency at the hospital last night…I hope everything is all right…"

But for the first time in her life, Rowena doubted anything would ever be right again. She leaned against the elevator wall, watching the numbers flash by. The trip seemed to take forever. But when the doors slid silently open, Bryony was waiting on the other side.

"Oh, sweetheart," Bryony said, rushing toward her in a cream silk robe. "What happened?"

"I love him, Bry. And I can't…we can't…be together." Rowena's voice cracked, sobs that had built up during the drive finally breaking free. "It hurts, Bry. It hurts so bad."

For the first time Rowena could remember, no "I told you so" left her sister's lips. Bryony's mouth didn't thin. She didn't even give a long-suffering shake of her head. Instead, Bryony's eyes filled with grief, with love, with understanding.

She opened her arms and pulled Rowena in.

CHAPTER TWENTY-ONE

ROWENA STOOD at the pet-shop window, peering at the playground beyond the chainlink fence. Snowflakes drifted in puffs of white. Bright red ribbons trailed from the lightposts marching down Main Street. Across the way, school windows were trimmed for the holidays, one boasting a snowman tall as any kindergartener. Every morning, some lucky kid got to change the number on its cotton batting tummy, counting down the days until vacation started.

But even Christmas had lost its luster. What was the sense in putting up decorations in her apartment when no one but her would see them? Besides, it only made her wonder what kind of tree the house on Briarwood Lane would have. Not an artificial one like her mother's interior designer had created for the sprawling house in Forest Park, decked with white flocking and cut crystal balls and no colors at all. A real pine would fill Cash's house with the scent of winter and the girls' memory with wanderings through a Christmas tree farm all blanketed in white.

She could imagine Cash carrying Mac up on his shoulders as Charlie earnestly inspected each prospect. Could see him seating Mac on a stump, then kneeling in the snow to cut down whichever tree his girls had chosen.

It was so easy to imagine him selecting the gifts Santa would leave. His beautifully shaped hands putting together a doll's house or a scooter or a new bike. She wondered what it might have been like to creep out to the new green living room with him long after midnight and fill stockings together. Curl up with him and share kisses flavored with peppermint and hot chocolate and the passion she knew would never cool between them.

But the chance for that kind of magic had passed Rowena by. No, not passed. She'd given it up herself. Hadn't done as Cash had asked her, giving Charlie a chance to adapt, get used to…what? Her daddy's love being divided up one more time? His precious time with Charlie subtracted away? Charlie spending her days afraid she'd become invisible again? No.

Charlie had been through so much. The little girl deserved this chance to make up for everything she'd missed. Rowena wouldn't be the one to take it from her.

But knowing that she'd done the right thing didn't stop the ache that kept Rowena awake at night, and none of the projects she'd tried to distract herself with could fill the hole in her heart left by Cash Lawless and his children.

Christmas just seemed to make the loss worse. Rowena couldn't muster the least bit of enthusiasm for the shopping that had once delighted her, finding whimsical presents that would make her too-serious sisters laugh in spite of themselves. And the prospect of one of her mother's elegant formal dinners where everyone would scrupulously avoid the subject of Rowena's latest disaster seemed about as appetizing as turkey-flavored cheesecake.

It wasn't that they were bombarding her with the usual round of "I told you so" phone calls. Or saying "I know this hurts now, but someday you'll see it's better this way." Rowena knew her reprieve was Bryony's doing. Her older sister must have threatened her mom and Ariel with something dire indeed.

Or maybe they'd just realized the truth, as well. That this time Rowena had finally really done what they'd all feared for so long. She'd gotten her heart so chewed up she wasn't sure she'd ever have the courage to risk being bitten again.

So why was she staying here in Whitewater? Because the

shop was finally starting to blossom, now that it had her full attention? The people in the town not only accepting her gift, but delighting in it? That she'd begun to make friends—Miss Marigold and her new fiancé, Vinny, Deirdre Stone and Ms. Daily? Those were logical enough reasons to give her family.

But Rowena had never been good at lying. Even to herself. She stayed because she could peer out of her pet-shop window and catch glimpses of the children she might have called her own and the man she would love forever.

She knew the girls were healing. She could see it for herself. The whole world was moving on. Even Cinder the cat and her litter of kittens had been swooped away from her. When she'd called the vet to ask about bringing them to the pet shop after they'd finished recuperating, Dr. Wilcox had laughed out loud.

Don't you read the newspaper? Every one of those animals is spoken for. At least, they are as of this Friday. That's when their new owners can pick them up. Big doings at the Holiday Program at school.

That little Lawless girl is a kid after your own heart. She found homes for every one of those kittens. Her best friend is taking Cinder on. Cat looks like something from a horror movie after the burns it suffered, but Hope is downright crazy about that animal.

So the little girl who had wanted the "prettiest kitty in the whole world" had come to love the bravest one instead. She wished she could hear Charlie's version of how that transformation had come about.

But when Cash and the girls had stopped by the shop for their monthly supply of dog food Rowena hadn't been able to bring herself to ask the silent, painfully stoic little girl. If you kept picking at a wound it would never heal. Even then, this was one she wasn't sure ever would.

Still, Mac had jabbered like a little jaybird the whole time. *I get to pick a pet of my very own. See, Destroyer can lick me and play dolls with me but he's Charlie's dog, not mine. Daddy e'splained it to me.*

That's wonderful, Rowena had told her. *Your daddy is a very wise man.*

Yeah, Mac had agreed, jumping right into the holiday season. *But he doesn't ride on a camel or anything like the Christmas ones. Maybe Santa Claus will bring me one of those dogs with a pushed-in face like Lucy. Or maybe a kitty. Which one do you think would look pretty in a tutu?*

The postman blotted out Rowena's view of the playground for a moment, scattering the poignant memory. She opened the shop door to take the mail. She sifted through the bills, the advertisements and Christmas cards, then suddenly glimpsed an envelope that made her heart stop.

Charlie's neat printing marched across the envelope. Rowena's fingers shook a little as she opened it.

The students and staff of John Glenn Elementary School invite you to Winter Magic, December 15 at 7:00 p.m.

Beneath it was a personal note. "Be there or else." In parentheses Charlie had noted "Mac made me write that. I just wanted to say please instead."

So Mac was behind the invitation being sent. Rowena could see Mac giving one of her comical regal commands. Charlie reluctantly doing her sister's bidding, trying to soften Mac's orders with "please" even though Charlie would doubtless have anybody come to the performance besides the threat she'd managed to get rid of six weeks before.

Why would Mac want Rowena there? Was the little girl performing somehow? One thing Rowena knew for certain was that Charlie had only sent this under duress.

Rowena didn't want to go. Didn't want to see everything she'd never have.

But when the night of the program came, she watched the cars turn the playground into a parking lot, families spilling out in their holiday finery. Little girls in poufy dresses, boys with their hair neatly combed. Fairy lights twinkling, the winter wind piping a haunting tune.

What if Mac *was* going to be performing again somehow, not dancing yet, but still on her feet? What if Rowena missed this chance to hang back in the shadows and see…see how much stronger Mac had grown, see how much happier Charlie might be. See Cash. Drink in the sight of him, remember the feel of him, his mouth, so hard, so tender, his eyes that hadn't dared look up from duty for so many years. She hoped he was seeing rainbows again and tree houses high overhead.

The clock over the counter read quarter to eight when her resistance finally snapped. Rowena grabbed her keys and locked the door, not even stopping to put on her coat because she was afraid she might change her mind. She dashed across to the school door, snowflakes in her hair.

The school gym was dark, quiet, and for a moment she feared she'd missed the whole program. But then, a teacher announced "We'll close tonight's program with a reading by the winner of our holiday essay contest. Miss Charlotte Lawless."

Charlie. Her hair in French braids, her dark green dress decorated with a puppy in a Santa hat. Rowena glimpsed something silver sparkling in the stage light. Cuchullain's pipe making magic real for another little girl. Charlie crossed the stage, the heels of her patent leather Mary Janes clicking, a look of intense concentration on her face. She adjusted the microphone, then unfolded a piece of paper, its edges crumpled by her hands.

"*Winter Magic* by Charlotte Rose Lawless," she announced. Rowena saw the child look up, knew Charlie had seen Cash when some of the tension melted out of her little shoulders.

"People talk about magic like reindeers that fly," Charlie read. "I never met a single person who saw one. But magic is tricky that way. It doesn't come from big bangs out of magic wands. It would be lots easier to know it was magic if it did.

"Sometimes magic sneaks up on you. Magic is when your sister can't walk but your daddy makes her dance. Magic is getting to keep a dog even after it gave your daddy a black eye. Sometimes magic is somebody seeing you, even when you feel like nobody can.

"Magic can make an ugly cat look pretty. My friend Rowena told me that. I didn't believe her, but the cat my daddy saved from the fire is going to live at Hope's house. Hope thinks Cinder is the most pretty cat in the world.

"That kind of magic is better than being able to turn someone into a frog.

"Turning people into frogs is a very bad idea. Later you get sorry and wish you could change things back. You would even trade your magic whistle if you could. Maybe Christmas is a good time to try."

Rowena's eyes burned, a tiny cry rising in her throat. She saw parents glance up at her. She turned and fled out of the hall. Cold air hit her face and she stumbled, a hand catching her elbow, keeping her from tumbling to the snow-spattered asphalt.

She felt herself being hauled up into strong arms. Cash. She could smell the woodsy scent of his aftershave, feel the familiar hardness of his body. She turned and found herself staring up into dark eyes full of yearning. Why on God's earth had she put herself through this? Seeing him hurt too much. Charlie's words haunted her, making Rowena want to hope. But she didn't have the courage anymore.

"I kept watching for you," Cash murmured. "I was afraid you weren't coming. Mac was sure you would."

"She threatened me." Rowena tried to keep it light, put space between them. "I found out in the grocery store just how harrowing one of her 'or elses' can be. Tell her I'm sorry I missed... whatever it was that she did."

"She got to be a snowflake. It involved wearing a tiara. Jake and Deirdre are taking bets as to how long it'll be before I get that thing off her. Jake's got Halloween. Deirdre's going for a year from this Easter."

"Then maybe I'll get to see it sometime after all. When she's on the playground or…or you're picking up dog food."

"Actually, it was Charlie who wanted you to come to the program so much. Her teacher made her shorten her essay a little for the performance. I thought you might want to read the rest."

Cash reached in his jacket pocket. Rowena took the note, but couldn't read it in the dim light.

"I can't see…"

"I know it by heart," Cash said. "If I really could make magic, there are things that I would do. My sister would dance even without Daddy holding her up. Dr. Malley says she will. I would change Rowena, too. I would turn her into my mom."

Cash cleared his throat. "I didn't put her up to this, Rowena. I swear. One night she just asked me to check her spelling. We talked about it. She told me about your fairy godmother and the magic whistle and we thought maybe all our love and all your magic together could be so strong it could make this appear on your finger."

Rowena stared as she saw him uncurl his hand. The engagement ring lay there against the callused palm she'd felt search every inch of her body during nights filled with his love.

"I thought you'd take the ring back to the jewelers."

"I might have given up before I knew you. But someone very wise told me that nothing is impossible. That a little girl can disappear even though she's still sitting right at the kitchen table. That demon dogs have destinies and love happens even if you don't have time to find it. It barrels into you and leaves you with a black eye to go with your—your broken pieces inside. Pieces the right woman can put together and make whole. It's a gift, you know. Seeing all of that in a world that seems so—so shattered sometimes. Your gift, Rowena."

"Oh, Cash."

"You gave that gift to me. To my children. Do you have any idea how amazing that is? You showed me that if that monster of a dog can find someone who loves him even after all the mistakes he made…maybe it's not impossible to believe that I can, too."

Rowena caught her bottom lip with her teeth, hearing the awe in Cash's voice, sensing the wonder in him. Redemption, pure and sweet.

"You might want to know that we finally settled the great doggy-name war. We decided to call him Destroyer. It's ironic, I know, since he put a broken family back together and healed us in so many ways. Charlie says it's like a secret joke every time she calls him that." Cash swallowed hard. "Who would have believed it six months ago? My Charlie making a joke?"

Rowena's eyes burned. "That's wonderful, Cash."

His hand closed warmly over Rowena's. She felt the smooth kiss of his ring against her finger. "Marry me, Rowena. I want you in my bed. In my life. In my kitchen making me coffee."

"We're back to coffee again, are we?"

"No," Cash said, sliding the ring home. "We're back to *this*." He gathered her up onto her tiptoes, then against his chest, his mouth coming down on hers with so much joy, so much love she drowned in it. Hungry, hot, he kissed her as if he never wanted her to forget this moment. And in spite of the wintry wind and the coat she'd forgotten, Rowena doubted she'd ever feel cold again. She didn't even notice the crowd from the program spilling out the school doors, never felt eyes watching them until she heard a warning whistle.

Cash and Rowena sprang apart, flustered, to see Jake Stone approaching, Mac up on his broad shoulders and Charlie and Hope beside him.

"Woo-ee, baby!" Mac's high-pitched voice split the air. "Daddy's kissing Rowena in front of the whole school! Can you get arrested for that?"

Laughter rose from the crowd.

"How about you let us off the hook this one time?" Cash took Rowena's hand and held it into the light. The diamond shimmered, chasing rainbows into the dark. "Look, girls. Rowena's going to marry us."

Applause broke out and Rowena could feel the affection these people felt for Cash, felt for the first time that she belonged here, too. She'd found her destiny right here, just as her fairy godmother had promised. Whitewater was home.

"What do you think of a wedding as a Christmas present?" Cash teased, tugging one of Mac's shiny pink shoes.

Mac wrinkled her nose. "Well, I guess it's okay as long as I get to wear my tiara. But don't be trying to give me a baby for Christmas like Tyler James got last year. I'd like a kitty better."

"Some kids are lucky and get both," Charlie said softly, slipping her hand into Cash's. Her optimism made Rowena's heart soar.

"But you said you only got *bad* luck, Charlie," Mac complained.

"Now I've got magic instead." Charlie tugged the silver chain, and Cuchullain's pipe sparkled in the twinkling fairy lights. Suddenly her brow wrinkled, and Rowena could tell she was deep in thought. "I don't 'spose you've got any *more* magic stuff lying around somewhere, do you, Rowena?"

Rowena thought of her sisters, Bryony with her earrings and Ariel with the dagger centuries old. Magic, as yet not spun. It was hard to think they might not ever dare to give Maeve MacKinnon's gifts a chance. Rowena could only hope her happiness would give her sisters the courage to try.

Cash drew Rowena into the crook of his arm, into a future twinkling bright with love. "You think you'll need more magic than this, Charlie?" he asked, kissing Rowena's cheek.

"The magic's not for me, Daddy," she explained earnestly. "It's for Mac and Hope and a baby if we have one. It never hurts to be ready just in case."

REQUEST YOUR FREE BOOKS!

2 FREE NOVELS FROM THE ROMANCE/SUSPENSE COLLECTION PLUS 2 FREE GIFTS!

Kimberly Cates

| 77189 | THE WEDDING DRESS | ___ $6.99 U.S. | ___ $8.50 CAN. |
| 77178 | THE GAZEBO | ___ $6.99 U.S. | ___ $8.50 CAN. |

(limited quantities available)

TOTAL AMOUNT	$ _____
POSTAGE & HANDLING	$ _____
($1.00 FOR 1 BOOK, 50¢ for each additional)	
APPLICABLE TAXES*	$ _____
TOTAL PAYABLE	$ _____

(check or money order—please do not send cash)

To order, complete this form and send it, along with a check or money order for the total above, payable to HQN Books, to: **In the U.S.:** 3010 Walden Avenue, P.O. Box 9077, Buffalo, NY 14269-9077; **In Canada:** P.O. Box 636, Fort Erie, Ontario, L2A 5X3.

Name: _____
Address: _____ City: _____
State/Prov.: _____ Zip/Postal Code: _____
Account Number (if applicable): _____

075 CSAS

*New York residents remit applicable sales taxes.
*Canadian residents remit applicable GST and provincial taxes.

HQN™

We *are* romance™

www.HQNBooks.com

PHKCI207BL